When Katryn looked up to see the man's dark form blocking the slanting rays of the sun, she had felt her heart twist queerly inside her chest. It couldn't be—couldn't be—but no one else could make her pulse jump so. The shock of it made her mouth go dry. Despite the leaner frame, the ragged clothes, the longish, roughly cut hair, this was the shape of the man she would know in her dreams. . . .

And when he spoke, the voice was the same, deep and ringing with a natural authority. She had to blink hard to hold back the tears.

"Did you think I would not know you, Robert?" Her own voice sounded strange and faraway to her ears, and she barely concentrated on the words they exchanged after, because inside she was singing paeans of joy, like a lark waking the world at dawn. After such a long darkness, daylight was breaking. . . .

after such a long darkness,
daylight was breaking . . .

ROBERT'S LADY

Nicole Byrd

JOVE BOOKS, NEW YORK

This is a work of fiction. Names, characters, places, and incidents are either the product of the author's imagination or are used fictitiously, and any resemblance to actual persons, living or dead, business establishments, events or locales is entirely coincidental.

ROBERT'S LADY

A Jove Book / published by arrangement with
the author

PRINTING HISTORY
Jove edition / May 2000

The Penguin Putnam Inc. World Wide Web site address is
http://www.penguinputnam.com

ISBN: 0-515-12853-8

A JOVE BOOK®
Jove Books are published by The Berkley Publishing Group,
a division of Penguin Putnam Inc.,
375 Hudson Street, New York, New York 10014.
Jove and the "J" design
are trademarks belonging to Penguin Putnam Inc.

PRINTED IN THE UNITED STATES OF AMERICA

10 9 8 7 6 5 4 3 2 1

For my husband, Bradley. Je t'aime à vie, *darling.*
And for mothers and daughters.

1

He'd never thought to see England again.

He braced himself as the ship rolled, then pulled against the restraining drag of the anchor. The air stunk of brine and dead fish, and the docks were a blur of noise and movement: hot-pie vendors and whistling errand boys, brawny men rolling barrels toward waiting gangplanks, a drunken sailor taking one more swig from a dark bottle.

He was also keenly aware of what was missing. Warships bristling with cannon no longer prowled the coastline. The columns of soldiers were gone, the war over. Tradesmen were back crowding the docks, along with merchant sailors and their shiploads of wares ready for distant shores. After all, Napoleon, the ogre who had been used to frighten a whole generation of misbehaving children, had at last been defeated. The channel was safe for trade and travel once more.

All around him on the deck, sailors moved briskly, bringing the worm-ridden old fishing boat in for one more berthing. The tall man in the ragged clothes stood silently, while the tars traded ribald jests.

"Fat Molly's awaiting you in the bawdy house, Bones," a big sailor with a scar on his chin called to his skinny companion.

The other man laughed loudly and clutched his grimy hands to his heart in mock sincerity. "Aye, that she is, I'll wager, eager for me loving embrace."

Behind them, the quiet man held his breath as the gangplank dropped, clunking against the wooden dock, then shouldered his way past the two men. He had no trunks to wait for, no manservant to call. He left behind only a borrowed hammock and a greedy captain now a few pounds richer for this quiet passage.

"Here, now, wait your bloody turn," one of the seamen called after him, cursing.

But he'd already taken a big step—too big—onto the dock itself, slipping on the wet wood and falling to one knee. He heard guffaws behind him, but he didn't care. He put one hand to the splintered wood beneath him, almost caressing the rough worn planks.

England! England was home, England was family, England was a girl with golden hair and big blue eyes, eyes he'd last seen overflowing with tears when he'd told her good-bye. Eleanor—Eleanor would be waiting! He would have leaned down and kissed the rough wood beneath his feet, except for the crowd of people around him who might think him demented. His appearance was rough enough, anyhow, his dark hair shaggy and unkempt, his face streaked with grime, and he stank of the prison even yet.

He got to his feet, staggering just a little, and hurried past the curious stares, eager to get through the formalities of landing. The Customs officer gave him a cursory glance, then wasted little time on such a poor wretch.

Back in the fresh air, the traveler put one hand into his pocket and felt the small lump of coins. He badly needed a bath and a change of clothes, but he had only enough money to pay for a coach seat to London, and he was too impatient to linger in Dover, anyhow.

But as he strode through the streets, the babble of voices

all around sounded as gentle and sweet as a nightingale's song—they were speaking English, with many different accents, but English nonetheless. The words sounded strange to his ears; he had been away so long.

After he paid for his fare, he had a few pennies left with which to buy a hot meat pie from one of the vendors on the street. He took the pastry with him into the coach, sitting beside a fat merchant who pulled his coattails back quickly to avoid touching the newcomer's grimy garments.

The man whom his fellow prisoners had called Mannie hardly noticed. He crammed the pie into his mouth—he still relished every bite of decent food, and this was hot and savory, still steaming with the rich aromas of beef and dough—and the prim-looking woman in the snuff brown traveling gown who sat across from him sniffed and looked away.

What would Eleanor think to see him such a savage? Frowning, he ate the last crumbs of the pie more slowly, wishing for a drink of good wine, lacking even a handkerchief to wipe away the food stains. He rubbed his chin absently and felt the rough stubble; he had hacked off his beard aboard ship with a borrowed razor.

No one on the coach spoke to him, though he felt the stares of the other passengers. He tried to keep his long legs tucked out of the prim woman's way. Laying his head back against the wall of the coach, he shut his eyes; his eyelids felt leaden. He'd been unable to sleep on the voyage across the Channel, somehow fearing that they would find him, snatch him back before he reached home and did what he had to do. He had so little time. . . .

But now he was beginning to believe he was actually here. He was in England. Soon, he would be home. Soon, he would see Eleanor. Despite the jolting as the coach clattered over the rough road, his eyes remained closed, and he slept.

When the coach rumbled into London, he was the first

one off, not even waiting for the hatchet-faced woman across the aisle to exit the coach. She sniffed again and shook her head, but he ignored her, hurrying down the steps and jumping onto the cobblestones.

It felt as if he'd been away for a lifetime—in a way, he thought grimly, he had—and for a moment, his head whirled, and the crowded streets looked like one giant maze.

Then he shook himself mentally and everything settled back into place. He knew the office of his family's man of business, he knew the street, and though it would be a long walk—he had no money left for any other transport—the thought didn't faze him. He set off, his strides long, enjoying the luxury of walking unfettered.

He reached the office as the sun sank low in the late afternoon sky, hoping that Mr. Malbry would not yet have left for his bachelor establishment and the dinner his housekeeper would have waiting. The heavy outer door swung open when he pushed, but there was another obstacle—in the outer office, a new clerk sat on the high stool, ginger-haired and with a faint trace of mousy whiskers above his narrow lips.

"And what is your business with Mr. Malbry?" The clerk looked down his nose at the rough, dirty garments of this impertinent stranger who had demanded to see his employer.

"That is between Mr. Malbry and myself. I can promise you, he will want to see me." Mannie took a deep breath, trying to restrain his anger, his impatience.

"I think not. As if Mr. Malbry would trouble himself with the likes of—here, you ruffian, you can't go in there!" But the clerk was too slow, fumbling his way down from his high perch behind the writing desk.

Mannie pulled open the door and glanced quickly around the familiar inner office. The sight of the empty chair behind the big cluttered desk made his heart beat faster. If Malbry were already gone—but no, there, his hand on a ledger on the bookshelf at the side of the room, there stood the neat black-suited figure that he had hoped to see.

"What's this?" The old man was balder, if that was possible, but otherwise little changed. He held his ground at this unexpected invasion, but his expression revealed alarm.

"I tried to stop him, sir, but he wouldn't listen," the clerk was saying, waving his hands.

"Don't you know me, Malbry?" Mannie asked gently.

Silence, then a gasp. "Robert! I mean, my lord—Lord Manning—is it really you?"

The name felt awkward to his ears; he'd almost forgotten its sound. He let it slide over him for a moment, then reached out, trying to slip back into its shape as if it were a favorite old coat, left half-forgotten in the back of the wardrobe. It seemed like another person, almost, another life; it had all begun to seem like a dream, drifting away into nothingness—except for Eleanor. She had been his reality, his touchstone for those long, empty years.

Robert Manning, Viscount Holt, heir to the earl of Stonesbury, shut his eyes for an instant, then sank into the wide wing chair reserved for important clients. His clothes were too filthy to touch the silk upholstery, but relief had weakened his knees. Gaping, the clerk shut the door reluctantly behind him.

For a moment no one spoke. Malbry still stared as if Robert might be an apparition—a will-o'-the-wisp—who would disappear again if he removed his gaze.

"It is really me, come back from the wars, more or less whole," Robert said into the sudden quiet. "I need money to get myself the rest of the way home, and news. My family—are they well?"

Malbry, his brown eyes still as shrewd as a magpie's, hesitated. "You know about your brother's accident?"

Robert nodded. "I got the news of his death just before I was captured." It had perhaps been his shock that had made him careless, he thought for the hundredth time, with useless regret.

The other man relaxed subtly. "Your mother and sisters are in excellent health. Your father is not as strong as he was, though he will be better now, I think, when he sees you. You know they think you dead?"

"I feared as much." Robert took a deep breath, exhaled it. The last male heir, their last hope. "Do you have any wine?"

"Forgive me, my lord!" The old man bustled to the door, and shouted, "Bring the brandy, Wilkins, the good bottle, at once!"

Shutting his eyes again—his father was alive, all was not yet lost—Robert heard rather than saw the clerk return with a still-dusty bottle of brandy and two glasses on a silver tray.

Malbry poured a generous amount into the first glass and passed it to him. Robert sat up straighter and accepted the wine. He brought it to his mouth so quickly that the liquid inside sloshed the sides of the glass and drank it down in one quick gulp.

The old man looked shocked. Malbry closed his gaping mouth and poured more brandy into Robert's glass.

Controlling himself—no one was going to take it away; he must shed those habits he'd acquired to stay alive in that hellhole of a French prison—Robert took a sip, rolled the brandy on his tongue, and savored its deep body.

"Excellent," he murmured. "Deep-flavored, yet smooth. You haven't lost your ability to choose a wine, Malbry."

The attorney looked reassured at this more normal behavior. "Shall I send word to your father's estate, my lord, before you journey on? Stay the night in town. You might like to visit your tailor and—"

Robert was surprised into a laugh. "What, you don't think I could start a new fashion?" He glanced down at the filthy rags that barely kept him decently covered.

Malbry permitted himself a slight smile. "Not precisely, my lord. And indeed, the shock of seeing you—"

Robert's laughter died. "You may send word, of course," he said. "But I cannot tarry here, I have no time to waste."

"My lord?" The old man looked puzzled.

Robert took another sip of the brandy, feeling the fire of it burn through his weariness, as the other man's words tempted his resolution, prompting thoughts of a clean bed, a warm bath. . . .

No, he could not. He had no time, no time. The words came unbidden to his tongue, but he pushed them back. He couldn't explain. He trusted Malbry completely, but still, there were some things the man of business did not need to know. No need to put his head into the noose, too.

"I am impatient to see my family and my home again, Malbry," he said now. "I can visit my tailor another day. If you can extend me funds—"

"Of course, my lord, it goes without saying," the old man interrupted. "Whatever you need, my lord."

Robert nodded. "Thank you."

"If you don't wish to go to your club"—Malbry glanced at his client's beggar's costume, then quickly away again—"I would be honored to offer you a bed for the night, my lord. And dinner, and a bath . . ."

"I had thought to travel by night," Robert told him. "The moon is just waning; there will be light for some hours."

"And after that, my lord? Besides, you are barely able to stand," the other man told him bluntly. His long employ and trusted status allowed him to speak so. "Better to rest tonight and start early tomorrow."

Robert pushed himself to his feet, ready to argue. But the room spun for an instant, and he had to catch hold of the arms of the chair. He waved the old man away. "I'm all right."

But he was weak as a newborn pup, and the brandy roared

inside him, searing his too-long-empty stomach. In the end, he lost this argument. He rode home in the older man's chaise and shared Malbry's roast pork and mint jelly.

While he ate, forcing himself to chew slowly, not wolf down the tender meat that seemed to melt into his tongue, Robert brought up the question that burned inside him. "Do you know the whereabouts of my commander, Colonel Richmond?"

There was a silence; Robert heard a log pop in the fireplace and a slight creak, like a door opening. Then the footman, a skinny, raw-boned fellow who seemed to ill-fit his livery, reappeared to offer him another spoonful of jelly. Robert took it, though his stomach already felt tight with unaccustomed bounty.

"I'm afraid he was killed at Leipzig, my lord," the old man said slowly. "I am sorry indeed to be the one to acquaint you with his death."

Robert felt his throat tighten. Struggling to keep his expression even, he took a sip of wine to ease the ache in his throat. "I feared as much," he said. "He was a good man." And I should have known it would not be as easy as that, he thought bitterly. Of course not. His one hope for peaceful nights and dreams not haunted by the gallows . . .

He saw that Malbry stared, his forehead wrinkled with concern. Robert forced his fears to the back of his mind. "You were telling me about the prince's argument with the prime minister?"

They passed the rest of the dinner with gossip of the London society that Robert had once known so well. Then he had a long, luxurious bath with real soap and scrubbed himself over and over—not sure he'd ever feel clean again—and he slept in a borrowed nightshirt that was barely long enough to cover his muscular thighs.

In the morning—since nothing that Malbry owned would begin to cover his long-limbed, broad-shouldered frame no matter how much weight Robert had lost during his imprisonment—he put back on the clothes that the plump little housekeeper had scrubbed the night before and hung near the fire to dry. They were wrinkled despite her best efforts and still ragged, but a trifle cleaner than before, and at least he did not smell so rank.

The hired carriage with its job horses couldn't travel fast enough for him. He leaned forward in the seat often, as if he would thrust his head out the window and urge them on. If he had been stronger, he would have ridden, Robert thought, and hang the distance.

But by late afternoon, he was at last rolling into the drive that crossed one of the bigger parks in Hertfordshire and curved past the small lake where he had taught his sisters to fish. There was the oak tree beneath whose sturdy limbs he had kissed Eleanor for the first time, the day he had proposed. Eleanor—her family's estate bordered his family's holdings; he had been tempted to go to her house first. But he could hardly drive past his own home, and his parents would understand if, after a quick greeting, he hurried on to find his sweetheart, to kiss away her tears and at last make plans for the wedding they had both awaited for so long. And the wedding night—the wedding night, thoughts of which had sustained him through so many desperate hours—the old ache in his groin returned, and he took a deep breath at the thought of at last bringing his golden-haired love to bed. He would teach her all the secrets of lovemaking, and the passion they would know . . . He exhaled slowly and forced himself to think of more sedate matters. Not long, now, not long. . . .

At last, the carriage was slowing. Robert sat up straighter as they neared the big house. Glancing out of the carriage, he caught a glimpse of a figure in a sprigged muslin gown entering the walled garden. Perhaps it was one of his sisters, but still—still, could Eleanor be here? Her family and his visited often, it would not be so strange.

He couldn't wait to find out; his pulse was racing. Yelling "Stop, here," to the driver, Robert paused barely long enough for the carriage to roll to a halt before he jumped down. He took long strides across the drive toward the garden and the feminine form he had seen only from the corner of his vision. Inside the garden, a woman knelt by the formal flowerbeds, bending forward to pluck a yellow blossom from the just-opened daffodils.

"Eleanor!"

She started, then straightened and turned to stare at him. Robert ran toward her, then slowed, almost stumbling, though the turf of the garden was level and smooth.

It was not Eleanor, but her younger sister, Katryn. Why hadn't he seen that instead of gold, her locks were a soft brown, and her eyes a clear green instead of deep blue? Because he had wanted so badly for it to be Eleanor, he thought, cursing silently. He'd seen a vision of his own making, that was all. He'd waited so long for this reunion that now another hour apart seemed such exquisite torture.

Katryn looked at him with wide eyes, her face very pale. He realized that, despite the bath and a decent shave and the scrubbing of his ragged clothes, he must still present an alarming sight. She was not accustomed to roughly dressed strangers with long shaggy hair following her into a private garden. She must be struck dumb with terror.

"It's all right, Katryn," he said awkwardly. "I won't harm you. I just—"

"Did you think I would not know you, Robert?" she said, her voice trembling a little. "Are you real, flesh and bone—no ghost, no vision?"

"Quite real," he said, smiling, warmed by her perception. He took a deep breath, and some of his tension ebbed. He was home, he had lived to see home despite all the terrors, all the dangers. "Eleanor is not with you, I suppose?"

Katryn didn't seem to hear his question. She gulped audibly, then drew a deep breath as if she could not quite believe it. "Not dead, after all?"

"It is I, alive and well. Napoleon has not killed me, not yet."

She came forward slowly, touched the rough, ragged sleeve of his shirt with a trembling hand. "Oh, Robert, I knew it. Somehow, I knew you must be still alive. I told Eleanor—" Then abruptly, she fell silent. He saw the sheen of tears in her eyes, and she blinked hard.

Moved—he would not have expected so much emotion from little Katryn, who used to tag behind Robert and her sister when they walked in the garden, whom he had once teased lightly when she followed her sister into the drawing room uninvited, whom he had taught to dance, unknown to her mother or governess, before she was old enough to wear long skirts—Robert took her hand in both of his. "Then I must thank you for your faith in me," he told her, and he heard a huskiness in his own voice that took him by surprise. "My parents—are they inside?"

"They—your father is napping, and your mother and sisters are at Eastborne, my lord, paying a call on my family; they will return soon. Your brother William—" She hesitated.

"I know," he said gently, pushing back the old sorrow.

Katryn swallowed hard. He squeezed her hand, then released it. She was surely not in the schoolroom any longer; by now she would be out, a young lady, likely with suitors paying call. He must remember to treat her with more ceremony. He felt a stab of disappointment that Eleanor was not with her sister, but she was only a few miles away—he must act like a rational man, no matter how his blood warmed at the thought of touching Eleanor's hand, kissing those sweetly curved lips. . . .

"They didn't get Malbry's message, then?" With an effort, he pulled his thoughts back to the garden. He must have made almost as good time as the hired courier, Robert thought, he had been so impatient.

"The express came a short while ago, my lord. It's unopened, awaiting your mother's return. We didn't give it to your father; your mother doesn't like to excite him."

Robert frowned slightly.

"Forgive my ragged manners, Katryn. Perhaps I should call you Miss Worth? I was never 'my lord' to you before."

"I—of course not." She didn't quite meet his eye. "I am only—oh, so glad to see you, that's all."

"I know my return will be a shock to everyone," he told her. "I hope my appearance will not disturb my father's health. But it is a happy surprise, I hope."

"More than you know," she said, so low he almost did not catch the words.

"I hope my sisters will take it as calmly as you did," he said, thinking aloud. "Without shrieks or hysterics. How is my father, Katryn?"

"He is—is well, my lord," Katryn said, then stopped. "Shall I be honest?"

"Of course." But he braced himself.

"I think you have come back just in time, my— Robert," she said slowly. "Your cousin has visited often, twice in the last month, till your father finally forbade him the house."

Katryn's cheeks flushed with emotion and her green eyes were dark with ire. This time, she spoke with her usual force. "Cavendish is insufferable, Robert! Ever since William died, and we had the news of your—your death, your cousin has walked the house and grounds as if he is taking inventory; I half expected him to demand a count of the silver. He is only waiting till your father is—is gone, and he can turn your mother and sisters out. But you are home now, safe, and your cousin's hopes are dashed. And I am so glad!"

Robert felt a stab of alarm, but pushed it down. Nodding, he repeated his earlier question. "And Eleanor—Eleanor isn't here with you? She's at home with your parents?"

Katryn squared her narrow shoulders beneath her simple muslin gown and lifted her chin. Her eyes, green and clear as a southern sea, met his gaze.

"She—she is with our parents. That is why your mother and sisters are at Eastborne, to see Eleanor—and her new baby."

2

When Katryn looked up to see the man's dark form blocking the slanting rays of the sun, she had felt her heart twist queerly inside her chest. It couldn't be—couldn't be—but no one else could make her pulse jump so. The shock of it made her mouth go dry. Despite the leaner frame, the ragged clothes, the longish, roughly cut hair, this was the shape of the man she would know in her dreams. . . .

And when he spoke, the voice was the same, deep and ringing with a natural authority. She had to blink hard to hold back the tears.

"Did you think I would not know you, Robert?" Her own voice sounded strange and faraway to her ears, and she barely concentrated on the words they exchanged after, because inside she was singing paeans of joy, like a lark waking the world at dawn. After such a long darkness, daylight was breaking. . . .

He was alive, Robert was alive. The joy lifted her up, and not until she had to speak her sister's name and see his face change did her elation fade.

"Eleanor's . . . baby?" he said very carefully, and she saw the hope in his eyes dim.

"Eleanor is married, more than a twelve-month now," she

said slowly. "They told us you were dead, Robert. Eleanor was truly distressed—she wept for days."

And Katryn had wept for weeks, but no one noticed, because her family and friends had been busy petting and pampering Eleanor, whose engagement to their neighbor and lifelong friend had barely been announced. Katryn, with no such excuse for heartsickness, had struggled with her grief alone. But she could not tell him that, not now. He was pale with shock, and he swayed a little on his feet.

"You must come inside," she said quickly.

He shook his head, but he was trembling, and she took his hand, heedless of his frown, and pulled him gently toward a garden bench. He dropped heavily, as if his knees had given way, and she sat down beside him, still holding his hand. His skin was warm against hers, and she was acutely aware of his touch, which seemed to send shivers up and down her body, awaking a strange, unfamiliar ache deep inside her belly.

It was not at all proper, of course, but she was sure he didn't notice that she still gripped his hand, and she needed to feel his living flesh, reassure herself that he was really here. It was not a dream, like those she had woken from too often, to cry fresh tears when she remembered he would never again ride up to Eastborne, smiling and calling out Eleanor's name.

He leaned forward, breathing hard. She released her grip and watched him rest his face in his hands. Katryn looked away, then, not wanting to see how the naked grief twisted his face. How could Eleanor not have known, sensed in her heart, that her fiancé still lived? How had she given up on him, relinquished their future together so easily?

Robert pushed his palms hard against his eyes and drew deep, ragged breaths. He didn't trust his tongue; he could barely control his shivering. *His* Eleanor had believed him to be dead? Perhaps he could understand that, if the army had sent word, but—but to transfer her affections so quickly, so easily? She could not have loved him as he had loved her. No, her devotion had been shallow indeed. The pain of that knowledge seared his chest like a hot poker held to his heart. Nothing they had done to him in the prison had hurt this much. It was impossible; this could not be true.

Wearily, he raised his head and glanced at Katryn. Her piquant, heart-shaped face was solemn; her green eyes looked back at him steadily. The sweet child would not lie to him. The unbelievable had happened. His beloved had given him up for dead. She had surrendered all hope, just when he had been grasping every shred of it even in that hellhole of a prison. Eleanor, safe and protected, her family around her, had married another man with a sickeningly quick change of affections. Bitterness rose inside him like bile, sour and hot.

"So soon?" he murmured.

Katryn felt duty-bound to defend her sister. "They swore to us you were dead," she repeated. "Mama, Papa, they told Eleanor she must go on with her life."

He nodded slowly. "And she agreed, I take it." He rubbed his hand over his face and struggled for composure. "I should have—should have realized. Who was—is the lucky man?"

Katryn gazed at the velvety grass at their feet as if she didn't hear the tremor of fury and sorrow in his voice. There had been plenty of suitors for Eleanor's hand—fair, wellborn, biddable Eleanor, with her respectable dowry and abundant charms.

"Lord Whitmund," she said. "They are happy enough, I think, though what she will say when she sees you—" She stopped abruptly.

"It doesn't matter," Robert almost whispered. "It is too late. Too late for us all."

"No, no, Robert. You mustn't say that." Katryn turned toward Robert, slapping her hand emphatically on the bench between them, crushing the forgotten flower. "Your mother will be so happy, and your sisters, and your father—it will ease so much of your family's grief," Katryn said, trying to turn his thoughts. "There will be so much joy at your home-coming, my d— my lord."

He pushed back the shaggy hair and straightened, pain and bitterness still visible in his dark eyes, but his face now composed, though how much this exercise in self-control cost him she could only guess.

"Let's go inside. I will greet my father, and perhaps I can find some old clothes to change into before my mother returns so she will not have to see me like this. It will be enough of a shock without showing her such a disreputable appearance. Unless all my clothes have been thrown away?"

"I don't know. We must ask the housekeeper." Katryn was happy to turn her mind to practical matters, too.

They walked out of the garden and up to the front doors together. Inside the hall, the elderly butler hurried forward at their approach, then stopped, his face white.

"My—my lord!"

"God in heaven! It's a ghost!" Behind him, a footman shrieked and dropped the tray he carried. The crackle of breaking china brought another footman hurrying into the big front hall, and he stopped, too, his mouth agape.

"Mercy on us!"

As a homecoming, it was not the most propitious.

"It is really me, Samuels," Robert told the butler quietly. "And pull yourself together, man," he told the first footman more sternly. "I'm as real as you, and in need of food and drink, and I hope, fresh garments."

Samuels gave himself a shake and hurried forward. "My lord, I am so happy to see you, but how—why—" He paused and with obvious effort pulled his expression back into its usual calm formality. He bowed. "I will send orders to the kitchen, my lord. Shall I announce you to his lordship?"

Robert glanced at Katryn, raising his brows. "Will it disturb him too much, you think? It must be a great shock, and his heart . . ."

"Perhaps we should wait for your mother." Katryn tried to think. "Or fetch the doctor, in case—"

The butler cocked his head. "I think I hear him now, banging on the floor with his stick, my lord, desiring my attendance. Perhaps he heard the outcry and wishes to know its cause." Turning a stern gaze on the footmen, he watched as the two younger men flushed and hastily bent to clear away the wreckage from the tray.

"We must not leave him in suspense," Katryn decided. "That must be a worse strain on his heart than hearing such wondrous news."

Robert nodded in agreement, and the butler waved toward his underlings.

"Bring fresh tea and brandy and his lordship's cordial to the drawing room," Samuels told them. "I will go to his lordship, my lord."

"I will go too and try to prepare him," Katryn decided. "Wait just a moment more, Robert."

He nodded and followed her slowly up the broad staircase, to stand outside the drawing room where for some years now his father had spent most of his waking hours. Robert touched the intricately carved wood of the railing as he climbed the steps, trying to believe he was really here. But his long-awaited prize, the biggest joy of his homecoming, was lost to him forever. . . . He took a deep breath and waited while Katryn opened the door and slipped inside.

She found the earl frowning, as if frustrated once again by his body's infirmities. With one hand, he clutched the walking stick so tightly that his knuckles were white. His tall frame sat in a specially built wheeled chair; his heart could not bear the strain caused by any exertion.

"What's all that caterwauling, Katryn?" he demanded, his

voice thin and querulous. "No way for a respectable house-hold to behave. It's not that beetle Cavendish returned to plague us, is it? I said I'll not have him in my house—he doesn't own the place till I'm in my grave, and I'm not there yet!" His face was dangerously flushed, and she hurried to calm him.

"Of course it's not your nephew, my lord. Do not distress yourself."

The old man took a calming breath. "If it's not that rascal trying to force his way into my hall, what was that racket about?"

"A surprise for us all, but a very happy one," Katryn said, watching him closely for the bluish tinge that crept into his face when his heart began to fail. "You must brace yourself for a shock."

The earl lifted his thin brows with characteristic arro-gance, so much like his son that she had to bite back a smile.

"What do you mean?"

"Your younger son—Robert has returned, my lord. He was not killed after all. The report was false."

The butler had entered the room quietly and was pouring out a glass of the cordial the doctor had prescribed. He held out the glass, but the earl waved it impatiently away. His eyes had widened, and his voice was suddenly hoarse. "My s-son, my—Robert? Can it be?"

She turned to go to the door and bring Robert inside, but he must have heard, because it opened before she reached the threshold. Robert came quickly into the room and hur-ried to drop to his knees beside his father's wheeled chair.

"Sir." Robert's voice shook; his father must look even more frail than when he had left, over three years before, riding away to fight the French.

The earl touched his only living son's ragged coat, put a shaking hand on his shock of over-long dark hair. "It is true," he said. "Oh, my son."

The butler held the glass closer, and Katryn was glad to see Robert take it and hold it to his father's lips, urging him to drink.

The earl sipped it and, to her relief, his breathing steadied. "How did it happen? How dare they give us spurious news? And where have you been all this time?"

"In a damnable French prison, sir," Robert told him. "It is a long story, and I will explain it all later."

"Yes, yes." The old man patted his shoulder, as if afraid Robert would vanish. "Oh, my dear boy. You know about William?"

Robert sighed. "I got your letter before I was captured. A senseless accident, you wrote, going over a middling fence."

His father's eyes glistened, one tear rolling down his cheek. "Yes, so hard. But now you are here. God has listened to me, and I can die happy. You have returned to us— what greater gift could I have? And this will save us all, you know."

"I know," Robert answered, but his voice sounded grim.

Samuels cleared his throat discreetly. "My lord, Mrs. Lawford will have fetched a change of clothes for your lordship. You might wish to change before Lady Manning returns."

And the earl would have a moment to rest and calm his agitated spirits, Katryn thought.

Robert must have been thinking the same thing. "Yes, a good notion. I will return very shortly, my lord."

The earl looked ready to argue, then he laughed, a thin chuckle that shook his fragile frame. "No need to show your mother such a sight, eh? Though you know she would welcome you wearing haircloth or beaten bark, my boy. But go along and see what Mrs. Lawford has unearthed. Should have known she would have refused to empty your wardrobes completely. Go on, go on. I will await your return."

"My lord." Robert bowed and pressed his father's hand. He looked up at Katryn. "You will wait with him?"

"Of course," Katryn told him.

Robert nodded and strode quickly out of the room.

She walked over to the window, looking down at the drive to give the earl time to wipe his face with his handkerchief and compose his features. No sign yet of her ladyship's carriage. What rejoicing there would be under this roof tonight! But Eleanor—what would she say when she heard the news? Would she weep anew for the fiancé she had put aside, for the loss of the life they could have shared?

Katryn should have been more anxious about her sister's regrets, but she found that she could barely control the smile that played at the corners of her mouth. What could distress her for very long when Robert was alive?

The butler was given quiet orders and left the room, and Katryn came back to sit with his lordship, but they spoke little, both no doubt lost in wonder over this incredible change of fortune.

It was not long before Katryn heard the sounds of the carriage in the drive. She looked up expectantly, and the earl smiled. They sat silently, listening to the chatter of female voices in the entrance hall below.

"Told Samuels not to spill the news," the old man confided. "Told him to bring my wife and daughters to me at once."

Katryn nodded, hearing the voices now ascending the staircase.

The countess swept into the room, pulling off a fashionable silk bonnet as she hurried to her husband's side. Her forehead was slightly creased. "My dear, are you ill? Samuels said that we should come up at once—"

"No, no," the old man said impatiently. He gripped his lady's hand, and a broad smile replaced his usual dour expression. "Something to tell you. A surprise for you, a most happy surprise."

"What?" Looking puzzled, her ladyship glanced at Katryn, who tried not to laugh.

"Wait, wait, you will see," her husband insisted.

After a quick assessing glance at their father, the two girls came to plump down beside Katryn on the settee.

"Oh, the baby is such a dear thing," Marianne, who was the elder, said. "He doesn't look much like Eleanor, though."

"No, poor thing, I think he favors his father," Dora said with less tact, then colored to the roots of her dark hair. "I beg your pardon, Katryn, I meant—"

"I know exactly." Katryn smiled at her. "He seems to have the Whitmund ears."

The girls laughed, but their mother was still trying to pry the secret from her husband, who watched the doorway expectantly.

"What is it?" she demanded. "Really, sir, you are too vexing." She turned to the girls. "Katryn, what are you keeping from me?"

"We have had miraculous and most unexpected news," Katryn answered, glancing cautiously at the earl, whose expression was still mischievous. "But I think his lordship wants to—"

At last they all heard the footsteps in the hall. When Robert walked into the room, his blue coat slightly out of fashion but an immense improvement over the ragged suit in which he had arrived home, his thick, wavy hair still long but brushed back behind his ears, Lady Manning gasped and sat down very suddenly onto a silk-upholstered chair.

The girls shrieked.

Robert hurried forward to take his mother's hands, then to hug her fiercely, while his sisters clustered around them, everyone embracing and babbling and no one able to speak coherently.

The earl beamed, and Katryn watched, damp-eyed. She wondered if she should call for a vinaigrette, but the countess, a sensible woman, was recovering rapidly, though her cheeks were wet with happy tears.

"My dearest boy, how is this possible?" she cried. Lady Manning cupped his square jaw in her still-unsteady hand. "Oh, I don't care at all. As long as you are here, alive and well, nothing else matters. Dearest Robert, how I have missed you!"

It was just what Katryn longed to say, but could not. She watched them silently, enjoying the sight of so much happiness, her eyes fixed on Robert's face. She was delighted to see his expression lighten.

When she stood up, ready to slip away and grant them privacy for their family reunion, Robert turned his head.

"I shall leave you, my lord, my lady," Katryn said. "I am so happy for all of you."

"Thank you for coming, dear child," Lady Manning said. "It was kind of you to keep his lordship company so we could all visit your family, since Cousin Mary is indisposed today."

"As if I was a babe needing constant minding." The earl sniffed. "Ah, but you're a good girl, Katryn. Give your parents my best wishes."

"Yes, my lord," Katryn said.

"I will walk you out, Katryn," Robert said unexpectedly, patting Dora's shoulder and putting Marianne gently aside.

"There's no need—" she said quickly. "Your parents, your sisters—"

"Will still be here." Robert smiled at his mother, who was wiping her eyes. "But I haven't forgotten all my manners, you know."

So she accepted his arm and they descended the wide staircase side by side. Did he have a private message for her sister? Katryn waited for him to speak, but not until she had donned her bonnet and gloves and he had called for her carriage did he break the silence.

"About Eleanor—" He paused.

"Shall I give her a message for you?" Katryn asked, keeping her tone pleasant even though her throat felt tight with emotion.

And what could he say? Inside him, bitterness struggled with deep chasms of regret. Robert pulled his thoughts away from the dangerous gulf of anger, of recriminations.

"Give her my felicitations," Robert said, holding his tone steady. "Tell her I am happy for her—since I have no choice. But it can't be mended. I must—must think of something else."

"What do you mean?" She gazed at him, perplexed.

Beneath his breath, almost to himself, he said, "I am in urgent need of a wife."

Katryn thought she could not have heard properly. "What?"

He didn't answer. The footman had opened the carriage door, and Robert took her gloved hand to help her in.

Katryn settled herself into her carriage and smiled her thanks. He could not have said what she thought she had heard, she told herself. It was nothing, had to be nothing. She would not think of it. So, of course, she thought of nothing else on the short ride back to her own estate.

When they pulled up at Eastborne, she alit from the carriage and hurried inside. She found her mother and Eleanor in the small drawing room with the baby and his nurse. Eleanor was cooing to her son and looked up with a smile when she saw her sister.

"Hello, Katryn. How was the earl?" Her tone was gentle, her blue eyes guileless; it was impossible to be angry with Eleanor, Katryn thought, no one could be.

Her mother was more astute; she looked at her younger

daughter, frowning a little. "Why do you look so, my dear? Has the earl had one of his attacks again?"

"No, he's well, considering the shock. Where is Whitmund?"

"With your father down at the stables, looking over the new colt. What shock?" Mrs. Worth demanded.

"The family has had a very big surprise, but a good one. It's about Robert. . . ." Katryn paused to glance at her sister. She had been absorbed in the baby, but she looked up at the mention of Robert's name.

"Have they found his grave at last?" her mother asked, sighing.

"No, it seems the news of his death was incorrect."

Her mother's eyes widened, and Eleanor blinked.

"You don't mean—"

"He is alive, not killed after all. Robert has come home," Katryn told them, her voice rising with ecstatic emotion she was unable to fully contain. "He has been locked away in a French prison, for years apparently."

Eleanor flushed and said nothing. Her mother paused, then said, "I am so happy for them, especially after William's sad demise. Robert is well, no permanent injuries? Prison life is most deleterious to the health, I am told."

"Of course!" Katryn trembled at the thought, then recovered her composure. "I mean, he's very thin, but as far as I can see, he looks perfectly well."

"I am so glad," Eleanor murmured. Her flush had faded, but now she looked very pale. The baby began to wail—perhaps Eleanor gripped it too tightly—and Mrs. Worth frowned.

"Take the child back to the nursery," she directed the nanny, who jumped up quickly to take the baby from its mother.

But Eleanor shook her head. "I will take little Fitz up myself," she said. Followed by the servant, she walked out of the room, her head bent down to whisper to the baby—or to hide her expression. They both watched her leave.

"Do you think—" Katryn began, keeping her voice low, but her mother interrupted.

"We did it for the best," she said, her tone almost too confident, as if trying to reassure herself as well as her daughter. "Eleanor is a sensible girl; she will understand that this could not be expected. And whatever she—any of us—feels, it is too late to look back now."

"Yes," Katryn agreed. Too late for Eleanor, who had married "till death do us part," like any respectable woman. And as for Robert—would his heart heal? How long would it take for him to consider letting another woman into his life, and how could Katryn manage to be that woman?

Upstairs, Eleanor sat in the rocking chair in the old nursery quarters, where she and Katryn had once squabbled and played and had their tea and their lessons. She held little Fitz, her dear, dear son, more gently, and his wails subsided into drowsy gurgles as she rocked him. She waved the nurse away.

"Go tell my maid that I shall be there very soon to change for dinner," she said. "She may lay out my dress."

It was an unnecessary errand, as Camden, her dresser, was most certainly already preparing her evening ensemble. But the nanny curtsied and hurried out of the room, leaving Eleanor and the baby alone for a blessed moment of privacy. For a minute or two, she could stop guarding her expression and give rein to her deepest feelings.

Robert was alive! Come home by some miracle, and it was too late. The thought made her heart ache. How could she face him? How could she explain that the pain of his death had been so great that it seemed best to leap into marriage with another man, any man almost, since it wouldn't matter whom she pledged herself to if she couldn't have her first, her earliest love? And her mother and father had been insistent that she choose from among the many suitors that news of Robert's death had brought crowding around her. Perhaps her parents had feared that she would go into a decline and die herself, otherwise? Oh, how could she make him understand?

Her eyes flooded with tears, and she sniffed them back. She could not face her husband with tears in her eyes. Oh, dear lord, she would have to tell Whitmund, she thought in distraction.

The nanny was back all too soon. "Your dresser is waiting, my lady," she said. "Shall I take the baby now?"

"Yes," Eleanor said reluctantly. Little Fitz was almost asleep; he cooed slightly and blinked at her. She kissed his forehead before handing over the precious bundle. Dearest Fitz. She must be brave, for her son's sake.

Suddenly, she remembered her mother's conversation earlier about hiring a local woman as wet nurse for the baby. Eleanor had gone against convention by nursing her infant herself, enjoying the close contact, the quiet times together. But the Season was about to begin, and if she had to be at the baby's side so often, it would be difficult to take her place among the Ton . . . perhaps she should reconsider. Eleanor had not expected to care about attending balls and teas and socials. Now, perhaps she had changed her mind. Perhaps she would hire the wet nurse, after all.

When she reached the room she shared with her husband, she was relieved to see that he had not yet returned. Eleanor hurried into the dressing room and shut the door. As Camden stood behind her and unfastened the simple day dress, Eleanor glanced at her own image in the looking glass. Her breasts were fuller than usual because of her motherhood; would Robert approve of the way she looked, ripe and womanly?

She shut her eyes for a moment, remembering how the baby had been made. She had wanted it to be Robert who taught her how to love, only Robert. . . . Pushing the thought away, she accepted the silk evening gown that Camden lifted from the chair and slid her arms into the short, capped sleeves. What on earth was she to say to Whitmund?

In the end, she told her husband very simply, and she thought she kept her tone admirably composed. But Whitmund paled as he listened, and he turned abruptly to stare out the window into the back courtyard, his shoulders straining against the superfine of his coat. He stood motionless for so long that Eleanor bit her lip. "My lord?" she said, hesitating. And when he turned at last, his face was that of a stranger.

"We should go down to dinner, my dear," he said, but there was a look in his eyes she had never seen there before.

Dinner conversation was brisk, and, though the amazing return of their neighbors' last male heir was much remarked upon, Eleanor added nothing to the chatter. Not until the ladies removed to the drawing room did Katryn at last have a chance to speak to her sister. She drew her to one side while their mother was speaking to the butler and whispered, "Are you all right, Eleanor?"

"Of course."

"You are very calm," Katryn blurted, then wished she had been less blunt as she watched Eleanor bite her lip, obviously struggling to maintain her usual serene expression.

"I must be calm. There is no use to repine," Eleanor answered, but she didn't meet her sister's anxious gaze.

"Are you very unhappy to have given up your engagement?" Katryn watched her sister's averted face; she needed to hear her answer.

"If you mean am I sorry that I didn't wait a while longer, yes, you could say so. But no one could have foreseen this, and there's no point now in wishing myself back," Eleanor said, her voice trembling just a little. "After all, it's not so bad. Of course I am glad that Robert is alive. And Whitmund is a pleasant husband, and we deal very well. And now I have the baby; I could not wish him away, Katryn. Since there's nothing to be done, there's no point in making a fuss, is there?"

If there was a slight tremor in her voice, it was kinder to pretend not to notice. Katryn nodded. "I'm glad you are not too distressed," she whispered.

Eleanor's eyes flashed for a moment, and Katryn paused in surprise to see her usually serene sister look so agitated. But then their mother came to join them, and it was necessary to talk of other matters. The conversation turned to baby Fitz and the imminent appearance—Eleanor was quite sure, though the nanny thought it too soon—of his first tooth.

They heard no more from Manning Hall till two days later, when an invitation came to dine and was of course accepted. Katryn had been able to think of little else but Robert, and she prepared for the dinner party with a good deal of nervous anticipation. Likely, he still would not notice her; she could tell he still thought of her as a schoolgirl. How long would it take him to get over his disappointment over Eleanor, and would he have fallen in love with someone else before she could shake the blinders from his eyes? And what, oh what had he meant by that cryptic remark about needing a wife?

It was not by accident that she chose her lowest cut, most fashionably seductive gown. Katryn dabbed her best perfume in the hollow between her breasts and stared for a long time at her reflection in the looking glass, thinking that Robert must be made to see that she was a child no longer.

Mrs. Worth came in while Katryn's maid arranged her

heavy hair in an elaborate upsweep; her mother raised her brows at the daring cut of the silk. "Perhaps a bit much for a quiet dinner with old friends, Katryn? I thought you were saving the new gown for London?"

"I have a mind to wear it tonight," Katryn said, frowning into the looking glass.

Her mother's expression appeared thoughtful; she went away again with no more protests. When they drove over to Manning Hall, the men riding before them, the women sitting inside the carriage, Katryn was the last out of the carriage, and she followed her family slowly inside. It was proper to allow Eleanor and Whitmund to walk into the drawing room before her, but she also wanted to watch Robert's response as he had his first reunion with his lost love. She was glad to see that he looked pale but composed as he bowed to her sister.

"I am so happy to see you, Robert," Eleanor said in her gentle voice, but her smile seemed stiff. "To see you alive and well and home again. Your family is so relieved, I know."

Robert bowed to her. "And I am glad to see that you are well, and that your mourning period was not prolonged."

Eleanor's blue-eyed gaze flew to his face, and the silence in the room seemed charged. Katryn held her breath. Eleanor's mouth trembled, and her eyes glistened.

Then a muscle jerked in Robert's face, and before Eleanor's obvious distress, his tone softened.

"It cannot be helped, I know that. I wish you only the best. My felicitations to you," he said. "And to you, Whitmund."

The two men exchanged stiff bows, and then Eleanor moved on to speak to the countess. Robert made his bow to Katryn, but she was afraid he hardly noticed her becoming gown; his expression was set and his eyes hard, his thoughts seemed far away. He greeted her absently, as if he was still the genial friend of her childhood, no more, and she sighed in disappointment.

She made conversation with his sisters and tried not to watch Robert and Eleanor too closely. Once, they spoke briefly as they stood together in front of the big windows, and she saw Eleanor blush and bite her lip, and Robert's face settle into even more rigid lines. But in a moment, he bowed slightly, and Eleanor turned and came back to rejoin the rest of the party. No one else made any comment, though Katryn thought that Whitmund frowned.

Katryn was seated across from Robert at dinner—the table was of necessity a bit uneven, as only their two families were present and there were too many ladies to match the gentlemen—and had no chance to talk to him, though she glanced at him as often as she dared. He looked a little more at ease now, but some thought still troubled him, she would swear to it. Behind his determinedly even tone, behind his smile, there was a darkness—or was it only his grief, his bitterness over losing Eleanor?

Not until the gentlemen rejoined the ladies after dinner, and the earl was wheeled off early to bed as usual, by his doctor's orders, did she have the chance for conversation with Robert. Robert's elderly cousin Mary had also excused herself. Her parents, the countess, and Whitmund sat down to a quiet game of whist. Across the room, Eleanor and Robert's sisters discussed the latest fashions and made plans to meet later in town as the Season began.

Robert walked across to one of the windows and gazed out into the deepening dusk. In a moment, she rose and joined him.

Was he looking at the dark groves of his estate or watching Eleanor in the candle-lit reflection thrown up against the windowpane? The thought brought a pang to Katryn's heart, but she pushed it aside.

"You stare as if you have never seen the park before," she

said softly. "Are you beginning to feel yourself more at home, my lord?"

He turned and gave her a somewhat forced smile. "Slowly," he told her. "I still wake at night and wonder if this is only a dream."

She swallowed hard. "Was prison so—so very bad?"

He nodded. And through the very worst, he told himself, his salvation had been memories of his fair-haired angel. And now his hell was knowing that his sweetheart had freely given her heart and her soft body to another. While dreams of her had kept him sane, she was learning love from another man—all the pleasures he had thought to teach her. With an effort, he pulled himself back to the present. "Not a subject fit for a lady," he said lightly. "Let us talk of more pleasant topics."

"Of course. Have you been out riding? I know your parents have kept your favorite mount; your father could not bear to part with him."

Robert pressed his lips together and gazed once more into the darkness. "Yes, indeed. I was delighted to see Shadow still in the stable."

Katryn added, "And there are improvements in the home farm you should see, my lord, if you have not yet ridden that way. My father says your steward could use overseeing, with your father unable to leave the house. Now that you are home again . . ."

He nodded, but didn't seem to be attending. "Yes, though in fact, I plan to leave for London very shortly."

"Oh," Katryn said, her heart sinking. "Because Eleanor and her husband are returning to their town house at the end of the week?"

Robert must have heard her mother mention that information at dinner, she thought, trying not to show the wave of despair that threatened to overwhelm her. He would never forget her sister, and who indeed could blame him? Eleanor had always been the beauty of the family. How could she expect him to take notice of Eleanor's less beautiful, less biddable sister?

This time Robert turned his head and gave her his attention. "No, not because of Eleanor. That is all in the past now. But I must marry."

She knew her eyes widened. "Then what you said the other day—you were in earnest?"

He nodded.

A proper young lady would not have pursued the subject, but Katryn pushed aside any thought of propriety. This was too important.

"Robert, you should not rush into a new engagement just because you are heartsore," Katryn protested. "How can you judge your own feelings so soon? You must give it time."

"Time, my dear, is what I do not have," he told her, lowering his voice and glancing back toward the rest of the party. No one seemed to be regarding them, and he went on. "It is not a matter of the heart. You know how the estate is situated, the house and property and income—all entailed. My father has little to will away from his lawful heir, and my sisters and mother must not be left virtually penniless."

"But there is no need to worry! You are here now, whole and healthy and—oh, Robert, you are not ill?" Katryn felt her heart seem to stop, and she could breathe again only when he shook his head.

"I am well, but there are circumstances that— I can't explain it, Katryn, I'm sorry. But I must take a wife and beget a son as soon as may be. The succession, and my family's welfare, must be ensured. My—my recent experiences have convinced me that this matter cannot be left to the mercy of an uncertain fate."

"But whom do you wish to marry?" Katryn asked, keeping her tone very low. "Forgive me for asking, but you—you have another love?"

Unbidden, his gaze sought Eleanor, sitting near his sisters at the other side of the room. Robert smiled grimly and turned back to the window. "My emotions do not change so quickly."

She bit her lip, and he continued after the briefest pause.

"Didn't I just say it was not a matter of the heart? Besides, I've been away a long time. That's why I must go to London: to meet some eligible ladies at once, and to find one who would be willing to accept a somewhat businesslike proposal. Love does not enter into it, but I have something to offer—a handsome estate, an old and respected family name."

Much more than that, she thought, shutting her eyes for an instant, though she could still see his masculine profile in her mind's eye, his newly trimmed wavy dark hair, his tall frame. She remembered how he looked astride Shadow, the man and the beast moving in unison, the very picture of leashed power. She remembered how his touch always made her quiver inside. So much more than that. With indrawn breath, she gathered her courage and spoke quickly, before she lost her nerve.

"Robert?"

"Yes, my dear?" He sounded absent again, as if already his thoughts had strayed, perhaps to the choice of well-born brides he might find in London.

"I am an eligible lady."

3

For a moment he stood very still, and she thought he was shocked, displeased. She should never have spoken. But how could she not, if he were determined to throw himself into such a cold-blooded and hasty marriage? When all her senses were so attuned to him that she felt as well as heard the soft rise and fall of his chest when he breathed, how could she lose him yet again?

He turned slightly to gaze into her upturned face, illuminated by the rich candlelight. The shadows that occasionally danced back and forth across her face made lovely green eyes more alluring, soft lips more red. In his carefree salad days, before the infernal war, Robert had known celebrated courtesans, always eager for young lords with old fortunes, who had only allowed themselves to be seen at night. The forgiving candlelight was a veil that softened edges grown rough and brittle. Sadly, their battle scars had not always been completely concealed. He knew something of battle scars, Robert thought bitterly.

Looking down now at Katryn, he saw the candles' glow only heightened Katryn's youth, her freshness. A freshness he could never touch. He sighed.

"Katryn, my dear. You are very young—"

"I have been out two Seasons," she interrupted, her tone indignant. "I have had *two* proposals of marriage, thank you, sir!"

"As many as that?" Robert asked, his eyebrows raised.

Katryn flushed, uncertain how to respond to the slightly mocking smile that twisted his lips. Her impulsive boast left her feeling as gauche as a schoolroom miss.

Suddenly contrite, Robert knew his smile had softened. "Forgive me, Katryn. I am quizzing you in a most ungentlemanly manner."

He turned more fully toward her. Katryn dared a step forward, closer than was seemly. She could almost touch him, almost stroke the thick nap of his jacket, savor the delicious contrast of its softness draping his hard-earned muscles.

"And neither of these gentlemen was fortunate enough to secure your affections?" His tone was formal, but he searched her face, and she lifted her chin to meet his gaze, her own eyes steady.

"No."

He smiled ruefully. "But there will be other men clamoring for your hand, Katryn. And you, of all people, I would not wish to condemn to a loveless marriage. There is no need for *you* to rush into matrimony."

Loveless! she thought, biting her lip to hold back the rush of words. *Robert, how can you be so blind?* She took a deep breath, but before she could answer him, a call from Lady Manning interrupted.

"Come and have tea, dearest boy." The card game had ended, and the butler had brought in the tea tray.

Katryn threw a quick, pleading glance at Robert, and he spoke very softly. "I will ride over tomorrow afternoon, if you really wish to speak about this."

She nodded, and they rejoined the family group. There was no more chance for private conversation, but as Katryn accepted a cup and sipped the hot tea, she shivered a little, thinking what she could say to him tomorrow, how she could convince him. She must, she must!

She slept little that night, tossing and turning beneath her linen coverlet, rumpling her smooth sheets, her mind all a-jumble as she rehearsed again and again all the arguments she could muster. She must be logical, as cold-blooded and rational as he. She could not break down and weep, allow him to see the despair she felt at the thought of losing him all over again. Certainly, she must not reveal the way her belly ached when he touched her hand, or the heat that rushed through her when his shoulder brushed her own. Perhaps he would think these responses improper; she wasn't sure what to make of them herself.

She would do anything—but she must not beg, she told herself in the dark hours of the morning, when her hope was at its lowest ebb. He might despise her. And the most pressing reason of all she felt very sure she could not admit. *Because I have loved you all of my life. . . .*

He might pity her, she thought bleakly, but love did not grow from pity, or else no suitors would be spurned, no ladies jilted.

She rose early, heavy-eyed and pale, hardly a good way to greet a prospective suitor. Katryn took a long time about her toilette, dressing very carefully in her favorite green-sprigged muslin with the crisp white lace accents. She had the maid thread a white ribbon through the cluster of dark curls pinned to the top of her head. When she came downstairs, she could eat hardly a bite of breakfast. Fortunately, the table was almost empty; the men had already eaten and ridden out early, and the baby was fretful, her mother said, so Eleanor was still in the nursery. Her mother didn't seem to notice Katryn's agitation, or if she did, she kept her own counsel.

The morning stretched on forever, and when she at last could begin to expect him, Katryn fled to the garden, walking up and down and trying to breathe deeply and compose herself for what must be the most important interview of her life. When she heard a horse approaching, she trembled despite herself. Her father and brother-in-law had returned long since; surely this must be Robert. She walked to the edge of the garden wall so that he would see her.

It was Robert, and he lifted his hat to her, then slid smoothly from his horse and tossed the reins to a groom who had hurried up. He turned away from the house and walked across the drive to join her. She stood at the gate and watched him come, and her heart pounded so hard she could barely breathe. She had never swooned in her life; she wasn't about to be a goose and succumb to the vapors now.

When he was close enough to speak, Robert bowed, and she made him her best curtsy.

"Katryn."

Robert looked grave; had he already decided against her? If so, how could she bear it?

Her mouth was so dry she almost couldn't speak. She waited a long moment for him to comment on her appearance, to pay her some pretty compliment like the sort he had never failed to give Eleanor. She waited in vain. Not an affair of the heart, he had said. Finally, Katryn swallowed and borrowed from her mother's matter-of-factness. "A fine day for a ride, my lord. Shall we take a turn around the garden?"

"Yes, indeed." He strolled alongside her through the formal garden. She stared down at the thick greenery, not really seeing it. She waited, but he was silent, and she rushed into speech, too nervous to dally any longer and too impatient to avoid the real subject of their meeting.

"Have you considered what I said? I mean, if you are still of a mind to wed?"

"I must wed," Robert said quietly. "Everything I said to

you last night is true, and I do not wish to waste any more time."

"Then why do you doubt my—my willingness?" she said, stumbling over the words. "Unless I do not suit, and you— you dislike the thought of marrying me?" She held her breath till the answer came.

She was such an innocent, Robert thought, sweet little Katryn, always tagging along behind when he had walked with Eleanor through this very garden. Her nervousness was so patent, he felt like a cad already, by even considering allowing her to make such an impulsive alliance.

"Of course I don't dislike you, Katryn. I've known you all your life, since you were in short skirts and pulled my hair when you didn't get your way. I've seen you kick your heels in quite marvelous tantrums."

His tone was lighter, and she dared to throw him a quick glance. He smiled, but the smile soon faded, and his dark eyes were somber.

"It's you I'm thinking of, Katryn. I don't want to do you an ill turn. I still fear that you're too young. After I heard of Eleanor—when I knew I must find someone else to marry, I was thinking more of some well-bred lady old enough to have given up any thoughts of romance, who would be willing to make a rational arrangement," he said. "If we married, and then you found someone more suited to you . . ."

As if that were possible. "Robert, I like you very much," Katryn told him, her voice husky. It was a pale version of the truth, but perhaps he heard her sincerity, because he smiled again, suddenly.

"I know that, my dear, and I value your friendship. But you've always looked up to me, and I'm afraid you still see me through a child's eyes. I was older, and I looked—forgive me—perhaps more dashing, more heroic, than you will find that I am. I should hate for you to be disappointed."

"I am willing to take the chance," she said, her throat aching with tension. She paused and gazed at him, and he stopped, too, and met her eyes. "I think you should allow me to make my own choice, Robert. Unless the thought of us— of—of such a union disgusts you—"

"Of course not!"

He reached to take her gloved hand, and she felt the light touch all the way to her bones. The familiar heat rushed over her till she felt that her face must have flushed, and she tried not to tremble.

"Who could I most desire to bear my name than someone I am already well acquainted with, an old friend? I only want you to be sure."

"I am quite sure, Robert," she said, holding her tone level with the greatest effort. "I am not a schoolgirl any longer, you know."

He nodded. "Very well. You don't mind a quick wedding?"

"As soon as you will," Katryn said, hearing a faint roaring in her ears. Was it really done, so simply?

"Then, my dear, I must solicit the honor of your hand in marriage."

He still held her hand. His light pressure made her heart soar, and the warmth inside her deepened into a strange heat that made her knees tremble and her belly ache. She blushed, but her voice was firm. "I am honored to accept."

He pressed her hand, but he did not, to her disappointment, bend to kiss her.

Robert pretended not to see the slight tilt of her face. He looked away, feeling like a criminal—she was so young, so unknowing . . . How could he do this to her? But after all, he reminded himself bitterly, the marriage would be of brief duration, cut short by forces outside all of their control, and she would recover soon enough and go on to a new love. Women did; he had Eleanor's example to teach him that.

His voice was more brusque than he intended. "I hope you do not regret this. I must speak to your father. I should have done it first, of course, but I'm afraid he may think me mad. He may still think so."

"I will marry you, Robert, whether my family approves or not," she said firmly.

He was surprised into a chuckle. "More tantrums? I hope that will not be necessary. I will suggest that my mother call upon you very soon, and we can make the necessary arrangements for the ceremony."

They walked together back to the house, and while Robert went to the study to find her father, Katryn went upstairs to the nursery. As she had hoped, she found her sister sitting in a chair and rocking the baby in his cradle, the nanny at the side of the room.

"Sshhh," Eleanor murmured, her eyes on the infant. "He is almost asleep."

Katryn waited a few moments, then whispered, "I must talk to you, Eleanor, at once."

"I shall be downstairs very soon."

"It can't wait!"

Eleanor sighed, but she nodded. "Very well." She signed to the nanny to come and take her place, and as the nurse took him the drowsy infant blinked, made a bubbling noise, then shut his eyes once more. Katryn led her sister out into the hall, then glanced up and down its length.

"Come to my bedroom," she said.

"Why such a to-do?" Eleanor asked. "Is this matter so urgent?"

"Yes!" Katryn ushered her sister into her own bedroom and shut the door. "I wanted to tell you first, before our parents speak of it." She paused—there was no easy way to say it—then the words rushed out almost of their own volition.

"Robert has proposed marriage, and I have accepted. I hope you don't mind?"

Eleanor gasped. "Proposed? Three days after his return? Are you both mad?" Her voice had risen, and Eleanor never shouted.

"Oh, do not be angry, Eleanor," Katryn begged. "I know—I know this must be hard, but he cannot marry you, and so—"

"You didn't misunderstand him? Are you sure that is what he asked?"

"Of course I'm sure," Katryn answered impatiently. "It's not the sort of question one can mistake, Eleanor."

Eleanor gazed at her, her blue eyes still wide, her lips pressed into a thin line. "I am glad to know that he has recovered from my loss, and so quickly." She sounded bitter, and so unlike her usual gentle self that Katryn gasped and for a moment didn't know how to answer.

"But, Eleanor, you waited hardly more than a year to marry someone else. How can you—"

Eleanor jumped to her feet. "I waited more than three days! And a year can be a very long time when your heart is aching. . . . I don't wish to talk about it anymore." She hurried out of the room, slamming the door behind her.

Katryn was left alone, feeling heavy with guilt. She didn't want to hurt Eleanor. But, barring Whitmund's death—and he was barely thirty, strong and hale—there was no hope for Eleanor and Robert. Robert had said he was afraid to wait. And to have the chance to marry Robert herself—she could not pass it by.

Her thoughts flew down to the study; what was her father saying right now? She paced up and down her room for some minutes, then went to hang over the stair rail. When she heard her father's voice, and Robert's, she gripped her hands tightly together and stepped back out of sight.

Robert was saying his farewells; surely, surely, her father had not refused to hear his suit? Katryn picked up her skirts and ran down the stairs. But Robert was gone and the door shut behind him before she could reach the ground floor. The sound of the retreating hoofbeats teased her, and she shook her head in frustration. She turned back toward the study and, when she entered, found her parents arguing.

"I'm not sure whether his mind has been affected after all," her father was saying. "Not home a week, and he can't have one sister so he'll take the other? I never heard of such a thing! We'd be the talk of the county!"

"Carlton, you are the one who has lost your senses," her mother retorted. "We have known the boy since the day he was born. He is good-natured, well-featured, of a good family—our oldest friends, I might add—with a handsome estate and income, and now he will even have the title. How could you possibly consider not granting your permission? It is a famous match!"

Katryn slipped inside and shut the door quickly behind her, hoping the servants would not overhear the heated voices.

"But so soon—if he had asked for her hand in six months or a year, I would have understood, smiled upon them both." Mr. Worth paused to rub his hands together, looking troubled. "The boy even talked of a special license. I will have no daughter of mine married in such a pell-mell way!"

"Of course not, the banns will be read, just as usual," his wife declared in a firm tone. "But you cannot withhold your approval just because he didn't wait as long as you think seemly."

"But why the haste?" her father repeated. He turned to see Katryn and waved her forward. "Oh, come in, come in, child. Are you certain of this? Such a quick proposal seems very strange to me."

"I am quite certain, Father," she said, putting one hand on his arm in entreaty. "Pray, say you do not dislike it. How could you be offended by the thought of Robert for your son-in-law?"

"Oh, I liked the thought just fine when he was engaged to Eleanor! Do you mean to tell me you don't mind that he was engaged to your sister first? People will talk, you know." Her father's hazel eyes were troubled.

"I don't care," Katryn told him. "I want to marry Robert. I know Eleanor had the first claim, but she has married someone else. I don't mind being his second choice, truly."

He patted her hand, his smile rueful. "If you are quite certain."

"I am, Father, I am," Katryn assured him.

Her father kissed her lightly on the forehead. "Well, then, who am I to stand in your way?"

Her mother sighed in relief. "Thank goodness. I am sure Katryn knows her own mind. Certainly, she always has. You will not regret this, sir."

"I hope not." Mr. Worth shook his head. "More to the point, I hope Katryn does not. She does not need to hang out for a fortune, you know, or even a title. I can provide for my own daughters well enough, even if not as grandly as our neighbors."

Katryn smiled at him. "I know that, sir; I am very fortunate. I make this choice of my own heart, I promise you."

"But why such a rush?"

"I think," Katryn told them both, "he has waited too long in that French prison, seeing empty days fly by. Perhaps he wants to waste no more time. He needs to go on with his life."

It was their own words to Eleanor, she remembered suddenly and blushed. Her parents exchanged troubled glances, but her mother straightened her shoulders and came across to embrace her younger daughter.

"I am happy for you, my dear. He is a fine young man and well situated. And you have known each other forever; why should he not make up his mind quickly? It's not as if you had been strangers—now, that would have been improper. I am sure you will deal very well together."

Katryn hugged her mother back, and the bubbling of happiness inside her grew. Surely nothing could impede the marriage now.

But she still threw anxious glances at her sister; Eleanor seemed very quiet at dinner, and when the ladies withdrew, leaving the gentlemen at the table, Katryn took her aside.

"Are you all right?" she said with her usual forthrightness. "I know Robert loved you first, Eleanor. Perhaps he always will. He makes this match now only from practical considerations. You must perceive that."

A trace of stiffness in Eleanor's stance faded. "And knowing that, you still want him?" she asked quietly.

Katryn nodded. "I do, I do. Even if he loves you most, perhaps I can win a scrap of his affection. But I don't want to wound you, truly I don't. Tell me you will not hate me for this wedding!"

"But would you be happy with only a scrap of Robert's affection?" Eleanor asked, her voice low.

Katryn looked at Eleanor with level eyes. "You mean, of course, would I be happy with a scrap when you have his whole heart?"

Eleanor glanced away. Unable as usual to share Katryn's bluntness, she sighed.

"How could I begrudge you a good match?" Eleanor said, her usual gentle tone almost back to normal. "I must wish you only the best, my dear. And Robert, too."

"Thank you!" Katryn gave her sister an impulsive hug. "I will be happy, I am sure, if only it does not trouble you."

Eleanor looked down to smooth the pale blue silk of her gown. "I—I was a little surprised, that's all. I hadn't expected Robert to make another alliance so soon. But how can I criticize, when I am already married myself. You do not think he does it only to punish me, Katryn?"

Katryn shook her head. "He's not like that, you should know better than anyone," she pointed out. "I am sure he has . . . other motives."

"Yes, the entailed estate, of course. And of course I knew that you—" Eleanor paused and looked around, murmuring, "Now, where is my embroidery frame?"

Eleanor had never been good at dissembling. "What?" Katryn demanded. "What did you know?"

Her sister met her gaze, her own blue eyes steady. "That you have always loved him, of course."

Katryn felt her cheeks burn. "Even—even before, you knew? You never said."

Eleanor nodded. "I believed you would outgrow it, I admit. I thought it was mostly hero-worship, a schoolgirl crush. But if it has lasted this long—and you have had other offers, did you not? Then perhaps I was wrong, and this— this was meant to be."

Katryn sat down beside her sister, for once left without an answer.

"What are you chatting about, girls?" their mother said, coming to sit across from them.

"Just wishing Katryn happy." Eleanor pushed her needle through the fine linen with more effort than it needed. She pricked her finger and, exclaiming, put it to her mouth to ease the stinging. "I think she will be, indeed."

"Yes," Katryn murmured, still staring at her sister's bent head. Surprises everywhere. "Thank you, Eleanor. It is very good of you not to begrudge me the match."

The next morning, her mother sent a note to Lady Manning bidding them all to dinner. The earl, of course, would not come. He never left his own house—any exertion was a risk for his frail heart—but his wife and children arrived at a good hour.

The countess seemed in good spirits—though Katryn wondered what Robert's parents had said to the news when they first heard of the engagement—and greeted her future daughter-in-law with a kiss on the cheek.

"My dear, we are very pleased."

"Thank you, my lady." Katryn curtsied and flashed an answering smile.

She knew that the girls were watching curiously as Robert came up to greet her. Katryn held out her hand, and he bent over it, in the French fashion, and kissed it gracefully.

"You see," Dora told her sister. "He is being romantic, after all, and you said it was all just a trumped-up arrangement."

Marianne blushed and gave her sister a quick pinch on her arm. "Hush, you simpleton! Katryn, I am very happy to think of having you for my sister." She came forward for a quick hug, careful not to crush the soft folds of Katryn's silk gown.

"Yes, indeed," the irrepressible Dora added. "Since we can't have Eleanor—"

"Dora!" her mother said sharply. "You forget that you are no longer a heedless child, my love. One would think you were still in short skirts."

"I only meant . . ." Dora made a face, but under her mother's stern gaze, her voice faded.

Robert took Katryn's hand and placed it inside the crook of his arm. "Shall we leave my poor sister to remove her foot from her mouth and go inside, my dear?"

Katryn had blushed, but now she could laugh up at him and forget her momentary twinge of embarrassment. It was all worth it, if Robert was to be her husband. His touch evoked the usual shivery feeling inside her, and she thought with a quickening breath of the intimacies marriage would bring. She would never have to leave him again. She didn't care what anyone said, and the gossips would say far worse than Dora.

Katryn sat through dinner in a happy fog, watching Robert and listening to his voice when he spoke. It didn't matter that he chatted only of the most commonplace events—he could hardly make love to her at the dinner table, with all the family gathered around. And talk of war would also have been ill-suited for such an occasion, if he could have been induced to speak of it at all; he seemed to want to put all his bad memories away. And why should he not?

When the ladies withdrew, Eleanor went upstairs for a moment to check on her baby, and Robert's sisters sat beside Katryn on the settee. "What about a wedding dress, Katryn? Where will you buy it?"

"Mama is taking me to London to buy my bride clothes," Katryn told them. "And we will send in the engagement notice to the papers, while the banns are being read at the parish church here."

"I wish we had more time to give you a big party," Marianne said, sighing. "We should have had a ball for you, and your family would have had parties, too, if Robert were not in such a stupid rush. Mother says it doesn't matter, but I would like parties whenever I marry."

Katryn smiled. "I don't miss them. We'll have time enough for parties later."

"But it will be boring when you're married," Dora put in. "Whitmund used to be so attentive to Eleanor; now he sits over the brandy with your father for ages!"

"I don't think Eleanor minds," Katryn said.

"No, all she can think of is the baby, and he is a sweet thing, though he screams too much, I think. Nanny says it is the colic," Dora told them wisely. "Do you wish for a baby soon, Katryn?"

"Dora, hush!" her scandalized sister hissed. "I shall tell Mama. You don't say such things."

"Why not? Everyone knows that married ladies may expect interesting events—oh, all right." Dora subsided with a resentful glare at her sister.

Katryn knew her face was flushed, and she had to glance down at the figured carpet. It was foolish to be embarrassed, she told herself. She knew that Robert wanted a son quickly, and so she did, too. How could she not want any child of Robert's? But for a moment she thought of the bridal night, and her cheeks flamed again. If she felt so strange when he only touched her hand, how would she feel when she put off her gown and petticoats and—no, she mustn't think of that now, with Dora watching with her innocent eyes and heedless speech.

Katryn told them about her plans for the trousseau, and the girls were immediately absorbed in details of silk and muslin and trimming, new bonnets and shawls and shoes. This kept their minds safely occupied until Eleanor returned.

"Fitz is sleeping very well tonight," she told them, her voice less strained and her blue eyes looking a little more serene.

The men followed after her into the drawing room almost at once. Mrs. Worth directed the butler to set up a table for whist, and the younger members of the party, except for Eleanor, who laughed and excused herself—"I am too old for such pastimes," she said—sat down at the round table to play a game of jackstraws.

The girls were soon giggling over the children's game, and Robert appeared to have lost none of his agility.

"You beat me the last time we played, do you remember?" Katryn asked her betrothed, glancing up into his dark eyes. It made her breathless to sit beside him, so close that she could catch a trace of his masculine scent and detect a tiny new scar on his chin. She wished she could reach up and touch it, feel his warmth, soothe the old hurt.

"No, I'm afraid I do not. How long ago was that?" He glanced at her as he bent over the table, and she had to remind herself to breathe normally. His dark eyes were as brilliant as a moonlit lake, and she wanted so much to touch his face. . . .

They were all waiting for her to answer, and she pulled her thoughts back swiftly. "It must have been three months or more before you went away. It was only you and me and Eleanor; your sisters were visiting their cousin Sophy."

"And I won?" Robert asked lightly, pulling yet another straw from the tangled pile.

"Yes, indeed," Katryn told him, smiling a little. "You refused to have pity on us at all."

She couldn't help glancing across the room at Eleanor, whose attention seemed fixed on her needlework as she sat close to the card table, close to her husband. Was Robert aware of her, did he sense her relative closeness, just as Katryn herself knew with every pore of her body that Robert leaned across the table, only inches away from her shoulder?

Something inside her quivered, and Katryn tried to focus her mind on simple things. But Robert had his hand out to take another straw, and she gazed at the newly tanned skin, the supple fingers—there was a fading bruise on his arm— she could just make it out beneath the snowy cuff of his shirtsleeve.

She swallowed hard, and it brought her thoughts back to the ordeals he had had to withstand alone. *Oh, never again,* she thought. *I will be at your side now, Robert, always.*

Robert glanced up as if sensing her thought and smiled at her. But somehow the smile never seemed to reach his eyes; they were somber, holding back.

Did Robert regret the engagement?

She was being fanciful, Katryn told herself. But when her turn came, Katryn's hand was unsteady, and she dislodged the pile of straws at once.

Dora laughed in glee. "My turn, my turn!"

When the butler brought in the tea tray, Robert had been victorious thrice, and his sisters were laughing and merry. Robert grinned at them and Katryn impartially, though he did not laugh often.

When he and his family departed, he kissed her hand again, and Katryn smiled as she told him good night. She kept hidden deep inside her real thought—when would he kiss her lips? Robert had never kissed her, not for real. She didn't count the birthday greetings when he touched her cheek—she wanted to see how a fiancé, a husband kissed. Soon, soon, she would know.

On Sunday the banns were read at church for the first time, and on Monday Eleanor and her husband and baby and servants ended their visit and left for London, followed closely by Katryn and her parents to attend to the important business of the bride clothes.

As Eastborne was left behind, Katryn gazed out the window at the familiar landscape, glad that Eleanor and her family rode in their own carriage, glad that her mother did not require answers to the questions she was posing aloud to herself about gowns and gloves and shoes.

Was Robert already sorry he had asked for her hand? Why did the somberness remain, why was he not wholly happy? Was it simply Eleanor he still pined for? If so, nothing but—she prayed—time would ease that hurt. Would he ever learn to love Katryn? She was gambling her heart that he would.

And if not? Perhaps she should offer him his freedom, Katryn wondered, blind to the groves and hills that flowed past outside the carriage, hardly hearing the steady pounding of the horses' hooves. Perhaps marriage with a strange woman who had no real feeling for him would be easier on both husband and wife. Perhaps Katryn should offer to release him, if she were truly noble. But only to think of ending the engagement made her hands clench into fists, and her lips tighten. She had waited so long, with no hope at all, and now she had his promise of marriage.

Nothing would induce her to give him up.

4

In London, Katryn was thrown into a whirl of activity, with dressmakers and milliners and shoemakers to visit, and endless bolts of muslin and silk and satin to peruse. She was feminine enough to delight in the array of soft, shining fabrics and the rolls of ribbons and laces. Every time she went to a fitting and tried on a satin ball gown or a silk or muslin day dress, she wondered what Robert would think when he saw her. Would he approve? Did he see her as a wife yet, as a woman? Or did he still see her as the chubby child who had followed him fearlessly through one scrape after the other?

Katryn gazed into the tall looking glass and pressed her lips together tightly. She could not make her brown hair golden, nor her green eyes blue. She could not be Eleanor. How long before her husband saw her, Katryn, and did not wish for Eleanor instead?

"Why are you frowning?" her mother demanded. "That shade of green does very nicely; it makes your eyes look particularly brilliant. We also need the crimson walking dress and the sarcenet—should it be the lilac or the purple, do you think?"

"The purple," Katryn decided, liking the way the deeper

color made her dark hair stand out against her pale skin. Unlike fair-haired Eleanor, she had never shone in the paler hues deemed suitable for unmarried ladies; now she had a fuller spectrum of colors to choose from. Marriage had many advantages, she told herself.

"I believe you're right." Her mother held up a swatch of the silk beneath Katryn's chin. "Yes, this is the one. And the deep blue-green evening dress, I think?"

"Yes, Mama," she agreed. "I like it very much." Katryn stood still while the seamstress positioned a pin carefully in the high-waisted design, then added, "Perhaps the neckline can be a little lower?"

Her mother's brow creased, but the modiste nodded. "Yes, indeed. Very fashionable. And the young lady has the shape to carry it off."

Katryn grinned at her reflection. If only Robert agreed!

By the time they left the dressmaker's shop almost two hours later, Katryn was limp with fatigue, and her mother's shoulders sagged.

"I shall be glad to go home and take off this hat and have a cup of tea," Mrs. Worth confessed as she nodded to their coachman, who had been waiting outside the shop. "We will do the shoemaker tomorrow, and check on the new bonnets, and you'll need more silk stockings."

"Yes," Katryn said and prepared to cross to the coach, when a new voice interrupted.

"Why, Miss Worth! I read about your engagement, my dear. My felicitations! A happy event, but so sudden." It was Melanie Forsyth, a well-born girl with sharp blue eyes and a thin nose, and a penchant for putting it into other people's business.

"Not really," Katryn said, managing to keep her tone even. "I was acquainted with Lord Manning before he went into the army. In fact, I have known him all my life."

"Yes, but he was betrothed to your sister then, was he

not?" Miss Forsyth smiled, but her eyes held a malicious glint. "Forgive me, but it seems so strange. Marrying so quickly, and with no betrothal party to share the news with your friends—but I'm sure you have your reasons."

Was she daring to stare at Katryn's waistline? The hussy! Katryn's palm itched to slap her face. She bit back her temper with enormous effort. "I'm sure," she said with deliberate sweetness, "my friends will understand."

Miss Forsyth blinked, and Katryn's mother added smoothly, "Lord Manning's father, the earl, has had a long illness. Of course the dear boy wishes to be wed while his father is still here to share our joy. But we will indeed be sending cards for a betrothal party; we will hope to see you there." She glanced at her daughter. "Our carriage is waiting, Katryn. Good-bye, Miss Forsyth, please bear my good wishes to your mother."

They entered the carriage and as they drove away, Katryn fumed. "The little gossip—I'd like to pinch out her tongue!"

"Already the talk has started. I didn't want to tell you, Katryn, but yesterday two ladies stopped in midsentence when we walked into the hat shop, and the stares they gave us . . . We shall have to have a betrothal party after all. I shall write to Lady Manning at once."

Katryn's mother snapped her fan open and wielded it vigorously to cool her flushed face. "The party will have to be put together swiftly, and goodness knows it must not be a shabby affair. We have enough tongues wagging as it is; we must make an effort to allay some of the wildest gossip."

"Marianne will be happy," Katryn murmured. Her mother, already muttering aloud about guest lists and menus, paid her no heed.

Katryn laid her head back against the padded cushion and wondered if Robert would mind. She wished she understood why he seemed so driven, so obsessed with a quick wedding. Was it only his need for a son to ensure the succession, or did it have to do with his lost love? Was he struggling to overcome his passion for Eleanor, and could Katryn endure this strange marriage with old memories standing always between them?

Yet if it were a choice between marrying Robert, while he was still in love with her sister, and not having him at all, she knew there was no real decision to be made. Sighing, she stared out the carriage window and tried to pay heed to her mother, who was worrying aloud about where to find an extra chef who could cook French dishes.

Now in addition to the trousseau, there were the cards to address and send out, menus to plan and musicians to hire, extra servants to engage for the night of the party. The servants unswathed the large crystal chandelier in the ballroom at the back of the house, and washed every crystal pendant so the chandelier would sparkle when the wax candles were lit. The hardwood floor was polished to a high gleam, and the housemaids washed glasses while the footmen polished silver.

"The Season is barely begun," her mother pointed out. "Many people are not yet in town. There is no need for a crush, but we should have enough guests for the party to be a reasonable success. I will not have anyone saying that we are being furtive about your engagement—the very idea!"

"Yes, indeed," Katryn agreed, content that the only person that mattered would be there. She had had a scrawled note from Robert, saying, "I will be in London late Thursday, and will be there Friday in good time for dinner and the party. I hope all goes well. Do not tire yourself, my dear."

The note was tucked into her reticule so she could see it often; he had never written to her before. As a love letter, it was mild, indeed, but at least he had added the last solicitous sentence about not exhausting herself over the party arrangements. She touched her small bag and smiled at the thought. If there was a quiet yet insistent voice whispering that it was more like an older brother's concern, not a lover's, she chose not to heed it.

On Friday, she woke early when one of the maids brought her a tray with a cup of steaming tea. She heard men's voices outside in the street, and she glanced at the girl.

"What's happening downstairs, Annie?"

"It's the extra chairs for tonight, miss," the maid told her, beaming. "And the flowers for the ballroom have arrived, very fine, indeed. You must go and see when you come downstairs."

Katryn sipped her tea and could swallow only a few mouthfuls of toast. Her stomach was already knotted with anticipation as she thought about the party.

As the maid took out the tray, her mother looked into her room. "Don't dawdle, Katryn. Madame Clair promised me your dress would be here by noon, and the hairdresser will come at three. We will have Robert and his family for dinner, of course, before the other guests arrive. But the fishmonger sent Cook only one fresh turtle, instead of two, and one of the underfootmen slipped on the back stairs and may have broken his leg—of all days!"

She hurried out again before Katryn could call, "I hope he is all right."

She got up right away, but even impatient as she was for the evening, there was so much to do that the day seemed to fly by. She lingered long over her dressing, changing her mind three times about how to arrange the fresh flowers in her hair, and fretting her maid almost past politeness. "Miss," she said at last, "the dinner guests are arriving!"

"Yes, yes," Katryn said, leaning closer to the glass.

She had decided on the new green ball gown; its deep lustrous sheen pleased her, and its low-cut neckline gave her confidence. Her hair was done up in a deceptively simple arrangement that had taken the dresser time and effort to achieve—a knot of hair at the back of her head, with small white flowers tucked into the knot, and a few artless curls tumbling over her ears to soften its severe sweep. She was putting on her pearl eardrops when someone knocked at her bedroom door.

Her maid, who was holding her shawl, her foot tapping with impatience, hurried to open it.

"Who is it, Annie?" Katryn asked, not looking around. "If it's Mama, I shall be there directly."

The deep masculine voice made her jump. "Only me, Katryn. May I interrupt your toilette for just a moment?"

"Of course, my lord! I am so happy to see you." She rose quickly from the stool in front of her dressing table and hurried to greet him. "Have you just arrived? You look very fine."

Robert's evening clothes fit him admirably, and she could see he was regaining some of the weight he had lost during his imprisonment. His wide shoulders filled out the well-cut lines of the black coat, and his pantaloons were taut over well-muscled thighs.

Robert bowed. "And you look a vision, my dear. I arrived too late yesterday to visit, and this morning I too have been enduring fittings. I visited my tailor and my bootmaker, and I had other shopping to do." He smiled at her. "But before you came down, I wanted to give you this."

He held out a flat box, and Katryn took it, her hands not totally steady. When she opened it, she exclaimed, "Oh, Robert, it—it is lovely!"

The necklace was cunningly wrought; emeralds and diamonds flashed against their gold setting. Matching earrings nestled against the black silk that lined the box, and she touched the glittering jewels with a reverent hand. "The set is magnificent. Thank you! They will be perfect with my gown." She held out her hand and clasped his for a moment. He squeezed her hand briefly and then released it.

"I have to confess, your mother told me you would be

wearing green tonight," he admitted. "I'm glad you're pleased. I thought they would go well with this."

He took a smaller box from an inner pocket, and she flushed as she took it. This time, she had no words, gazing at the ring with its handsome square-cut emerald surrounded by smaller diamonds.

"I thought it would match your eyes," he said simply. "Diamonds alone seemed too insipid for you, somehow. I hope you like it?"

"Oh, yes," she said. It was somehow hard to speak; her throat ached and she had an alarming impulse to burst into tears. The ring was beautiful, and his actions were all correct, but she heard only politeness in his tone, and his dark eyes seldom met hers directly.

He was only going through the motions, like a windup toy. How had she ever thought this counterfeit marriage would be enough?

Robert took the ring from its velvet nest and slid it onto her finger. Even at this light touch, her awareness of him increased tenfold, and she felt the familiar tingle.

Oh, Robert, she thought. *When will you feel for me what I am feeling for you?* She had a wild impulse to clasp his hand, pull him closer, and kiss him wildly and without reserve.

But he had already drawn back, and the maid stood behind them, her eyes bright with curiosity.

"I hope this evening does not try your patience," Robert was saying, "but I will be at your side."

Katryn took a deep breath, pushing back her impatience. *I will make him love me! I will!*

She lifted her chin. "I would face any danger with you beside me," she told him. "A raging lion, or a troop of French soldiers!"

He smiled, but she thought a strange sadness lingered in his dark eyes. "I hope it will not come to that. I will let you finish your preparations; your mother is fretting about the time."

"I'll be down soon," she promised, sorry to see him bow and shut the door behind him. She wanted to feel his hand on hers again, perhaps have him clasp the necklace around her neck himself—she shivered at the thought. Now she looked down at her ring, touched the necklace in its box, and, for a moment, her vision wavered and she had to blink hard. Robert's betrothal gifts—they were beautiful, yet she would have traded all the jewelry for one heartfelt kiss.

But she would wear them, of course. She quickly removed her simple pearl earrings and replaced them with the new jewels. Her maid clasped the necklace around her neck, and in a few moments Katryn followed Robert down to the drawing room, where their dinner guests were assembling. The first thing she saw when she hurried into the room was Robert, Robert bending over Eleanor's seated form while the two talked quietly.

They looked so intimate that Katryn's smile wavered. She looked away, forced her lips upward again, and walked more slowly across the carpet to say hello to the countess.

"I hope you left his lordship in good health?" she asked, accepting an embrace from her ladyship, who was elegant in lavender silk, with three tinted feathers in her headdress.

"As well as can be expected," Lady Manning said. "But his spirits are excellent. He insists he will be carried to the carriage and into the church next week for your wedding, my dear. And I haven't the heart to argue, though I fear it will tire him greatly."

"I hope it will not exhaust him," Katryn said. "But it will be wonderful to have him there to share the ceremony with us."

Marianne came up to greet her, sparkling with excitement; she looked very grown-up in pale primrose muslin. "I'm so happy your parents decided to give a party after all,"

Marianne said. "Dora is livid that she can't be here tonight; she is pining to come out at once, and her not yet fourteen. Oh, the emeralds are lovely." She leaned close to peer at the necklace, and Katryn held up the ring for her sister-to-be to inspect.

"Robert has wonderful taste," Katryn said. "I've never seen a design I liked better." She was careful not to look around for him, but in a moment, she felt his presence at her side.

Marianne pursed her lips and then gave her brother an approving nod. "Nicely done, Robert!"

"I'm so glad I have your approval," he told her with dry humor, offering Katryn his arm. "The emeralds suit you very well, Katryn. Your mother is directing us toward the dining room. May I take you in?"

She nodded, happy to grip his arm lightly, careful not to look back at Eleanor. Katryn had his promise, she would soon have his name. And the love would come, it must!

Katryn lifted her chin and flashed her fiancé a bright smile, clutching his arm a bit too tightly as they walked into the dining room.

Dinner passed with nothing else to try Katryn's carefully nurtured composure, but the receiving line for the party was an ordeal. All the guests were prompt to offer their felicitations on the engagement, but too many matrons were bright-eyed with curiosity, and even some of the gentlemen eyed her with obvious speculation.

"So nice," Lady Exeter purred, her narrow eyes gleaming with inquisitiveness, "that Lord Manning should be returned safely to his family. And then to find his heart recovered so quickly, as well as his other wounds."

Katryn had to struggle to maintain her too-brittle smile. "Perhaps," she said boldly, "he has had good reason to recover."

While the noblewoman blinked and raised her brows, Katryn's mother said, "We are all pleased with the engagement. Of course, our families have been friends for so many years."

Katryn watched Lady Exeter smile and move on, wishing she could pull out the woman's hennaed hair. And there were other comments, too.

"So this is Katryn?" an elderly countess noted. "Pity you're not more like your sister, dear."

Katryn bit her lip and forced herself to smile, though the effort made her cheeks hurt. She knew what everyone was thinking, even the ones polite enough not to speak their thoughts. What could have prompted a notable catch like the earl's only son to settle for the younger, less beautiful Worth sister? Katryn's family was well born but had no title, comfortably off but not rich. And Katryn had never turned heads, as Eleanor did when she entered a room. All her life Katryn had lived in Eleanor's shadow.

"But I am wearing Robert's ring, not my sister," she said beneath her breath. "And someday, I will have his heart, you will all see."

Katryn knew the whispers were flying around the elegant, well-dressed company more rapidly than the glasses of wine the servants carried on their silver trays. Her temples ached as she forced herself to keep smiling and nodding as she greeted each guest.

Once, glancing at Eleanor chatting with her husband, she wondered how her sister could look so serene. All the gossips were watching her, too, as Eleanor must surely know. The usually staid Whitmund seemed especially solicitous tonight, looking around with a fierce stare at the assembled company. Eleanor stayed unfashionably close to her husband, and if she looked a trifle ashen, she had always had a pale complexion. It could not be easy for Eleanor, either, nor for her husband. But at least they did not have to stand in this stupid receiving line for every guest to gawk at. Katryn sighed and turned back to greet yet another society matron.

"So happy to see you," she murmured to the woman. Her cheeks were beginning to hurt in earnest from the effort of maintaining her frozen smile.

When the reception line finally broke up, and everyone except a stray latecomer or two had been greeted, she accepted a glass of punch and turned to speak to Robert's mother.

"A nice turnout, Katryn," the countess was saying. "Don't worry about the small-minded, my dear. The malicious chatter will die, and the matter will be forgotten soon enough."

"Yes, ma'am," Katryn agreed, only hoping it was true.

Then the countess gasped and gripped her fan so tightly that Katryn distinctly heard one of its slender ribs crack.

"Katryn, surely your parents never invited him to the party!"

Katryn turned slightly to see who had entered the ballroom, and her eyes widened as well. The tall, well-featured man with the brown hair and the slight but unnerving resemblance to Robert . . . it had to be Jerod Cavendish, the earl's nephew and—until Robert's return—lawful heir.

"I'm quite sure they did not," Katryn said quickly.

"The nerve of the man!" Lady Manning sniffed. "I will not speak to him! I will fetch your father, Katryn."

She hurried off, but in fact Mr. Worth was nowhere in sight; he might have stepped into the library where the card tables had been set up for guests who didn't care for dancing. And who would stop this intrusive person in his absence?

Katryn looked around for Robert. He was talking to several gentlemen a few feet away, but he seemed to sense her glance because he looked up to meet her gaze. She made a slight motion, and he excused himself to his companions and came quickly to her side.

"Robert," she began, but before she could explain about the uninvited guest, Cavendish strode up to join them.

The two men stood only a foot apart. The air was suddenly tense, and Katryn took a deep breath, observing the surface likeness between the two men. Cavendish was a little thinner, his shoulders narrower, and just an inch shorter than his cousin. They had the same arch of brows, and both had strong noses, though Cavendish's had a slight hook at the end. Despite the family resemblance, neither man smiled.

Robert spoke first. "Cavendish, I admit I had not expected to receive the pleasure of your company this evening."

Cavendish's jaw was tight, and Katryn saw a glint of malice in his eyes, which were a paler hue than Robert's deep brown. "Ah, yes, my invitation seems to have gone astray. But as it was all in the family, I knew I need not stand on ceremony. I came to offer my felicitations on your marriage, Cousin. Indeed, upon your miraculous return to home and hearth. And, perhaps, to be sure that it is really you."

Katryn heard the undercurrent of less civilized emotions beneath his bland tone. Suddenly she thought that he did not look so much like Robert after all. She had never heard Robert speak with hidden malice.

"Did you think I could be an imposter?" Robert answered, his own voice level.

"I shouldn't have been surprised," Cavendish snapped, and for an instant she saw genuine fury beneath the polite facade. "Manning would do anything to keep me from the title. I was surprised enough he allowed you to buy your colors—the military life is not the most healthy. And then, after your poor dear brother's accident, when your death, too, was mentioned in the dispatches—well, I did put on black arm bands. But I could not pretend indifference to the upcoming change in my fortune."

"Your honesty is impressive, Cousin," Robert said levelly. "Of course, I'm not sure which grieved you more: the report of my death or my unexpected return to life."

"I'm sure you can guess," Cavendish answered, his voice low.

"How dare you speak so?" Katryn demanded. But to her annoyance, neither man seemed to take note of her; their eyes remained locked and their posture stiff.

"A shame about all this gossip," Cavendish continued. "But this unseemly rush into matrimony—"

Robert raised his brows. "A subject you are perhaps familiar with?" he murmured.

Cavendish's face flushed, and Katryn saw the rage flash in his pale eyes. There was something about his own birth—Katryn couldn't quite remember the details. . . .

"So I should wish you happy?" Cavendish was saying, his mouth twisted, more grimace than smile.

"Upon the occasion of my wedding, yes, indeed," Robert answered coolly, while Katryn was still trying to decide if Cavendish meant to be as insulting as he sounded.

Cavendish nodded, as if conceding the point to Robert. "I could not believe my eyes when I read the announcement of your engagement. Why the hasty wedding, my lord, if not for the most obvious reason—and you've hardly been back in England that long, have you? One hopes your mind has not been affected by your sojourn in prison. A mad earl would never do—the honor of the family, you know."

Katryn drew a deep breath, and she saw Robert frown.

"Your solicitude for my well-being is most affecting; I will only assure you that my health is excellent on all counts and accept your congratulations." Robert sounded as if he spoke through gritted teeth. "We won't detain you any longer from your previous engagements. And now that I am returned, I'm sure I don't need to point out that any further visits to Manning Hall are quite unnecessary? I won't have my father distressed."

There was a short silence, and the air seemed to crackle with tension; Katryn would not have been surprised to see Cavendish raise his fist.

"No need to remind me; I have no wish to look on what I cannot have. Only by an accident of birth . . . such a small thing to have such large consequences. But that accident may yet be mended. Stranger things have happened. Your good health, sir." Cavendish bowed with exaggerated grace. "Indeed, your family must all hope that it continues."

He turned toward the doorway, his gait stiff with suppressed emotion, and, in a moment, disappeared from their sight.

Katryn trembled; she had never encountered such anger, thinly hidden though it was beneath a veneer of courtesy. "What did he mean by that—that last comment?" She felt cold, as if a draft of icy air had swept through the overheated ballroom.

"Do not mind him; an envious man making empty threats, that is all," Robert told her, keeping his own voice low. Several people had watched the brief exchange with open curiosity. "Listen, they are striking up for the first dance. We must take the floor."

Katryn nodded and gave him her hand to lead her onto the dance floor. Of course they must open the ball. She was only sorry it was not a waltz. But when he bowed, and she curtsied, it was a relief to concentrate on the intricate movements of the dance, smiling at Robert when the pattern brought them together again, enjoying the touch of his hand, the reassurance of his smile. If only their life together could have the easy give-and-take of the dance, the rhythmic ebb and flow, and, most of all, the crisscrossing line that always brought partners back together.

Forgetting all the other guests who watched them, Katryn smiled up at Robert. In three days they would be wed. In time he would forget Eleanor and come to love her, Katryn. Surely nothing could threaten her joy.

When Robert left the party, he sat silently in the carriage as his mother and sister chatted. Marianne was in high spirits, and she chattered on about gowns and dance partners. The countess was less exuberant, still angry over the appearance of their cousin.

"How could he walk uninvited into the party? The man has no class, no conscience whatsoever," she fumed. "With his breeding . . . the earl's younger brother was never any good, you know, and that wretched woman he married—just in time, too. Well, blood does tell, doesn't it?" She turned to stare at her son. "I hope it did not ruin your enjoyment of the party."

"I would not give that cur so much satisfaction," Robert told her, his voice level.

Marianne narrowed her eyes in the dark carriage as if to make out his face. "I didn't think you looked as if you were enjoying the party very much, anyhow," she said. "I mean, you and Katryn made a nice couple in the dance, but you don't act much like you're in love, Robert."

"And I suppose you would know all about love-stricken suitors?" Robert answered, keeping his tone light.

His sister giggled, distracted. "I danced three times with the younger Mr. Wiggins, did you see?"

Robert shut his eyes and let the chatter flow past him. But when they alighted at the Mannings' London residence and his sister, yawning, climbed the broad stairs, his mother hesitated long enough to look him in the eye.

"Robert, you are not regretting this engagement?" She sounded troubled.

Robert shook his head. "No, I am sure that this is the right course."

She patted his arm and continued up the stairs, but he turned aside into the library and rang for a bottle of brandy.

When a sleepy-eyed footman brought his wine, Robert poured it with a lavish hand. He didn't care what his head would feel like in the morning; better if he couldn't feel at all.

How could he do this to Katryn, sweet innocent little Katryn, whom he had known all her life? Would she hate him, later?

Robert took another gulp of brandy and almost groaned. He had never thought to have this responsibility—it had always been William's duties, William's cares. Now, since his older brother's death, Robert was the one who had to provide for his family. And Katryn would still have the title, the estate—or she would if they could manage to start a baby, a son, before the letter surfaced, the letter that would end his life and all his hopes. There would be a scandal, but it would pass. She would get on with her life and most likely find another husband. Of course she would—hadn't her sister? With Eleanor to guide her, Katryn would not grieve for long.

And his sisters, his mother, would not be penniless after his father's death. It came down to that. Even if he sometimes felt he was buying security for three innocent women by sacrificing another just as blameless, the good would outweigh the bad. Katryn would not weep for long; she would have the trappings of widowhood to protect her, and she would soon find other men to amuse her. And yet—

"Oh, Katryn, I hope you can forgive me," he murmured into the half-filled glass. He tossed the rest of the brandy down his throat and coughed a little; the potent wine should be savored, not be so ill used. But tonight he wanted only to silence his uneasy conscience.

He put down the glass. A rush of weariness threatened to overcome him; he sat heavily in the nearest chair and stared into the flickering depths of the fire. In its ruby heart, he seemed to see Katryn in short skirts, with a torn stocking and skinned knee where she had fallen from an apple tree.

She hadn't cried, even then, he thought, grinning ruefully. Katryn had spirit, she had staying power. Maybe, someday, she would pardon him for what he was about to do.

And the wedding, and the wedding night, would proceed as planned. The vision in the fire's dancing depths changed, and he saw her again as she had been tonight, grown up indeed, the smooth white skin of her breasts alluring in the low-cut gown, her eyes sparkling with defiance as she faced the curious gossipmongers who had thronged to the party.

He felt his blood stirring, felt the beginning of arousal. He'd never thought of her as more than a little girl, but now—now he must see her as a wife and, truth to tell, if she wore any more gowns like the one tonight that hugged her body and emphasized her swelling breasts and narrow waist, it would be no very onerous task. Who would have thought that little Katryn would grow into such a beauty? She deserved better than this sham of a marriage, he thought again.

And Eleanor—a picture of her blond, blue-eyed loveliness rose before him, and he felt guilt of another kind. He had loved Eleanor so long . . . oh, gods, had any man ever had his heart twisted in so many directions?

For a long time, he stared into the dancing flames, till the fire burned low and all that was left was a smoldering mound of ashes hiding the glowing coals beneath. Much like his love for Eleanor, Robert thought glumly, unconsummated, but undying. What a tangle.

He rose at last, and when he opened the door to the hall he saw Marianne's handkerchief lying where she had dropped it on the tiled floor. When he bent to pick it up, he saw that the lace was torn. Robert stared at the flimsy little trifle, so delicate, so easily damaged. Like his sisters, like his mother, like Katryn herself.

He had no choice; he had to go on with this marriage.

5

Katryn and her parents left town the next morning to return to Hertfordshire for the wedding. Katryn was happy to leave; in London too many gossipy ladies and gentlemen stared at her wherever she went. So she left the city behind and took with her several trunks full of new clothes. She still struggled to believe that she was really to marry Robert, whom she had loved for so long, but with every bounce and jostle of the carriage, the ceremony drew closer.

After she and her parents reached home, Robert soon rode over to ask if she would like to spend a brief honeymoon at his parents' hunting lodge.

"There would be more privacy, and it's only half a day from here, so it will be an easy distance," he told her.

"It sounds charming," she agreed at once, but she didn't meet his eyes, and she had to bite her lip to keep herself from blushing. Thoughts of the wedding night evoked such surprising feelings inside her, it was hard to look him in the face.

But now the hours ran by with such speed that almost before she could credit it, she was standing at the altar in their local parish church, with only their families in attendance—the earl had indeed been carried downstairs by two stalwart footmen and placed carefully into the carriage, with his wheeled chair tied on behind. He beamed upon them as the rector intoned the service.

"To have and to hold, for better or for worse, as long as ye both shall live . . ."

They were beautiful words, Katryn thought, her heart swelling. She glanced quickly at Robert; his face was slightly pale, his expression grave.

I will do my very best to make you happy, and perhaps you will love me someday, she thought, making it as much a promise as the oaths they swore aloud to the vicar.

When the service ended, Robert touched her lips lightly, but the kiss was too brief to be the "real" kiss she had dreamed of for so long. Then she was being hugged by her mother and then by Robert's mother. Eleanor, looking very white, came up to offer her hand.

"I hope you will be happy," Eleanor murmured. She turned to offer congratulations to the groom, and if Robert grasped Eleanor's hand a moment too long, and if there was a sheen of tears in Eleanor's eyes, Katryn tried to look as if she did not notice.

They all returned to Manning Hall for a wedding breakfast, and then, before she knew it, luggage was being tied on to the back of the carriage, and Robert was helping her in.

She felt a stab of dismay when she found that he was not planning to sit beside her.

"You're going to ride?"

"It's such a fine day," he said, but he didn't quite catch her eye. "I always ride, you know."

"Of course," Katryn said, swallowing her chagrin. It was not a long journey, after all, no use to repine over something so small. She must keep her emotions under control. She had not slept well the night before, too excited, too incredulous to sleep, and now she dozed through most of the journey.

They reached the small house in good time. The servants

had been forewarned of their coming and were prepared to receive them. Dinner was ready to be served as soon as she had gone upstairs to take off her bonnet and wash her hands and face. Robert waited for her in the small drawing room and poured her a glass of Madeira when she entered. Katryn stared at the fire in the hearth—the day was fine but a little chilly—and couldn't think of anything to say. She was Robert's wife, but he was so silent. What was Robert thinking? Did he still see Eleanor's face, so pale and strained as she watched the ceremony? Katryn was relieved when the butler announced, "Dinner is served, my lord, my lady."

Dinner was quiet, with little conversation as they ate. The food was doubtless good, but afterward, Katryn could not remember one thing that she had eaten—it might as well have been grass and wild berries for all she knew.

What she was aware of was Robert seated across the small table, lifting his wineglass so that the candlelight glinted off the crystal, smiling at her briefly as he handed her a dish of some cunningly wrought confection. When their hands brushed, she felt as if she were burned, as if her skin were afire, torched by his passing touch.

She nibbled at her food, wondering if all brides felt this contraction of the throat, this strange trembling inside the belly, or if it was only brides with matches as strangely made as this one. But indeed, no one else could have been wed in such a way. Surely normal weddings were glad-met encounters with partners united in love, or at least mutually agreed-to convenience—not this strange half-twix, half-tween arrangement.

Robert seemed at last to notice her abstraction. "Katryn, you're not eating. You are not ill, I hope?"

"Oh no, I'm fine, just a little—a little tired," she murmured, looking down at her hands clasped tightly together in her lap. She could feel the heat rise inside her and color her cheeks. Perhaps Robert was looking for an excuse to avoid taking her to his bed, or else he thought her so missish that she would use any justification to elude his advances. She knew from whispered accounts that some ladies avoided the marriage bed, finding their marital duty distasteful. She would not be one. She had more spirit than to shrink from her husband and his desires. Besides, if the strange tremblings inside her were any indication, she just might have desires of her own.

Looking up through her thick lashes, she watched her new husband as he ate quickly, as if he dared not waste too much time on any one chore. A large pair of candelabra sat on the table between them, and the candlelight sent shadows dancing across the sharp angles of his face. He had no affectations; he was no dandy like many of the young men in London. No, indeed. Strength and purpose characterized every movement of his tall frame. Lost in his thoughts, he did not seem to notice her gaze.

She touched the gold band on her left hand with silent awe. Married; she was a married lady, she told herself for the hundredth time; she and Robert were husband and wife. How hard it was to credit. . . . The dreams she had had when she was very small—she had never really expected them to come true.

When the servants took away the dishes, she retired from the table, leaving Robert in his solitary state to another glass of port. But when she looked into the drawing room, she decided she could not bear to sit and make polite conversation. And it was late enough; she went into the hall and caught the eye of one of the maidservants.

"Tell his lordship that I will be awaiting him upstairs," she said, with as even a tone as she could manage.

It didn't help that the girl, her eyes bright and saucy, almost winked as she gave a quick curtsy. "Yes, milady."

The honorific still sounded strange to her ears. She was married, and a lady. . . . She was Robert's lady, Robert's wife. She went up slowly to the large bedchamber that had been prepared for them, and in a moment the maid followed to help her disrobe.

"I've unpacked your trunk, my lady," the girl said. "I have your gown and wrapper all laid out."

Katryn allowed the servant to help her out of the silk gown, undoing the rows of tiny buttons, and to brush her thick hair till it fell smooth and straight past her shoulders. Then the maid poured warm water into a porcelain bowl for her to wash and handed her a linen towel, and Katryn sent her away. Katryn washed herself with the finely milled soap she had bought in London. She hoped her husband would like the carnation scent she had always preferred.

Then, with anticipation building in her stomach, she donned the nightgown her modiste had made. It was unlike any gown she had ever worn before. The white silk was so thin she could see her hand through it, and its thin straps kept slipping down one shoulder. The neckline and back plunged into a deep V, leaving very little concealed. The French modiste had assured her it would please her husband very much, and Katryn knew it showed off the hollow between her breasts to advantage. Still, she felt suddenly doubtful. Perhaps it was too revealing. And would he be very pleased if the gown caused her to catch consumption? Oh well, she supposed the seamstress knew what she was about.

Katryn glanced at the bed, then away again. She was not bold enough to greet him from its nest of smooth linen. Pacing up and down for a moment, Katryn pulled her lacy wrapper close around her body, then sat in a chair near the small latticed window and stared out into the night.

Across the fields, the darkness seemed soft and deep, and she heard the distant bleat of a lonely sheep. She thought of Robert downstairs, sitting alone at the table. He would receive the servant's message and nod. Soon, he would stand up, leave the dining room, and walk through the hall and up the stairs, finally coming inside the bedchamber. He would come across and kiss her and then—somehow she couldn't see what came after the kiss, though of course she knew, in a general way, what marriage would mean. She found her shoulders were stiff with tension, and she couldn't seem to draw a deep breath.

It wasn't long before she heard footsteps in the corridor and heard the slight creak as the door opened. She didn't look around, but she knew at once it was he. She heard her husband close the door and latch it, and her skin rippled with awareness, her cheeks felt hot. Not wishing to show him such obvious confusion, she continued to gaze out the window, though she no longer was conscious of the night landscape.

Robert paused in the doorway, feeling as if he were a trespasser in his own house. Even with the flickering light of the fire and lit candles by the bed, the room was dim. His wife sat by the window, her form silvered by pale moonlight; she looked to him as delicate and illusive as the moonbeams themselves. Her profile was almost childlike, the brow untouched by care lines. Her eyes were lifted to the sky, her lips pressed together. She was clean and fresh and he did not deserve her. She should have more than a weary soldier who had wallowed in the filth of Napoleon's war and Napoleon's prison. But by a twist of fate, she was now his, and he would do all in his power to protect her from the dark memories imprinted upon his soul, as well as from the ugliness yet to come.

He walked across the room, pausing a few feet from her chair. "Katryn?"

Hoping that the redness had faded and her complexion had cleared, she turned and smiled up at him as normally as she could. "I await my husband, my lord."

Robert looked grave. "Katryn, you are not afraid of—of me?"

She trembled at the deep timbre of his voice, belying what she said next. "No, indeed."

He reached to take her hand. "If the situation were different, I would give you more time to—to get to know me, to be at ease in the marriage, but I fear we may not have that luxury. However, if you are truly reluctant . . ."

She could barely focus on his words, nor wonder what he could mean. He still held her hand, and his skin was so warm, his grip so firm.

"That is not necessary, Robert," she told him, trying to keep her voice steady. "I want—I want to be your wife." She shrugged her wrap from her shoulders and felt it fall behind her. Throwing all her fears and doubts to the devil, she stood, stepping forward to face her husband, to offer herself to him. "I wish to be your wife in every sense, my lord."

The candlelight threw her body into stark relief. Through the filmy gown, every curve she possessed was revealed. Robert's mouth grew dry. This was no child, no schoolgirl. He stood before her, drinking in the intoxicating sight of her full breasts and round hips. Her legs were long and slender and—God help him, but he could already feel them wrapped around him.

He had to remind himself to breathe.

Where was the little girl he had married? This goddess sent to tempt him could not be little Katryn. Any last charitable thought of playing the gentleman and giving her a few days to feel comfortable fled from his mind. Instead, the masculine desire to possess and dominate welled up inside him with alarming speed.

Katryn bit her lip, feeling an agony of self-doubt. Had she been too forward? Mama had said that one day her impulsive nature would get the better of her; perhaps she was right. Robert was so silent, his expression impossible to read. He must loathe her, repulsed by her unladylike behavior. Katryn stared mutely at Robert and wished she could take back her too-frank words.

If only he would do something instead of just stand there staring as if he had never seen her before. She wasn't going to wait for his censure. She would just—

All thought left her. She watched in astonishment as Robert ate up the remaining distance between them in one stride. Rough hands grasped both sides of her head, tilting her face up to him, then gentled.

Her wide eyes were fixed upon him, and Robert wondered why he had never fully noticed their beauty, their heat. Deep green—no ordinary green but the color of his long-yearned-for fields—pulled him close, then closer. He pressed his lips to hers, tasting her, learning her scent and flavor. With expertise, he parted her lips and slid his tongue inside to tease and please. She was heady, delicious, and full of surprises.

Katryn stood frozen in disbelief when his lips descended to her own. But disbelief turned to sheer delight. Robert was doing things to her mouth she had never heard of, never imagined. But, heavens, she liked it.

Even though he was only touching her with his cupped hands and his mouth, she felt as though she was being touched all over. Parts of her body were affected that she had never even noticed before. But most importantly, he wasn't repulsed by her actions. Indeed, he seemed pleased.

She let out a deep sigh as his lips descended to her neck. First his lips were greedy, but then they slowed as he nibbled a path to her shoulder. The strap slid just a little. Darn strap, she thought, until his lips found it, pushed it back into place. Ah, realization dawned. Perhaps the modiste knew what she was doing after all.

The world suddenly tilted as he slipped an arm beneath her legs and the other around her back. He lifted her and strode toward the bed, which the maid had thoughtfully turned down. Gently, he laid her down and stripped off his cravat and waistcoat and shirt before settling himself beside her. He propped himself on one elbow and touched her naked shoulder, sliding his hand down toward her breast.

It was all happening so fast. Katryn felt a surge of nervousness overwhelm her. "Ah, my lord," she interrupted.

Robert smiled down at her. "Yes, my dear?"

"Perhaps we—we should take this opportunity to discuss my duties."

Robert choked back a laugh. She looked so earnest; he did not wish to hurt her feelings.

"Your duties?"

Katryn nodded eagerly and pushed up the strap that he had just pushed down. "Yes, as your wife I shall have many new duties, and I—I don't wish to disappoint you."

She was making this too easy.

Robert stilled his hand and looked at her. Her widened eyes—windows to the soul, some poet had said—revealed her anxiety. His voice was gentle.

"Katryn, I promise you have nothing to fear from our marriage bed."

She watched him as he lifted her hand and kissed it gently. She still couldn't meet his eyes—this new wave of nervousness had chilled her first eager response—and her gaze dropped below his chin. Firelight flickered across the muscled planes of his chest. Silky dark hair spread lightly across his upper body before narrowing down into a thin line that led most disconcertedly into his breeches. She quickly raised her eyes to his.

"But, my lord—"

"Robert," he said firmly.

"Robert," she continued weakly, "it's just that I haven't done this before."

He could not contain his laughter this time. "My dear Katryn, I hope not. Otherwise, I'll have to make a dawn appointment, and I am not fond of early rising."

Katryn ducked her head, trying to hide her embarrassment. "That is not what I meant."

He smiled.

"I'm most relieved," he said with mock severity.

Robert took her chin between his thumb and forefinger, gently forcing her face level with his. Her green eyes stared stubbornly at his chest.

His voice was low and soothing. "You have my word of honor that nothing we will do is sinful or shameful." Her eyes finally met his, their expression doubtful. "It dismays me that I will have to cause you a little pain." She opened her mouth to protest but he would not let her speak. "Trust me that it is necessary, and not of my choice. I shall be as gentle and considerate as possible."

At this last, his tone was firm. She knew that what he said must be true for she had never known Robert to do anything unkind to anyone. And he had always told her the truth. Barring all that, he was her husband now. And she loved him. She would fear the unknown no longer.

Casting aside all the maidenly fears and strict virtues that several governesses, as well as her mother, had worked very hard to instill, Katryn took a deep breath, trying to ease the tension in her taut body. Deep inside, she felt her natural curiosity, her usual adventurous nature, reawakening. Slowly, she reached out and touched the chest that had so intrigued her since its unveiling. The unfamiliar texture of his warm skin and the softness of his body hair was so interesting that she forgot to be timid; she ran her long fingers in lazy circles around his chest. Her fingertips brushed a nipple, and she heard Robert stifle a surprised gasp. Intrigued, she raised her eyes to see his reaction to her exploration.

Robert drew a quick breath and felt his desire rush back with the ferociousness of a bursting dam. Whether his reac-

tion came from her shy touch or the absolute trust he saw in
the shining emerald depths of her eyes, he was not certain.
Looking down at her elegant hand, he was momentarily
thrown by the ring on her finger. His ring. His lady. His wife.
It sobered him, brought back the grim reality of his situation
and the reason for his hasty marriage to this young innocent.
The first step had been accomplished; he had wed. Next, he
must produce an heir. And he had to do it without scaring
her to death.

Perhaps he should say more to prepare her. "My dear . . ."
he began. But to his surprise, he was silenced by his new
wife's finger touching his lips.

"Shh," Katryn whispered. Her lips spread into a shy
smile. He savored the rosy color his kiss had brought to
those full lips.

"You needn't fear for me, my lord. I love—"

Swiftly, he covered her mouth in a rapacious kiss before
she could say the words he did not want to hear. They would
have further bound her to him and that he could not bear. He
would not break her heart. She was too young, too innocent
to know what love even was. And it most certainly was not
for him.

Katryn did not notice the silent rejection. She was too
busy tasting desire for the first time, and it was a heady
brew. Eagerly, she parted her lips for him and drew his
tongue into her mouth. So intent was she on his kiss that she
hardly noticed how her gown seemed to melt away under his
questing hands.

She tilted her head back as his lips forged a delicious path
down her neck. She sighed. When he slid his fingers down
her side and then up her torso to cup her breasts, she did not
pull away but opened her eyes to watch her lover.

Robert's eyes were glazed with an emotion she was just
beginning to understand, and his jaw was tight. Leaning
over her as he was, she could see the thick cords of muscle

on his arms and shoulders. The flickering fire played games, causing his face to be clearly visible one moment and shadowed the next. She wondered if he was pleased with her. And then she ceased to think at all. . . .

Robert leaned down and took her nipple in his mouth. Rolling it between his lips, he pleasured himself and her, holding back his surging desire with effort. She deserved every moment of exquisite delight he could give her.

Katryn's back arched off the bed, as if instinctively striving to get closer to him and the glorious things he was doing. Blindly, she reached seeking hands toward him. Burying her fingers in his dark hair, she held him next to her. He took long moments shaping and caressing her breasts before abandoning them in search of other delights.

Rising back up to take her mouth, he reached down with one hand and laid it upon the curly triangle at the base of her thighs. Katryn's eyes shot open at the intimate touch. Her languid limbs tensed. Automatically, her hand had gone down to shield herself from him.

Robert made a sound that was half-moan and half-laugh against her mouth. "Don't hide yourself from me, little Katryn. I would have all of you."

Katryn reacted more to the husky tenderness in his voice than his words. After a moment's hesitation, she pulled her hand away and loosened her thighs. She lifted her arms and wrapped them around his neck, offering herself to him.

Robert groaned. He pressed a proud kiss on her lips and whispered words of praise for her courage. With impatient hands, he reached down and unbuttoned his breeches. Swiftly, he stood and stripped off the rest of his clothing, leaving it crumbled on the floor in a manner that would have horrified his valet. Even in his passion, Robert remembered to keep his back from Katryn's view. He found his scars distasteful, and he had no patience just now for the questions, the shock, they might inspire.

Katryn had not surfaced from the haze of lust Robert had carefully created. When he joined her again in the bed, she turned eagerly to him and pressed herself full length against his body. The shock of their naked skin against each other was delicious. She raised her mouth to his and captured his lips in a fiery kiss. She sent her tongue deep and ran curious hands down his chest, then lower until she stiffened in surprise.

With a hoarse chuckle, Robert rubbed soothing hands down her back. "Do not worry, little one."

Katryn pulled away so that she could see his face. The masculine arrogance in his eyes strangely reassured her. Reminding herself of her promise not to be afraid, she began a light trail with her fingertips down his chest, then lower still until Robert laughingly captured her hand and linked her fingers with his.

"You little minx," he said admirably. "You've never been afraid of anything in your life, have you?"

As he ran strong hands over her breasts and stomach, she bit back her reply. *Oh, Robert,* she thought in that faraway part of her brain that was still capable of rational reflection, *if you only knew how afraid I am of losing you.*

Robert continued the path he had earlier abandoned. His fingers found her slippery with desire. He was glad, as he did not think he could take her eager, innocent caresses much longer before exploding.

Supporting his weight on his elbows, he spread her legs with a muscular thigh and poised himself at her moist entrance. Inch by inch, he slid slowly inside her tight warmth. Gritting his teeth against the incredible pleasure, he sought the barrier that shielded her secrets. He pushed gently, but it held. Laying his forehead against hers, he whispered to her, "I had hoped this would have been easier for you." Bracing himself, he surged forward, sinking deep inside her.

She gasped at the sharp pain. Tears welled into her eyes

and trickled down the sides of her face, but she did not try to pull away.

Robert tried desperately not to move even though it felt so damned good. He knew she needed him to be still so that she could adjust to the new invasion. He kissed the tears away. "It will be better in a moment, I promise."

She nodded, disbelief written all over her lovely face.

Robert cautiously withdrew, and Katryn tensed, expecting the same searing pain. But curiously, when he thrust again she felt no pain at all. In fact, his movement caused a strange, very pleasant sensation.

Carefully, Katryn arched her hips up to Robert and was stunned by the pleasure it brought her. Above her, Robert pressed his face close to her wet one.

"Sweetling, don't do that, not yet." His voice was gritty with checked desire.

In answer, she pushed against him again, and it was all the encouragement that Robert needed. Lost in the arms of an innocent, he thrust slowly in and out, reaching to give her the ultimate pleasure. Beneath him, Katryn eagerly met his hips with her own. Robert set a rhythm that had Katryn tossing her head against the pillow beneath her.

Katryn had never dreamed that such closeness was possible. Strange, exciting emotions gathered inside her with an unbearable force. She felt that she was close, so close to something wonderful that she should be able to reach out and grab it. She rode a cresting wave, no longer caring where it took her.

Breathing harshly, Robert grasped her hips and surged deep, spilling his seed deep inside her. He collapsed heavily on top of her, but she did not care. Not when he had his arms wrapped so tightly around her, not when she felt so cherished, so desired, so loved.

After a few moments, Robert rolled to his side, pulling her with him. They lay pressed close together, bodies still intimately joined. Such elation filled her that she felt she could not possibly contain it. A few tears escaped from her closed eyes, but if Robert felt them against his cheek, he did not comment.

She clung to him, with no need to speak and no words to express this new world of happiness she had discovered. She could not imagine why everyone was not married—how impatient young ladies would be, if they knew what joys they were being denied, she thought vaguely. Better not tell Marianne and Dora, not just yet. . . .

They lay together, she within his arms, resting her cheek on his bare chest and drowsily certain that she could stay this way forever. She shut her eyes and listened to his breathing become slower and more even. When she was sure that he slept, she glanced up at him, watching his face by the light of the one guttering candle Robert had left burning.

"Oh, Robert," she whispered. "I do love you so."

He blinked, and she held her breath, afraid she had awakened him.

His eyelids fluttered, and he murmured, "Eleanor."

Katryn lay very still till he had slipped back into sleep again, then carefully, not disturbing him, she eased out of his arms. She turned to face the wall and pulled the pillow over her face so that he would not hear, and then she wept.

6

The stealthy movements of the housemaid gradually penetrated the thick layers of sleep in Katryn's head. Lifting gritty eyes, she saw that the light coming through the window was weak. Trying to think why her maid would be disturbing her so early, Katryn reluctantly pushed herself into a sitting position. The young woman stopped midflight from her dash around the room to gaze in distress at her new mistress.

"Milady, I'm so sorry. I was trying to be quiet, I was." The servant's thick, red hand was raised to her mouth in uncertainty.

Katryn stared dumbly at her, trying to wake enough to ask an intelligent question. She had had precious little sleep. She was unsure how long she had wept, but she had stayed awake for hours after Robert, her husband, her newly married lord, had called out for another woman—her sister.

He would never forget Eleanor. Perhaps she had made a grievous mistake, dooming all three of them to lives of misery and frustration. Would Robert, sooner or later, seek out his first love for a clandestine affair? Such discreet liaisons were common enough among the Ton, blinked at as long as a man's succession was not in jeopardy. And Eleanor had al-

ready given her lawful husband an heir. Having done her
duty, she was free to follow her own desires, or so some of
the more licentious members of fashionable society would
believe.

For a moment, Katryn tormented herself with the vision
of Robert raining kisses upon Eleanor's fair skin, Robert
giving the same exquisite pleasure to Eleanor as he had to
Katryn on their wedding night. No, some part of herself rebelled, pushed the painful image away. Robert could not be
so deceitful; he was the most honest man she had ever
known. And Eleanor—could Eleanor wound her own sister
so deeply?

Katryn would not dwell on such nightmares—especially
when she might still have some hope of diverting Robert's
interest. It seemed impossible that he could be unaffected by
their night of lovemaking. Surely he must love her just a little? Never had Katryn felt her inexperience more keenly.

No, this thought still led into chasms of self-pity, reminding her that she would be forever his second choice, wed
only because her sister was out of reach and he needed an
heir. Katryn felt her eyes dampen, but she blinked hard
against the tears; she would not sit and weep. Robert was her
husband; the impossible had occurred, and if she had
achieved one miracle, why not two? Somehow, she would
also gain his love. Taking a deep breath, she gave herself a
mental shake; she would not give up so soon.

Katryn ran a hand through her sleep-tousled hair and then
used it to cover a yawn. She remembered the maid, who still
stared at her, her expression alarmed. "What are you doing
in here so early?"

The maid bobbed a belated curtsy and clasped her hands
in front of the clean white apron covering her dark dress.

"His lordship requested that I get you all packed to go,
milady, and as early as possible." She nodded twice as if to
strengthen the truth of her words.

Katryn lowered her hand from her mouth and stared at the servant. "But this is our honeym . . . that is, did his lordship say where we—I was going?"

"No, milady. Just that I was to get you ready as soon as I could." The unpleasant chore of explaining herself taken care of, the maid, temporarily serving as lady's maid while they stayed at the lodge, returned to her task of packing Katryn's belongings.

Panic welled up inside Katryn as the servant's words chased any lingering weariness from her. The determination she had fought to regain melted away, and again she was filled with doubt. He must be displeased with her, after all. But she had only done her wifely duty, had she not? And she had done it with all the love that still lay hidden in her heart.

Anger rose up to take panic's place, and Katryn welcomed it. How dare he treat her in such a way—did he mean to send her back to his home so that his parents and sisters could pity her? Poor little Katryn was such a bad wife that she had been tossed away after less than twenty-four hours of matrimony. Or worse, perhaps he planned to send her home to her parents. If he sent Katryn away, he could more easily bring home his beloved Eleanor for quiet trysts without a jealous wife in residence to notice.

The pain in her heart came near to piercing her through, but Katryn shuddered and fought for self-control. She would not meekly accept such a dismissal. Shoving the covers back, she flung herself from the thick feather mattress and marched over to the maid.

"My dressing gown, if you please."

The wide-eyed servant gasped and rushed to fetch the garment, but she soon looked up, her expression even more flustered. "My lady, I don't see it here. It might be with the few things I took to have laundered last night before we knew ye were leaving us so soon."

She stopped her frantic search and looked bravely at the

new wife of Lord Manning. "If I may be so bold, my lady, Cook wondered if maybe ye weren't pleased with the meal last even'. She heard as ye didn't eat more than a sparrow." The maid smiled shyly. " 'Course I told her not to worry herself none, just that you be fashionable and slight." With a bob of her lace cap she indicated Katryn's naked form.

Katryn looked down and gasped. In her fury she had forgotten she had fallen asleep without pulling on her night shift. Turning, she grabbed the nearest garment on the bench at the foot of the bed. It was her husband's discarded robe and she hastily covered herself with it, wishing she could hide her red face as well. It was that infuriating man's fault she had made such an exhibition of herself.

With angry motions, Katryn pulled the luxurious embroidered velvet tighter over her naked body and fastened it hurriedly. She was going to give her new husband an earful he wouldn't soon forget. Quickly, she walked toward the richly carved double doors at the entrance of the room and flung them open. Without missing a beat, she walked through them and straight into Robert's wide chest.

The impact stung. Katryn's hand flew to her abused nose. Doubly humiliated, she glared at him from behind her hand. Robert stared down at her, not even trying to hide the smile lurking at the corners of his mouth—the same mouth that had eagerly devoured her breasts only hours ago. Quickly, she pushed the memory away, trying to hold on to her anger.

"In a hurry, are we?"

His rich voice nearly distracted her from her fury, for it reminded her that she had once thought never to hear it again. After a quick glance to assure herself that no blood dripped from her bruised nose, she dropped her hand and pulled herself to her fullest height. Remembering a particularly stern governess, she tried to duplicate Mademoiselle's most disapproving look.

"Despite your wishes, no."

His eyes were wary, now; the shadow that so often seemed to separate him from her had reappeared too quickly. "I beg your pardon, Katryn. *My* wishes?"

Katryn was sickened that he would trifle so with her feelings. The treacherous tears she still refused to allow to fall reappeared in her eyes. Why should he be so obtuse?

"I am leaving Verdant Lodge, am I not?" Her dainty chin rose on the question as if daring him to agree.

His expression grew warier still. "Yes, my dear."

Now, of all times, when he was sending her away, he called her by an endearment. "I'm not going," she said decisively. "You will not have your way so easily."

Robert looked down at her petite form engulfed in his dressing gown and, for a moment, the almost-overpowering guilt over his own duplicity, the sadness that this newfound marvel, this delicious and unlooked-for passion he had awakened in his young lady wife could not last, receded. Again, he had to swallow a laugh he was sure would not be appreciated.

She looked like a bantam rooster, small but defiant, ready to spring on its larger prey and fight to the last breath. He watched Katryn clutch at the slipping lapels of his robe. Except for the occasional glimpses of her generous breasts, her slender figure was well hidden by the velvet folds. But it took little to provoke his memory of her delectable curves. The too-large, masculine garment only emphasized her womanly charms. And that was a memory Robert must force himself to forget.

But she seemed genuinely upset. He would hurt her soon enough, no need to inflict small wounds till fate stepped in to part them forever. Trying to appear at ease, Robert leaned a well-clad shoulder against the wide door frame and crossed his arms in front of his chest.

"You're not?" His voice was controlled, just a tinge of doubt creeping in.

Katryn squared her shoulders in a move already familiar to him; it was characteristic of her stubborn nature. "No, I most certainly am not."

Robert stroked his chin. "I see . . . if that's your decision."

"It is," she assured him, her lips still thin with anger.

"I'm afraid you'll get lonely all by yourself in the country." He shook his head as if in bewilderment.

Katryn suddenly felt totally at sea. What was he talking about? "I don't understand, my lord."

Robert looked down at her. "My father always said that when a woman made up her mind, there was nothing left but to accede to her wishes. So if you wish to remain alone at Verdant Lodge, I shall not question your decision."

Katryn lowered her head and felt like a child not yet out of the schoolroom. "You mock me, my lord," she whispered.

Robert put out one hand and lifted her chin. Standing so close, he could see the slight whisker burn on her face, and indeed, on the cleft of her breasts, just visible beneath the folds of the robe. He wished they were alone, that the maid packing industriously in the dressing room were not so close by. But no, there was no time. He had pressing business in London. It might be a hopeless case, but now—looking at his flushed and almost naked bride, her heart in her face— he knew he had to try. Besides, it wasn't fair to tease her like this.

"We are both going to London," he told her gently. "There are parties, balls, alfresco outings happening every day now. I thought you would wish to enjoy the gaiety."

The relief in her face was so obvious that again guilt struck him. He had to take a deep breath. *Oh, little Katryn,* he thought, *sweet Katryn. I hope someday you will forgive me for what I have done!*

"We are both going?" she repeated, as if not sure she'd heard him right.

"Of course, what else?"

"What else?" Katryn repeated. She was being a fool, she thought. Robert was not unhappy with her; he had no wish to push her away. Happiness swirled inside her, lifting her spirits high. She was aware of his closeness, of the deep masculine smell of him, of his chest rising and falling, and she had a sudden wild desire to—

No, the little housemaid was in the next room, packing Katryn's clothing, and the connecting door was still open. Katryn took a deep breath, trying to look dignified, serene. Even married people, newly married people, could not make love every moment, she supposed. Katryn stifled a grin. Too bad.

They were on their way within the hour, first returning to Manning Hall to take their leave of Robert's family. If Robert's mother seemed a bit puzzled that they were traveling to town so soon after the marriage, she quickly schooled her features not to show it, and she welcomed Katryn with such genuine warmth that Katryn again felt reassured.

"We are so happy to have you as part of our family," the countess told Katryn, squeezing her hand.

Katryn felt a glow of happiness, and she knew her smile was wide. "I will do everything I can to make him happy," she told Robert's mother, her voice low but heavy with sincerity, as if this were another vow, like the ones she had made on their wedding day. And I will be happy, too, she thought, if only he can come to love me!

For a moment, the countess looked troubled, then she smiled again and turned to speak to Robert. Katryn thought she might have imagined that look of concern, or did Robert's mother also fear for their mutual contentment?

No, it was all going to work out, she told herself, this strangely conceived marriage would be as happy as the union she had always longed for. After all, she had Robert, and what else really mattered?

So they talked merrily all afternoon, and played at lawn bowls in the garden. Dora squealed when she managed to place a ball just right, and Robert teased both his sisters, laughing and seemingly at ease. After dinner, when the earl was wheeled off to bed, Robert bade his father a tender farewell.

"We will be gone early tomorrow," he told his father. "I will not disturb you then. But take care of yourself, my lord."

"Dear boy," the earl said, patting Robert's hand, "I can't begin to tell you how happy I am that you are restored to us. And your marriage—dear little Katryn—I wish you both many happy years." The elderly earl yanked on Robert's claret sleeve to pull him closer. Startled, Robert leaned forward to afford his father the privacy he seemed to desire and turned his broad back to cut off the view of the rest of the family.

Under lowered brows, his father's eyes grew serious. "Do not be disturbed if you do not hold the same tender feelings for Katryn as you did for her sister. They will come with time." He nodded his head for emphasis.

"Yes, sir, thank you," Robert agreed and rose to his full height, suppressing the frown that might give too much away.

Katryn, who was sitting close enough to hear the quiet exchange, sighed to herself over her teacup. Eleanor, always Eleanor. But she pushed back the small pain. Soon enough she could forget her concern.

When Dora demanded it, the rest of them played spillikins and other silly children's games. Robert made his sisters laugh, and even his mother smiled at his nonsense as he teased and joked. Katryn played, too, but always she watched her husband, her heart full of contentment that he was so near. This was what her life would be, she thought happily. Robert was kind and considerate; someday he would play thus with his own children, their children, and the thought filled her with delight.

And the nights—the love-filled nights that would make those children—she felt a thrill that made her look down at her own hands, hoping his sisters could not discern the direction of her thoughts. The ache inside her belly at the thought of Robert coming to her once again—it made her wish for the clock hands to speed their way around the circle.

At long last they said good night to the rest of the family. After Dora and Marianne had clung to their brother, been kissed on the cheek and playfully advised to spare the young gentlemen's hearts when they came to London in a few weeks, after his mother had said good night to her only surviving son, they climbed the steps together to their bedroom.

With eager anticipation, Katryn accepted the help of one of the housemaids to take down her hair and change—she would look for a new lady's maid when they got to London, she told herself. She wanted someone new, someone who would know her only as Robert's lady wife, not someone from her parents' household or her own village, who would remember her as the ignored little sister of Robert's first love. And anyhow, a London maid would be more sophisticated, would know more about fashion and the latest hairstyles, as she had explained the decision to her mother. There hadn't been time to engage a new dresser before the wedding; there had been too much else to do.

Now she nodded to the girl. "That will be all, thank you."

The servant curtsied and took herself away. Her pulse quickening, Katryn opened the door of the dressing room and walked into the bedchamber, only to find it empty.

Her heavy hair swung across her shoulders as she looked around the room. Her shoulders drooped with disappointment. Where was Robert?

Sinking down on the edge of the bed, she crossed one leg over the other and bounced her foot up and down in rhythm with the clock on the bureau. She stared absently at the ivory slipper dangling from her toes and wondered what could possibly be keeping her husband. Robert had said his good-byes; his father was in bed asleep, dosed by his usual cordial at the doctor's orders. What could be more alluring than her bed?

With mounting impatience, she waited while the minutes crept by, hearing the sounds of doors shutting and footsteps fading as the rest of the household settled into sleep. And still Robert didn't come. Was he avoiding her? Had she been right after all, and she had somehow displeased him during their bridal night?

The slipper finally flew off its precarious perch and landed a few feet away from her. She could no longer bear the uncertainty. She would find Robert and *invite* him to bed. A nagging voice inside her head told her this was not really something a lady would do. She pushed back the voice—to hades with ladies and their namby-pamby ways!

Retrieving her slipper and pulling her dressing gown—an older and more modest affair suitable for their visit to his family—firmly around her, Katryn took up a candle from the bedside table and opened the heavy bedroom door. The hallway was dark and empty; the guest wing was very quiet and, as far as she could tell, the family quarters, too. She made her way slowly down the wide staircase, hoping all the servants were abed. What would she say if she encountered one of them? It didn't matter; she had to find Robert.

The large chandeliers and the sconces on the papered and paneled walls had been extinguished; the big house was dim with shadows, and she was glad to have her candle. It cast a wavering circle of light as she made her way silently, her slippers making no noise on the thick rugs and polished floorboards. Only the big clock in the hall ticked its steady measure of time passing.

She looked into the parlor, where they had played their

games earlier, but all was quiet. The dining room likewise stood empty, and the library smelled faintly of dust and old books and leather bindings, but no one loitered in front of the banked ashes over one last glass of brandy.

Where could he be?

She continued through the first floor, glancing into the gun room, the billiard room, all the masculine haunts where a man might have some reason to linger. Finally, she climbed the steps again, baffled and worried. This time, she turned away from the family quarters and went into the long gallery, where scores of Manning forebears looked down from the row of portraits on the wall. Here was the history of Robert's family, men and women eloquent in their haughty grandeur and old-fashioned costumes, though speechless now as they hung captured in thick oils and gilt frames.

And here was Robert, standing in the musty dark with one lone candle lighting a small circle, gazing at the long line of his family, at the grand portions of the hall itself, as if he viewed it for the last time.

The thought was absurd, yet it frightened her. He was so still, his face lifted, his eyes distant, and he seemed not to notice her quiet arrival.

But her candle cast its feeble glow into the cavernous shadows of the long room, and at last he turned his head.

"Robert?" she whispered. "Is something wrong?"

She was shocked by his haggard expression. Surely it was only a trick of the shadows playing over his face. Surely he could have no reason for such a deep despair, for pain that darkened his eyes and left them bleak and empty.

He put out one hand, and she found his touch on her arm infinitely reassuring. "Come, my dear," he said. "Let us off to bed."

Yet, when they came together on the cool linen sheets, though his body moved smoothly, though he was as gentlemanly and as concerned for her pleasure as he'd been the previous night, she felt that his mind, his heart, was somewhere else. And when the lovemaking ended, and he slept, he spoke no betraying name, but it didn't matter.

Katryn knew that Eleanor still held his heart, and the bed they shared was not big enough for three.

7

They arrived at the handsome mansion that was the
Mannings' London residence in time for dinner.
Robert again had ridden, while Katryn sat in solitary ele-
gance in the carriage. He seemed to avoid being alone with
her, except at night. Did he despise her so much? He had
to share her bed; their lovemaking was necessary to start a
baby. If it were otherwise, would he leave her alone then,
too? Katryn fought against the depression that occasionally threatened to overwhelm her. After all, she had never
expected it to be easy; she had chosen this marriage with
her eyes open.

Still, when the footman opened the door, and Robert came
forward to help her down, she knew that her expression was
grim.

"Are you tired from the trip, my dear?" Robert asked,
courteous as usual. But his gaze was guarded; always she
felt the barrier between them; if only he would lower his de-
fenses and let her glimpse his deeper feelings!

"A little," Katryn admitted. "But I will be fine after we
dine." She paused on the steps to look up at the large house
that loomed before them, feeling suddenly nervous. She had
visited here before, when both their families were in London

for the Season, but she had somehow forgotten just how large it was, twice the size of her own parents' town house.

And now she was the mistress of this house! Robert's father could not travel, and his mother came to town only for brief visits. It would fall to Katryn to run this establishment.

When the footman opened the double doors, and a stout butler hurried to take their outer garments and hand them on to yet another liveried footman, Katryn took a deep breath and willed her stomach to stop its churning.

"Katryn, you remember Mason; he has been with us for many years."

"Yes, indeed." Katryn smiled at the elderly servant, whose shiny bald head barely topped her own petite form. "How nice to see you again."

"Welcome, milady," the man said, bowing deeply. "And this is our housekeeper, Mrs. Simons."

The older woman had been standing discreetly at the side of the hall, but she moved forward to curtsy. "Milady," she said, her tone more reserved. "We hope you will be very happy here."

"I'm sure I shall," Katryn agreed, giving the woman an even warmer smile. "Perhaps we can sit down over a cup of tea tomorrow, and you can instruct me about the running of the house. I shall depend upon your expertise to guide my decisions."

The housekeeper's glacial features relaxed noticeably. "I would be honored, milady."

Katryn glanced at Robert, catching what she hoped was approval in his dark eyes. And when they went up the wide stairs together to the big bedroom reserved for them, he leaned closer to whisper, "Well done, Katryn. You have captured their loyalty already."

If she could only do the same with their master! She felt the familiar pang, but she smiled at him, warmed by his praise.

They ate alone together in the big dining room, talking little. She watched him covertly after the servants had brought in a savory of sweetbreads with mince jelly, which she knew was one of Robert's favorites. He grabbed a morsel of the food with his bare hand and gulped it down, then another—and then he stopped with his hand midway to his mouth, fingers still clutching another sweetbread. His strong features frozen with self-disgust, he slowly, deliberately put down the food. Wiping his hand on the linen napkin, he picked up his silver fork and ate more slowly, with his usual decorum.

Katryn stared down at her own plate, not wanting him to see how startled she was to see him forget the proprieties. For an instant, he had looked like a starving man, intent only on easing the hunger of the long ride. What memories of prison, of pain and deprivation, were locked inside him still? It was another wall between them, and she grieved for him, for them both, that his years of hardship should form a gulf she might never bridge.

But it also made her own worries seem petty. At the end of the room, a fire crackled in the fireplace, and the silver serving dishes, heaped high with meats and breads, vegetables, and stewed fruits, gleamed in the candlelight. The multitude of aromas from the course rose to tempt her: roasted pork, sweet berries, mint sauce, and more. A thick rug cushioned her feet, and footmen hovered, ready to offer the next course. Whatever happened in their marriage, she would be warm and well fed and safe. Robert would always treat her courteously; he had a kind heart, she had known him long enough to know that. And if he did leave her bed later to have affairs, he would do it with gentlemanly discretion. And she would hide her pain, Katryn thought, and continue to be his attentive wife. But the well-prepared food in her mouth turned tasteless as sand as she considered this polite and dismal future.

But he had not left her side yet, and she would fight for

him with all her heart. Katryn took a large sip of her wine, and when the last course had been consumed, she rose from the table and met her husband's eyes.

"I will go up to bed," she told him. "And await you."

Robert nodded, and she turned away, trying to pretend she had not seen the wave of sadness that for an instant had passed over his face.

Robert waved to the footman standing nearby with the crystal decanter of brandy. The servant poured the deep ruby liquid into the glass. Robert took a large swallow as he watched his wife's graceful exit. She was so sweet, so giving; he did not deserve her, he thought with a wave of resurgent guilt. She deserved better than this sham marriage.

He still held a different image in his heart of hearts; Robert's thoughts drifted once more into forbidden territory. His first love was blond and delicate, blue-eyed and soft-voiced—and married to another man. No, he could not think like this.

Perhaps this marriage had not been such a wise plan, after all. Yet, what else could he have done? Robert took another long drink of the powerful wine, feeling it warm his throat as he swallowed. Painfully, he pushed away the memories of Eleanor, thought of Katryn instead. As he pictured her upstairs in their bedchamber, his body betrayed him and he felt passion awake as he imagined Katryn slowly disrobing, dropping her bodice and her petticoats and allowing the maid to pull her lacy shift over her head. . . .

He had no more thirst for the brandy; a headier delight awaited him in his chamber. Mason and the footmen might think it odd that Robert would leave the table so soon after his wife, or they might smirk about it later in the servants' hall. He didn't care. Katryn was waiting, and he could already smell the sweet scent of her skin, almost feel the satiny smoothness of the hollow between her breasts. . . .

Robert put down the glass and pushed himself back from

the table. Taking long strides, he followed his wife's path toward the staircase that led to their bedroom, and all the delights that awaited him there.

The next morning Katryn woke to find the other side of the bed empty, again. This time she didn't panic; they were in London, she reminded herself, blinking at the handsome crimson bed hangings that had remained pushed back—for some reason, Robert did not want the bed enclosed. He had come to her last night, and their joining had been deeply pleasing. Already she was learning his body, what gave him pleasure, and the small aches and soreness of her wedding night were easing. Marriage was indeed a wonderful thing!

Smiling, Katryn saw the door open; was it Robert?

Instead, a maid entered with a breakfast tray. "Good morning, milady," she said in a soft voice.

"Good morning," Katryn answered. "Is it fair outside?" She picked up a buttered crumpet and bit into the toasted breadstuff with a strong appetite; lovemaking was a strenuous activity, she told herself. Her appetite had never been so strong.

"Oh, very nice, milady. Only a bit of fog in the early morn, and now the sun 'as come out."

Katryn could see sunlight shining through the polished windowpanes as the maid moved around the room, pulling back the heavy draperies. Outside, she could hear street noises—carriages passing, a dog barking, children shouting in play.

The maid left the room, then returned with a silver salver piled with notes and letters. "You've had a slew of mail, milady; it's been coming in all week."

Katryn looked up in surprise. She swallowed and licked a crumb off her lips. "Put it there," she said, and when the maid went into the adjoining dressing room to lay out a morning dress, Katryn reached for the stack.

Invitations to parties, dinners, lunches, breakfasts, theater outings, picnics, and masked balls. Good heavens, they could fill every hour of every day with social activity, if they so desired. Katryn and her family had always been part of polite society, but this glut of hospitality still surprised her. She had never really considered what Robert's rank would entail.

She shuffled through the gilt-edged, elegantly scripted pages, feeling a strange mix of emotions. On one hand, she would be proud to go into the Ton as Robert's wife, Robert's chosen lady. There would be gossip still, and sharp-eyed and sharper-tongued matrons ready to note any deficiency in his attention to her. On the other hand, she almost begrudged the lack of private time that this socializing would necessitate. She'd gladly give up all of the parties to sit alone with Robert and talk quietly of things that really mattered—their feelings for each other, their memories of the past, their hopes for the future. Someday, she prayed, there would be children to cherish, babies to bounce and cuddle, small boys who would toddle after their father in adoring imitation, little girls who would smile when he entered the room.

Katryn's heart melted at the thought of Robert's children, at the mental picture of Robert holding a baby or smiling down at a child who would bear his deep brown eyes, or his unruly dark hair. Then perhaps they would at last be a real family, secure in their love for each other. Oh, would it ever come to pass?

Still holding one elegant invitation, she gave herself a mental shake. How could she be so unfair to Robert? He had been locked away from his own country, his friends and acquaintances for so long, with nothing but hardship and isolation. Of course he would enjoy dinners and theater parties and balls and races, and whatever new event an imaginative hostess could devise. She could not possibly suggest that she was not eager to share such gay times; indeed, for Robert, she would go willingly and never dull his enjoyment of the festivities. No one could deserve such gaiety more.

So when, dressed and coiffed, she went downstairs to find him about to go out, she held up the stack of mail and smiled brightly at him.

"We shall have our choice of amusement, Robert. You must tell me which friends are the oldest and which parties you prefer to attend."

Robert looked almost ruefully at the thick pile of invitations. "Nay, my dear. That onerous task will fall to you; you know my family as well as I, and I have no friends you are unaware of."

He said it lightly, but she felt her heart swell. No secret assignations to hide from his wife, she told herself, happy again. Dear Robert!

"Are you on your way out?" she asked, observing his dress and careful to keep her tone light. She would not start out as a demanding, nagging wife; she would not have Robert regret their bargain so soon.

"I'm going over to the War Office," he said. "There are army comrades that I wish to trace—if they survived the wars. I'm very much out of touch."

His voice sounded grim, and she shivered at the reminder of his miraculous return from the dead. "I wish you good luck."

Robert nodded. She had no idea, he thought, how much their future happiness depended on this feeble hope. Now that his commander was dead, it was doubtful that anyone else could swear to Robert's innocence, but he had to try. With an effort, he made his next words light. "And what will you do today?"

Katryn smiled. "Oh, I shall be busy enough. I have to talk with the housekeeper—and agree with all that she suggests, I have no doubt! Then I must begin interviewing for a new lady's maid, and, of course, go through this enormous pile of mail and try to decide which to accept."

"Anything you like," Robert repeated, turning back at the door to add, "oh, one thing—I did agree that we would dine with old Scabbytoes on Thursday. I spoke to him at the club when we were in town before the wedding."

"Scabbytoes?" Katryn looked bewildered at the strange nickname.

"Lord Emory," Robert explained, smiling. "He shot off the tip of his little toe in a hunting accident when he was fourteen."

"Of course," she said, laughing.

He saw the sweet curve of her lips and wished for a moment that he could walk back to her and kiss that luscious mouth, lift her in his arms, and carry her back up the stairs, back into the bedchamber and then—

No, he must behave like a rational man and put these thoughts aside. As for the invitations, even though he still felt uncomfortable amid civilized people after his long years of isolation among the dregs of a foreign prison, though the thought of parties and of too-large, chattering crowds held no attraction for him, Robert told himself that he could not deprive Katryn of the normal parties of the Season. It would hardly be fair. Her life would be shattered soon enough; he must allow her some innocent pleasures while he could.

And though he longed to walk back and beg her forgiveness for the disgrace that was to come, perhaps kiss her soft lips just one more time, he forced himself to continue out the door and nod to the groom holding the reins of his horse. Not only because even newlyweds could not revel in each other's arms for every waking moment, but because something much more serious hung in the balance. His life, their future.

● ● ●

Katryn's day passed swiftly. Her first task was to find the invitation from Robert's old friend. It was not a small, intimate dinner, as she had expected from his words, but a large party, probably already planned before Lord Emory knew that his childhood friend had returned. She sent the reply off in the hands of a footman, spent an hour going through the rest of the invitations and deciding which ones to accept, then had her meeting with Mrs. Simons, which passed more smoothly than she had feared.

"His lordship," Mrs. Simons said, pouring out the tea, "is very partial to fresh fish, but it must be truly fresh, milady."

"Of course," Katryn agreed, hiding a smile at the seriousness of the housekeeper's tone. "I'm sure you know how to procure only the freshest."

"It's all in the choice of fishmonger, milady," the older woman advised solemnly. "Now, I only patronize O'Toole, even though 'is prices are a mite higher. . . ."

Katryn tried to pay strict attention, but her thoughts did keep wandering to the sweetness of Robert's kisses, and how much she had longed to call him back when he left the house this morning. . . . But one could not live on love alone; there was also fish. With great effort, she concentrated on Mrs. Simons's words.

From fresh fish to bread to the new pantrymaid who was not working out and would have to be replaced, the subject turned to the lady's maid that Katryn had need of.

Mrs. Simons promised to see about filling the post at once. "Believe you me, milady," she said, "I know all the best lady's dressers in London; you shall have your pick of the crop, I shall see to that."

Katryn thanked her, and finally could leave to eat a light luncheon all alone in the big dining room—Robert had not yet returned; had he found any of his missing comrades still alive? The thought saddened her, and reminded her of the miraculous return that had brought him back to her. They had been given a second chance, and now, praise heaven, they could grow old together. . . . She found herself humming over her cup of vichyssoise.

Robert spent the day at the War Office, searching for any trace of the mission in which he had posed as a French agent. He could not admit the real reason he pored over the dusty records—he could not give himself away if there were as yet no doubts about his loyalties—and he found nothing. Dejected at his lack of success, he was silent at dinner. He had been relieved to find that Katryn had not accepted an invitation for that evening; they had another blessedly quiet meal together, and then afterward he forgot his worries briefly in their lovemaking. Yet he knew that some part of him could not surrender to the pleasure of Katryn's smooth skin and open arms; some part of his mind was still braced against the Damocles sword that hung over them. And also, in some hidden part of his heart, there was still a vision of a fair-haired, blue-eyed beauty who could never be his. In fairness to his wife, he tried not to think, never to think, of Eleanor. . . .

The next few days he resumed his search, seeking out any fellow officers who had survived the war and its final bloody battles, but though he rode across London and once into Kent to locate old comrades, none had any knowledge of the secret mission that had led to his capture.

He had not really expected to find an easy answer—Colonel Richmond had promised the utmost secrecy when he had asked Robert to volunteer for the delicate assignment—but Robert's spirits plunged nonetheless.

He was even more silent at home, and he sometimes found Katryn staring at him, her delicate brows creased in worry. But he could not burden her with the fears that kept him tense with anticipation as he waited for the fatal blow to fall.

The dinners and dances and alfresco outings that filled the week became almost a welcome distraction. Katryn was holding up well to the gossipy matrons who watched them both with malicious eyes. And there were some old friends, of course, who did not offer barbed comments or too-close scrutiny, and at least Katryn seemed to be having fun.

On Saturday, he escorted his wife to a large ball at the home of Lord Swindon. The street outside the mansion was crowded with carriages and chaises.

One of the grooms held the door while Robert took Katryn's hand as she stepped down from the carriage. "Mind your step," he told her quietly, guiding her satin-clad feet away from the steaming mound of manure that another carriage team had left behind them. He led her safely inside the big entrance hall, where they left their cloaks with a footman.

When Katryn shed her outer garment, she exclaimed in annoyance. "I caught my hem getting out of the carriage," she said, showing him the fine fabric that dangled at the edge of her skirt. "I must go and pin it up."

"I'll await you at the foot of the steps," he told her and watched her disappear with a housemaid into an inner room. He stood idly near the marble steps that led up to the next level with its large ballroom; he could hear murmurs of talk and laughter and the melodic notes of stringed instruments.

He spoke to several guests coming into the house, answering with only half his mind the questions that still met his return to society. Once he saw a man in the scarlet coat of an army officer, and he stiffened. But the man walked past him without even meeting his eye, calling out greetings to a friend on the stairwell and going up without a glance in Robert's direction.

Robert took a deep breath, knowing that his brow was damp. Not yet, not yet, his secret had not yet come to light. Dare he hope that no one would find the incriminating letter? The worst of it was, he would live his whole life still waiting for the document to surface, never knowing if he were truly safe.

Give me a few months, he prayed. *Let us start a baby, a son, so Katryn and my mother and sisters will be provided for. My family must be safe. Just a few months.*

Someone spoke his name. Robert exchanged greetings with a baronet he knew slightly from his club. And then, then he looked toward the door and saw a vision of loveliness that drove all thought of ordinary courtesies from his mind.

It was Eleanor, ravishing in a deep-cut gown of pale blue, with a wispy, silver-embroidered shawl circling her shoulders like a veil of frosty mist and her golden hair swept up and topped with a delicately wrought diamond-studded tiara. She looked like a fairy queen. When she saw him, her pale cheeks flushed with emotion, and her lips flew open.

"Robert!"

It had been bound to happen sooner or later, Robert told himself grimly. Of course they would meet; they attended the same parties, knew the same people. But he had not braced himself enough, had not thought it would be so hard.

For a moment he remembered only the years of longing, and he knew his face revealed too much. To give himself time, he bowed more slowly than usual. When he lifted his head, he saw that Whitmund had come up to take his wife's arm, and Eleanor's expression was once more under control. The moment had passed; they both had to remember that all had changed; they were no longer affianced sweethearts, longing for the day they could consummate their love.

Robert felt an instant of fierce hatred for Whitmund, who stood between him and his lost love. He wanted to push the man aside, thrust a sword into his belly. . . .

He took a deep breath. He was a civilized man, not a prison ruffian. He must remember who he was.

"My lord," Whitmund said, his slight bow just deep enough not to be a calculated insult.

"Whitmund," Robert answered, keeping his tone civil with great effort. "Lady Whitmund." He said her married title with grim emphasis, and he thought that Eleanor's lips tightened, but she managed a ghost of a smile.

"I hope Katryn is well?" Eleanor said, her tone brittle. "I shall call upon her shortly; the baby has been fretful, and I've been busy at home."

Robert nodded. "She is very well and I'm sure will enjoy a visit," he answered. But he felt a stab of guilt; for a few minutes, he had forgotten his wife's existence. He watched as Eleanor and her husband climbed the staircase side by side, then realized that Katryn had returned, her gown mended.

Katryn had come into the room just in time to see her husband and Eleanor a few feet apart, both faces flushed with emotion. The naked yearning in Robert's eyes, the haunted look of a man who sees what he can never have, pierced her like a knife through her heart. It was a physical pain, and she had to pause on the threshold of the hall and take a deep breath to steady herself. While she hesitated, Whitmund came up and gripped Eleanor's arm, more tightly than necessary Katryn thought, and Eleanor's expression became immediately more guarded.

As was Robert's, Katryn found when she could bear to glance at her husband again. She watched them exchange pleasantries, then Eleanor and Whitmund moved on up the steps. Katryn waited another moment before walking across the marble floor to rejoin her husband.

"It's done," she said, looking down at her skirt to indicate the pinned-up hem, not wanting to meet his gaze just yet. Some trace of suffering, of regret, might linger in his eyes, and she didn't want another reminder of how much he still loved Eleanor, how he longed for the sister he could not have. It was harder than she thought, being second best.

But when he offered her his arm to go up the wide staircase, Katryn rested her hand lightly upon the superfine cloth of his coat, feeling the firm muscle beneath it, and some of her pain eased. He was here, he was her husband. Surely the rest would come.

They were announced at the entrance to the ballroom by a white-wigged footman with a deep voice, and heads turned inside as they greeted their hostess and then moved on into the crush of elegantly clad guests.

Katryn took a deep breath, almost choking on the strong scents of perfumes and powders that hung over the crowd; candles in large candelabras flickered at the edges of the room and in crystal chandeliers hanging above, and the air was much too warm, heated by too many bodies. She could hear music from unseen musicians, but the voices of the guests almost drowned out the tune.

Her instinct was to cling to her husband's arm, but that would look strange, and it might annoy Robert. At some level of her mind, Katryn knew that to keep Robert, she had to leave him free. So instead, Katryn turned aside deliberately to talk to a young lady she knew slightly from the last Season and allowed Robert to be absorbed into another group of party guests. If he drifted toward the side of the big room where, she knew by some instinct, Eleanor stood, Katryn would reveal to no one how much that knowledge pained her.

Robert spoke a few words with an old army acquaintance, then joked with a friend from Eton and exchanged greetings with several fellow club members of White's who had not yet retired to the card tables set up in the library. He made his way from group to group without admitting to himself whom he hoped to find in the swirl of brightly hued gowns and somber dark coats. When he spotted Eleanor at the side of the room, for once without Whitmund standing guard at her side, surely it was only natural to walk over and speak briefly to his own sister-in-law?

This time, he had his expression carefully under control; no gossiping biddy watching them would have reason to talk. He owed that much to Katryn, and to Eleanor, too.

His lost love did not seem to see him walk closer; she stood at the edge of the big room, fanning herself idly with a wispy confection of lace and silver thread. She seemed lost in thought. But when he paused beside her to speak softly, she gave no start of surprise.

"Eleanor," he said, keeping his voice low. "You look very lovely tonight."

She raised her eyes, and he thought her expression softened, as if in pleasure at his words. But she met his gaze for only an instant, then her lids lowered again to veil the soft blue eyes, hiding her thoughts from his too-probing scrutiny.

He remembered when she had hidden nothing from him, when every thought had been shared. The memory made his throat feel tight; they had lost so much. Why had she not waited?

As if she still had the power to guess his thoughts, Eleanor said, her tone equally low, "I had no way to know that you still lived, Robert . . . except in my heart, where I knew I would keep your memory always."

He could not answer; his throat tightened even more and choked his voice, and he fought to keep his expression even. He knew there would be eyes in the crowd watching them, eager for some lapse in decorum.

She went on, her gaze on the fan she held. "My parents urged me to pick another suitor; they were afraid I would slip away, I think, go into a decline from the grief I felt at your loss. Their intentions were good, though it's hard not to blame them now. Yet I blame no one more than myself."

Her voice was still quiet, but the anguish was obvious.

Robert felt a wave of compassion that pushed aside all his own anger, his bitterness.

"Dear heart," he said very softly, "I do not fault you, truly. I was only . . . so unhappy that I could not—that we could not—"

The crowd undulated, and Whitmund's large, stocky frame reappeared, carrying two glasses of champagne. He frowned when he saw Robert standing beside his wife.

"Here you are, m'dear." He handed Eleanor one of the glasses. "Sorry to take so long; dashed crush around the tables."

"Thank you," Eleanor murmured, accepting the glass and taking a sip. She was pale again, except for two bright spots of color in her cheeks.

Robert knew he must walk away, not make it harder on his lost darling. But he had to clear his throat before he could say to Whitmund, as casually as he could manage, "Quite a turnout."

"Indeed," the other man agreed. Turning to Eleanor, he added, "Saw your friend Lady Wessex, said she'd like to speak to you." He offered his arm, and Eleanor took it, not glancing at Robert.

She had no choice, of course, Robert told himself, trying to push back an irrational anger. He could not step forward and pull her away, could not challenge Whitmund, could not put his hands to the man's thick throat and choke the life out of him, leaving Eleanor free. . . .

He pushed aside these criminal thoughts and smiled for the sake of the crowd, though he knew that his lips felt tight and his expression might appear more like a grimace. He should seek out his own wife and stay by her side, avoiding the dangerous pleasures of any more stolen moments alone with Eleanor. He edged through the tangle of silken skirts, speaking absently to several acquaintances, and the music behind him changed to that of Eleanor's favorite tune. He wondered if Whitmund would know, if Whitmund would end the boring conversation they were no doubt engaged in and pull his wife onto the dance floor, as Robert would have done, could have done, if only he'd had the right. . . .

At last he found Katryn. She was chatting with three other women, two plump sisters with similar snub noses and round cheeks, and a tall lady in bilious green, with three ostrich feathers rising from her stiff headdress. The tall woman laughed at some witticism of her own. Katryn didn't seem to see him for a moment, then she focused on him and turned away from the other women.

"Would you like a glass of wine, my dear?" Robert asked, reassured that she had not apparently thought anything strange of his absence.

Katryn tried to stifle the wave of relief that almost turned her knees weak. In no way would she reveal her apprehensions, especially not in the midst of a sea of curious faces. It had been Mrs. Fleming—the yellow-green hue of her over-trimmed dress well representing the envious nature that it contained—who had hastened to her side a few minutes earlier to remark in a smug voice, "I see your husband chatting with your sister just now, dear Katryn. It's wonderful that you have so much trust in them, considering their history, you know."

Katryn had bitten back the angry words she wanted to hurl in the woman's face. Malicious cat! Instead, she'd spoken with deliberate unconcern. "I know my husband very well, Mrs. Fleming. His loyalty and respect for me are apparent, unlike some men's."

Since Mr. Fleming's love affairs were conducted with notorious lack of discretion, this was a point obviously taken. Mrs. Fleming recoiled, and her eyes glittered with spite. "No doubt. Personally, I'm happy to have no sisters, especially one so fair!"

"Yes, Eleanor is admired wherever she goes," Katryn agreed coolly.

Mrs. Fleming's dyed plumes seemed to droop, then she pulled herself together and embarked upon a brittle exposition of the foibles of any of the other guests unfortunate enough to catch her eye, laughing often at her own small-spirited jibes. The timid McEllvy sisters simply nodded and did not try to stop the flow of vitriol. Katryn was about to make her escape when Robert reappeared.

She was pleased that he should return so soon. Mrs. Fleming glared at them both but seemed to have no criticism ready, and Katryn nodded to the women and turned away.

In no way would she reveal her uncertainties, Katryn told herself. She clutched Robert's arm when he offered it, and if her smile was forced, no one would ever know the wild maelstrom of emotion that swirled inside her. Of course Robert would speak to Eleanor, Katryn told herself as she had so many times before. How could he pretend Eleanor didn't exist; how could his love for her end so soon?

But would it ever end? As Robert led her through the milling crowd of party guests, the thought tormented her. Perhaps Robert would love Eleanor till he died, till she died, till Katryn died. Stop it, she told herself, stop it!

Deep in thought, conscious only of Robert's reassuring presence and trying to keep her already-damaged hem safe from being trodden on again, she walked right into Robert's back when he stopped suddenly.

"Robert?" She pushed forward to look at his face. He was white as a ghost. "Robert, what is it?"

Could it be? Robert's thoughts had still been on Eleanor as he parted the thick crowd of guests, his wife just behind him, and he had scanned the faces in front of him with only half his attention.

But the familiar face of the petite woman with the dark hair and the almost too big eyes had jolted him out of his reverie. For a moment he thought it was a vision, that he might be slipping into madness. Had his prison years stolen his wits, as he had sometimes feared they must?

No, she stood there, sedately gowned in lavender, with no jewelry except a modest string of pearls, clutching the arm of the short, gray-haired man who stood beside her. The costume was very different, but this was a face from his past, from the dangerous days of his time in France. This woman knew him as a supposed spy for the French and, even more importantly, as a British double agent. She knew!

A witness for his defense! Robert's blood rushed to his head and he thought that he gasped. He had stopped in midstride and was vaguely aware of Katryn bumping into his back. But he concentrated only on the woman a few feet away, separated by several groups of chatting women.

Her name . . . her name was Minette. Robert dragged it from a distant memory, trying to place her more clearly. She had sheltered him one night when Napoleon's agents had been hot on his trail; she'd hid him and fed him thick homemade soup; she had been kind. Surely she would come to his defense now?

Then Minette looked away from the stout matron who had been talking loudly to her and caught his eye. She, too, went pale with shock. Recognition was there in her face; it was obvious she did know him, did remember.

His heart in his throat, joy birthing after long despair, Robert stepped forward, his hand outstretched. She could save him, could testify to his innocence—

Minette turned, her eyes dark with fear, and fled into the crowd.

He had to find her! Robert found that a small hand tugged at his coat. He looked over his shoulder to see Katryn frowning up at him.

"Robert, what's wrong?"

"I'll be back," he said quickly and hurried through the

crowded chamber after Minette. But her small form had already disappeared behind tall gentlemen with pomaded hair and women whose lofty hairpieces bobbed and danced as they chatted and sipped their glasses of wine.

"Minette!" he shouted. Heads turned toward him at his cry, but he ignored the stares as he scanned the room desperately. The chatter around him drowned his cry; the din of shrill voices lifted to be heard over the many conversations seemed to thicken the air itself, as sweet perfumes and the faint tinge of wood smoke from the room's fireplaces already were doing. She couldn't hear, worse, she didn't seem to want to hear. Why had she run away?

He pushed through group after group of silk- and satin-clad ladies, brushed past dark-coated gentlemen arguing politics or racing, but could catch no sight of her. Minette had disappeared. Minette who? He did not even know her last name, he realized, his heart sinking. He certainly did not know why or how she could have turned up in London. And something else nagged at him—

Of course, how could he have forgotten where they had met? His wits were indeed working slowly tonight. That could explain a great deal, he thought. But he must locate her!

Finally, he made his way back to Katryn waiting at the side of the room. This time she looked obviously concerned.

"Robert, what's wrong?"

"That woman, do you know who she is?" Robert demanded. "I have to find her."

Katryn looked ever more alarmed. "What woman? You were in front of me, Robert. I didn't see who you meant. Who are you trying to find?"

And why? she wanted to add, but she bit back the words. Did he have another old sweetheart that she knew nothing of? Katryn had to fight to keep from stamping her feet.

He looked down at her, his expression abstracted. Why

did he keep so much from her? What other parts of his life had been hidden? And how had she thought that she knew him so well; perhaps she had been mistaken in that, as in so much else, Katryn thought, her spirits plummeting.

She heard a stir at the other side of the room, a sudden hush, then voices raised. Had some political discussion become too heated, ended in fisticuffs? At least such an episode would divert some of the gossip of the night, Katryn thought. Surely she and Robert and Eleanor had contributed more than their share to the talk of the Ton.

Then the crowd parted, and out of the kaleidoscope of gaily hued ball gowns and black and dark blue gentlemen's coats, she saw the flash of scarlet.

"Arrest that man!" someone shouted.

8

"What on earth . . . ?" Katryn glanced toward Robert to ask what could be happening, but when she saw his face, her words died away.

Thus might he look gazing up at the scaffold, she thought, the blood turning icy in her veins. He was in danger, terrible danger; she knew it with every fiber of her being. Whirling in a flash of skirts, she grabbed Robert's arm. "Come! We must go."

But it was too late. Striding across the room, Jerod Cavendish approached them, his arm outstretched. "That man, there. Arrest him at once!"

Two scarlet-coated troopers were right behind him, long rifles in hand. "Robert Manning, Viscount Holt, I arrest you in the name of the Crown, for treason and other seditious acts," his cousin announced loudly.

There were gasps, then the whole room went abruptly silent. So silent Katryn could hear a log crack apart in the hearth, and a startled musician scrape his bow across his strings, the raspy sound like a cry of pain. Katryn had to take a deep breath to steady her voice.

"What are you talking about? How dare you speak such lies! It's not true!"

Cavendish turned to face her, and she saw the glint in his

eyes; he was enjoying this, she thought, had engineered this arrest in front of all their acquaintances just to humiliate her husband even further.

"Alas, dear Lady Manning, I fear it is true. Your husband has not, I suspect, been honest with you."

She looked at Robert despite herself. His face was still wooden with suppressed emotion, and his eyes looked blank, as if already he were dead. No, no, it couldn't be; he had come back from the grave once, had been lost to her and then returned; they could not snatch him away like this.

"Robert, tell them," she whispered, shaking his arm. "Tell them it's not true!"

He didn't seem to hear her; he watched Cavendish instead. "Family honor, cousin?" Robert said, very low, speaking directly to the man whose brow and hairline were so similar to his own, like a dim reflection in a dusty mirror.

Cavendish smiled, his lips stretched very thin. "Needs must what needs must," he answered. "I like not the method, but . . ."

A faint murmur of talk rose, swelled, and flew round the crowded room like a flock of startled sparrows. Katryn could hear the furious whispering, the nervous titters of laughter, see the shocked expressions already melding into speculation as the other guests glimpsed the unfolding of the biggest scandal to hit the Ton since Lord Byron had eloped with his own half-sister.

"Robert is not guilty of treason," Katryn spoke loudly, trying to divert Cavendish's attention. This nightmare could not be true. "This is a complete fabrication."

"No indeed, Lady Manning, I would not stoop so low," Cavendish told her, his tone smooth with the barely contained joy of victory.

A rustle in the crowd, then the host of the ball, Lord Swindon, hastily retrieved from a whist table in another room, hurried forward. "What's this, what's this?"

"I apologize for the disruption of the festivities, my lord." Cavendish bowed slightly.

"What do you mean, bringing these common soldiers into my house, without so much as a by-your-leave?" Lord Swindon demanded, pulling his white shirt cuffs back into place and glaring at the troopers.

The two men stiffened and looked visibly unhappy. Cavendish was more resilient. "Their lieutenant will be here shortly; we could not wait, in case Manning should guess that we suspected his duplicity."

"Duplicity?" Swindon transferred the direction of his frown from the soldiers to Cavendish.

"Treason, my lord. During Lord Manning's long absence in France, he was actually working for the emperor himself." Cavendish drew a crumpled letter from an inside pocket and held it up, though no one else could possibly read the faint writing. "The proof has just surfaced!"

A chorus of gasps, and the murmurs at the edge of the crowd grew louder. Katryn, still gripping her husband's arm, felt the tremor that ran through his body. This was serious, then, not just a spurious charge manufactured by Cavendish. But Robert could not be a spy. Katryn took a deep breath. "That's nonsense!"

Her voice was hoarse, but no one seemed disposed to listen. Frowning, Swindon stared at her husband's accuser. "Find that hard to believe," he said bluntly. "But whatever the case, Cavendish, why announce this in the middle of our party? M'wife will be much distressed."

"I do apologize, my lord." Cavendish bowed again. "I could not risk Manning's flight."

"Bosh." The older man snorted. "Manning's a gentleman, not a bloody gypsy. Everyone knows his address. No need for such twopenny theatrics."

Cavendish's face darkened, but he did not argue. "I am on

the Crown's business, my lord, and we *will* remove him. Your entertainment can continue—"

"No!" Shoulders braced, Katryn stepped in front of her husband as the troopers moved forward. "Lord Swindon, you cannot allow this man to take Robert away for some hidden purpose of his own. Jerod Cavendish's enmity is well known; he stands to inherit Robert's title, his estate, all his wealth. If some convenient accident occurs on the way, before this ridiculous charge can be resolved, his blood will be on your hands!"

Her voice cracked with the emotion that threatened to overcome her, when a large hand wrapped around her clenched fist, warming it. Robert pulled her back to his side. In a low, terse voice he spoke.

"That will do, Katryn."

She looked up into his dark eyes and drew strength from his silent composure. She waited impatiently for Robert to speak out and refute the absurd charges. But he said nothing.

Still, Katryn's angry words had made an impact. Swindon's frown deepened. The older man chewed on his heavy mustache,

"Some sense to that," he finally said.

"But, my lord"—Cavendish's voice lost its thin veneer of smoothness as desperation made him careless—"you can't mean to pay heed to the ramblings of an hysterical woman. It is obvious she is as immoral as he."

Katryn sputtered, but before she could speak, Robert, with one smooth movement, stepped in front of her. Cavendish's eyes widened in anticipation.

Robert spoke slowly as if Cavendish were a simpleton and might not catch his meaning. "Take care, Cousin. I can forgive stupidity and even understand greed; but you will not speak of my wife in such a way ever again. Better yet, don't speak at all unless you mean to sing her praises and call yourself a fool."

"I'm not the fool here! Nor the traitor, either."

Robert's hands clenched, and he took another step closer to his accuser, then stopped, his jaw tight with the effort it took. "A fine effort, Cuz: anger me into violence and make it simpler for you to detain me."

Cavendish's face was alight with rage. "I have no need to anger you. I have the proof to set your treasonous neck swinging." Satisfaction rang in every word.

The two men were squared off, unmindful of the crowd and totally focused on the rising violence in each other. Watching, Katryn found it hard to breathe.

"It will be a glorious day when I watch you climb the steps of the gallows, Mannie," Cavendish said, slurring Robert's nickname. "I shall be watching, in your phaeton, driving your fine pair, mayhap escorting your fine wife. What say you to that, Manning?"

It was too much; it was more than enough. "I say it's a damned pity I must delay the pleasure that running you through would bring me." Robert drew a steadying breath, then continued, deadly intent in his voice. "We have an appointment, you and I."

The whispers around them soared into deafening proportions as Robert's quiet words were eagerly passed from one person to the next.

Cavendish shook with fury. "Much as I would like to give you a lesson in swordsmanship, Cousin, I fear the business at hand is too vital to wait."

He kept wary eyes on Robert but spoke to Lord Swindon. "It would be madness to let him go, not now, when he knows his guilt has been exposed."

"You cannot send my husband off with this snake," Katryn repeated.

"Neither," their host decided. "Put him into my study till this officer of yours shows up, Cavendish. And I expect him to have some papers, proper papers. In the meantime, you, come along now."

He motioned to the soldiers, who looked distinctly relieved to be leaving the ballroom. Robert grimly followed.

One of the women tried to take Katryn's hand, patting it in sympathy, but Katryn shook her off. She had to see what was being done to Robert, had to protect him. He still seemed to be stunned, and there was no one else here to look out for him.

Swindon led the way through several hallways and into a study whose walls were covered with family portraits, a boxed set of dueling pistols from more contentious ancestors, and old swords mounted against the mahogany-paneled walls.

Cavendish looked around the room at the antique weapons, shaking his head. "I hardly think this is the right place—"

"Not here, you fool," Swindon said shortly, opening the door to a smaller inner study. "In here, Manning. Apologize about this, you know, sure it will all turn out to be nothing."

Robert nodded. Watching him, Katryn thought in alarm that his face seemed drained of blood; he was as white as his immaculate shirtfront. "There is no window," he muttered, then, visibly bracing himself, he walked inside.

They left him sitting in a leather-covered wing chair, staring at the wall. There were indeed no windows; the room was little more than a large cupboard, and it had only one door, which led to the other study.

To Katryn's horror, they would not allow her to stay with her husband. "No, my dear," Swindon said, not unkindly, preventing her entrance as he shut the heavy door and locked it, putting the big key into his own pocket. "My wife—ah, there you are, my dear. You must see to Lady Manning."

Lady Swindon hurried in, her face flushed with distress,

her solitary ostrich feather leaning precariously to the side. "I only went to check on the jellies for the second course," she said, her tone miserable. "The new cook is so—and then everything happened. In the middle of our biggest ball of the Season, I can't imagine how this—oh, my dear"—she looked at Katryn, genuine concern mingling with her agitation—"my dear, I have smelling salts in my boudoir; if you would come up . . ."

"You, stay here," Cavendish was saying to the first trooper; turning to the second, he added, "you, wait outside on the front steps for the lieutenant to arrive. Then we will take the prisoner away and lock him up for good."

For good—for evil, you mean. For the first time in her life, Katryn thought she might truly swoon. Lady Swindon grabbed her arm. "Oh, my dear, it is too much for you, of course it is. Swindon!"

Her husband put his head out into the hall and barked for a footman; the servant hurried to hold up Katryn's other arm, and between them she was ushered up the steps to her hostess's private parlor. Lady Swindon, still babbling beneath her breath, waved the pungent vial of smelling salts under Katryn's nose. "I only went to check on the jellies; it's the new cook, he's not very—oh dear, oh dear."

Katryn jerked her head back when she sniffed the strong ammonia odor. "I'm quite all right," she said, coughing a little, and indeed, the room had steadied around her. She could not lie back on the chaise as her hostess urged while they took her husband off to hang him—behead him (what did the Crown do to an accused peer?)—for a crime he had not committed. She must do something to help Robert!

First she had to get rid of this well-meaning woman who had pulled up a small stool to sit beside her and chafe her hands.

"Please," Katryn muttered, "if I could rest, alone, with no one near me. My head pounds so."

"Of course, of course, I do understand." Lady Swindon patted her hand one more time. "You poor child, such a scandal, such embarrassment. I'm so sorry."

Katryn wanted to bite the small plump hand—her husband was in danger of his life, who cared a fig for the scandal? But she smiled feebly instead.

"I'll leave Wilton outside the door; just call if you desire a glass of wine later." Her hostess pushed the smelling salts into her hand. "I must get back down to the party and see if the evening can be saved. At least the jellies were coming along nicely, and, one must say, they will have plenty to talk about." She glanced down at Katryn, her expression guilty. "Not that I meant—oh, dear, just try to rest."

At last she went out, but Katryn heard her give directions to the footman to wait outside the door; that was not what Katryn had had in mind. She must get down to the study where Robert was locked up before the lieutenant arrived and took him away, past any help she could give him. Where did they put important prisoners, Katryn wondered, in the Tower, like the poor princes of long ago she had heard about in nursery tales? The little royal hostages had died alone, disappearing into the mists of time, their puzzle never revealed.

They would not kill Robert, she would not allow it!

She jumped to her feet and paced up and down the small parlor, tossing the vial of salts onto the silk-covered chaise. How could she release Robert? The key was in Swindon's pocket; impossible to obtain. Was there any other way to open a locked door? She had no idea; too bad she had not studied lock-picking instead of fine embroidery as a girl, Katryn thought ruefully. And there was the soldier outside the study door; he would not watch idly while she tried to pry open the lock. And also the footman outside her own door, who could raise the alarm if she did something suspicious.

The footman first, Katryn decided. She had no more time to waste. Looking around the room, she spotted a handsome marble bust on a side table. Lord Nelson? Perhaps, but it was a good weight in her hands. She lifted the bust carefully and pushed the stool to the side of the door before calling, "I would like something to drink, if you please."

The door parted, and the footman stepped in. "Yes, my lady, what would you—"

She stood on the stool, her weapon ready. She clipped him neatly on the side of the head and, despite the padding of his wig, he collapsed at once, falling into a heap on the Persian rug.

Katryn found her pulse beating so hard, she could hear the thump of it ringing in her ears. Was he dead?

To her relief, she saw his chest rise and fall. But he did seem unconscious; she was free to hurry downstairs to the study and—and what? The soldier standing guard at the door would not step aside and wait for her to knock him in the head. He was much bigger than she was, and he carried a weapon. And indeed, all he had to do was shout for help. What could she possibly do?

Katryn felt a moment of doubt. Any sensible woman would—but when had she ever been sensible? It had to be done, Robert's life depended upon it; therefore, she would find a way.

She stared absently at the servant still lying at her feet. Shaking her head, she looked at his face for the first time, thinking vaguely that she hadn't observed before the wart on his nose. No one looked at servants, not really. Then she thought, with her heart beating fast again, *No one looks at servants.*

His wig had already been loosened by the fall; it came off easily. The coat was harder to tug off the limp figure; it and the figured waistcoat underneath cost her precious minutes. The cravat she untied easily enough; if she arranged it care-

fully, it would cover up the gap above the waistcoat; she did
not need the shirt. But his trousers—taking a deep breath,
and praying that the man wore undergarments, Katryn un-
laced the pantaloons and peeled them off.

She shed her own gown, ripping off some of the tiny buttons in her haste, and put on the borrowed livery. She tucked
her dark hair up beneath the powdered wig—thank goodness Lady Swindon's private parlor had a looking glass on
the wall—and soon thought that she could pass for a servant,
if no one inspected her too closely. The shoes were too big;
she stuffed her handkerchief into one of the toes and a scrap
of writing paper from the desk into the other. Then, bundling
her own clothes into a ball beneath her arm, and holding the
invaluable marble bust in the other, she shut the door firmly
behind her, leaving the servant still oblivious, laid out on the
rug in his shirt and smalls. Trying to keep from tripping over
her own feet in the awkward, stiff shoes, she hurried down
the back staircase.

After one wrong turn, she found the study and paused outside the door. She thrust her bundled-up clothes under a side
table, first pulling out a silk stocking and bunching it into an
anonymous—she hoped—wad of cloth. Then she opened
the study door and walked inside.

The soldier stood at the door of the inner room; he looked
up when she entered, his expression suspicious.

"You there, this is not the time for cleaning," he said, his
voice gruff.

"Got my work to do, I do," Katryn replied, in as deep a
tone as she could manage. She did not meet his gaze; she set
the bust on the mahogany desk and began to dust the glass
cases behind it, completely ignoring the trooper as if he
were simply another piece of furniture. Her shoulders felt
rigid with tension, and she fought to keep her hands steady.
From the corner of her eye, she saw him look away, apparently deciding to ignore her.

She worked her way slowly closer to the man, but could not decide how to get a blow in without his knowledge. He was tall and more alert than the footman. And the gilt clock on the mantelpiece ticked away the passing minutes, bringing the lieutenant closer with each swing of its pendulum.

What could she do? The closer she got to the guard, the more nervous Katryn felt, yet she had to keep cleaning; it was her only excuse to be in the room. In the end, her nervousness betrayed her. She lost her grip on the silky fabric, and it fell almost at the trooper's feet.

She saw him focus on the delicate stocking, his eyes narrowing with suspicion.

"Here, what's this?"

He bent to pick up the revealing garment, and Katryn took her chance. Snatching the bust from the desktop, Katryn brought it down upon his head.

He gave a muffled exclamation, then fell heavily. Katryn dropped the bust, which hit the floor with a thud, and put her hands over her own mouth, holding her breath. Had anyone heard?

She waited long seconds, but there was no outcry from the corridor, no one rushed inside to arrest her, too. But the inside door was still locked. Now what?

Katryn looked around, then ran to pull an old-fashioned dagger from the display of antique weapons on the wall. She shoved the tip of the heavy blade into the large keyhole and pried and pushed. At first she thought it might not work, then, after long anxious moments, she felt something give, and the handle turned. She pulled open the door.

"Robert!" She hurried inside.

He was still seated just as she had last seen him, his head now buried in his hands. He didn't seem to hear her.

"Robert, we must go; they will be here any moment!" She shook him, and at last he looked up, his expression so bleak that her heart twisted.

"Robert, it's me."

His blank stare frightened her more than the rest of the nightmare all together. To her relief, he slowly focused on her face, blinking at her in surprise.

"Katryn?"

"Yes, come on, we must get away."

For a moment, she thought he might argue, then he stood up suddenly. "There is still one chance."

"Yes, yes," she agreed, with no idea what his meaning might be. She only knew they had no chance if they stayed.

Taking his hand, she led him toward the outer room. At the threshold, Robert paused in surprise to see the soldier lying sprawled on the floor. They stepped over his body carefully—he was breathing, Katryn was happy to see— then Katryn led her husband into the hallway. Pausing only to grab her bundle of clothes, and, hopping on one leg, then the other, to discard the footman's too-big shoes for her own satin slippers, she hurried toward the back of the house.

They met a couple of surprised maidservants, but no one tried to stop them. At last, they found a side door that led them out into the courtyard.

They needed horses, transport, but to call for their carriage would certainly give them away. There was the other soldier, and Cavendish, too; if he caught a glimpse of Robert at liberty, he would be sure to sound an alarm.

The night air was cool, and Katryn shivered. She could hear the muffled sound of voices and music from within the house, and outside, somewhere, a horse neighed.

Could they steal horses from the stables in back without alerting the whole house? But if Cavendish heard or suspected, he would be there at once with the remaining trooper.

She took one step toward the stable, then Robert grabbed her arm. "Wait, someone's coming!"

•   •   •

When they had taken Robert away, Eleanor had instinctively moved toward him. Someone grasped her arm in an unshakable grip and brought her up short. Startled, she looked up and met her husband's clear hazel eyes.

"Do not make it worse, my dear," he said softly. "There is nothing you can do."

There was sympathy in his voice, she thought, but also perhaps a glimmer of satisfaction in his gaze. It made her want to jerk free of his clasp, but there were too many people around them; she could sense the eyes watching her, the busy tongues ready to wag. It wasn't fair, she thought. How could she not feel for Robert, for the man she had once promised to marry? And this charade of treason was so absurd that it made her want to laugh.

She did laugh, and was alarmed to hear the shrill tinge of hysteria in the sound. "This is nonsense," she told her husband. "I do not believe a word of it!"

Perhaps he heard the dissonant tone, too, because he put one arm around her shoulders and led her toward the side of the room. "Perhaps we should withdraw, Eleanor. The evening has been unusually taxing."

This was so ridiculous that she laughed again and, to her alarm, found that she could not seem to stop. Her laughter rose till it sounded almost like a scream, shrill and desperate, and the faces around them turned to regard her.

Whitmund pulled her hastily to the nearest door; outside in the hallway, he slapped her cheek.

Shocked, Eleanor gasped. She put one hand to her stinging cheek and gazed at him in surprise. But the manic laughter at last faded. "Edward!"

"It was for your own good," he told her, his voice heavy with concern. "This has been too much for you. I understand your regret for Lord Manning, but—"

"You cannot believe this to be true?" Eleanor snapped, feeling the tingle still in her abused cheek. "You don't know

Robert, Whitmund. He would never do anything of the sort; he's the most loyal person I've ever known."

Her husband stared at her, his expression hard to read. "Whitmund," she said more softly, "you must believe me."

"I believe *you*," he told her, with only the slightest emphasis on the last word. "But you must not add to the scandal; I do not wish to see your name besmirched along with your sister's, and Manning's himself. We will find him the best solicitor—"

"No, there must be more we can do—" she interrupted. A young maid appeared, and Whitmund nodded to the servant, who struggled to keep her expression free of curiosity; her eyes were wide.

"Fetch our cloaks, at once. And send a footman to bring our carriage around."

"I don't wish to leave," Eleanor argued.

"You want to remain here and have every guest at the ball staring at you, speculating?" Her husband's tone was firm.

Eleanor tried to marshal her thoughts. "Katryn—we mustn't forget about Katryn. I must see about my sister first. I cannot leave her here all alone; if they take Robert away, she will be in total despair." She glanced at him quickly, then looked away from his steady gaze, knowing she should have remembered her sister's plight earlier. But she had been thinking of Robert, Eleanor told herself; it had not been selfish unconcern that had made her overlook Katryn. And anyhow, it was an excellent argument.

Whitmund hesitated. "Very well," he said. "Go to your sister; see if she wishes to leave with us. We will take her home with us, or to her own house, as she wishes. She can hardly desire to stay here once Robert has been removed. I will wait for you in the front hall."

Eleanor nodded and turned for the stairs. She was so intent on getting out of her husband's too-vigilant sight that she had gone up one flight before she realized she did not know where Lady Swindon had taken Katryn. She hesitated on the next landing, wondering if she could summon a maid to ask, when she glanced over her shoulder and saw her hostess coming up the wide staircase.

"Lady Swindon," Eleanor said, thankfully. "I wish to speak to my sister."

"Oh yes, my dear." The older woman looked pleased. "I was about to check on her myself, but you're just the person she will wish to see, I'm sure. That is—well, you are her sister. She's in the small parlor next to my bedchamber, just along the corridor there."

Lady Swindon pointed, then picked up her skirts and hurried back down to her other guests. Eleanor paused for a moment in the hallway, wondering if she would find Katryn fuming, crying, or weak still with shock. What if she demanded to go to prison along with Robert? Eleanor knew her sister was capable of anything; she'd never had a sense of what was proper. Eleanor sighed. Perhaps for once Katryn would listen to an elder sister's counsel.

As long as she could remember, Eleanor had been the good daughter, and now the dutiful wife, doing what was expected of her, never causing concern. And Katryn had been the baby, cosseted and indulged, running heedlessly through life, doing just what she pleased. Really, it was too bad, Eleanor thought, cross again despite herself. But she must remember to be sympathetic; this time even Katryn could not escape her predicament.

Taking a deep breath, Eleanor put her hand on the silver knob and turned it, pushing the door open. Taking one step inside, she stopped, her hand flying to her mouth as she gasped. Katryn was nowhere in sight; instead, the body of an almost-naked man sprawled across the rug.

God in heaven, were there murderers in the house? Had everyone gone mad?

Eleanor bit back an instinctive scream. Who was this

man, and why had he no clothes? Well, almost none. She looked at him quickly. He had thin, hairy legs, she noted absently, and a hole in the heel of his long stockings. Blushing, she averted her eyes. Why had he no shoes, no outer garments at all? And where on earth was Katryn? Had she been kidnapped, murdered as well? Her mind racing, Eleanor tried not to panic. She must call for help! But her mouth was dry, she wasn't sure she could make a sound.

Eleanor edged around the man's body toward the bell rope at the side of the room, then jumped when the man stirred. Surely he had shifted his arm? He moved again and moaned. He wasn't dead, after all.

Eleanor forgot about the bell rope; she knelt by his side. "Are you all right? What happened? Where's my sister? Where is Lady Manning?"

The man opened his eyes; they were dazed with shock. He blinked at her and rubbed his head. "That deceitful Jezebel what clobbered me w' the marble?"

"What?" Eleanor gasped again. "How dare you speak of Lady Manning in such a way!"

"Uhh, beg pardon, milady," the man said, groaning.

He was a servant, Eleanor realized from the uneducated accent. And as for her sister—had Katryn really hit the poor man? Had she lost her wits? As if they did not have enough of a scandal brewing, now this—

Eleanor bit her lip, exasperation replacing her first instinctive surge of concern. Katryn had not been kidnapped, injured; she was the one inflicting the mayhem! Eleanor should have known.

"Stay here," she told the servant. "I will fetch help; you have a big lump on your head."

"Guess I do, God love us!" He touched his sore scalp gingerly, then lowered his voice and added, "Yes, milady."

Eleanor stood, feeling the weakness in her knees, and left the room, shutting the door firmly behind her. The man inside could wait a few minutes; he was in no danger. She had to locate Katryn and keep her sister from doing anything else equally rash. If she could attack an innocent servant, she was capable of anything.

Whitmund—Eleanor's thoughts flew to her husband. He would be waiting downstairs; she should go and make some excuse. They could not leave yet, not till she knew what had happened to Katryn, what was about to happen to Robert. Although her spirits sank as she thought of Robert hauled away to some ignominious prison, Eleanor knew she could not look the other way. Once, she had failed him; this time, she would be there when he needed her. Robert must know that she had stood beside him, had held her head high in belief of his innocence.

She flew down the staircase, intent on finding her husband. But the foyer was empty except for a parlormaid who waited patiently, holding Eleanor's ermine-trimmed evening cloak.

"Lord Whitmund has stepped outside to check on the carriage, milady," the servant said.

"Thank you," Eleanor answered automatically. "I'll go and tell him I'm not ready to leave just yet."

"He's in the side courtyard, milady," the girl told her, adjusting the cloak around her shoulders. "That—that gentleman and the soldier-person are still on the front steps."

Eleanor hurried to the side entrance the servant indicated; she had no wish to run into Cavendish and his guard dog, who might have the impertinence to question her. And just now, she had no wish to have to explain anything, with Katryn up to who-knew-what.

She found Whitmund just outside the door, pacing up and down on the cobblestones.

"Is your sister not coming with us?" he asked, looking up as she emerged from the doorway. "Is Lady Manning too ill to be moved?"

"No, I—that is, I don't know; I couldn't find her," Eleanor explained, her words almost as jumbled as her emotions. "We can't leave just yet."

"But—"

Eleanor jerked her head; she had seen a motion in the shadows. "Katryn?"

It was her sister's face, a pale oval in the darkness, and she motioned to her.

"Why is she out here, alone?" Whitmund demanded.

Eleanor waved his words aside. "I think—I think she is very agitated in spirits," she said quickly. "Wait here; let me speak to her privately."

She hurried across the courtyard, dragging her cloak on the uneven stones and trying not to trip. When she reached the darker shadows, she felt her sister reach out and grasp her arm, pulling her closer.

"Eleanor, we need your help!"

9

"Why? Are you going to hit me on the head, too?" Eleanor demanded crossly. "And what on earth are you wearing? Is there not enough gossip about us already? Have you lost your wits, Katryn? This is no way to help Robert."

Then she saw that Katryn was not alone, and when she recognized who stood in the deeper shadow, Eleanor gasped. "Robert!"

Stepping away from her sister, she reached for him, she could not help it. Robert took her hands, holding them so tightly that she bit back an instinctive protest. But the pressure of his grip, the warmth of his skin pressed against her own—indeed, she had no wish to be released—if only, if only . . .

"I know you are innocent of the charges." She wanted to cling even closer to him, but she knew it was forbidden. "I know it cannot be true."

His eyes glinted in the dimness, and she felt him tremble; they stood so close, still linked by his tight grip of her hands.

"Eleanor," Katryn said from the side, raising her voice a little. "Eleanor, we need a carriage."

"Why? You cannot run away; that will not help your case," Eleanor protested, still looking at Robert.

"You think he should stay and be locked up by that hateful man?" Katryn argued hotly.

"We'll get him the best solicitor," Eleanor answered, not taking her eyes off Robert's face, but irritated again by her sister's impulsive behavior. "Whitmund says—" She faltered when she felt, as much as saw, Robert wince. Slowly, he released her hands.

"We can't wait," Katryn said. "Can you get your carriage for us without alerting Cavendish?"

"It's already ordered," she answered.

"Eleanor," Robert spoke quickly, his voice a harsh whisper. "There's a woman at the party—a Frenchwoman—I saw her only for an instant. She's slight of frame, small as a child, with dark hair and very large dark eyes. She's wearing a lavender gown. Her Christian name is Minette, or it was when I knew her. She was with a short older gentleman who wore a blue old-fashioned coat. I need to know who she is and where I can find her."

Eleanor wrinkled her brow, trying to think. "I don't know anyone of that description, Robert. Why is it so important?"

"She might be able to furnish information about my real mission in France," Robert explained, glancing over his shoulder. "She knows the truth; it might save my neck, and our family. Look, here's your carriage. I must take it, Eleanor, forgive me for dragging you into this contretemps, too. Katryn, I'm sorry. Go with your sister, my dear; Eleanor will look out for you. I will send you word when I can."

Robert strode forward to hail the carriage, and both women ran after him.

"Take this gentleman up, Watkins, and take him where he wishes to go," Eleanor informed the driver quickly.

"Yes, milady," the man said, his expression puzzled but obedient.

The groom hopped down to open the door and hold it for Robert to climb in. Eleanor turned in time to see Katryn scrambling into the carriage.

"Katryn!" she and Robert exclaimed, almost in unison.

"Do not think you will leave me behind again!" Katryn spoke to her husband, ignoring her sister's gasp of outrage. "I am your wife, Robert. I swore an oath, for better or worse, remember?"

"It's too dangerous, I cannot allow it," Robert told her, frowning.

Someone shouted behind them.

Katryn reached for his arm. "Get in; there is no time to argue!"

Robert jumped inside, and the groom slammed the door.

"Spring the horses!" Robert shouted to the driver, who raised his whip. The carriage lurched forward, and the groom had no time to hop back onto his perch.

"Hey, here now," the man protested, but the team of horses had broken into a run, and the carriage rolled across the courtyard and clattered into the street.

"Wait," someone shouted.

Hearing footsteps, Eleanor, still gasping over Katryn's rashness, lifted her skirts to hurry back to the house, but within a few paces she came face to face with her husband.

"Eleanor!" Whitmund said, breathing quickly as if he had been running. "What—wasn't that our carriage?"

"Yes," she agreed, trying to meet his gaze. But the anger, the hurt that she saw in his eyes made her look away too soon. "I—I have lent it to my sister."

"I saw a man get into the carriage."

Whitmund paused, and Eleanor tried to summon all her most persuasive arguments. But she felt her stomach clench itself into knots, and her tongue seemed too thick. She couldn't think of the right words to say.

"It was Lord Manning, was it not?" His voice was very quiet, but the emotion evident beneath his steely self-control made Eleanor tremble. Was he very angry? What would he do to her? She thought of the blow he had given her in the hallway when she could not stop laughing, and she felt cold inside.

"Yes," she said, her voice tremulous. "I told him he could take our carriage."

"You wish me to go to jail, too?" Somehow his terrible self-control was worse than the ranting and shouting she had expected.

"Of c-course not," Eleanor objected, her voice still trembling. "But I know this charge is untrue, and Robert said— he said he had one last chance to prove his innocence. I could not stand in his way."

Whitmund stared at her, then turned and took several quick steps before pausing to look back at her. The dim light of a flickering lantern cast his face into shadow, but she did not like the grim lines that she could make out. "And when Cavendish finds out, he will think we are all in league together, French spies the lot of us."

"That's insane," she tried to protest. "No one could think such a thing!"

"I might remind you that it is your son's reputation you are risking, along with mine and yours." Her husband's implacable voice came out of the darkness. "If you have no concern for my honor, since it is obvious you care more for Manning than for me, you might think of your child."

Eleanor wished he had struck her again instead of throwing hateful accusations; a physical blow could not hurt more than this. She felt tears slip down her cheeks, and it was hard to speak. "That's not fair. How can you speak so? When Robert's innocence is known, this will all be forgotten, and we will go on as before."

She heard a harsh sound—a laugh or a groan, she wasn't sure—and his dark figure, silhouetted against the torches that lined the far side of the courtyard, turned away from her.

"Edward, where are you going?" she cried, panicked. Was he leaving her? Was he so angry he would petition for a divorce? She would be shamed for the rest of her life, ostracized by polite society, a pariah living at the fringes of the only world she had ever known.

"Edward!" she called again, but all she heard was the faint sound of his boots on the stones of the courtyard, footsteps fading as he walked away into the darkness.

Eleanor thought she might faint, might die, even, right here, alone and with no one to help her. It wasn't fair, she thought again. Katryn—how dare she!—had gone off with Robert, and Eleanor, who had only tried to help, was left to face the stares, the whispers, and the alarming wrath of her own husband.

She sobbed and hid her face in her hands, swaying a little on her feet. What could she do? Go back inside and face the eyes of the crowd? No, no—but how could she get home? Their own residence was only a couple miles away, but the streets were dark, and she had never been out at night alone—

"Milady?" a male voice said cautiously, from the dimness.

She jumped. "Who is it?"

"Me, milady, Parson." He stepped out of the shadows, and she recognized their own livery. She had forgotten the groom, who had been left behind when Robert and Katryn drove off so precipitously. "What, um, do you wish me to do?"

She felt relief flood over her. "You can go home and fetch the other carriage—no, no, I don't want to wait. You can escort me home."

"On foot, milady?" he said in surprise.

"Yes, it's a fair night." She tried to sound rational, tried to pretend it was her usual practice to walk through the streets of London at night. "Wait—you can hail us a hackney cab if one passes by."

"Yes, milady," the groom agreed.

Eleanor heard the sound of voices as the door opened behind them, and a long shaft of light shot into the dark courtyard. "Oh, someone's coming."

It might be Cavendish. He might already have discovered Robert's absence, but did he know in whose carriage his prisoner had escaped? Eleanor felt guilt rise inside her; had Edward been right after all, would they all go to prison for this? Trembling with fright, she motioned to the groom. "Keep silent!"

She lifted her skirts and hurried into the shadows, away from whoever approached. When she stood deeper in the darkness, the groom an invisible presence just beyond, betrayed only by a faint smell of sweat—she must ask the housekeeper how often their liveries were cleaned, Eleanor thought in some corner of her mind—she turned to see who was emerging.

But it was only another couple from the ball; the woman had a shawl thrown over her slightly outmoded ball gown, and the man paced up and down, watching for their carriage.

Was the whole party breaking up? Eleanor wondered. She had pictured the rest of the crowd gathered around the supper tables, talking as hard as they ate, like ravens picking clean a rabbit's bones while they snipped at Robert and his whole family, devouring the scandal as if it were the main course.

No, it was only this one couple, she saw; the door had shut behind them, and no one else emerged. The man walked up and down impatiently, stopping only to pat his wife's shoulder.

The woman—if she was his wife—was very short, and—With a shock, Eleanor remembered Robert's instructions. He needed to find a woman of short stature with dark hair and big eyes. Eleanor crept forward just a little, trying to see this woman better.

Yes, her hair was dark; wisps flew around her face, released from its pins by the rising breeze. From the little she could discern of the woman's gown, it did look to be lavender colored. And her eyes were large and hollowed in the light from the lanterns by the side door; the man was short and stout and elderly. Perhaps this was the very woman that Robert sought. But what was her name?

"Parson," she whispered, and she heard a rustle in the darkness as the groom came closer at her summons. "Hurry to the stable; these people awaiting their carriage—find out who they are and where they are from. Some of the stable lads must have chatted with their driver. Hurry!"

"Yes, milady." She heard him patter away through the darkness, stumbling once, and she waited in the shadows, trying to make out more about the mysterious pair who were for some reason important to Robert.

They both seemed nervous, and the gentleman—he had to be a gentleman if they had been invited to Lord Swindon's ball, Eleanor told herself—was very impatient.

At last the man stopped his pacing, and an old-fashioned chariot rolled up, with only two horses pulling it. The servant who jumped down helped them in, while Eleanor held her breath. Had her groom had time to find out the information she sought?

By the time the unknown lady was handed into the vehicle, with the man taking his place beside her, Eleanor's groom had returned. The chariot was rumbling away as she impulsively clasped his arm.

"Milady?" His surprise was apparent, and she dropped her hand.

"Did you find out their names?"

"Yes, Lady Whitmund. Them's Sir 'enry Grabble and his wife; 'e's a distant connection of Lord Swindon, not very important, and they 'ail from York, tho' them are staying in a rented 'ouse in Cheapside for the Season."

"Good," Eleanor breathed. The courtyard was quiet again, then she heard a muffled shout from the front of the house. Her heart leapt. Had they discovered the wounded half-naked servant upstairs in the boudoir? She must get away. Yes, there were more shouts.

"Let us go," she told the groom with as much semblance of dignity as she could manage.

"Yes, milady," the servant agreed, though he craned his head toward the house, his expression curious. "Do you want me to inquire—"

"No," she said sharply. "I have no stomach for any more outcries tonight."

And pulling her cloak more closely about her, she walked as quickly as she could out of the courtyard and into the street, the groom following respectfully just behind her.

Katryn gripped the edge of the seat as their borrowed carriage bounced over an occasional pothole; they were traveling too fast for a London street, but she had no wish to slow their pace. They were free, Robert was free! By some miracle, her barely thought-out scheme had worked, and he was here by her side. She wanted to lean into his embrace and feel his heartbeat against her cheek, but Robert still seemed lost in his own thoughts. His unusual lethargy was as alarming as the shock of Cavendish's announcement. How could Robert's cousin have come across such a letter, and why did it purport to expose Robert as a spy? Robert could not have done such a thing; she was as sure of that as she was of her own name.

Though, glancing down at the ridiculous livery she still wore, Katryn told herself that anyone else observing her just now might doubt even that. She tried to stifle a nervous giggle.

But the slight sound made Robert turn. In the jolting carriage and the faint flickering light from an occasional lantern outside, he seemed at last more alert. She felt an enormous relief to see him somewhat restored to his normal demeanor, and some of the tightness in her chest eased.

"Robert, are you all right?"

He looked over the incredible outfit she wore and nearly smiled; her powdered wig slanted crookedly to one side, and the pantaloons were too big, drooping at the knees. When would Katryn ever cease to surprise him? Then he remembered their desperate predicament, and the smile died before it could lift his lips. "Katryn, I appreciate your help—indeed, I hardly can understand how you have done so much. You may have saved my life. But I deeply regret your presence here."

His gentle tone brought tears to her eyes. Robert was not happy that she was with him? When she needed him so badly—would this marriage always be so one-sided? Perhaps she had done the wrong thing in asking for this union, Katryn thought, not for the first time. But regardless, she could hardly leave him to Cavendish's clutches.

Robert saw the liquid glint in her eyes and felt a tremor of remorse. "I thank you for all your brave efforts," he repeated. "But it is too dangerous for you, my dear. And now you will be a fugitive, too. This is no way for me to treat the woman I have sworn to honor and protect. The scandal is bad enough—I never thought to expose you to physical danger, as well."

Katryn swallowed hard, and some of her pain eased. He was concerned for her—that moved her deeply. It was a moment before she could steady her voice.

"Oh, bosh on the scandal," she said, lifting her chin. Her last governess would have washed out her mouth with soap, but using cant terms was such a mild transgression compared to her exploits of the night that Katryn again felt a wild desire to giggle. "I would share whatever comes, as long as I can be with you, Robert. And besides, you might need my help again."

The words, coming from such a diminutive form, should have been ludicrous, but she had saved his neck once already tonight. Now he must put this unexpected opportunity to good use.

"I must find Minette," he muttered. "But where I must go to find the information is no place for a lady, certainly not for my wife. I will have the coachman drop you at our house, first; stay out of sight; the servants will tell no one you are at home."

He leaned toward the door to call to the driver, but Katryn grabbed his arm.

"No, Robert! You said yourself, I'm a fugitive, too. Do you really think that Cavendish would hesitate to search our whole house? The servants would not be able to protect me. I will be safer with you."

"You could go to Eleanor—"

This time, Katryn knew her tone was sharper. "Cavendish will consider that possibility, too! Your cousin is selfish and greedy, but he's not stupid."

Robert seemed to give this thought, but again he shook his head. "But to take you to a place that no respectable lady would frequent—"

"Just as well." Katryn nodded toward her odd costume, and pushed the wig back—it made her head feel hot and itchy. "I'm not exactly dressed for anyone's drawing room."

Robert smiled briefly. "I suppose you're right," he said. "Though I do not like this course of events."

But she was still at his side, Katryn thought, keeping her own smile demure. He was still here, still alive, still free. For the moment, that was enough.

Robert gave the driver new orders, and then they rode for some time through streets that Katryn had never glimpsed before. She could tell by the narrower lanes and the rank odors that drifted into the carriage that this was a poorer section of London than she was accustomed to frequenting. Despite the late hour, light glinted from alehouses, and she glimpsed slatternly women lounging against the buildings that lined the street, some lifting bottles to their lips and laughing shrilly.

When the carriage drew to a stop, Robert opened the door and helped her down. She carried her bundle of clothing beneath one arm and tried to watch her step. The street was thick with mud and offal, and the smell was almost overpowering.

But the house that rose before them was respectable in appearance, if not overly large; its front door was painted neatly and the knocker polished to a high gleam. A lantern still burned brightly, and, by its light, Robert lifted the brass knocker and rapped.

Within a few moments, the door swung open. Robert spoke briefly to the servant, and then they were being ushered inside.

Katryn glanced around her; the hall was narrow, then they were led directly into a small but handsomely appointed salon.

"Madam will be with you in just a moment, milord," the footman said. He glanced at Katryn once, his eyes curious, but his tone was correct as he bowed himself out of the room and closed the door behind them.

The room was pleasantly warm; it held brocade armchairs and a settee, and a fire danced on the hearth. Katryn turned to her husband to ask more about their destination, but at that moment the door opened again, and a woman of uncertain years swept into the room.

Katryn's gasp was audible in the stillness. After a quick look, she averted her eyes to the fire. The woman, for lady she could not be called, had dampened her skirts in the French style, to such a degree that the thin material clearly delineated her round thighs and the V between them. The thin muslin gown was high-waisted with short, puffed sleeves, otherwise very correct and stylish. Katryn had heard of this scandalous practice but had never actually seen it done. She hoped the fire would be blamed for her reddened cheeks. Cautiously, Katryn looked back at the woman but was careful to keep her gaze focused on the stranger's face.

With no sign of the shame Katryn would have felt at receiving callers in such a state, the woman held her head high. She had such a regal presence that Katryn wondered at her living in such a poor part of the city. A widow of meager fortune, perhaps? But the muslin of her gown was of good quality, and the thick strand of diamonds and amethysts that glittered around her throat did not appear to be made of paste.

Her coppery hair showed no signs of gray; it was upswept into a cascade of curls and rolls, and her eyes were bright with intelligence. But her cheeks were perhaps a trifle too highly colored—could it be this woman wore rouge? Katryn peered closer, but the weak light of the fire and the one candelabra kept her from being sure.

Katryn jumped when Robert's hand touched her arm. She met his amused eyes with chagrin. He seemed to know exactly what she was thinking. She tossed her head. Unfortunately, this caused the heavy wig to slip low over her forehead, cutting off her view of the woman entirely. Quickly, Katryn shoved it back and paid no attention to Robert's quiet chuckle.

Ignoring Katryn, the woman glided up to Robert and took his hands. "Robert, dear one! It has been much, much too long."

Robert smiled too warmly at the woman for Katryn's liking. "It has been a long time, indeed; I wasn't sure you would remember me."

"As if I could forget such a brave and charming gallant." The woman glanced up at Robert from beneath her long dark lashes, her coquetry obvious. "I'm delighted to see you back in my modest establishment, dear Robert."

Katryn, blinking in surprise to hear her husband addressed so intimately, tried to pull herself together as the woman glanced in her direction.

"But to bring a footman? Really, Robert, have you become so pompous in your advanced years?"

She tittered, and Katryn felt a flicker of jealousy. "I am not a footman," she declared, her voice louder than she had intended.

Robert's brows lifted; she thought he was trying not to laugh. "No, indeed; Lucretia, may I introduce my wife?"

Lucretia's too-red lips parted for a moment, then her eyes narrowed. "Indeed? I am pleased to make your acquaintance, Lady Manning." She gave Katryn a slight curtsy, and Katryn, blushing at the odd appearance she knew she must present, couldn't decide whether to bow or curtsy, and finally just inclined her head as if she were royalty. When she realized the implications of that, she blushed even more deeply.

Lucretia (did the woman have no other name, or were she and Robert on such close terms that—no, no, Katryn did not wish to pursue that thought) stared at her.

"You have changed a good deal, Robert, if you choose to bring your wife"—she made the word a question, and Robert nodded firmly—"to my humble establishment. Or is this some new game that the Ton has evolved to alleviate its boredom?"

"No game, it is a desperate move, I'm afraid, for desperate straits." Robert's tone was grim. "I need information, quickly, and I thought you might know the woman whom I seek."

Katryn opened her mouth to demand a private room so that she could change back into her own clothing—she felt increasingly ridiculous in the servant's livery—then realized she didn't really want to leave these two alone together. So she remained silent and listened to Robert explain quickly about the attempted arrest, the spurious charge of treason, the woman who might be able to save him.

"Why do you think I would know her?" Lucretia demanded. Her smile had faded, and she looked alarmed to hear of such serious accusations.

Katryn felt a flicker of concern. What if this woman turned them in? How could Robert trust her with so much of the truth?

"Because of her, uh, occupation," he said quietly. "And I know how wide your circle reaches. I met her in Paris, but if she is in England, I thought you would know of her, if anyone does, even though she now seems to be married."

Lucretia paced up and down the small parlor, her skirts almost transparent when she passed in front of the fire. She paused at last and looked up at Robert, putting one hand to the heavy necklace at her throat. "Yes, I do know Minette," she said slowly. "And if it were anyone else, or if your situation were not so grave, I would not admit to it. She is respectable now, you know."

Robert nodded. "I will be discreet, I promise."

"Very well." Lucretia seemed to come to a decision. "She is married to Sir Henry Grabble; he has a small estate in York, but they are in London for a few weeks; they usually stay in a rented house in Cheapside. I have the address, though nowadays we rarely correspond, of course."

"Thank you, Lucretia." Robert breathed a sigh of relief. "We will be on our way at once. I will not endanger you by staying any longer."

Lucretia nodded, but Katryn decided she had bided her time long enough. "Just one more favor, if you please. May I have the use of a private chamber so that I can change my clothing?"

Lucretia laughed. "What, tired of your servant's garb, my lady?" Her tone was mocking. "Of course. I'll have my man show you to an empty room. Robert, you had better go with her."

"I should think so," he said with some emphasis, offering Katryn his arm.

Why could she not change her clothes alone? Was there no lady's maid available to assist her? Puzzled, Katryn put one hand on Robert's arm, and they followed Lucretia into the hall.

On the other side of the hall, the double doors were now open, and she could glimpse another, larger salon. Several men lounged on the settees, and a number of young ladies, dressed in sheer and deeply cut gowns, all of them remarkably handsome of face and form, were sitting unusually close to their male friends. One young lady played a pianoforte with some skill, and the laughter and talk was loud.

They had interrupted a party, Katryn thought, embarrassed at such a social blunder, even while she wondered at such a fast set of people. No wonder Robert hadn't wanted her to come. Of course, Robert had explained to Lucretia how urgent their mission was, but obviously he wanted to leave as soon as may be.

They were led quickly up the stairs—Lucretia's haste to be rid of them seemed a little extreme—and into a small bedchamber. The room had pink roses on the paper, and thick draperies covered the window.

The bed, to Katryn's surprise, was unmade, the covers tumbled back in disarray. The servants of the house must be behind in their chores. She scratched her head again absently, happy to pull off the heavy wig, and prepared to shed her borrowed clothing.

"May I help you?" her husband asked after Lucretia's servant had departed.

Katryn shook her head. She was surprised that no maidservant had come to assist her, but the house must be short-handed, with the party downstairs, and all. "I will be out of these things in a moment," she assured him. Robert walked across to peer cautiously out the window, pushing the curtains aside. Surely Cavendish would not find them here? But there was the borrowed carriage standing on the street, its emblazoned crest proclaiming Whitmund's name. She must hurry. She began to unbutton the jacket, stopping only to scratch her head one more time. That dratted wig had left her—

Then she felt something strange. Bringing her hand down, she looked more closely at what she had found in her hair, and screamed.

"Katryn! What is it?" Robert was at her side at once, his expression alarmed.

She held out the tiny but all-too-alive insect she had discovered on her scalp and tried not to shriek again. Her stomach rolled, and she had to swallow a wave of nausea. "Oh, Robert—look!"

He knew at once what she held. A wave of distaste crossed his face, then he had himself under control. "I see. You must be more careful next time whose wig you borrow, my dear."

"It is not funny!" she snapped, tossing the thing into the fireplace, shuddering as she did so. She scratched futilely at her head, pushing her much abused hair even further out of place. "I've never had—what am I to do?"

Robert went back to the door and called for the servant. When the man reappeared, Robert said, "We shall need a hot hip bath prepared, if you please, and fetch us a fine-toothed comb."

The man nodded—did no request surprise him?—and went off to order the hot water.

Katryn found she had to blink hard to hold back the tears. She had never felt so dirty; how would Robert ever want to touch her again? She didn't want to touch herself! "Robert, I'm so sorry."

He came to her side quickly and took her hands. "What do you have to be sorry for? That while you were busy saving my life, you put on the wrong wig? The only one to blame is Swindon, who must see to his servants' grooming."

"But you must be so disgusted . . ." Her voice quavered.

He pressed her hand. "Believe me, my dear, I have seen much worse. There was a time when my appearance would have repulsed any woman of breeding."

Prison, she thought; despite the apparent lightness of his tone, she could detect the emotion he kept under careful control. Her head itched; she tried to pull out of his grasp.

"No." He still gripped her hands. "Don't scratch your head; we will take care of the problem shortly."

When the servant returned to lead them to another room, one with a large and surprisingly elegant bathtub filled with clean water, Katryn could hardly wait for the footman to depart before shedding all of her clothes and stepping into the warm liquid. There were small soaps and bath salts in glass bowls nearby, and thick towels on a stool beside the tub.

Katryn washed herself vigorously with handfuls of lather and scrubbed her hair especially hard. Robert poured a pitcher of clean water over her to rinse away the soap, then he ran the narrow tines of the comb through her wet hair over and over, till they were both reassured that no vermin remained.

Katryn was about to reach for a towel when the door flew open, and they both jumped in surprise. Katryn's heart beat fast. Had Cavendish found them?

But the man was a stranger, his face ruddy with drink and his cravat undone. He leaned unsteadily against the door frame and leered at Katryn. "Well! What have we here? Madam's been hiding her most delectable morsel from me, shame, shame."

Katryn felt her cheeks, her neck, even her chest turn red as she blushed deeply, sinking low into the tub to try to hide her nakedness. How dare he burst into a private room? Who was this unmannerly lout, and how had he come into their bath?

Robert moved swiftly to grab the man by the lapels of his jacket.

"Hey, wait," the stranger protested, his voice thick with liquor. "You had your turn, now it's my—"

Robert tossed him out into the hallway, shouting for the footman. The servant—Katryn hadn't remarked before on how brawny the man was—picked up the drunk easily and shoved him toward the stairwell. They passed out of Katryn's line of vision, then Robert came in and shut the door, leaning against it.

"You'd best get dressed, my dear," he said, not quite meeting her eye. "I am sorry for that."

Suddenly, it all came together. They had taken refuge in a bawdy house! No wonder Robert had not wanted her to come. Those women downstairs were common whores (well, maybe not so common) and Lucretia—Madam, the stranger had called her—oh dear, oh dear. After one dismayed glance, Katryn looked away from her husband and stared at the prints on the wall, which she had not inspected earlier, and saw that their subject matter only made her cheeks burn more hotly. She glanced down, but her own nudity now seemed disgraceful, too.

Biting her lip, she grabbed a towel from the stack and, with a great splashing of water, climbed out of the tub. Robert guarded the door as she rubbed herself hastily dry. Before she could reach for her shift and underthings, she heard a light knock at the door.

"Who is it?" Robert demanded, holding the door shut.

"Just me."

Robert eased the door open a crack, and when he was satisfied, opened it wider. Lucretia stood in the doorway, her expression concerned. "I am sorry for that, me lord," she said, formal for the first time. "but you know 'ow it is when the gentlemen have been too long in their port."

Robert nodded. "I know. I just hope he didn't recognize us."

Katryn bit her lip at this new worry.

But Lucretia shook her head. "He's so drunk, he won't remember anything of a morrow, except how his head aches." She seemed to have recovered her poise, and her control of her *h*'s.

Robert looked thoughtful. "You're probably right. But we had better be on our way as soon as may be."

Lucretia turned to Katryn. Katryn, still wrapped in the towel and feeling both indecent and ridiculous, found herself, for once, speechless. What did one say to a madam, a prostitute?

"My man told me of your little, um, problem," she said. "I suspect your underthings should be scrubbed, milady. You may have picked up a few fleas, as well."

"Fleas!" Katryn gasped, for a moment forgetting the rest of their worries in a rush of total revulsion.

"I have some new shifts just back from my own seamstress—never been worn," Lucretia added quickly. "I'd be happy to offer you a set of undergarments, milady."

"Thank you," Katryn said with real gratitude.

Lucretia picked up the elegant gown, now sadly crushed, in which Katryn had started the evening. The madam touched the fine silk, the delicate stitching and pearl trim, with obvious appreciation. "And this is not much of a dress to travel in, if you'll pardon me for saying. I could lend you a nice clean traveling gown, milady, that might be less, um, remarkable."

Robert had lifted his brows, but Katryn said quickly, "That would be very kind of you."

"And I'll wrap up your gown for you to take," Lucretia went on, but this time Katryn knew what to say.

"I'd be pleased if you would keep it; perhaps you could make use of it?"

Lucretia's smile widened. "That's very genteel of you, your ladyship. A beautiful piece of work, it is." She was out the door quickly, still carrying the ball gown, as if to forestall Katryn from changing her mind.

Katryn glanced at her husband, hoping he was not considering just how much that dress had cost him, its delicate silk and fine embroidery a creation of one of London's top modistes.

Instead, Robert was smiling. "You continue to surprise me, Katryn," he murmured. He came closer to touch her bare shoulders, then lowered his head to kiss her neck. She shivered in delicious appreciation of his caress, almost dropping her towel. She leaned into him, delighting in his touch. That woman might have known Robert at some point in his life, but now—now—

Someone in a nearby room shouted, his drunken voice heavy with lust. Robert jumped and looked around. The sounds of revelry from the rooms around them were too loud; this was not the place to tarry. Looking reluctant, Robert kissed her again quickly, then released her and went back to hold the door.

Lucretia was back very soon, carrying a brand-new set of underwear and stockings, as she had promised, and a clean but very plain gray gown, with a matching pelisse.

Katryn dressed quickly, then regarded her reflection in the long looking glass at the side of the bathroom. "I look like someone's governess!" she said in dismay.

"The better to escape attention," Lucretia told her, looking her up and down with a professional glint in her eye. "She's too pretty by half, your lady wife," she murmured to Robert.

Robert grinned. "I will not quarrel with that."

"I'm afraid I have no clothes for you, Robert," Lucretia added. "My man is too broad in the back, and his trousers would be too short for you."

Robert looked down at his own evening wear. "It can't be helped. Thank you for your invaluable aid, Lucretia."

The madam put one hand to her neck and, this time, pushed the wide necklace aside an inch. Katryn knew her own eyes widened. A scar showed white against the woman's olive-toned skin, then disappeared again as the thick necklace slipped back into place.

"Saved my life he did once, your husband," Lucretia said bluntly to Katryn. "Some customers, they get mean when they're drunk. I remember my friends, I do. He's quite a man, your lord and master. You make sure he lives to turn the tables on this cousin of 'is who wants the title and the money."

"I'll do my best," Katryn answered, taking the charge as seriously as Lucretia seemed to offer it.

Robert looked at them, his brows lifting as he fought back a smile.

"Women have more wits than men sometimes think," Lucretia told him, her tone tart. She touched her neck as she turned toward the door. "It's almost dawn. Best get that fancy carriage of yours out of sight, now, and you both on your way."

"We will. Come, my dear," Robert told Katryn, his expression sobering as he remembered all the dangers still ahead.

10

Eleanor slept little that night. She had arrived home in a hackney, to the consternation of the servants, to find that her husband had not returned, nor had he sent any message. She retired to bed but lay awake, listening for the sound of his footstep on the stair, till the sky began to lighten. Then, sick at heart at the thought of what could ensue if Edward did not forgive her, she had finally fallen into a restless doze.

When she woke, the morning was still fresh, and she felt heavy-eyed and miserable. She threw on a wrapper over her thin gown and went up to the nursery. Her small son was just finishing his breakfast at the breast of the wet nurse. The village girl, who had just weaned her own child when she'd happily agreed to come to London with them, leaving her several children at home with her husband and grandmum, was cheerful and red-cheeked with health, apparently viewing her brief employment as a great adventure. But Eleanor watched their close bond with envy, almost wishing she had not given up nursing her son herself.

When the girl had changed the baby's soiled wrappings for fresh ones, Eleanor took her son and sat down with him in the chair, holding him close. The baby made faint sounds of contentment, and she kissed the downy head. If Edward divorced her, he would take their son away, too. Eleanor would have nothing, and her heart went hollow at such a thought. She trembled and held the baby too tightly, till he squirmed and fussed in protest. Eleanor loosened her grip and kissed him again, overcome with anger at the unfairness of it all.

She cuddled little Fitz for some time, then with a sigh handed him to the nurse and went back to her room to dress. But the anger still burned inside her; she wasn't even sure who was the object of her rage—Cavendish, for raising this ludicrous charge against Robert; Whitmund, for not supporting her, not understanding; Katryn, for her rashness; Robert—no, she could not be angry at Robert.

When she went downstairs, she walked into the dining room then paused abruptly on the threshold. Whitmund was seated at the table, holding a cup of tea, his expression grim.

She stared at him, not sure what to say. Was he still angry, or had he recovered from his unfair fit of temper? And where had he been all night?

He looked up at her, but his expression did not change. "Good morning."

A footman brought in a tray of eggs and kidneys. So, they were not to quarrel in public; her husband was always proper. He might destroy her life, but he would not rail at her before the servants.

It was so ridiculous she wanted to laugh, but remembering her hysteria at the ball, she forced the nervous giggle back.

"Good morning," she replied, though her voice sounded strange to her own ears. She took her seat and poured out a cup of tea, her hand trembling.

The footman offered her food, but she waved it away. Her throat was too constricted to allow her to swallow anything solid. She added a lump of sugar and stirred her tea, looking down at the fragile china cup. "Did you go on to another party last night? I hope the scene was festive." She kept her tone light with some effort, but she was afraid to meet his gaze.

She thought he would not answer, but at last he said, his tone heavy, "No, I was in no mood for festivity."

Then where were you? she wanted to shout, but she would not give him the satisfaction. *You accuse me of not caring, and then you walk away—*

She could say nothing, only stir the tea till her cup rattled from the vigorous motion.

"Are you going to Lady Elizabeth's luncheon party?" he asked.

She looked up in surprise, then remembered she had accepted the invitation weeks ago. But the thought of facing acquaintances who would stare and whisper, perhaps question her bluntly about the arrest and Robert's disappearance—she could not face it. And she certainly dared not give away the fact that she might know something about his escape. "No," she said, dropping her spoon with a clatter. "I— I don't think I feel well. I will send Lady Elizabeth a note with my excuses."

Whitmund nodded with approval. "I think that would be wise, and perhaps you should send a note about the dinner at Mrs. Castle's this evening, as well."

So she was expected to hide herself indoors? For how long? Despite the fact that she herself had just chosen to avoid the first party, Eleanor felt a new wave of resentment. Whitmund was acting like—like a schoolmaster whose young charge had broken his slate. Was she to be sent to her room without supper, too?

"And you, my lord?" she asked formally. "What are your plans for the day?"

"I'm going to my club," he told her, his tone still grim.

"And shall no doubt spend my day trying to squash the rumors that are flying about London like pestilent rats."

He met her angry gaze, and Eleanor was irked to find that she was the one who dropped her eyes first. Before she could think of more to say, her husband had risen from the table. To the footman, he said, "Tell the groom to bring my horse around."

"My felicitations," he said to his wife, just as if she were a stranger, then walked out of the room.

Eleanor stared down at the cooling tea in her cup and blinked back angry tears. She sipped the tepid liquid and tried to compose herself; their servants already had enough to remark upon. And she should stay at home anyhow, in case Robert contacted her, she tried to cheer herself. She had, after all, found out the name of the woman that he wished to see.

But though she waited in her sitting room all morning and most of the afternoon, no word came. Edward did not return, and Robert sent her no message, though she often scanned the street in front of their town house with a desperate hope.

When at last she heard a rap on the door, the shadows were lengthening in the street. Eleanor jumped at the sound and hurried to the hallway to lean over the railing of the staircase and listen. Surely it would be a message from Robert!

When the butler came up the stairs, carrying a note on a silver salver, Eleanor snatched it and broke the wax seal, pulling open the folded sheet.

"Dear Lady Whitmund, I have information that you will wish to know. If you can visit my rooms this afternoon, it would be to our mutual advantage." The note was signed *Cavendish*.

Eleanor felt the blood roar in her ears, and she thought she might swoon. What was this—a veiled threat? Had he found out already whose carriage Robert had used to flee? Perhaps he intended to blackmail her. If only Whitmund were here—no, Whitmund would not take her side, she thought bitterly. She must face this villain herself, even though she trembled at the very thought. But to protect her marriage—hollow as it now seemed—and her child, to protect Robert, she would go and try to convince Cavendish to hold his tongue.

She hurried to her bedroom and rang for her maid. "Quick," she told the woman. "I need to change; I am going out."

Eleanor ran up to the nursery again before she left the house and bent to kiss her baby son gently on top of his head; he was asleep in his cradle, looking angelic with his eyes closed, the faint curve of lash touching his smooth cheek. "Take good care of him!" she told the nurse, then hurried down the stairs before she could lose her nerve.

She had called for their second, smaller carriage, and she was pleased to see the same groom, Parson, from last night; somehow he seemed an ally.

With her lady's maid, Eleanor drove to the address included in Cavendish's note; it was a respectable street, though Eleanor felt a little strange going up to a single man's rooms, even with her maid coming just behind. But she climbed the steps doggedly and knocked on the door, her hands cold inside her kid gloves.

Cavendish himself opened the door; he smiled when he saw her. "Come in, Lady Whitmund," he said, his voice smooth.

She hesitated, and he stepped back as if to demonstrate his civility. She saw a totally unremarkable if somewhat bare sitting room, with a desk at one side and a settee and two chairs on the other. "Wait for me outside," she directed her maid quietly. The girl looked surprised, but she obeyed, of course. Eleanor entered the room slowly, feeling a crawling sensation on the back of her neck as he shut the door behind her.

"I have asked you here to apologize," Cavendish was saying.

She had been bracing herself for threats, and Eleanor's mouth dropped open. "What?"

"I was too precipitate in my accusation, and I am deeply ashamed." He dropped his gaze as if in contrition.

She stared at him in suspicion. "Why this quick change of heart, sir?"

"I have done more research in the military files that have just been brought back from the Continent; I found another letter"—he picked up a sheet from the desk, gazed at it, then laid it back on top a stack of papers—"that will clear Lord Manning's name completely."

Her heart leapt, and Eleanor knew she could not keep the joy from showing in her face. "Is it true? I knew the charge had to be mistaken," she exclaimed.

"Yes, indeed, and I must try to make amends for my too-hasty accusation." He glanced at her again, his smile too smooth for her liking. "If you could only tell me where to find my fugitive cousin . . ."

Instantly, she was suspicious again. "I do not know," she told him slowly, but he continued to regard her, and she could not tell if he believed her. "Truly, I do not."

"But if he should contact you—"

Eleanor blushed and looked away—angry at herself for the instinctive reaction.

"If he should," Cavendish continued, "you will tell him that his flight was unnecessary, that he may return?"

"I will, of course," Eleanor agreed. She took a deep breath, feeling herself sway slightly; she was dizzy with relief. Soon this would all be behind them; Robert's name would be cleared, Whitmund would forget his anger, her child would not be snatched away—

"Let me fetch you some wine," Cavendish said quickly. "This news has overpowered you, I fear."

Instead of ringing for a servant, he walked out of the room, and Eleanor looked again at the letter that lay on his cluttered desk. She could not totally trust Cavendish; even if she had known where to find Robert, she would not tell his cousin. But if she had the letter—if she could take this vital letter to Robert and show him his innocence was known, could be proven—perhaps that would make up for her inadvertent betrayal; perhaps Robert would at last forgive her for marrying another man.

Before she could quail at such a step, she was up and standing at the desk. She snatched the letter and thrust it into the pocket of her pelisse, then ran back to take her place on the hard wooden chair.

When Cavendish reappeared with a glass of wine—did the man not have a personal servant?—she sipped it quickly, afraid he would look back at the desk and notice the letter's absence.

"I must go," she said. "If someone saw me here, they might—leap to the wrong conclusion."

"Of course," Cavendish agreed, some glint of amusement showing in his light eyes. "If the circumstances had not been so dire, so urgent, I would not have dreamed of asking you here."

She wondered why he had not just come to their house; perhaps he had feared she would not admit him, and he would have been quite right. Suddenly she wanted to be away from here. Eleanor said her good-byes as hastily as she could and almost ran down the steps to her waiting carriage, her maid hurrying after her.

"Home," she cried to the driver when they had boarded the chaise. He slapped the reins and the horses surged forward. She thought she saw Cavendish watching from the window of his sitting room, but she turned her face away, thinking instead of Robert. How could she get him this vital piece of evidence?

When they reached home, she was disheartened to find that Whitmund had sent a message that he would not be home for dinner. He was still avoiding her, still angry. Her new elation faded; she was still faced with this tangle, and the sooner to sort it all out, the better. She scribbled a hasty note, then called for the groom, Parson.

"Did they tell you last night just where in Cheapside Sir Henry Grabble and his wife are staying?" she asked when he stood, cap in hand, looking awkward and ill at ease in her private parlor.

"Um, I know the street, milady," he said.

"Good, then take this note to Lady Henry; I must have a reply as soon as possible," she told him. "Knock at every house on the street, if you must. Someone will know of them, to direct you on."

"Yes, milady." He bowed and went out, and Eleanor felt a weight lift; she was taking action. The thought got her through a slow, solitary dinner, sitting by herself at the long dining table. Afterward, she went up and spent time with her baby in the nursery, taking comfort in his coos and smiles.

When the groom finally returned and asked to see her, he looked as weary as she felt, and he had bad news.

"I found the house, milady, but them's left."

"Left?" she repeated in surprise.

"Yes, milady. Went back north, the housekeeper said, all in a rush, like." He held out the rumpled note she had given him earlier.

Eleanor took the paper, feeling a rush of defeat. "Did you get the directions for their home estate?"

"Yes'm; it's on the northern border of Yorkshire, milady. A long way from here."

Now what? When she retired to bed, unable to sleep, the

hours crept by. Whitmund did not return—just where was he sleeping!—would he turn up at the breakfast table again with no explanation? Eleanor burned with chagrin, deeply humiliated at the thought that her husband was resting in some other woman's bed—just to punish her. He should not be so cruel. And meanwhile, why had Robert not sent word to her—had he been recaptured? The all-important letter now rested in her reticule, she had scanned it to be sure of its contents, and she must get it to Robert.

When the darkness in her bedchamber began to lighten, she made a decision. It was possible Robert had found another way to locate Sir Henry and his wife. Eleanor wished he had confided more in her—why was this stranger important? But there had been so little time. Perhaps Robert was on his way north even as she pondered what to do. But Robert still needed the letter that Eleanor had snatched from his cousin; it was essential to prove his innocence. Very well, if he could not come to her, she must take it to him.

She rose, and by the time her maid came in with her morning cup of tea, Eleanor had packed a few necessary items. Fortunately, she still had almost half of her quarterly allowance; money should not be a problem. When her dresser found her shutting a small valise, the girl stared in surprise.

"Are you going away, milady?"

"I have decided to accept an invitation to spend a few days with friends," Eleanor told the servant, trying to keep her tone light. "My lord is—much occupied at the moment; is he downstairs?"

The maid looked away. "No, milady; Lord Whitmund is not at home just now."

Indeed. Eleanor swallowed the lump in her throat. "Order the carriage, and make sure Parson is the groom who accompanies me."

"I won't be going with you?"

"No, it is only a short trip," Eleanor answered lightly, hoping her dresser would not comment on how unorthodox this was. "I will be home very shortly."

"Yes, milady," the dresser said, sounding confused as well as slightly miffed. But she went away to carry the message.

Eleanor ran up the steps to see her son for a few precious minutes, then she wrote a brief, evasive note to her husband—he would not have the excuse of saying he had been left without any word, despite his own heartless abandonment of her these last days—and went out to the carriage.

They would have to change horses, of course, but the driver would know where best to get the necessary fresh teams. Eleanor looked back up at her home, picturing her small son drowsing in his cradle on an upper floor. For a moment, she wanted to get out of the carriage and run back to safety.

Then she remembered Katryn, running madly off with her fugitive husband. Katryn was not the only sister who could be outrageous; Eleanor had courage, too! Robert must see this, must know she too could risk herself to help him.

With a firm voice, she called to the driver, "Let us away!"

When Whitmund returned home, weary from a long night at cards, which he had enjoyed not at all even though he had come out the winner in the early hours of morning, he climbed the steps to his house without enthusiasm. What was he to say to Eleanor? How could he look at her and not remember that she loved another man? If only Manning had not returned from France! If he had died, as everyone first believed, Eleanor would eventually have put away her first love and have grown to love her husband. Or that was what he had told himself when he had courted her, Whitmund thought wearily, his mind running through the same well-worn paths like oxen circling a mill.

Then he felt a moment of shame, to wish death on a man who had suffered enough. Manning had lost Eleanor, after all; it was Whitmund who had claimed her hand and her soft, fair body—but if he was never to have her heart, as well, was there any point to it? He had been so triumphant, so sure, when she had agreed to his proposal, that she would in time forget her childhood sweetheart.

Frowning, he went into the hall and gave his hat and gloves to a footman.

"Would you like breakfast, my lord?" the butler inquired. "The table has been cleared already, but I will send word to the kitchen—"

"No, no," Whitmund answered absently. "I'll have a cup of tea presently, that's all."

He looked into the large sitting room, but found it empty; was Eleanor abovestairs? He went up the wide staircase, but Eleanor's private parlor was also unoccupied, as was the bedroom.

He climbed another flight of steps to look into the nursery; the nursemaid was rocking his son. Whitmund paused to touch the top of the baby's head gently, then asked, "My wife is not here?"

"No, milord," the young maid said, clucking to the baby.

He returned to Eleanor's suite, and this time came upon her maidservant putting away some fresh linen.

"Ah, have you—that is, did her ladyship go out this morning?"

The dresser flushed and looked suddenly tense. "Ah, yes, my lord. She has gone to visit friends, she said."

Something about her tone alerted him. "Friends? For the afternoon, perhaps, or for a luncheon party?"

He had been too restrictive, he told himself; Eleanor was tired of staying at home. How could he blame her?

"Perhaps—perhaps longer, my lord," the woman said, faltering a little as she flashed a quick glance at his expression, then looked back at the clothes she folded. "She took a bag with her, my lord."

Whitmund felt his whole body go stiff with alarm. A bag—a change of clothing? She was going somewhere overnight? Was Eleanor so totally disgusted with him that she would leave her own husband? No, no, she would not abandon her baby, he was sure of it. But still—the evidence was in front of him, and there was no way to ignore it. Eleanor had had no invitation to visit friends; they would have gone together if that were so. And in the middle of the Season, no one went out of town. She must be greatly agitated—he should have come home sooner, spoken to her earlier. His own hurt and anger had been too strong.

And now she was gone. To where—and to whom—had she fled? One name came immediately to his mind, but he pushed it away.

He had to clear his throat; he tried to speak normally. "Did she say where she was going?"

"Ah, no, my lord," the maid said, clearly ill at ease. "She left a note on your dressing table, my lord."

Whitmund strode into his dressing room and snatched the sheet of paper. "I am going out of town to stay with friends; I will be back soon." Nothing of her direction. Frustrated, he went back to locate the maid. "How did she leave? Did someone come for her?"

"No, my l-lord," the woman answered, stuttering. "Sh-she took the second carriage."

"I see." Whitmund turned abruptly and hurried out to the stables in back of the house. He found the head stable boy cleaning saddles. "Do you know where Lady Whitmund went this morning?" he demanded bluntly.

"No, my lord," the young man said, looking up in surprise. "I weren't there to hear her directions."

Whitmund took a deep breath, holding in his alarm, his

anger, with great effort. He wanted to lash out, but it was not the servant's fault that he had lost his own wife.

Thinking hard, he asked, "Did her ladyship go out yesterday, at any time?"

"Yes, my lord. She were out just before twilight and 'twas back within the hour." The man looked relieved to have some information to impart.

"Do you know where she went?"

The stable hand nodded. "I heard the driver remark upon h'it; she went"—he swallowed nervously—"her ladyship went to see a gentleman in Derry Street. And I'm sure it was nothing," he blurted.

Whitmund fixed him with an unwavering stare. "No doubt, and you will not repeat this to anyone else."

"No, my lord, not a word, my lord," the servant agreed quickly.

Who lived in Derry Street? Had Eleanor gone to see Robert? Perhaps he had sent her word he was hiding out in cheap apartments. But she had taken a bag—surely she had not run away with her first love? Whitmund felt a quiver of fear and forced it back.

He had to find out more. He questioned the hapless stable lad further, then barked out orders for his horse to be saddled. "And be quick about it!" he snapped.

Shortly, he was swinging into the saddle, and he spurred his steed into a quick canter, despite the crowded London streets. Narrowly avoiding a cartload of potatoes on its way to market, checking slightly to avoid a pushcart of hot pies, Whitmund rode on.

When he reached Derry Street, he soon found the building the stable lad had informed him about; it held suites of rooms for gentlemen of fashion; it was adequate if not lavish, suitable for men who possessed more breeding than ready cash.

Whitmund rang the ground-floor bell and questioned the

housekeeper. With his usual forceful personality, and the help of a few coins changing hands, he soon had the list of occupants, and there was only one name he recognized.

Cavendish! Could Eleanor have come to see Robert's cousin? Why?

There was only one way to find out. Whitmund took the steps two at a time and banged on the door of the second-floor flat.

When Cavendish opened the door, he blinked in surprise to see Whitmund in his doorway. And was that a tinge of alarm on the other man's face?

"An unexpected surprise, Whitmund," Cavendish said with a slight bow. "Unfortunately, I am just on my way out."

"Your business can wait," Whitmund told him, his tone curt. "I need to speak to you."

"Perhaps later? This business is rather urgent." Cavendish looked uneasy; he glanced at the small clock on his mantel and nodded for Whitmund to step aside.

Whitmund didn't move. "No, not later, now," he repeated. "And what I have to discuss should be said in private." He strode into the room, and Cavendish was forced to give way before him.

"My lord, I really—"

"My wife was here yesterday," Whitmund interrupted. "Would you like to tell me why?"

For a moment, he saw a glint of malice in the other man's eyes. Cavendish shrugged. "I'm sure I would not presume to speculate upon a lady's motives. You know her better than I, and—"

Whitmund took one step forward and grasped the man's lapels, jerking him until his teeth chattered. "The truth, man!"

Cavendish had paled. "It's not—not what you think," he said hastily. "I have no designs upon your wife's virtue, Whitmund. I swear it!"

"Then why was she here?"

"It's about Lord Manning."

Whitmund felt as if he'd been hit in the stomach. He released the other man and stepped back, trying to marshal his thoughts. Perhaps he had been right after all, and Eleanor had run away with her first love. He had to force himself to speak calmly.

"What about him?"

Cavendish had regained his own composure. "I fear I cannot break a confidence—"

Whitmund lifted one hand, and Cavendish spoke quickly. "That is, I had information to give her which she thought Manning would need, that is all. I was only trying to be helpful."

"After arresting your own cousin, you expect me to believe that?"

"Indeed, Lord Whitmund, you should trust me. I think we are after the same purpose, are we not?" Cavendish said, his tone very smooth.

"And that is?"

"To see Manning out of the way." Cavendish's eyes glittered, and this time, his emotion was clear. "But if you will forgive me, I really must leave now."

There was a knock at the open door, and both men turned. A small man in brown stood there, a cloth cap in his hands.

"It's just as you thought, sir, she's taking the Great North Road. But you'd better hurry or you'll be too far behind. I've got a hired carriage in the street, sir."

Cavendish's expression was wooden. Whitmund looked back at him, feeling his own face flush. "You are following my wife?"

The other man blinked and took a step backward. "Only to find where Manning has gone to. I thought"—he glanced at Whitmund's raised hand, which had without his volition folded into a fist—"I thought she might know."

"Indeed," Whitmund muttered. "So you did."

Cavendish was easing around him. "So, if we are both to be served, I will be on my way now, before the trail grows too cold."

"Certainly." Whitmund nodded in sudden decision. "Lead on, my lord."

Cavendish picked up the valise sitting by the doorway and paused on the threshold. "Lead on?"

"I'm coming with you," Whitmund said.

11

It was a fortunate thing that Whitmund kept a good carriage and decent horses, Robert thought. He rested his head against the padded cushion of the seat, feeling the well-sprung chaise sway beneath him, hearing the steady clip-clop of the team that pulled them, but he was too tense to sleep.

Katryn dozed on his other side, looking ridiculously prim in her gray gown. Simple as it was, the garment was just a little too tight, and the lines emphasized the curve of her bosom. He thought, as he had many times when they made love, how much she had changed while he was away. When had the schoolgirl he remembered grown so womanly?

He watched her breasts rise and fall as she slept, and glanced at her half-open lips, her mouth slightly pursed as if she were about to taste a new dish. That thought led inescapably to others, and he felt the stirrings in his loins that almost any reflection on his wife seemed to produce. He would like to reach across and—no, not now; they had a difficult journey to make, and Katryn should not even be here. He had failed her again in allowing her to accompany him. He should have put his foot down, Robert told himself yet again, and insisted that she stay behind.

The trouble was, Katryn never paid attention to ultimatums—he no longer wondered that her parents had agreed to their hastily arranged marriage. Stopping Katryn when she had her mind made up was no simple matter.

As if his gaze had disturbed her slumber, Katryn moved slightly, her eyes blinked open, and she yawned. Then her eyes widened and she glanced quickly around the interior of the carriage, relaxing when she met his gaze. Taking a deep breath, she turned to the window and adjusted the drape so that she could look out.

"How far have we come?"

"Only about fifty miles," Robert told her. "After you dozed off, we stopped the carriage in one of the byroads to rest the horses overnight, as we did the night before. This morning I bought some feed for the horses from a farmer, but it has taken the last of my coins."

Katryn nodded slowly. Her own stomach rumbled with emptiness; they had eaten only bread and butter bought from a farm wife the day before; it was more important that the horses and coachman be fed. They had been forced to go slowly, pacing the team, as Robert had not had enough money on him to hire new horses. He had not been expecting to take a cross-country journey when he'd dressed for the ball, she thought, sighing.

At first, Robert had been reluctant to tell her just how perilous their position was, but when he had explained, although Katryn had looked grave, she'd shown no tendency to panic, to shriek or swoon or whatever it was that gently bred ladies did. He should have known she would face the situation calmly, Robert thought.

"Robert," she said now, stretching her cramped shoulders, "why did you not tell me before about the letter that Cavendish has discovered?"

His smiled faded, and it was hard to meet her steady gaze.

He could not lie to her—had he not lied, by omission, long enough?

"I should have told you," he agreed. "I apologize, my dear, though it does little good now. I should have been candid about the scandalous revelations that lay in wait for me, for us. It was not fair to you—"

"Oh, bosh," she said, shrugging. "Robert, do talk sense. I don't care about the scandal; I know the charge of treason cannot be true, and if a bunch of henbrains want to gossip, let them. But having my husband thrown into prison—worse, having your head separated from your body—that I do care about, and I do think you might have told me!"

He swallowed; he had a mad desire to laugh, and her expression was too serious; he could not wound her pride yet again.

"It was very wrong of me," he agreed. "I earnestly beg your pardon, my dear."

He was always so punctiliously polite, Katryn thought, watching his face. But why couldn't he just once call her *my love,* or some other really personal endearment. Robert would always treat her with honor, but she wanted passion, real emotion, not just the surface civility that held their marriage together. Even now, running for his life, Robert would not take out his worries by yelling at her. But he would not open his heart to her, either. She longed to ask—demand—that he tell her more about his time in France, but she clamped down on the questions that wanted to spill out. He should want to confide in her; she should not have to ask.

So they rode in silence till clouds hid the sunset and Robert and the driver had a hurried consultation about what to do about shelter for the night.

Once again they turned off the main road and drove several miles to a village where a small inn sat at a crossroads. "Where are we?" she asked yet again.

"Umm, a few miles from Lichfield, I believe," Robert told

her. "This is not the best type of hostelry, my dear, but I thought you needed to get out of this carriage and rest properly. And the rates here may be more manageable in our present straitened circumstances."

"It will do very well," she assured him, her spirits lifting at the thought of a real bed, of food and drink. "I find it quite liberating to travel off the beaten path. What shall we be, Robert? You can be a gentleman farmer, perhaps, and I shall be a vicar's daughter?"

Despite the demure gray traveling costume, she looked so unlike a clergyman's daughter that Robert smiled. Then he glanced down at himself, and the incongruous evening wear, now wrinkled from their nights and days in the carriage, made a stranger sight. "I doubt that I will pass as any kind of farmer," he said. "But we will try."

When Katryn stepped down from the carriage, she found that her back ached from traveling for so long, and her stomach felt hollow; how long had it been since their last meager meal? And her throat was dry with thirst; she suddenly hoped almost desperately that the hostelry owner would not turn them away.

They went inside the small inn while the driver took their borrowed carriage and horses around to the stables in the back. Katryn felt self-conscious, though she could thank Lucretia that she no longer wore the servant's livery nor sported a ball gown in these totally inappropriate circumstances.

Inside the building, a narrow, dimly lit hall led into a small taproom; the room stank of cheap tallow candles and unwashed clothing, and the chimney didn't seem to draw properly; a haze of bluish smoke hung near the ceiling. A couple of local farmers, drinking ale before the fire, turned to stare at the newcomers, and the inn's owner looked them over with obvious suspicion.

"We need a room for the night," Robert was telling him in

a low voice. "Dinner for ourselves and our driver, and provisions for our team."

"We got no vi't'als suitable for gentry," the man said, scrutinizing Robert's odd costume, so out of place in this third-rate inn. "And anyways, 'ow do I know you got the coins to pay?"

"We were called north on a sudden family emergency," Robert told him. "So I am low on funds. But"—Robert paused to take out a pocket watch and click it open, the gold case bright in the flickering light from the candles—"this will more than compensate you."

The stout man scratched the stubble on his chin. "Well, now, I dunno. Not much traffic here for such baubles. But them pearls on your, um, lady friend are right pretty."

Katryn's hand flew to the pearl drops that hung from her earlobes; they had been her grandmother's. She felt a stab of grief, then put it aside. Their perilous situation allowed no room for small sorrows. She pulled off the pearls and put them on the counter.

The man blinked at them greedily. "Me wife, she'll be most pleased," he said, scooping them up before Robert could object.

"And that will cover breakfast tomorrow as well," Robert said, frowning. "What about our meal tonight?"

"We got some nice rabbit stew," the man told them. "And a bit of mutton left over from yesterday, and some cold gooseberry pie. Real tasty. Me wife's a good cook, you'll see, best in the district."

He led them up the narrow stairs to a small bedroom, its ceiling sloping down on each side of the room, the bed narrow for two, but neatly made up. A tiny table and two wooden chairs were tucked under one side of the sloping ceiling, and a washstand with an earthenware bowl on the other.

"We'll need water to wash with," Katryn told the landlord

firmly. "And I suspect we had better have our meal upstairs, don't you think, R—my dear?" she amended hastily.

Robert nodded. "Since I doubt our landlord has a private parlor, yes, I think so."

The innkeeper seemed disposed to argue about carrying the food upstairs—extra labor, he protested—but Robert stared him down. And when the man went back into the hall, Robert stepped outside, too, and pulled the door shut behind him.

"I would suggest that your wife does not grow too fond of those pearls," he told the man quietly. "In a few weeks, I shall send someone to redeem them—for a handsome profit on your side, of course."

The man's eyes glittered with avarice. "If you say so, me lord."

Robert descended the narrow staircase and went out to the stables to check on the horses. He found the driver rubbing down the tired steeds. Robert pulled off his jacket and pushed up his sleeves and gave him a hand. When the horses had been groomed, Robert used the driver's pocket knife to check the horses' hooves to be sure they had not picked up any stones, and he felt for any heat in their limbs.

Then, when the team had been settled with fresh water and grain, he washed his face and hands and arms at the outdoor pump. The cold water felt good against his skin, washing away the dust. Staring curiously, a plump, bright-eyed matron brought him a rough cloth to dry himself with and invited the driver into the kitchen for his own meal.

Robert thanked her pleasantly, then climbed the winding staircase to the small bedroom. On the stair, he felt a hard object against his thigh and realized he still had the driver's small knife; he had put it into his own pocket without thinking. No matter, he would return it on the morrow.

At the top of the stair, Robert encountered the landlord huffing as he knocked on the door. When Katryn opened it, the man carried in a tray of food and a pitcher of tepid water for the washstand. He deposited his load and departed, and Robert latched the door behind him.

"I have inspected the bedding," Katryn told him, competent with her newly acquired worldliness. "The linen is rough and much mended, but it does appear clean, for a wonder, and free of vermin."

"I think our landlord married above himself, in skills if not in class," Robert said. "The kitchen looked spotless, and this actually smells good."

They sat down to the simple repast and both ate hungrily, without talking. The landlord had brought them pitchers of ale, as there was no wine in the house. Whether it was the cook's skill or their own hunger, the food tasted delicious, and by the time they finished, having torn apart a round loaf of brown bread to sop up the last of the stew, the crockery gleamed as if just washed.

Robert put the tray outside their door and latched it again. When he turned back, he saw that Katryn had shed her dress and was washing her face and arms at the washbowl. For a moment desire stirred as he watched the delicious curves revealed as she worked, clad only in her thin shift, then a giant yawn overpowered him. They had been traveling for the better part of two days, and he had not slept last night, standing watch when they had stopped to rest their team. Now, fatigue lay heavily upon him, and his arms and legs felt like stone.

Katryn had finished her sponge bath; she turned back the coverlet and beckoned to him. "Come to bed, Robert." She pulled out a silver comb and, with no looking glass to help her, shook her hair free of its knot.

He nodded and shed his clothing rapidly, till he wore only his drawers. When he slid beneath the covers, he stretched—his feet touched the footboard of the small bed too soon—and felt the sheets rough against his bare skin. He meant to wait for Katryn to curl up beside him, but his eyelids were too heavy.

Katryn stood beside the bed, holding up the one narrow taper that had come with the tray, using its feeble light to scrutinize her husband. He looked so tired, so worn; it made her heart ache to see him like this. If only their journey was successful, and they could find a way to prove his innocence. She would do anything she had to do to help him. Her jewelry was a small sacrifice, she told herself, though she sighed when she touched her bare earlobes.

She blew out the candle and climbed into bed, trying not to wake him. But Robert slept heavily, overcome by his exhaustion; his breathing was slow and he did not stir as she lay her cheek against his shoulder. The warmth of his skin was like a talisman, and this tiny bedchamber felt safe, a haven from their pursuers. For the first time since Cavendish had marched into the ballroom with soldiers behind him, Katryn felt that she could relax. She shut her eyes, too, and slept.

She woke to find morning light brightening the drab little chamber. The one small dormer window was bare and it faced the east, she deduced, as sunlight streamed through its panes. She could hear Robert breathing evenly beside her, and she lay pressed against his side. The small bed gave her little choice, in fact, but she enjoyed the contact with the warmth of his body, and she touched his chest lightly with her fingertips, feeling its rise and fall. His skin was smooth, with only a light sprinkling of hair curling beneath her fingers.

The sound of horses' hooves was the first warning. Katryn sat up in bed quickly; how many mounts did the clatter foretell? And why were so many riders coming to this out-of-the-way hostelry?

"Robert!" She turned to shake him awake, but found that his eyes had flown open before she spoke. Pulling on his shirt, he jumped out of bed and ran to the window. Frowning, he turned back and shoved one of the chairs beneath the knob of their bedroom door.

Katryn watched him in bewilderment. They could not expect to hole up here; the door would soon give way to a determined assault. Then she saw him snatch up the rest of his clothing and shoes and head for the window, and she understood. But it was so small—could they make it through?

"Get your clothes," Robert told her as he pushed up the sash. Katryn could slide through it, he thought rapidly. His own passage was more problematical, but he would try. The roof sloped steeply away beneath the window, but he thought they could negotiate it safely.

"I will go first and help you out." He dumped his bundle of clothing outside on the rooftop and began to thread himself through the narrow opening. His shoulders were almost too broad, and for a heart-stopping moment he thought he was stuck half in, half out. But he strained and twisted till he felt his skin scrape, and at last he cleared the window and scrambled out onto the sloping rooftop. The stone shingles beneath him were slick; he had to hold to the edge of the sill as he aided Katryn outside.

She took one step onto the smooth surface and bit back an exclamation as she slid a few inches. Robert grabbed her, holding her by one arm as he clung to the windowsill with the other. Then, as Katryn found her balance, he took a deep breath and let himself go. He slid down the angle of the roof, catching the roof's gabled edge before he could fall, and looked around the courtyard. So far, no one had appeared in the back of the inn, though he heard loud voices at its front door: the landlord arguing loudly and a voice that was surely Cavendish's raised in shrill dispute. There was not a moment to waste.

He nodded to Katryn. "Come."

She grabbed their bundle of clothing and half slid, half

crept down the rooftop till he could stop her descent, then he whispered, "Hold on." He dropped the bunched-up garments over the side, and then jumped.

On this side of the inn, the angle of the roof was low, and he hit the muddy ground with a thump. He grunted despite himself, but in a moment found that he could stand. No bones broken, though he would bear the bruises of this unconventional exit, and his arms and shoulders were scraped and scratched. He motioned to Katryn, who was peering fearfully over the edge of the roof. "Now!"

She lowered herself over the edge, her legs waving beneath the thin shift—at any other time he would have enjoyed this unusual view—then let go and dropped. He grabbed her and broke her fall, sending them both sprawling back onto the soft muddy ground, then Robert jumped up and pulled Katryn to her feet. Snatching up the bundle of clothing, he grabbed her hand and they ran across the bare dirt, past a small outbuilding, a privy, and another shed, and then trees closed around them.

Robert drew a deep breath of relief, but he knew they could not stop yet. "We must put as much distance as we can between us and our pursuers," he told Katryn in a low voice.

Katryn, her hair loose and disordered around her face, her cheeks flushed, nodded. "Was it Cavendish?" she whispered.

"I believe so," Robert told her. He pulled on his shoes and motioned for her to do the same. They would have to dress later, when they had gotten farther away. "I'm sure I heard his voice; it is hard to mistake."

"He must have troops with him; I heard more than one horse," Katryn added, her breath coming quickly. "Oh, Robert, we have no mount; how can we get away from them?"

"We must go through the woods, try to avoid the road," he told her. "And hope they do not pick up our tracks."

She nodded, as if determined to overcome her moment of fear. "Then we'd better go," she agreed. She shivered as a gust of wind cut through her thin shift; Robert draped his own jacket around her shoulders and carried their other clothing under his arm. He could ignore the cold for a time; he had known much worse—the dampness of an underground cell, where his very bones ached with the chill. He pushed the memory away. They must find a passage northward. At least the undergrowth was not so dense as to prevent them from finding a route through the woods.

Robert led the way through the grove of oak trees, their tall trunks shadowing the sunlight, their limbs blooming with newly unfurled spring leaves. Happily, the growing foliage would offer them better concealment from prying eyes. And at this moment, their predicament had never looked so desperate; they needed every scrap of advantage they could grasp. But he refused to give up, not when even the smallest hope remained, elusive but tantalizing in its existence, like a will-o'-the-wisp beckoning them on into dangerous and unknown terrain.

"This way," he said, and he led his wife through the cluster of trees.

Cavendish's hired cattle was of poor quality; they made indifferent time the first day but were able to stay only a few miles behind Eleanor's carriage, stopping often to question innkeepers and anyone by the roadside to make sure they were still on her trail. They had already quarreled once; Whitmund wanted to sprint ahead and stop his wife's flight; Cavendish preferred to wait and watch to see where she might go.

"You know whom she seeks," he told Whitmund, his tone vicious. "If we wait, we will find not only Lady Whitmund, but Manning, too."

Only because Cavendish held the reins did Whitmund

hold back his anger; he wanted to slam his fist into the man's leering face, but a runaway carriage could kill them both. So his anger and his frustration simmered.

Then the right leader picked up a stone in his hoof just before Leicester. By the time they limped into town, they had lost the trail completely. They spent the night in a second-rate inn, and the next morning Whitmund hired a replacement for the injured horse, glad he still carried his gaming winnings. Then they had again wasted valuable time quarreling about which way to seek the lost carriage.

"She will have needed to change teams," Whitmund pointed out. "Someone will have seen her. The horses would not have lasted for such a distance. It is a good team, but they have their limits, man. We have gone too far."

They turned back to question the hosts of all the bigger inns, and some of the smaller ones, too, but no one would admit to seeing Eleanor or the carriage. When they had crisscrossed the market town, they were forced to admit a dead end.

"Perhaps she may have turned off into one of the country lanes," Cavendish suggested, his brow knit in a deep frown. "Perhaps Lady Whitmund fears pursuit. Or perhaps the driver took a wrong turn. Or perhaps"—he glanced at Whitmund and said carefully—"perhaps she is meeting someone, in some secret rendezvous."

Whitmund felt his face flush with anger. "Mind your tongue!" he snapped.

Cavendish lifted his brows, but said nothing.

Whitmund wrestled with his anger, with the burning desire he felt to put his hands around Manning's throat and wring the life out of him. When he could command himself, he continued slowly, "It is possible the driver went astray. We will try some of the back roads."

They hurried through their meal, both too intent on their mission to linger over indifferent beef and overdone pastries. Then they backtracked, beginning a tedious search of any smaller villages and hamlets that lay not too far off the main road to London.

At one crossroads, they argued again, Cavendish sure the carriage would have gone to the left, Whitmund thinking that the right lane seemed broader and showed more evidence of traffic. A cowherd ambling down the lane, guiding several heifers before him, came into view and was hailed.

"Is there a small inn in the neighborhood, man?" Whitmund asked, his tone holding the instinctive note of command to which his own tenants always responded.

The herdsman pulled off his cloth cap. "Aye, sir, but not fit for the likes of the gentry. You'd need go on to Lichfield, sir."

"We want something small and off the path," Cavendish put in. "Is there nothing along this road?"

"Only ol' Masserson's place, sir," the cowherd explained. "It's two, three mile yonder way."

"We'll check it out," Whitmund said, tossing the man a coin.

Leaving the herdsman beaming, Cavendish slapped the reins and the rented team moved on, a trifle uneven in their gait, which made Cavendish mutter beneath his breath.

When they reached the small inn, Whitmund eyed it dubiously. It was not the sort of accommodations he could picture his wife patronizing. On the other hand, if she were meeting Manning—and Whitmund's blood roared in his ears at the thought—the man was on the run, probably short of funds. It was worth a look.

Whitmund jumped down from the carriage and pounded on the front door; he knocked again, then waited impatiently till he heard bolts being pulled back. A stocky man still in his nightshirt rubbed his eyes and then stared in suspicion at the early arrivals. "What do ye want? I got no rooms to let."

"I wouldn't stay here if a blizzard blocked the highway,"

Whitmund said bluntly. "I want to know if you have seen anything of a lady traveling this way, a tall, fair lady with golden hair in a chaise and four."

" 'Aven't seen no golden-haired lady," the man told them, eyeing them as speculation grew in his pale eyes.

"Have you seen someone else?" Cavendish interrupted, his voice eager. "Perhaps a couple traveling this way, the man dark and slim, taller than me. And he may be with a woman who is shorter, handsome of face, with brown hair."

"Maybe I 'ave and maybe I 'aven't," the man said, his eyes gleaming with greed. "What is it, an elopement? Reckon the lady's family would pay well to bring her 'ome, eh?"

Whitmund stepped forward, forestalling Cavendish's move. "If you have seen them, you'd best tell us everything you know—if you value your cursed hide!"

The man tried to break free of the iron grip on the front of his nightshirt, but ended up dangling like an overplump rabbit in Whitmund's grasp. " 'Ere now," he protested. "No need for that. I can tell you exactly where to find 'em. I just wanted a little compensation for my trouble."

"Tell us!" Whitmund snapped. If he could find Katryn, she might know of her sister's whereabouts.

"Upstairs in me best bedchamber, 'at's where," the man wheezed. His Cockney accent betrayed his origins, even though he was now a country landlord. "Now, let go me best nightshirt, for God's sake! H'it's only a fortnight since me wife sewed it special."

With a strangled cry, Cavendish pushed past them and took the twisting steps so quickly that he almost stumbled. Whitmund dropped the innkeeper and followed. At the top of the stairs, they found a door shut firmly. Cavendish rattled the doorknob, but it would not open.

Despite the protests rising behind them, Cavendish put his shoulder to the door and pushed. At first, it would not budge, but when Whitmund added his weight, the door creaked and then gave way.

A wooden chair went tumbling aside; they pushed it out of the way and almost fell into the tiny room. But the chamber was empty, the bedclothes were pushed back on the narrow bed, and—

"The window!" Cavendish exclaimed, hurrying to look out the narrow dormer. "I see them! They're getting away!"

They both ran back down the steps, their way blocked for a moment at the bottom by the stout landlord, who croaked in dismay as Cavendish pushed him bodily back. They hurried outside and around to the back of the inn, where Cavendish led the way past several outbuildings and into the woods.

But within a mile, even Cavendish had to admit defeat. All the trees looked the same, and there was no way to tell which way the fugitives had gone.

"We'll be lost ourselves if we don't turn back," Whitmund warned. "We're wasting time here."

They retraced their steps to the inn, Cavendish cursing under his breath, Whitmund thinking hard. When they reached the inn yard, they found Whitmund's carriage, his arms emblazoned on the door, and his driver peered sleepily out from the doorway of the stable, a strand of hay in his hair. He flushed when he saw his master.

"Milord!"

Cavendish swung round to glare at Whitmund. "What's this? You had a hand in this, then? No wonder you tried to lead me astray."

"Don't be an idiot, man," Whitmund answered. "Manning took my carriage without my consent. Do you think I would abet a crime?"

Cavendish glowered at him. "How do I know what to think?" He turned to the driver. "Who gave you orders to drive these people from London?"

The driver gulped, glancing nervously at his master, then back to Cavendish. "Uh, it was Lady Whitmund, sir. I hope I did right, milord."

Whitmund nodded, knowing his expression was stiff. "Have you seen Lady Whitmund?"

"No, milord," the man said, looking bewildered. "Not since we left London."

Whitmund felt some of his tension relax. But if she was not with Manning, where was she?

Cavendish turned and seemed ready to head back into the woods once more. "To be so close and to let them escape my grasp! We have to go after them."

"We cannot take the carriage through the forest, and on foot we'd be lost before we were over the first hill. Don't be a fool," Whitmund repeated. He spoke to the driver. "Do you know where they were headed? What directions did you have?"

The man swallowed visibly. "North, milord. We were traveling into Yorkshire."

"Prepare the team," Whitmund told him. "We will be leaving right away."

"For London, milord?" the driver asked. "Home?"

"No," Whitmund answered. "We're going north."

12

They half-walked, half-ran through the trees till Robert
decided they had put enough distance between them and
their pursuers to stop long enough to dress.

"Quick, get into your clothes," he told his wife.

Katryn shivered as she put aside Robert's jacket. She
pulled on her demure gray gown and pelisse, wishing for the
warm furs that hung in her wardrobe back in their London
town house; would they ever see it again? No, she could not
think of that; as long as Robert was free, and she was with
him, she must not give up hope. She buttoned her clothes
while Robert dressed; the fine lawn of his white dress shirt
was wrinkled and dusty from their travel, and his evening
coat much creased. They must present an odd appearance.
And now they had lost their borrowed carriage—how could
they continue?

She spoke her thought aloud, and Robert shrugged. "We
will do the best we can," he told her. "I wish we had money
to buy a ticket on the Mail. Still, Cavendish will probably
have the coaches watched, so it may be just as well. Anyhow, we are out of funds. Too bad I'm not one of those men
who adorns himself with bejeweled fobs and gold chains."

The thought of Robert as some overtrimmed dandy made

her giggle, despite the seriousness of their predicament. If
they had to go north on foot, it would slow their journey im-
measurably. But they would not give up, not while there was
a chance to prove Robert's innocence.

They walked through the trees till they came to cleared
land and had to skirt a farmer's plowed fields. Next they
reached a sloping pasture dotted with placidly browsing
sheep. They paused to scan for a shepherd, and, finding no
one in sight, edged past the flock, moving slowly so as not
to frighten the animals. The sheep took little notice, contin-
uing to graze and regarding the strangers with placid eyes.

When they climbed the next hill, Katryn scrambled up the
rocky ground and cleared the top first; she saw more sheep
on the slope, and this time—though she still saw no shepherd—Katryn was alarmed to hear a low growl. Then a
sheepdog sprang up from where he had been sitting patiently beneath a gorse bush, watching his charges.

He bared his teeth and snarled at her. Katryn held her
breath, afraid to move.

"Down, boy," Robert said sternly from behind her. "We
are no threat to you. Down!"

Robert's instinctive note of command seemed to work;
the dog's low growl faded and he looked confused. His ears
drooped, and he whined.

"I know you have a job to do, but we shall not harm your
charges. Sit!"

The dog obeyed and made no more threatening sounds as
they walked slowly down the slope of the green hill.

Katryn drew a deep breath of relief when they had left the
dog behind them. "I thought he might attack us," she confessed to Robert when they reached a small stream winding
its way through the dell.

"Rest a little," Robert said, looking around them to make
sure they were not observed.

Katryn dropped to her knees and bent to dip some of the

clear cold water to her lips—her mouth was amazingly dry, and her empty stomach growled. But they had nothing to fill it with, and she told herself to be grateful just for the water—her throat felt parched and scratchy. Robert drank deeply, too, and sat on the cold ground beside her.

"You haven't spent enough time in the fields, Katryn," Robert told her lightly. "Dogs always know if you are afraid of them, just like horses."

"I am not afraid of my sweet mare," she told him, frowning. "But she does not nip my fingers. I was knocked down by a dog when I was not yet five. He made a terrible noise and he bit my arm—I still have a scar to show from it. My mother was frantic that I would get the rabies and die." She rubbed her right forearm absently, as if the old wound still ached. "So, yes, dogs make me nervous."

"And I thought you frightened of nothing," Robert teased her gently. He lifted her arm and pushed back her sleeve to kiss the faint white line of the scar tenderly.

His touch quivered through her. He looked at her as if really seeing her, and Katryn was so happy to see the wall between them seem to drop, at least for a moment, that she almost could not regret their present plight.

She turned her hand to touch his cheek, her palm feeling the prickle of the slight stubble of the beard he had not had a chance to shave off.

"I look like a ruffian, indeed," he pointed out. "An unfit escort for a lady."

"You are always fit to be my escort," she argued, her tone as light as his. "You always come to my aid, do you not?"

"With growling dogs, at least." His dark eyes smiled at her. *Oh, Robert,* she thought, *dearest love.* When the silence seemed almost too poignant, she spoke quickly, and rashly. "Dogs are my weak point, I'm afraid. But everyone has fears."

His eyes clouded over, and he looked away. She dropped

her hand, wishing she could take back the impulsive words. Robert, she knew, had more reasons for fear, more outcomes to dread, than the average man.

"Come," he said, pushing himself up. "We'd better be on our way."

Sighing—the respite had been too short—she rose, too, though she winced when she put her weight back on her abused feet.

Leaving the stream behind, they headed north again. Katryn's feet ached with every step, and she limped slightly from the soreness, but she tried her best to hide her discomfort. She had insisted on coming; she would not be the reason that Robert fell behind and became vulnerable to capture.

The countryside became increasingly more rugged: the hills, dotted with large boulders, were steeper and difficult to climb. By the end of the day they had skirted two stone farmhouses and otherwise had not set eyes on another person. At least they seemed to have evaded Cavendish, Katryn told herself, though she doubted he would give up this easily. They must find this woman first before Robert's cousin could overtake them, this Minette that Robert sought, and pray she would bear witness to his innocence.

When the sun dropped behind a rocky crag, casting deep purple shadows over the green meadows, it became increasingly hard to walk; the dimmer light veiled the rabbit holes and rocks that littered the hillside. Katryn stumbled over a patch of loose stone and barely escaped a serious fall. Robert grabbed her arm and steadied her before she pitched forward onto her face.

She gasped and clutched him, getting her balance.

"We must find a place to spend the night," Robert told her, his tone concerned.

They walked on and, before the light had faded completely, came across a rough stone hut on the side of the hill; it seemed deserted.

"Is there no one inside?" Katryn asked, rubbing her aching shins. Her feet were swollen and blistered from their long walk, and her thin-soled shoes had provided little protection from the rough terrain; the soles were already worn half through.

Robert put his head through the doorway; the door had fallen away long ago. "No, I think it's an abandoned shepherd's cot. There are no furnishings, but it will give us some shelter from the elements."

The building's thatched roof had gaping holes, but still offered some protection from the light rain that had begun to fall. As the lavender stripes of sunset darkened into night, the wind that rushed down from the hilltops all around was increasingly chill, and the dampness made the cold more penetrating. Katryn shivered. She limped inside and leaned against the rough stones that made up the wall of the cot, glad to escape the cutting edge of the wind.

Robert stood in the doorway and held out his hand to catch rainwater to quench his thirst, but the rain was little more than a heavy mist. In a short time, it stopped, and a half moon peeked between intermittent dark clouds.

Robert went back out and in a moment returned, shaking the moisture off his coat. "I think I see a stream at the bottom of the hill; come and quench your thirst, my dear; I regret I have nothing to hold the water, or I would bring it back to you."

She yawned and nodded, despite the fatigue that seemed to pull at her shoulders, and followed him slowly down to the brook that curved through the rough pasture. The water tasted good to her, and after they both drank deeply, Robert bade her sit on a boulder beside the stream so that he could examine her feet. The light was too dim to see much, but he shook his head as he touched her swollen limbs.

She winced as he lightly probed the blisters that the long passage had produced.

"Let's bathe your feet in the water," he told her.

Katryn nodded, though she shivered when the ice-cold water touched her aching feet. Robert's touch was very gentle; he dried them with part of his own shirt, and ripped off shreds of his increasingly tattered costume to bandage the worst of her blisters.

"You shouldn't," Katryn argued. "You'll freeze!"

Robert ignored her protests. He wrapped her feet, taking care not to press too hard on the blisters, and then helped her to her feet. She was light-headed with hunger, and she swayed as she tried to stand.

"Lean on me," her husband told her, taking her arm. With a sigh, she did.

Watching her try to walk on her abused feet was worse than his own aches. Robert winced as she made her way gingerly back up the hill.

Inside the cot, they both sat down on the hard-packed earth, in the farthermost corner from the drafty doorway. He held her in his arms and tried to cushion her as best he might, warming her with his own body heat. The darkness was complete, and the air, musty from years of damp, reeked with the odors of long-dead sheep. But they were protected from the wind that whistled outside the walls of the hut, and Robert tried to relax, just a little. Rain fell again, more heavily this time, and the smell of it on the wind lightened the stench inside the cot.

"Sleep," he told Katryn. "I will keep watch for a while."

Katryn nodded and rested her cheek against his chest. "You must sleep, too," she murmured.

"I will. I'm sorry about this, Katryn," he told her, feeling a renewed wave of guilt that she must share his misfortunes. "I never meant for you to be so ill-treated."

She didn't answer; glancing down, he saw that her eyes

were shut and her breathing even. He watched her sleep until his own eyelids grew too heavy.

Someone screamed.

The high-pitched sound held pain and fear and a desperation that trembled at the edge of madness. He shuddered at the sound, feeling the whip again as if it were his own flesh that ripped and shredded beneath the blows he could hear from the next cell. He shook so hard that the half-healed scabs on his back pulled painfully, and he leaned against the rough stone wall of the prison cell, trying to hold on to his sanity. Eleanor, he must remember Eleanor; she was waiting; he could not give up.

Despite the constant darkness, the tiny cell was too familiar; he knew every inch of it, had paced back and forth as far as the leg irons would allow, had felt every rock in the wall behind him as if by some miracle an opening would appear and he could crawl through, into fresh air and freedom.

Now he sagged back against the wall; the jagged stones pricked his shoulder through the tatters of his coat, and the ragged beard that covered his face itched. He itched all over, and the rank smells of human excrement and bodies long unwashed that hung over the whole prison almost choked him. What would Eleanor think if she could see him like this? How repulsed she would be. Perhaps she would not want him any longer, seeing him this way—she must never know—

With enormous effort, he pushed back the panic, the overwhelming despair, and tried to focus on the vision of his beautiful, fair-haired fiancée, the privileged life he had once taken for granted and which now seemed so far away. But the screams came again, and the sound of the beating; he lost the wisp of memory as he struggled against the leg irons that held him chained to the stone wall. If he could pull off his own limb, he would do it. If he could crawl beneath the

*iron grate of the door like the insects and lizards that slith-
ered and skittered through the fetid darkness, he would. Oh,
Eleanor—if only the screaming would stop!*

Robert fought his way out of the dream with as much difficulty as if he were pushing through the prison wall itself. At
last he emerged from the vision like a drowning man coming up one last time for air; gasping with great effort, he
pushed open his eyes.

Still there was darkness, and rough stones against his
cheek, and a heavy, rancid smell that almost choked him.
For a moment, he thought he truly was back in the prison,
and the terror of that sent him lunging to his feet.

But no chains held him down, and now he could see a rec-
tangle of less dense darkness, a doorway. He scrambled for
it, bursting into open air with a relief so tangible it brought
tears to his eyes. A cold wind touched his face, and he found
that he shivered, but with relief as much as from the chill.

He was in England, on a lonely hillside, taking shelter in an
abandoned shepherd's hut. He remembered now, Katryn had
been sleeping curled up beside him. He took long, deep
breaths, trying to calm himself, but the shaking continued. He
should get out of the wind—the rain at least had stopped—but
he found he could not force himself to go back inside the tiny
hut. It was too small, too rough; it had evoked too much of his
prison memories, brought back too much of the nightmare.
He wrapped his arms around himself, willing the shuddering
to stop, and walked round the edge of the hut till he was at
least sheltered from the wind, then sat down on the bare earth
and waited for the sun to rise. The moon had dropped behind
the horizon once more, and thick clouds hid the flickering
stars; it was so very, very dark. And inside the blackness, the
memories lingered. . . .

When Katryn woke, she blinked in surprise at the heavy
darkness. She had become accustomed to Robert's habit of

sleeping with one candle always lit. Where was the candle? And the smell—had someone let a flock of sheep gather beneath her bedroom window? She wrinkled her nose, then nodded slowly as she remembered where they were.

Her body still ached from the long walk, and her feet throbbed, though the cold-water wash had helped a little. Despite the spring green of the pastures, the air felt wintry inside the cot, with no fire to warm the tiny room. She missed the warmth of Robert's body; he had been beside her when she'd shut her eyes. She reached for him now, but felt only hard-packed earth and the rough stone wall.

"Robert?" she called in alarm. Where had he gone?

It was so dark she could not see her own hand as she searched all around; in a moment she scrambled upright, wincing as she put her weight on her abused feet. She must find Robert—had something happened?

She felt around the edge of the walls till she came to the open doorway and made her way outside. She could make out little in the blackness, and she stumbled over a grassy root, barely catching herself before she fell. With one hand on the outer wall of the cot so that she wouldn't wander out onto the moor and get lost completely, Katryn made her way slowly around the perimeter of the small building.

She sensed him at the last moment, just before she walked into him. Katryn dropped to her knees—why was he outside in the cold and damp? Shivering, Robert sat on the ground, his legs pulled up, his arms wrapped around his knees as he curled into a knot. Was he ill?

She touched his arms, feeling the tightness of his muscles, then lightly stroked the side of his face. He seemed to have hidden his face against the top of his knees, and he did not raise his head.

"Robert?" she said again, worried at this strange behavior. "Robert, are you all right?"

He trembled again, and she wondered if he had a fever;

yet his skin did not seem warm; indeed, rather the opposite, he seemed deeply chilled. If he caught a sickness of the lungs and died here in this wilderness—

Katryn put her arms around him and pressed hard against him, trying to share her own warmth.

He did not lift his head, but he muttered something very low, and she strained to hear.

"I mustn't tell," he was repeating over and over. "I mustn't tell, no matter how bad it is. My company will suffer for it; my own men will die. No one is to know why I am here. My commander said—no one must know, no one must know."

"No one knows, Robert," she told him, stroking the lock of hair that always fell forward into his face. She felt cold inside, frightened at this suggestion of madness. No, it was only a bad memory, she told herself. What nightmare was he caught up in?

"If we can find the route Boney's army is to take, we can cut him off—" Robert took a long shuddering breath. "They will bring the whips again. Mustn't tell, mustn't tell. But I don't know if I can endure it, not again."

"It's all right, Robert," Katryn told him, trying to penetrate whatever hellish vision he had conjured up from his years of imprisonment. "It's all right; you're safe now."

"Mustn't tell," he droned. "Mustn't tell."

"You didn't tell any secrets," she assured him, touching his hair lightly as he rocked back and forth, her own voice shaking with tears that she had no time to shed. "Everyone is safe, Robert."

Except you, she thought. *My poor darling, you kept your mission secret, and you were the one who suffered.*

Somewhere in the darkness a night bird cried, and Robert's body jerked. "They're coming!"

"No, no, my dearest." Katryn shook his arm, trying to penetrate his waking dream. "You're safe; you're with me! I'm here."

"Eleanor?" His voice held so much hope that she forced herself to put aside the pain that pierced her whole body when he spoke her sister's name: Eleanor, his first love, always to be closest to his heart.

"No, it's me, Katryn," she answered as steadily as she could. "Your wife. I am here for you, my dearest, I will not leave you alone. You will be safe now, I promise."

He seemed to hear her at last; he raised his head. "Katryn?"

"I'm here," she repeated.

He lay his head on her shoulder and she held him, and after long moments his trembling seemed to subside. Katryn clung to him fiercely as the last tremors shook his body. For a brief while their positions seemed reversed; she was the one who could be strong, he the one who showed undreamed-of need.

It crossed her mind that this was not the strong young hero she had dreamed of when she was still in short skirts, the handsome young man wearing his first brightly hued scarlet uniform. She pushed the thought away. It didn't matter; Robert needed her, Robert had turned to her—to her, not Eleanor. Katryn loved him even when he was human and weak, and the warmth that filled her at his willing response to her embrace allowed no space for any disappointment. She knew his strengths, his kindness, his courage; seeing his fears for the first time only seemed to draw them closer.

"It's so black," she heard him whisper. She held him even tighter, as if he were a child afraid of the darkness.

"The sun will rise soon," she assured him. "See the flush that rims the hilltops?"

Robert shifted so that he, too, could see the first sign of returning light, and she felt him sigh deeply. Then he lifted his head and pulled her against him. They sat wrapped together while the blue-black sky lightened, as it became streaked with layers of rose and peach and lavender, and at last the golden ball lifted its face above the hilltops.

Sounds filled the stillness. One bird trilled, then others joined in. Birds wheeled and sang in the fresh light, and tall grasses waved in the wind. Once, Katryn saw a small deer trot across the crest of a far hill, and, closer, a hare rose on its hind legs to sniff the air, then—alarmed at the sight of them—dropped back to all fours to scurry away.

Outside the rank odors of the hut, Katryn could smell the growing grass and the scent of the water in the small rill below them. Her mouth felt dry, but she could wait to quench her thirst. Robert had dropped into a more peaceful sleep, leaning against the wall behind him, his arms still wrapped around her. She rested her cheek on his chest and she, too, shut her eyes.

The next time she woke, the morning was well advanced. She rested against the outside wall of the cot, and she was alone. Where had Robert gone to now?

She stood up gingerly, her feet still sore, and walked around to peer inside the hut, but saw no one. She gazed down the hill and located Robert kneeling beside the small stream.

She made her way slowly down the hill to the gurgling water. Robert turned as she approached and watched her come closer, frowning a little.

Was he regretting the nightmare he had shared with her, the brief letting down of his guard? *Please, Robert, don't put up your wall again,* she thought. *Don't shut me out.*

He didn't seem to want to meet her eyes.

"How are you?" she asked cautiously.

"Well enough," he said evenly. His tone was formal, and Katryn bit back a sigh. "I regret that I—that my nightmare was too vivid."

"Don't apologize, Robert," she said more forcibly than she had meant to. "You *should* talk to me; I am your wife."

"All the more reason you should be protected," Robert told her, his tone stubborn. "You should not be prey to the visions that fill my dreams, Katryn. I've done you enough ill turns already."

"I wanted to be married to you, Robert!" Katryn's temper suddenly flared; she was tired of his excuses.

"Yes, and much comfort the marriage has brought you," he pointed out, gesturing at the beautiful but desolate scene around them.

He still did not meet her gaze. "It's all right to be frightened, Robert," she said deliberately, controlling her moment of anger. "You have endured a great deal; it's no disgrace to be afraid."

She saw his lips tighten. "I should not give in to it," he muttered. "I am—I *was* a soldier."

"But still a man," she reminded him, "no god, no machine." Turning away to hide her sadness—would he ever want to let her in?—she knelt and drank from the stream, dipping her fingers into the water and cupping the cold liquid in her palm. Then, shaking the last drops from her hands, she walked to his side.

"We must get on our way; we are wasting time."

He shook his head; this time his tone was regretful but firm. "Today, my dear, we rest. Your feet are still too swollen and sore to travel."

Katryn grimaced; it was true that her feet throbbed and each step was difficult, and yet—

"What if they find us?" she demanded. "Perhaps you should go on alone."

"And leave you lost in the middle of the Yorkshire hills? I hardly think so." Robert's smile was rueful. "No, we stay together. I think we are far enough off the main road so that Cavendish is unlikely to appear. And he does not know where we are headed, after all."

Katryn saw him frown briefly, then shake off the thought. "He could not know," Robert repeated, as if to himself.

She certainly hoped not. She saw, lying on the bank of the

stream, that Robert had been weaving together some kind of knotted string. "What are you doing?"

"Making a rabbit snare," he told her; he now wore his jacket over his naked torso; he had shredded what remained of his shirt. "I learned the skill when I was a boy."

"From your father's gamekeeper?" Katryn guessed, trying not to show how her empty stomach clenched at the thought of food.

Robert shook his head, grinning. "From Black Ned, remember him? He lived at the edge of the Home Wood in that tumbledown hut."

"The one the village children used to whisper had been sired by a passing gypsy?" Katryn drew the old memory up with some effort. "I always felt sorry for him, even if he did shout at me once when I rode too close to his cottage."

"Probably afraid you would see a poached deer. He was a rascal, no doubt about that, but he took a liking to me," Robert told her. "We used to make trips into the woods together to put out our traps."

"I'll wager your mother did not care for you keeping such company." Katryn tried to push her hair back in place, combing it with her fingers.

"She never knew about it; even at eight years old, I was no fool," Robert retorted. "I'm going to go off into the grass and set up the snare; cross your fingers that it works."

She would cross her fingers and all of her toes, Katryn thought, yawning, considering how empty her belly was. And while Robert was gone . . . She glanced around. Despite the fact that the countryside was deserted, she searched for a clump of trees to hide her as she took off her clothes and tried to bathe a little in the chilly water.

Robert set out the snare with all the woodsman's skill he possessed, picking a grassy spot where they had not walked and which would be relatively empty of their scent. Then he came back to the stream, glancing around for Katryn.

She had retreated behind a knot of small trees, their branches twisted into strange shapes by the ever-present wind. Despite the chilly wind that moved the grasses around them, she had shed her clothing and was washing the dust and dirt of their travels off her well-shaped torso. He stood still and watched her arm raise, revealing the sweet curve of her breast, the nipple erect in the cold, and he felt a deep longing, and also a deep sense of unworthiness.

The prison nightmare had been too vivid; it had all come back too swiftly. He felt unclean, damaged, totally unworthy of Katryn's love, unfit for her embraces. How had he thought he could put his imprisonment behind him, emerge unscathed by those years of privation and misery?

Katryn deserved better. He watched her bend over the stream, shivering as she rubbed herself dry with a petticoat, then pulled the rest of her clothing back on. She should not be here, subject to such hardship. He had failed her yet again.

He turned and walked away, feeling absurdly guilty about watching her ablutions; he should not intrude upon her privacy. Instead, he sat on the bank several yards downstream, and she found him there when she came searching.

"Robert?" Her tone was questioning. "Would you like to talk? If you could speak of your past, I think it might help you."

He glanced at her, but did not meet her candid gaze. "You look very fresh, my dear," he said, avoiding her comment. "I think I should follow your example and try to rinse off some of the dirt of the road." He walked away, pretending he had not seen her expression of disappointment, perhaps of hurt. But what good would it do to share his painful memories? Had he not infringed enough upon her life of safety and comfort?

He stripped off his increasingly tattered outfit. Soon he would be as ragged as he had been in prison—he winced at that thought—and almost took pleasure in the icy cold water that he dashed over his body. He deserved the discomfort; Katryn did not.

They rested the remainder of the day, and in late afternoon Robert was pleased to find a fat hare caught in his snare. He used his borrowed pocket knife to skin the animal, and risked building a small fire outside the hut, using a dusty flint and stone left behind on a windowsill to start the blaze, and some of the fallen thatch that littered its earthen floor as kindling.

They roasted the hare on a rough wood spit and, when the meat browned, ate it hungrily. It was tough and gamey, but nothing had ever tasted as good. They had devoured every scrap; Katryn accused Robert of giving her the greatest share, and he shrugged off her words.

"No, indeed, I divided the animal into equal parts," he assured her gravely.

"I think mine was more equal than yours," she retorted, licking the grease off her fingers. "I never cared much for rabbit meat, but today . . ."

She didn't finish the sentence, but he knew her meaning; hunger was indeed the best spice of all.

They walked down together to drink from the stream and wash their hands, then lay down together outside the cot, taking shelter beneath its overhanging roof. Katryn did not mention his aversion to the tiny stone hut again; she simply came to lie down beside him. Together they lay, side by side, sharing the warmth of their bodies against the cold of the ground.

Robert held her close, but he felt no inclination toward passion; he still felt somehow injured, in his soul if not his body, no longer capable of making love to his wife.

Katryn stroked his face and kissed him once before they slept. Robert smiled at her, but he did not, as he usually did, return her embrace with a rising passion. And when she put one hand on his chest, running her finger down the center and feeling the hard muscle beneath the remnants of his coat, he put his hand on top of hers and stopped her inquisitive fingers. The wall was back, and wider than before, she saw with a sinking heart.

She tried to smile at him, but he did not kiss her hand, nor pull her closer. Instead, he held her smaller hand within his own grasp and said gently, "We should sleep."

Katryn tried to hide her disappointment. How long had it been since they had made love? Time might have stopped in their lonely hillside cot; they seemed to have been fugitives for half their lives, on the run forever. If Robert continued to pull away from her, to hide behind his own fears, how would they ever bridge the gap that lay between them? She would have liked the reassurance of his lovemaking. But that, too, she was to be denied. If they lost their passion for each other—or if Robert lost his desire for her, to be more apt—what on earth would they have left in this sham of a marriage?

The injustice of it stung her, and she had to bite back angry words. But his eyes looked hollow and wounded, his face heavy with fatigue and lack of food; how could she rail at him now? Still, it was a long time, as she lay on the cold, hard ground, before sleep came.

13

When they woke the next morning, Robert found another rabbit in his snare, so they ate again, then Robert inspected her feet. Her blisters were healing, and her feet no longer were quite so tender. Robert rewrapped them and decided that they would set out on their trek once more.

Katryn was happy to be back on the move, even though they perforce gave up their temporary shelter. Little good it had done them, she thought, bringing back Robert's prison terrors in full force.

The day was sunny, though big puffs of cloud floated across a deep blue-gray sky, and once they had to take shelter beneath a clump of small trees when a sudden downpour drenched the countryside. Despite the slight protection, they were both soon wet through, and when they came across a small road, Robert decided to follow it for a time.

"We need to check and be sure we are going in the right direction," he told her.

"What about Cavendish and his soldiers?" Katryn asked, trying to smooth out her sodden skirt. She felt a quiver of anxiety as she thought of Robert's cousin.

"If we wander in circles, we will never find Minette,"

Robert answered, his voice grim. "We must keep our eyes open, that's all."

By the middle of the day, they came upon a tiny village of gray stone houses, with one small church at its center, its spire reaching valiantly for the sky. They approached it cautiously, and Katryn looked over the hamlet, happy to see no sign of soldiers, no carriages waiting by the side of the road.

Robert knocked on the door of the largest house, and when the door opened to reveal a stout matron with a double chin and narrowed eyes, he made a polite bow.

"I'm wondering if you have any chores that I could do, for a few pennies," Robert asked, his voice quiet. "My wife and I have suffered an accident as we traveled, and—"

The woman looked over their travel-stained clothing, still damp about the edges. Robert's ragged coat showed little sign of its once-fashionable tailoring. She frowned. "Away with ye! I have naught to do with pilfering gypsies!"

"We are not—" Katryn began hotly, but the woman lifted her apron and shook it at them.

"Off with ye, or I'll put the dogs on ye!" She slammed the door in their faces.

Katryn wanted to stamp her foot, but her feet were too sore to consider such an action.

"Come along." Robert took her arm. "I thought it was worth a try, but she may indeed release the dogs."

Katryn quivered at the thought of the woman's threat. The sound of baying from the back of the house hurried their steps as they left the house behind. Katryn sighed, trying not to lose hope as her hunger returned in full force. How would they ever get to Sir Henry's estate like this? They would die of hunger, or at least be old and gray before they reached the northern reaches of Yorkshire.

The village fell behind them, and they walked on. A few miles past the hamlet, they saw a building a short distance from the road. As they came closer, they saw it was a farmhouse of weathered stone, with several outbuildings around it, and a large barn built on to the back of the house itself. Robert paused to consider the scene.

Katryn was glad to take a moment to rest; she sat down on a rock beside the road and looked cautiously around. There was no sign of dogs, but every farm had one about, somewhere.

"What are you going to do?" she asked as Robert's face hardened.

"Since honest labor is not in demand, I fear I must resort to dishonest."

Katryn stared at him in surprise, then nodded slowly. Their case was so desperate—and they were already fugitives before the law.

Robert headed around the side of the house, and then she saw what had tempted him. The farmwife had spread her laundry across a hedge at the edge of the yard; garments flapped in the breeze, and Robert seemed ready to improve their wardrobe. She had hoped for food, but without breaking into the house itself, perhaps this was the best they could do.

Robert ran across the yard, all his senses attuned for any dog barking or goose hissing at the intruder. He grabbed a handful of clothing off the shrubbery and turned to make his escape.

"Here now! What do you think you're doing!" a woman demanded, her voice shrill.

Robert would have run for it, but the low growl of a dog—judging by the bass tones, a very large dog—made him hesitate. Feeling both guilty and ridiculous, Robert turned slowly to face the back door of the farmhouse.

A woman in a blue dress and checked apron frowned at him. She gripped the collar of a mastiff, whose eyes glinted with eagerness as he strained to be released. The dog came almost to the woman's waist, and he growled again.

Robert sighed. He was likely dogmeat with or without an apology, but he could at least make the effort.

"I'm sorry," he said. "We had need of these."

"And you think I don't?" The woman raised heavy brows. "What are you doing in my yard?"

"Traveling north; we have friends I wished to reach," Robert told her honestly.

"On foot? You sound like a man of class," she said, suspicion in her voice.

"We have had some, um, downturns in our fortune," Robert told her. He put the pile of laundry back on top of the hedge. "And we have been reduced to walking, yes."

" 'Oo's that?" the woman demanded, looking past him to where Katryn waited at the edge of the farmyard.

Robert wished Katryn had hidden herself from view while there was time. Still, it must have taken great courage for her not to flee from the presence of the dog; he should have known Katryn would be too loyal to leave him, but—

"My wife," he said quietly.

The woman was silent for a moment, but at least she had not yet released the dog, though it still pulled against her clasp.

"Be ye a soldier?" the farmwife demanded suddenly.

Robert looked at her in astonishment. "I was, yes," he answered slowly.

She shook her head. "Too many soldiers left penniless to wander the roads, now the war's over," she muttered. "I've seen 'em, even in our northern shires." She mulled over some thought that Robert could not guess, then lifted her head. "Go on, take the stuff if you have need of it, and I reckon you do; half-naked you look."

"Ma'am?" Robert said in surprise.

"My brother was a soldier," she said gruffly. "Died at Waterloo, he did."

"Then he was a brave man, and he gave his life for his

country," Robert told her quietly. "Thank you. If you'll tell me your name and the name of your farm and closest village, and if I live to the end of this journey, I promise you I'll send recompense for what I have taken."

"Margarie Flanders," she told him crisply. "At Hilltop Farm, Thirskon Moor. Come on in, then, afore you go, you and the wife. I've soup on the hearth, and fresh bread."

Her voice was too honest, he thought, for this to be a trap, her face—reddened from the constant wind and weather—open to his gaze.

He bowed to her, and Katryn came forward to join him, though she eyed the big dog nervously. "We thank you for your hospitality," Katryn told the woman. "It is most kind."

Mrs. Flanders looked at her in pity. "My, you're a young thing to be in such straits," she said, sighing. "No family of your own to go to for help, have ye?"

Katryn blushed and didn't answer; she walked inside, while Robert lingered outside long enough to change his rags for a rough-cut shirt and trousers; there was also a soft cap to protect his head from the sun and rain. Then he followed Katryn into the well-scrubbed kitchen. Mrs. Flanders took bowls from an oak dresser against the wall, and they sat down at a stout table. Using a ladle she filled the bowls with thick soup, and they ate the savory soup and brown bread that she put before them. Katryn tried to remember a little decorum, but it was difficult; her stomach seemed suddenly to remember how empty it was, and she had to force herself to spoon up the liquid, thick with vegetables and barley, instead of lifting the bowl to her lips and slurping it all down like a barnyard pig. She sensed from the tight grip that Robert kept on his spoon that he was having similar difficulties.

Katryn felt the warmth of the hearty soup all the way down; it was better than the rangy rabbit that had been her only sustenance for two days. She used the rest of the bread to wipe up the last trace of soup in the bowl, and thought she had never enjoyed food more.

As they ate, Mrs. Flanders clucked under her breath at the sight of Katryn's swollen feet, still wrapped in rags, her shoe soles worn through. The farmwife brought out two pair of thick, much-cobbled farm boots. The larger she gave to Robert, the smaller fit Katryn's feet almost perfectly.

"Me brother's, from when he was a lad. I kept them," the woman told them, her tone gruff, not inviting sympathy. "But my boys are big'uns now, with feet like oxen, so someone might as well get some use of them."

"Thank you," Katryn told her. "You're very kind."

The farmwife waved away their thanks and glanced at the open door. "Me husband will be home soon enough, may not be pleased to see strangers."

The broad hint hastened their departure, but Katryn found walking easier with new, heavier shoes to protect her sore feet, and she felt much stronger after the meal.

They made good time through the afternoon, then came to a crossroads—Robert had gotten new directions while they ate their soup—and turned onto a more traveled road.

"Can we risk being on the open road?" Katryn asked him, uneasy as she glanced about, as if Cavendish would appear from behind a bush.

"I think we must," Robert answered, his brow knit in thought as he, too, peered to the side. "We have wandered a little out of the way, walking cross-country. I think we must take a more direct route lest we waste too much time."

Katryn nodded, but her back rippled with apprehension as they turned into the broader byway.

But it did not seem heavily traveled. They had walked another mile when they rounded a curve in the road and came upon a curious sight. A gig sat in the middle of the lane, its shafts falling forward into the dirt, with no horse attached to the small vehicle. In the slanting passenger seat, however, two slightly built old women sat, their backs as straight as ramrods.

"What on earth?" Katryn murmured. Robert had already quickened his step.

"You in need of help, ma'am?" he asked, remembering this time to pull off his cloth cap and roughen his speech, to look and sound less like a gentleman.

The two elderly ladies appeared as stiff and prim as if they were seated at their own tea table. Both had white hair pulled up into a knot on the back of their heads; both wore neat, old-fashioned gowns; and both had thin, wrinkled faces beneath their antiquated bonnets. They could have been two peas in a pod; only the color of their dresses set them apart.

"No, we're just fine, thank you." The one on the right, who wore blue, clutched her ivory-tipped cane firmly.

"Our groom will be back shortly," the one on the left, who wore puce, added. Her cane was of dark ash.

Robert raised his brows; their situation was most peculiar. "If you say so," he agreed doubtfully. "I am happy to hear that aid is on the way. Did your horse go lame?"

The diminutive woman on the right suddenly lost her ladylike impassivity. "No, indeed. Our sweet mare has never been lame a day in her life! It was those black-hearted thieves—"

"Ruffians!" her twin added. "I hope they rot in hellfire for a thousand eternities!"

"Sister!" The first woman looked mildly shocked. "It's not for us to judge their immortal souls. What would Papa say?"

"Papa would never have permitted himself to be set upon by such soulless hooligans," the second sister retorted. "Even a rector may show godly anger when the forces of evil rise up against him. And Papa, God rest his soul, always had a strong right arm. Mama used to call him into the pantry to beat the soufflés, if you remember."

"Yes, indeed," her sister agreed. "But since we are mere women, and our groom a cowardly sort, the thieves were able to waylay us and make off with our poor Mollie."

"Though Sister did get one good whack with her cane, when the first man came too close," the woman on the left added with some satisfaction. "He will sport a bruised face if he dares to let himself be seen again."

Robert had to hold back a smile at the thought of these tiny, small-boned women brandishing canes at their attackers.

Katryn came up to pat the woman's blue-veined hand. "You poor things," she said impulsively. "What a terrible ordeal for you. We must wait here with you until help comes. Where did your groom go for help?"

The first woman quivered and her eyes glistened with tears; her sister patted her arm. Robert could see now that beneath their surface calm, the two elderly women were deeply upset.

"If he has any sense—which I do not guarantee," the second sister answered, "he will go to Squire Akers and ask for help. The squire is our local magistrate, you know."

"No, I think the Joshlen farm is closer, Sister," her twin put in, sniffing a little to keep the tears from betraying her. "And there should be some men about the place, if they are not all at work in the fields."

"If they are, I'm sure someone will be able to fetch them," Katryn said, her tone still soothing.

Robert sighed. It seemed they were committed to succoring the women until more help arrived. If their own need for speed did not nag at him continually, he would not have begrudged spending half the day here while Katryn lent a sympathetic ear to the women's plight. As it was, he hoped the rescuers would hurry up about it.

"Such a sweet mare she was," the first woman was telling his wife. "A nice roan, she had a star just in the center of her forehead, and perfectly sound for her twelve years, too, though she had a small scar on her right hind leg where my sister overturned the gig years ago, before we decided that at our age it was better to be driven."

Katryn appeared fascinated by the women. "Did you drive your own gig?" she asked. "How resourceful."

"Oh, yes," the second woman agreed. "I had a nice light hand, Papa always said so. And Sister is no mean whip herself. Certainly better than that idiot groom of ours, who stopped at the first hail from those awful men."

They sounded calmer already, Robert thought. Katryn was working her usual magic, and the three women seemed perfect friends already.

Nonetheless, Robert was pleased when he caught sight of a couple of stout farm lads coming up the road from the opposite direction, hurrying toward the stranded gig and leading a donkey behind them.

"Miz Ludwig and Miz Ludwig," the first one said. "Be ye ladies all right?"

"We are well, thank you, Joseph," the first sister answered. "Where is our groom?"

"He mun went on to inform the squire," the farmer said, eyeing Robert with obvious suspicion. "Be this the man what stole your Mollie?"

"Of course not," the first Ludwig sister answered sharply. "This lady and her servant were on their way to the village; they stopped when they saw our distress. The two ruffians were low types, with dark hair and ragged clothes, gypsies mayhap, terrible villains."

Katryn caught Robert's eye, her glance rueful. Robert realized he had missed whatever story she had spun to account for their appearance, he with the rougher clothes and Katryn neatly, if not richly, dressed. He swallowed his smile and pulled off his cloth cap again.

"Aye," he agreed, in his best West Country accent.

"Oh," the farmer said. "All the horses be out in the field, but we brought mother's donkey; it will pull the gig back to our house, and you can bide there till your man returns with a rented beast."

They hitched up the donkey, which gave a half-hearted kick then settled down to pull the gig at a sedate walk. Robert thought they could now take their leave, but the Ludwig sisters wouldn't hear of it.

"No, no, you must come and have a cup of tea before you leave us," they said, looking positively agitated at the thought of giving up Katryn so soon.

There seemed no way to escape the offered hospitality without arousing suspicion. And truth to tell, his stomach rumbled at the thought of sustenance; already the soup and bread they had eaten at the middle of the day seemed a distant memory. So he and Katryn walked behind the gig, while the two farm lads pulled the recalcitrant donkey along when he wanted to lag and escape his burden.

"I'm sorry," Katryn whispered, giving him a quick glance. "But they are so sweet, and really distressed despite their attempts to hide it, and I—"

"It's all right," Robert told her, smiling a little. He could not press her hand in his present demoted status, and he kept his voice low. "At least we'll get a cup of tea out of the delay."

They all trekked another mile or so to a pleasant thatched farmhouse, where the goodwife waited, a pot of tea already brewing.

Her round face flushed with excitement over such high crimes in their own district, she filled crockery cups with the dark liquid. "Never have heard of such," she said over and over. "In our own neighborhood, too. Gypsies, I'll wager, or maybe some discharged ex-soldiers with empty pockets and bloodstained hands."

Katryn glanced at her husband anxiously, but his expression was bland. The farmer's wife was cutting thick slices of home-baked plum cake, and that drew his attention much more than the woman's artless insults.

"Be murdered in our beds next, God bless us," the woman said, fanning herself with a much-washed apron. "I hope the squire sets out a hue and cry for these villains." She paused to urge more cake on one of the Ludwig sisters, and Robert caught Katryn's eye.

She couldn't quite make out the words he mouthed, but she could guess their import. These people might accept their story easily enough, but the squire could be less gullible. She ate her cake—sorry that she had to rush through such a delicious treat—as quickly as good manners allowed and finally was able to make her farewells to the Ludwig sisters.

"You will be careful, won't you?" the first sister said to Katryn. "You're so young and pretty; you mustn't be attacked, as well. Did I tell you they took Mama's pearl pin right off my person? You've no jewelry, but still—and your man doesn't look too stout." The old woman touched the torn lace at her throat and sighed.

They all glanced toward Robert, who blinked at this insult to his well-built frame. Katryn tried not to giggle. "I assure you," she said, trying not to picture Robert's naked, well-muscled body in her mind's eye, "he's a stout fellow indeed, and will offer me protection against any ruffian."

"If you're sure, then," the first sister said, and her twin nodded. "Do take care, my dear."

At last Katryn said her good-byes, and they walked on and reached the next village before dusk had fallen. When they saw the buildings ahead, Katryn turned to him.

"Should we go around it?" They had been trying to evade notice as much as possible.

Robert shook his head. "Faster to go straight through, and less suspicious, if the Ludwig sisters should ask."

Katryn nodded. "I'm afraid I made us more conspicuous," she said. "But I couldn't walk past those poor ladies—"

"Of course not," he agreed. "Nor would I."

His smile was genuine, Katryn saw, and her guilt lessened. She had not planned to compromise his safety to help the stranded women.

"You've always had a kind heart, Katryn," he added. "I would not expect you to change, nor would I wish it."

The unexpected compliment warmed her, and she felt her cheeks flush with pleasure. She wished she could lean closer and kiss him quickly, but they were close enough to the village now that she had to remember their pose. He was dressed too roughly to be anything but her "servant," and they must maintain their disguises a little longer.

They walked through the village green without eliciting any apparent suspicions and kept walking till twilight descended. They slaked their thirst at a brook that paralleled the road for several miles, and Robert looked about for a place to spend the night.

Katryn made no comment when he chose a sheltered spot beneath a hedge; there were no abandoned huts in view this time, and just as well, considering Robert's reaction to the last one. But the thick bushes blocked the wind, and the grass was soft and clean; it could be worse. With luck, she thought, it might not rain.

They lay side by side, but since the incident of Robert's nightmare, he seemed even more detached, and he did not pull her as close as usual. What had happened to the passion that had sparked so easily between them since their marriage night? Katryn felt a new sense of loss; instead of growing closer, as she had hoped, they seemed to be falling further and further apart.

Sighing, she put one hand beneath her cheek and tried to find a comfortable spot where a pebble did not protrude through the grass. She reached out to Robert, who lay a few inches away from her—it might as well be a mile. His arm felt tense. Then she heard it, too.

Sounds of footsteps on the dirt road, and a murmur of a low voice. Who was coming? Had they been spotted? Surely it couldn't be Cavendish?

She strained to hear. A horse whinnied, and a man, louder now, spoke in low tones. She could not identify the voice.

"Here's a stream yonder," the unknown man said. "Let's water the animals afore we go on."

Katryn blinked at a sudden flash of light; a lantern's shield had been lifted, and the dancing light wavered over the slanting stream bank as the strangers picked their way carefully down the slope.

Robert touched her arm, and she jumped. "Be very quiet," he whispered, but the warning was unnecessary. Katryn lay pressed close to the grass, hardly daring to breathe, afraid even to lift her head and try to observe the intruders.

She heard the muffled hoofbeats as one, maybe two horses were led to the water, and the noisy slurping as the steeds drank. How many men were there? She heard a second voice, accusing in tone.

"We'd be in the next shire a'ready if you hadn't gotten us lost in your dash into the moors," the man grumbled.

"Well, we'uns are back to the road," the first man retorted. "The moon will be out soon, and us can make good time. No one up 'n' about at this hour."

The other man grumbled something, but neither spoke loudly, and Katryn couldn't make out the answer. To her alarm, she saw that one of the men was walking too close to where they lay hidden. As he encountered Robert's body, the man stumbled and cried out in alarm.

Robert jumped to his feet as the two men drew together, their posture threatening. The moon, fuller tonight, peeped over a hill behind them, and its faint light added to the flickering rays of the lantern. Katryn could see the two strangers for the first time, their dress rough and their hair long and shaggy.

"Who's this, then?" the first man demanded.

"Stalking us, are ye?" The second man's tone was threatening.

"No," Robert said. "Just resting a while before the moon rose; we are travelers, too."

Could these be the two men who had stolen the old ladies' horse, Katryn wondered. She turned her head to stare at the two mounts, tethered to a sapling by the edge of the brook, now placidly grazing on the thick grass near the water. One was a shaggy beast of medium height and undistinguished ancestry, but the second mount was trim and could be a roan; the dimness made it difficult to tell. But though she strained her eyes, she could perceive no star on its forehead.

One of the men had glimpsed her. "Two of ye? 'Tis a maid," he added in surprise, walking closer to Katryn.

"My wife," Robert said, his tone a warning. He stepped between Katryn and the strangers and gave her a hand. She stood, straightening her skirt, and ignored the two men's rude stares.

"We suffered an accident, and our horse went lame," she said, as if talking to strangers amid the hedgerows was an everyday occurrence. "Are these your horses? They are not for sale, are they?"

"Mayhap," the first man said. "What would ye be offering?"

They had no money to buy a mount with, in any case, but it gave her an excuse to turn away and walk closer to the grazing animals. She walked up to the larger horse, and sensed the men's frowns. Robert came just behind her, and she heard him whisper, for her ears alone, "It has no star on its forehead."

He was thinking the same as she. Katryn touched the horse's head, and it allowed her to run her fingers down its well-shaped face. Then she put her hand to her own nose and sniffed. Beneath the usual horsey aroma, there was something else, and her fingers felt gritty.

Soot! They had painted the white mark on the horse's face with soot to cover the too-distinctive marking.

"Robert," she muttered. "They have covered its star with ashes and soot."

"What's the wench up to?" the first man demanded. "Here, they're not for sale. But I think ye should show us your money, nonetheless." He was not tall, but his shoulders were wide and his arms thick with muscle. The man took a step closer to them, and Robert stepped in front of Katryn.

Katryn detected the flash of a blade as the second man drew a knife from beneath his shirt.

"Robert, look out!"

14

Even in the dim moonlight, Katryn could trace the path of the knife as the blade lifted, then fell with deadly intent toward Robert's chest.

Time seemed to stop; she had never been so frightened, not even when Cavendish had appeared at the party with soldiers at his back. Then, Robert's danger had been real but his death at least still in the future. This time, the peril was instant, immediate. He could die now at these villains' hands, outnumbered and with no weapon with which to defend himself. She remembered his tiny knife, but Robert had had no time to pull it from his pocket, and it was too small, anyhow, to be effective against the lethal blade the other man clutched so expertly. She wanted to scream, but her throat seemed to have closed. They were helpless. All she could do was gasp in horror as the knife came down, down, down—

Robert threw up one arm and deflected the blow, pushing the first ruffian back. The man grunted in surprise, and Robert crouched, then rushed the man before he could attack again.

Taken off guard, the vagrant tried to lift the knife once more, but Robert caught his arm and twisted, using the hold that he had learned in the common cell among thieves and murderers and street thugs of the lowest description. It all came back, without conscious effort—the prison lessons he had learned over time, when they had given up on extracting information from him and, because his life was no longer important, thrown him into a larger cell packed full of felons. He had learned, with many bruises and cuts to hasten his attention, the street fighting that he would use to keep himself alive through the rest of his imprisonment. Now, without even wishing it, he reacted, twisting the other man's arm behind him. The man cried out in pain, then fell back.

Katryn, still gripping the horse's lead with one hand, heard the sharp sound of bone breaking. The first thief muttered a curse as he dropped the knife, his arm hanging at an odd angle, and his fingers going suddenly slack.

It all seemed to have happened in a heartbeat—and now the second stranger, at first too surprised by Robert's unexpected resistance to react, appeared to summon his wits; he approached Robert from the rear, lifting a stout cudgel.

"Behind you, Robert!" Katryn called. The horse shifted restlessly at the fear in her voice, and she stroked its gritty head absently, unable to take her eyes off the fight.

At her warning, Robert turned, sidestepped the second thief's charge, and tripped him neatly, sending the man sprawling into the layer of dried leaves that lined the ditch. While he tried to struggle up again, the first man took the opportunity to scoop up the fallen knife, holding it awkwardly in his other hand, and approach Robert once more.

But he had been seen. Robert twisted aside, the blade sweeping past him as the thief thrust forward, overreaching and losing his balance. Robert kicked him soundly in the rear, and the first thief lost his footing completely, sprawling forward.

The second man tried to regain his footing, but Robert swept up the thick club the man had dropped. When the thief lifted his head from the ditch, dried leaves sticking to his scraggly, unwashed hair, a trace of greenish moss staining his beard in the lantern's flickering light, Robert lifted the club that had first been aimed at him and cracked the villain soundly on the head.

"Oh, well done," Katryn exclaimed despite herself. But the first thief had jumped up and, though one arm hung uselessly, the knife was clutched firmly in the other. He circled Robert, looking for an opportunity to use the blade, and Katryn held her breath. The horse thief's expression was intent, as if killing were nothing new to him. She was amazed that Robert had so far held his own.

When the thief moved, he moved swiftly, his good hand reaching for Robert's chest. He stabbed, but Robert deflected the blade with the club he still held, following the first swing with another. The thief jumped aside, and the second blow just missed. The two men circled, eyes on each other, and Katryn was afraid to make a sound lest she distract Robert.

The thief raised his good arm to plunge the weapon toward Robert's heart. Robert used the cudgel to again turn aside the thrust, but the other man changed the direction of his attack and with a vicious swing came up from beneath Robert's torso, trying to gut him like a hung pig.

Katryn gasped, but Robert had seen the movement coming, and he turned his body out of the knife's path. But though he evaded the slashing metal, his foot hit a damp spot that Robert—his eyes on his opponent—had not been able to note.

Katryn shrieked as Robert slipped and fell, his body open to the thief's next charge.

The robber stepped forward to take advantage of his foe's moment of weakness. Robert was trying to get back to his feet, but he seemed to have twisted his ankle, and he did not move swiftly enough.

Katryn had to do something, but she had no weapon, and
no knowledge of fisticuffs. What—

She suddenly realized she was still gripping the roan's
lead; she had hundreds of pounds of muscle at the end of the
rope. She pulled the horse sharply forward and ran toward
the thief.

Taken by surprise, he gaped at her for an instant, and that
was enough. Neighing, the horse reared slightly, alarmed at
this obstacle in its path. Katryn lost her hold on the rope, but
the thief was also forced to leap back.

Robert had jumped up, and while the horse thief scrambled out of the mare's path, Robert brought his own weapon
to bear. Katryn heard the clunk as the robber's head met the
thick wooden cudgel, then the hollow thud as he collapsed
onto the grassy bank. She sighed with relief, then ran to
Robert.

"Are you all right?" she demanded.

"Right as rain," Robert told her, grinning in the dim light,
though she saw that he still favored his left ankle. He pulled
her unexpectedly into his arms and lifted her for a hearty
kiss.

Surprised, it was an instant before she responded, then
she kissed him back with all the pent-up passion of the last
desperate days. She could feel the change in him, the renewed sense of his own vitality. Overcoming the two robbers seemed to have helped heal the lingering doubts inside
him, restored his sense of his own strength and potency—
she could feel his body respond to her own as they clung together, and for a moment she forgot everything, drinking in
his kiss as if it were nectar and she the victim of long thirst.

Then she heard one of the fallen men groan, and Robert
released her with obvious reluctance.

"See if you can lure the horse back," he said. "I will tie up
these two before they regain their wits."

Nodding, Katryn stepped away, though she ached to continue the kiss. While Robert ripped up the vagabonds' filthy shirts into sturdy strips of cloth, which he used to tie them both securely, she approached the horse, now once more grazing placidly on the lush grass. It allowed her to put her hand on its neck and take up the lead.

"I hope this is indeed the Misses Ludwigs' horse," she told Robert when he came to take a closer look at the animal. "If these are not the horse thieves, I would feel somewhat contrite."

Though not much, she thought, remembering how they had attacked Robert. And what they would have done to Katryn herself—she shivered and put that thought away.

"We will make certain," Robert told her, though his tone revealed no misgivings. He took a leftover shred of cloth and dipped it into the stream, coming back to scrub at the mare's forehead. Sure enough, the rag came away even blacker, if possible, and now they could both see the white mark on the horse's face. Robert lifted the animal's right hind leg and ran his hand over the smooth skin, finding the small scar that the Ludwig sisters had described.

After that, he went through the men's pockets and found a few coins, which he transferred matter-of-factly to his own, though he saw Katryn's eyes widen. Another pocket yielded a small pearl broach.

"That's Miss Ludwig's," Katryn said from behind him.

Robert nodded.

"How are we going to return her horse and her breast-pin?"

"I fear we shall have to backtrack a little and return to the last village we passed," he said.

"Now?" Katryn looked around at the dark countryside.

"Yes, now. I don't want to be seen too closely," he told her. "We must hurry, before the moon sets and makes passage too difficult."

Grunting a little from the effort, he lifted the men, one at a time, and slung them bodily over the stolen mare while Katryn held the reins so that the horse would stand still. The two hung over the horse's back like overfilled bags of grain, moaning and protesting through the cloth strips with which Robert had gagged them; their hands were tied behind their backs, and their feet similarly bound, so they could do little except produce muffled complaints.

He gave Katryn a leg up, and, with no sidesaddle available, she lifted her skirts enough to straddle the smaller steed. Then, with Robert limping a little, carrying the lantern, and leading the mare burdened with the two bound and gagged thieves, they headed at a fast walk back toward the village.

When the buildings came into view, Robert nodded toward the shadow of a tall oak tree. "Wait here," he told Katryn. "No need for you to be seen, too; there will be enough gossip about this."

She pulled up her mount and slipped off his back to wait for Robert's return. "Take care," she whispered.

Robert walked on into the village, stopping at the largest cottage of the half dozen that surrounded the green. He knocked loudly on the wooden door and waited, the mare standing behind him, shaking her head now and then but otherwise patient of her strange burden.

He pounded again. One of the thieves groaned. It seemed a long while till Robert heard voices inside. When at last the door creaked open a few inches, Robert saw a stout man in a nightshirt and cap, a thick walking stick in one hand and a candlestick in the other, peering cautiously past the half-open door.

"What's this, then?" the man demanded in a thick Yorkshire accent.

"These men stole the Misses Ludwigs' mare; I am returning it," Robert said calmly.

Speechless, the man gaped at him. Behind the farmer,

Robert glimpsed a woman and a younger man, both also in nightclothes, who had joined the head of the family. They craned their necks, trying to peer over his short, stout frame.

Robert held out the pearl broach. When the farmer gave his candle to the woman behind him, he dropped it into the man's hand. "They also stole this; be sure that it is returned to its rightful owner, as well as the mare. If not, I shall know who to blame."

The man stared at him. "What—"

"Take these two men to the magistrate," Robert continued, ignoring the stammered question, "and release them at your peril; I've no doubt they are murderers as well as thieves."

The woman standing behind her husband uttered a shriek, and the man paled. "Ah, yes," he said. "But who—"

"I am a friend of the Ludwig family who was also beset by the thieves, but I have no time to linger," Robert said firmly. He pressed the horse's reins into the man's hand. "You will likely receive a reward for your aid; just keep these men bound till you can turn them over to the squire."

The man nodded dumbly, and Robert stepped away. Within a few strides, he was out of the circle of candlelight and soon had left the village behind. To his relief, he heard no sound of pursuit.

Katryn awaited him in the darkness beneath the oak tree; the moon was slipping fast toward the horizon. He paused to kiss her quickly; the strange exhilaration he had felt when he had vanquished the two scoundrels lingered. He had come through for Katryn this time, and he felt stronger, almost renewed, as a result.

"Come," he told her. "Let us make haste."

"Will this beast hold both of us?" Katryn asked as he blew out the flame, then tied the lantern to the back of the saddle. He put his hands on the horse's wide rump and, with a lunge, scrambled onto his back. He swung his legs around and settled himself, his thighs gripping the horse's sides.

"I think so. He's not pretty, but he's a stout-looking cob," Robert told her, reaching down to grasp her arm and pull his wife up behind him. "Hold onto my waist."

Katryn was happy to do so. She leaned into his back, her face against the scratchy linsey-wool of his jacket. Then, as Robert turned the horse away from the village, a sudden thought made her lift her head.

"Robert?"

"Yes?"

"Do you suppose this horse is stolen as well?"

"Quite possibly," Robert told her. "But since we don't know from whom, we may as well keep him a bit longer, on loan, as it were."

She made herself as comfortable as she could as the horse moved forward. The gelding's pace could not be called smooth, but at least they were no longer on foot. She leaned against Robert's back, her arms gripping his waist, and smiled.

Whitmund and Cavendish reached Doncaster by late afternoon and began the usual round of post houses and inns, asking for information of a fair-haired lady traveling alone.

The first two inns yielded no sign of Eleanor, but at the third, the head groom looked them up and down, and something in his dark eyes made Whitmund's pulse leap. This man knew something; he was sure of it.

Cavendish seemed to have the same instinct. He stepped forward, and the groom transferred his gaze from Whitmund to Cavendish.

"And why would tha be wanting to know about the lady?" he asked in his Yorkshire brogue.

"We are friends of the lady's—" Whitmund began, when his traveling companion interrupted.

"That's none of your concern," Cavendish snapped.

"How dare you question a gentleman? Just tell us if you have seen her, and where she was headed!"

"Dunno," the man said, his accent getting even thicker, if possible, his eyes now veiled. "Dout that I can recall."

Cavendish, his city-cut coat now dusty from travel, his once-pristine shirt collar long wilted, lost his last shred of patience. He grabbed the smaller man by his worn leather apron and shook him. "Tell me, damn you!"

The groom gaped in surprise, but he didn't answer. Cavendish drew back his right hand, which still held his driving whip, and then found he had been gripped by his own coat and hauled unceremoniously backward.

"Whitmund, let go of me," Cavendish demanded, his voice shaking with rage. "This man knows something, and if you don't allow me—"

"To horsewhip him for holding his own counsel?" Whitmund demanded, his tone disgusted. "No surprise that he might wonder about your motives!"

He released his hold on Cavendish, then looked back to the groom, who watched them both with narrowed eyes. The man had taken a step back, deeper into the large stables that stood behind the inn, like a rabbit ready to bolt into its hole.

"She is not a friend," Whitmund said, meeting the man's dark eyes squarely. "She is my wife. We quarreled, and she has gone to stay with friends."

"Umm," the groom said, his tone still unconvinced. "Tha wants to wallop her, fer running away?"

"No indeed!" Whitmund raised his brows in shock at the thought. "I want to beg her forgiveness and ask her to come home."

"Hmmph," the smaller man said, rubbing the bristle on his jaw. "Well . . . She were a soft-spoken lady, thanked me nicely, she did. And a face like an angel's. Wouldn't want her to be fatched nor knocked about."

"I have never, would never beat my wife," Whitmund told

him. The statement had the ring of simple truth, and the servant nodded slowly.

"Ah well, then. She were asking the way to Squire Grabble's estate."

"Do you know where the squire lives?" Cavendish put in, then at a stern glance from Whitmund, subsided again, his expression sullen.

"Nay, but 'tis up toward Richmond way, think on." The groom scratched his jaw again. "Someone thereabouts mun know."

"How far, do you think?" Whitmund asked, before Cavendish could interrupt again.

"Day, day and a half, maybe," the man said, glancing toward the gray lowering skies. "If it don't rain too much, and th' roads don't mire up."

"Then we'd best be on our way," Whitmund said. They had already changed horses at the first post house and had supped quickly while the teams were switched. "We have no time to waste. Thank you for your help."

He gave the man a handful of coins, and the groom touched his cap in deference.

When they were back in the carriage, Cavendish snorted in derision. "He deserved a sound thrashing, not a reward! We are low enough on funds already."

"They are *my* funds," Whitmund pointed out dryly. "And he did give us the information."

"I could have gotten it out of him if you'd left me alone," Cavendish complained. "Without wasting money on his drivel." He brushed uselessly at his travel-stained coat and tried to straighten the sagging points of his collar.

Whitmund looked out the window, away from the man sitting across from him, holding on to his own patience with increasing difficulty. He had thought much about Eleanor, about Robert, even about Katryn on this journey, and there were questions still to be answered, but of one thing he was certain: he hoped never again to spend three days in close company with Jerod Cavendish.

"He was an insolent dog," Cavendish muttered, apparently still smarting from Whitmund's public rebuke. "You should have let me dust his jacket." The driving whip twitched in his hands, as if eager to find a warm body beneath its lash.

"Is this the way you always treat your servants, Cavendish?" Whitmund asked him coldly. "You must be very much loved at home."

The other man jerked his head back and glared at him. "Don't mock me, Whitmund!"

Whitmund glanced at the glittering, angry eyes and sullen expression. The surface resemblance between his soft-voiced brother-in-law and this man had faded as Whitmund spent more time with Cavendish; the heart and mind inside the body bore no relationship at all to Robert's. But fighting with Cavendish now would only waste more time.

Whitmund leaned forward to rap on the front side of the carriage, and almost at once he felt its pace slow. They were still on the outskirts of town, and though the streets were not as crowded as a London thoroughfare, still the carriage had to edge around carts loaded with farmers' produce and shop-keepers unloading wares from wagons piled high with goods, so it had not yet picked up speed.

"What are you doing?" Cavendish demanded. "Why are we stopping?"

"I'm going to take the reins myself for a while," Whitmund said. "I need some fresh air."

"What about your driver?"

"He can ride inside." Whitmund reached to push open the carriage door.

"With me? You'll leave me to sit with a servant?" Cavendish's face flushed with anger.

"Unless you wish to hang on the back," Whitmund suggested dryly.

"I have warned you not to mock me, Whitmund! Think I would suffer your insolence or anyone else's? Just because my mother was the daughter of a shopkeeper, just because my parents were barely wed before I was born—because I didn't inherit the fortune that I should have, you think I am dirt beneath your feet—you and all the rest."

Whitmund frowned; the man was obsessed, he thought. "Your father lost his fortune at cards and dice, and you must make your own reputation, Cavendish."

"I will, mark my words. When I have the title, the estate, the wealth, it will be a different story," Cavendish fumed.

Whitmund felt his own brow furrow as he stared at his traveling companion. "How convenient for you, then, after Robert was so inconsiderate as to survive the French wars, that this charge of treason should arise. It will solve all your problems, will it not?"

Cavendish jerked, pulling his lips back into an almost feral snarl. "Manning will get what he deserves, and so will I! But only if we find him quickly and stop wasting time."

"My purpose was to locate my wife and bring her safely home," Whitmund told him coldly. "You knew that when we left London."

"And if we find your wife, think you that we will not find Manning there as well?" Cavendish sneered.

Whitmund reached for the man's jacket and shook him like the cur he seemed increasingly to be. "Watch your tongue, Cavendish!"

"Why, because I speak aloud the thoughts that haunt your sleepless nights?"

"My wife is a virtuous lady, and if you wish to live to the end of this journey, you will remember that fact," Whitmund told him through clenched teeth. "And besides, Robert is married to her own sister."

Cavendish shrugged, trying to pull away from Whitmund's iron grip. "Perhaps his wife doesn't care about his affairs; she has the title and his money—at least for now—and that's enough for most women."

"Do you think he would dishonor both sisters in such a fashion, or that Katryn would put up with such treatment? You don't know her very well, do you?" If he hadn't been so angry, Whitmund would have laughed at the thought of Katryn complying meekly to such a scandalous arrangement. "And you don't know my wife at all, if you think—"

"Perhaps he wants them both," Cavendish said, very low. "He is just back from France, after all, and I hear the ménage à trois is quite the thing in some Parisian circles—"

Whitmund struck him hard across the face. "If you ever say such a thing again, you won't live to hear the echo of your malicious and groundless gossip, do you understand?"

Cavendish rubbed his cheek, reddened from the force of the blow. "I will send my second to call upon yours, sir! You will not treat me in such a fashion."

"Don't waste your time," Whitmund said, his blood still raging in his own ears as he struggled with his desire to choke the life out of this man right now, right here. "I only duel with gentlemen." He pushed him bodily toward the carriage door, which still stood open, and shoved him through.

Cavendish fell with a yelp and lay sprawled in the mud of the street, while several urchins gaped at them, and a matron in a bonnet, her shopping basket on one arm, stepped farther back from the street, out of danger's way. Cavendish gulped like a hooked trout, seeming for a moment too angry to speak, then finding his voice as he pushed himself up onto his elbows.

"You can't leave me here—"

"I can and will," Whitmund told him shortly. Already the air inside the carriage seemed fresher. He leaned forward to call up to the driver, who leaned over the side of the carriage to stare at them both in astonishment. "Drive on!"

Cavendish's curses and shouts dwindled into the distance, muffled by the steady rhythm of the horses' hooves, and soon the carriage was outside of town. The carriage picked up speed and the hired team settled into a dependable if not record-breaking trot.

Not much longer, and he would find his wife, find Eleanor, and then he would say to her—what, what could he say to break the spell of the first man she had promised to marry, the first man she had loved, still loved?

Whitmund shut his eyes and leaned back against the plush seat. As his anger slowly abated, he had to face a cold fact— that the depth of his rage at Cavendish's accusations sprang from his own terrible fear, the fear that some truth might hide beneath the libelous assertions.

Would he be able to bring his wife home again, would he ever have her love, or was sweet, gentle Eleanor already lost to him forever?

They rode as long as they could see the path, and when the moon dipped below the skyline, Robert lit the lantern again and held it in one hand so that the flickering light lit up the road in front of them. When his arm ached with fatigue, and he knew only a few hours remained till sunrise, Robert turned off the road into a copse of trees. He pulled up their mount, and Katryn slipped off the horse. He swung his leg over and dropped the short distance to the ground. The horse lowered its head, its weariness obvious. After Robert removed its bit and saddle and rubbed it down with a dirty rag, he tied the lead to the trunk of a small tree, and the horse dropped its head to crop the tall grass.

The cob was not well-bred, but he was sturdy, Robert thought, and might survive such rough treatment when a more finely built steed would not.

Robert found a patch of soft grass far enough away from the horse so that they would not be trampled in their sleep, and Katryn came to join him. She stretched and yawned, and he could see the outline of her breast against the deeper darkness behind the faint circle of lantern light. Desire, long absent, surged to life inside him, but he tried to push away the thoughts. Katryn needed sleep; he could not be so selfish. He patted the ground beside him, and when his wife came to sit down by his side, he turned down the lantern's light till the flame died.

The darkness was thick around them. Katryn could hear little sounds as the horse munched grass a few feet away, shuffling its feet. The grass was soft, though it only half-cushioned her body against the harder dirt beneath. She could smell the crushed grass, the scent of the horse that clung to them both after their ride, and above all, the male scent of Robert's clothing, Robert's body, so close to hers.

She felt a longing for the intimacy they had not shared for days, and then tried to stifle the thoughts. It wouldn't be fair to expect lovemaking tonight; Robert must be exhausted. She could not think of her own yearning at such a time. In a few hours, they must be up and on the road again.

She shut her eyes and nestled into Robert's open arms, leaning her cheek against him. She could feel the rise and fall of his chest, and his skin warm beneath the shirt—he had removed his rough-cut jacket to lay over them against the night air.

She loved him so much, wanted him so much—no, no, she would not think of it now. But he was too close, and she couldn't help putting up one hand to touch his chest lightly, drawing lines down the coarse, much-laundered shirt and feeling the firmness of his chest beneath the cloth.

Robert almost groaned; he wanted her so badly that he had to force himself to lie still. He knew Katryn, despite their few weeks of marriage, still had little idea how she affected him. And she lay so close, tucked into the circle of his arms, her breasts touching his chest, her legs warm against his own limbs; in his mind, he thought of all the things he wished to do to that smooth-skinned body. . . .

Katryn felt his breathing quicken. Had he heard someone coming?

"Robert, is something wrong?" she whispered, turning her head slightly to listen for any sign of more intruders.

Robert shifted enough to kiss her cheek; it was too dark to find her mouth easily. "Nothing, except that my wife is so enticing I cannot close my eyes," he murmured. He ran his lips across the smooth curve of her cheek till they found the petal-soft lips he knew so well, and when he kissed her, she responded with a fervor that only fed his rising passion.

Katryn pressed against him, delighting in the force of his kiss—this was the Robert whom she had first met in their marriage bed, his passion for her seemingly restored. She could almost bless the horse thieves who had startled him into remembering his own passion. She opened her lips beneath his, and his kiss deepened; she held back a moan, trying to remember her resolution to spare his few hours of sleep.

When he dropped his head to kiss the soft skin beneath her chin, to trace the line of her throat down and down, she shivered with delicious sensation. If he reached her breasts, if he put his lips around her already-straining nipples and touched them with his tongue, she knew that she would be lost.

"No," she said, summoning her last shreds of resolve. "You need some sleep, Robert. Perhaps I should turn away, so the temptation to us both is not so strong."

She shifted as she spoke, turning her back to him, and put one hand under her cheek as if to sleep.

Robert had to choke back a laugh; the sweet innocent—

she still had so much to learn. If God only gave him the time, he exulted in the thought of teaching her.

But she was right, they should sleep. He shut his eyes resolutely and tried not to hear the soft sound of her breathing—but it brought into his mind a picture of her breasts rising and falling, and he thought of the smooth hollow of skin that lay between them, and how Katryn would quiver if he kissed her just so . . . and if he touched her breasts—

Sleep be damned! He opened his eyes and ran his hands over her back, feeling the quiver that she tried to control, then let his touch slip down till he cupped her sweetly rounded buttocks in his palms. He stroked them, running his hands up and down, till he felt her shiver again.

"I fear, my dear wife," he said gravely into her ear, kissing the lobe, then biting it very gently, "that this may not be the wisest way to quiet my passion."

Katryn exclaimed in surprise at the nip, though it was not sharp enough to be painful, and then gasped once again as she felt him pull up her skirt, her petticoat, push down her drawers—until his hands were caressing the curves of her bottom, all too close to the secret places where she already knew his touch could bring such delight.

"Should I stop, lady fair?" Robert whispered into her ear, kissing it again. She quivered with indignity at the thought.

"No," she whispered back, her voice thick with a combination of desire and laughter. "Stop at your peril, my lord."

The last word left Katryn's mouth in a rush as Robert flipped her on top of him in one quick movement. Finding herself stretched full-length against the hard planes of his body, she looked into his darkened eyes and could not stifle her startled giggle.

"This is no laughing matter, I assure you, my lady." Robert's mouth quirked in direct opposition with his words.

Reaching for her hands, he loosely circled her wrists and brought them around his own neck. Then he slid his hands back down her body until he cupped her buttocks in his palms. He surged up, pressing his hardness against her melting warmth. Katryn released a shaky sigh at his sure touch.

For several minutes, his hands moved surely, intimately, until his heated kisses and leisurely caresses left Katryn shaking and all but pleading for his possession.

"Oh, please, Robert, please!" Impatiently, Katryn tried to roll over so that they might end this glorious torture, but Robert held her firmly. Robert groaned low in the back of his throat as Katryn innocently inflamed him further with her enthusiastic efforts to switch their positions.

Just as she was anticipating that Robert would roll her onto her back, he cupped the back of her thighs with rough palms and pulled her legs up so that she was straddling his rigid body. Robert let out a husky chuckle as the moon peeped out from behind a cloud; her loosened hair did not completely veil Katryn's confused and frustrated expression. The sight of her rising above him, skirts pulled up and billowing around them, dark tendrils sticking to her damp skin and kiss-swollen lips, had Robert burning with a sense of urgency and need such as he had never felt before . . . not even in his dreams of Eleanor. Ruthlessly, he smothered that thought.

"Don't worry, little one. You'll catch on," he whispered, then, with the pad of his thumb, found that sweet spot which had Katryn squirming to get closer. Slowly, deliberately, Robert pleasured Katryn with the tips of his fingers until she was dizzy with the glory of it.

With his other hand, Robert reached to free himself from his trousers. But Katryn, seeing his intent, pushed his hand aside and tore open the fastenings herself. Beyond thought, she acted on an instinctual need to reach whatever she was reaching for together.

"God help us!" Between sweet curses and pleas hurled into the night sky, Robert suffered the exquisite torture of his wife's hesitant, yet eager caresses. "Remind me never to fault your impetuousness, my love," he said with a heartfelt groan. Gripping her hips, he surged into her snug wetness with one sure motion.

Katryn gasped, then she began to realize the advantages of her position. She moved, slowly at first, then more quickly, finding the pleasure of it, watching her husband respond.

When Robert felt his passion erupt, he almost groaned. It was so exquisitely sweet, and yet it was so soon, too soon. He wasn't ready to end this joining.

Katryn lay her head against his chest, and neither spoke. She heard him breathe long, deep breaths, and she felt the sheen of perspiration that coated his skin. She felt like a land-locked shepherd who had first glimpsed the ocean—a whole new world lay before them, full of promise and unlooked-for delight.

"My love," she murmured. She slipped off him, cuddling close to his side. He held her against him, and for a few minutes they lay without speaking. Then, to Katryn's surprise and delight, he pulled her close once again. She felt his body hard against her. She put out one hand tentatively, unsure if she had read him correctly.

Robert caught the hand, kissed the palm, caressed the smooth skin of her arm, pushing her sleeve up.

Suddenly her clothes seemed a hindrance. She undid her buttons, working by touch in the faint moonlight and biting her lip when the silly things would not fall away quickly enough.

What a marvel she was! He could not get enough of her, Robert thought; she was like the sweetest nectar, the smoothest wine. And she met his passion with a heat as consuming as his own—he wanted to laugh, he wanted to shout her name into the dark clusters of trees. Instead, he slid out of his trousers and shook off the rest of his hand-me-down clothes until he lay bare against the grass, feeling the prickly smooth blades against his back.

Katryn laughed a little, seeing the firm outlines of his body in the faint light. She had never before lain with him completely naked; he'd always kept on a shirt, a nightshirt, something. Hurrying to join him in this total release, she pulled off her borrowed dress and tossed it into the grass; her thin shift soon followed, then her stockings, everything. Eager to retaste this new pleasure, she needed little urging to slide back onto his body, fitting herself neatly into him, gasping a little with the intense pleasure it gave her.

Robert groaned in delight as he felt her tightness encompass him. He watched the smooth curves of her breasts appear above him. The moonlight touched her skin, gilding the smooth ivory with silver. His desire surged; it was all he could do to hold himself back.

"Beautiful," he whispered, his voice husky, "so beautiful."

Katryn felt the air against her bare skin, smelled the grass they had crushed beneath them. She had never felt so totally free, so completely abandoned. They might have been wild creatures themselves, ancient demigods following Pan's pipe into the forests for mindless revels. Her skin prickled with anticipation; they would become one here, in a union so glorious and free that all the wonderful nights they had shared up to this moment paled by comparison.

Katryn's eyes widened and her blood roared as it pulsed through her body. Their heartbeats, their breaths, even the night sounds around them seemed to match the slow, hypnotic rhythm Robert set. Every sense was heightened and every muscle screamed for release. Katryn felt its nearness in every movement. Neither granting the other any quarter, their bodies met in sweet battle.

As they moved, Robert touched her cheek, ran his fingers over the sweet, plump curves of her mouth. Katryn took his finger between her lips, sucking the pad of his finger between her teeth.

He trailed the abused finger down her neck, in between her damp breasts, to the darkest shadows. With the barest of pressure, he touched where their bodies were joined.

The stars above them became a kaleidoscope of light and color as Katryn arched her back and raised her arms above her in pagan revelry.

Robert knew he would never see anything as magnificent as Katryn when she came undone. And then he ceased to think at all. Together, their passion soared, their souls united as intimately as their bodies. . . .

She had never felt so powerful, so weak. She pulled Robert up so that they could cradle each other in their arms. He laid his head on her shoulder and took deep, bracing breaths.

Katryn smiled against her husband's arm as he murmured, "Congratulations. You have accomplished what Boney's men could not. I am vanquished. Utterly and completely. Any information you want? It's yours."

Katryn chuckled. There was a quality to her laughter, a knowing, which even she could hear.

"Your money or your life?" Then she held her breath, wishing she could take it back. Neither laughed. Her thoughtless jest had fallen flat as they recognized the truth of her statement. After a moment, Robert laughed recklessly. "My dear cousin wants both. And you have stolen the rest."

If possible, her heart seemed to pound even harder than it had a moment ago. Afraid to reveal too much when everything was going so superbly, she only tucked her head into his shoulder and ran her hands down his well-muscled back.

"A thief, am I? I'll thank you not to lump me with the villains we've just met—"

Her words and her questing fingers stopped. Robert stiffened in realization of what she felt. He tried to draw away but Katryn clung tighter.

"No." Her voice was strong with command.

His shoulders shrugged in resignation. She would have to find out sometime. It was the height of absurdity to suppose they could go fifty years without her noticing his shame.

Gently, she felt again the ridges of scar tissue that criss-crossed his back like a trellis. In growing horror, she raised her body to look past him and tried her best to see in the darkness what she felt all too clearly with her hands.

"My God, what did they do to you?" Anger filled her voice, made it tremble.

"Whipped me" was Robert's terse reply. He steeled himself for her disgust that he could let himself be beaten like an animal in the gutters. Or worse, for her tears of pity.

But, as always, his young wife surprised him.

Raising that stubborn chin with the adorable cleft he was growing to love, she looked directly into his eyes. "And what did you do to them?"

He decided if she was brave enough to ask, he should be brave enough to tell her.

"Before my escape, I wrapped his whip around his neck and made certain he could never torture anyone again." Cautiously, he awaited her reaction.

She could not stop the shudder that shook her slender shoulders but she met his gaze firmly.

"Good."

Then with gentle fingers and gentler lips, she kissed the old hurt away, and it was Robert's turn to tremble.

15

Before they found the squire's estate, the driver had to stop twice more to ask directions, once from a shepherd who blocked the road as his flock of bawling, blank-eyed sheep passed by, later from a woman working in her garden near a roadside cottage. When at last they turned into the driveway of the old-fashioned manor house, its faded mortar and wood facade draped in climbing roses and thick ivy, its small Tudor windows sparkling in the pale sunshine, Eleanor suddenly felt a spasm of nervousness.

What on earth would she say to this woman? What if the Frenchwoman denied knowing Robert; what if she had no interest in helping him? How on earth would Eleanor explain her precipitous journey?

Eleanor sighed. She missed her baby son, missed the weight of him in her arms and the smell of his sweet head beneath her chin, missed the slight, contented sigh he made just before he fell asleep. She wanted to go home, but she had come too far to turn back now. What was Edward thinking, alone in London? Had he taken notice of her absence, or was he still spending all his time with goodness knew which loose women? Had her heedless flight only fueled his anger?

She had never done anything like this in her life. The thought engendered a strange sense of pride. Eleanor lifted her chin and swallowed hard against the quiver inside her stomach. When her footman opened the carriage door, she stepped down and approached the house.

When a hatchet-faced woman in a plain bonnet and apron opened the front door, Eleanor straightened, trying to look as if her coming were expected. "I am Lady Whitmund," she told the servant. "Please announce me to your mistress."

Gaping, the woman's eyes widened for an instant—surely she was not so ill-trained as to question a guest of obvious rank and breeding? But she shut her mouth quickly and opened the door wider.

Eleanor expected that she would be shown into a parlor and asked to wait. Instead, after a moment's hesitation, the housekeeper said, "If you'll follow me, my lady," and led her through a modest hall to the very back of the house, then down a narrow set of stairs to one of the cellars.

The woman must have lost her head, Eleanor thought, she must be rattled by the unexpected titled visitor turning up on her doorstep; guests were not shown into a stillroom where the lady of the house had her arms elbow-deep in milky whey.

"Lady Whitmund," the housekeeper announced and stepped back to motion Eleanor into the small room, its walls lined with shelves of curing cheeses. The air smelled musty but clean, and the sharp scent of the cheese was not unpleasant.

Minette, Lady Grabble was a petite woman whose sleeves just now were pushed up high on her slender arms. She wore a kerchief over her hair and an apron over her day dress, and she looked startled at Eleanor's entrance, as well she might, and also slightly guilty. Most gentlewomen did not dirty their hands in menial kitchen chores, and this was not how anyone would wish to greet a stranger.

Instinctively, Eleanor glanced back at the housekeeper; the older woman's expression was smug. It had not been surprise that had made her forget proper procedure; she had done this on purpose, had wanted to embarrass her mistress, Eleanor thought, anger kindling inside her. She tried to think what to say to ease the situation.

Her narrow face flushed with embarrassment, Lady Henry jerked her hands back from the vat and wiped them dry on a clean cloth. "*Excusez moi*—I was just checking the cheese," she said, her English only slightly slurred by her French accent. "My—my family had their own way of . . ."

"Of course. I always oversee the butter-making in my own kitchen," Eleanor lied gallantly. "But I have never attempted to make cheese. I would love to taste yours."

"It will be months yet before this batch is ripe," Lady Grabble said, the tightness around her mouth relaxing at Eleanor's gracious tone. "But I have some of last year's that came out *très bon*."

"How nice. You must explain the cheese-making process to me sometime." Eleanor smiled at the other woman. She could sense the servant's disappointment without even looking back, and she was pleased when Lady Grabble regained command of herself enough to turn to the housekeeper.

"Show Lady Whitmund into the front parlor and bring us a tea tray, *s'il vous plaît*."

Looking toward Eleanor, the Frenchwoman added, "If you will excuse me *un peu moment,* my lady, I will remove my apron, then I will join you there."

"Of course." Eleanor inclined her head, but sweetened the formal gesture with a genuinely warm smile. She already liked this woman, even though it was obvious she had married above her station. Her father had likely been a wealthy farmer, or even a shopkeeper. But she had a sweet smile, and whatever her birth, it did not give her housekeeper the right to embarrass her in front of strangers.

Eleanor followed the stiff-backed servant along the hall to the front parlor, where she should have been taken in the first place. The housekeeper went out again, and Eleanor sat down on a chair in front of the fire; despite the spring greenery outside, the air was chilly and, after the coolness of the cellar, the warmth of the fire felt good on her outstretched hands. Her gloves were thin and she had left her muff in the carriage. Eleanor shivered, her anxiety returning.

Where was Robert? Was he lying beneath some tree, cold and hungry and too weak to move? Unable to return to his house or his man of business, he must be perilously low on funds, and how could he survive once her carriage team had gone as far as it could travel? He would never make it this far; she should have waited in London, sent out runners to track him and tell him to return—tell him that she had the proof of his innocence he needed. She touched her reticule and the precious letter inside. Once the charge against him was dropped, Robert could come back to his own life, not skulk about like some highwayman in fear of the noose. She shuddered at the thought of the lethal punishment.

And what about Katryn? Was she cold and miserable, too? Eleanor felt a pang for her sister, really, she told herself, she did, but she still felt irritation as well that Katryn would insist on accompanying her husband into his dangerous exile. It was so like to Katryn to leap first, and think afterward. . . .

Katryn must be only a burden to him in his flight, and might even cause his capture. If her scamp of a sister ever did what she was supposed to do, it would be a shock to her whole family, Eleanor thought crossly.

The fire popped, and she pushed her chair back a few inches, so that she didn't become too warm. She did not want to greet Lady Grabble with reddened cheeks.

• • •

When Katryn woke, she felt the unaccustomed prickle of grass beneath her cheek. The smell of fresh greenery met her as she took a long breath, then slowly opened her eyes. She blinked in confusion. Why was she lying on cold earth beneath a tall oak tree, with the first faint rays of dawn lighting the eastern horizon? A few feet away, the cob munched grass contently, paying no attention to their supine bodies.

Then she remembered, and she turned her head, seeking her husband. Robert lay beside her; one arm had been draped loosely over her shoulders, but it had slipped off as they had slept. His eyes were still shut, and his breathing was even and unhurried. The usual lines of tension around his eyes were missing, and his brow was unfurrowed. For once, he looked completely relaxed, at ease with the world. Remembering their night of passion, Katryn smiled, feeling a rush of joy mixed with triumph. She had done that, she thought, she had given him the release from his worries that he so desperately needed. They had come together and found the bliss of complete love; they had created their own bubble of peace, separate and apart from the rest of the world.

Remembering the pleasures of the night, the revelations, the new honesty they had shared, her smile deepened, and she felt her body come awake, too, as if longing were already rekindling deep inside her. She wanted to lean closer and kiss his closed eyelids, nibble on the stubble that covered his cheeks and chin, slip lower to stroke his bare chest with its light sprinkling of soft hair.

No, she must let him sleep as long as he could, Katryn told herself firmly. He had had too little rest during their frantic flight north. But despite her good resolve, she reached across to push back that one unruly lock of hair that always fell across his forehead. He sighed in his sleep, and she drew back her hand.

When they came together in love, it stirred her to the depths of her being; the marriage bed only grew more satisfying as time passed, she told herself, then laughed a little, deep in her throat. If anyone had ever predicted that her marriage bed would be a mossy bank beneath the open sky, she would have thought the tale impossible, mad. Yet here they were, and despite all the danger that swirled around them, she was happy. Robert was here, and he loved her—they had never achieved such a vibrant, intense coupling before—she knew his heart was engaged now, it had to be.

Robert loved her, as she loved him. All her life, she had dreamed of this moment.

Her whole being warm with contentment, surfeit with love given and returned, Katryn leaned closer to kiss his forehead very lightly. But his eyelids fluttered, and she bit her lip, instantly contrite.

When he opened his eyes, he smiled at her, a slow, sleepy smile, and she relaxed again.

"I didn't mean to wake you," she said, very low. "Sleep again, if you can."

"No," he muttered. "We have a long way to go yet; we must make our start." But instead of pushing himself up, he leaned closer to kiss the lobe of her ear, then let his lips wander down to the tender skin of her neck. The stubble of his growing beard prickled a little, but it did not take away from the pleasure she felt. She shivered at the delicious sensations.

"But you tempt me greatly, Wife," he whispered with mock gruffness. "How can I greet the business of the day, when you evoke other feelings in me? Waking to see you lying close beside me is the best antidote ever concocted for nightmare."

He had not had nightmares, Katryn realized, her heart light with new reason for happiness. They had loved, and loved again, and he had slept easily afterward, with no muttering or thrashing or crying out, as he did when the prison dreams returned to haunt him. Perhaps the inner wounds were healing, as well as the outer.

"My dearest," she whispered back, her voice husky with the mingling of her heart's love and her body's desire. Above them, just visible through the branches of the tall oak tree, the dawn had erupted across the eastern sky, and bands of lavender and rose chased the fading darkness. Somewhere a lark sang, celebrating the morn. As Robert pulled her closer, she lay her hands on the warmth of his bare chest, delighting in his touch and content to live forever in this golden moment.

The tall oaken door opened and the housekeeper brought in the tea tray and set it on a small table in front of the fireplace. Behind her, Lady Grabble entered, looking more composed. She had removed her apron and the kerchief that had bound her hair, and had pulled her sleeves back into place. Her hair was dark, Eleanor saw, and her eyes, so brown they looked almost black, were very large, giving her face a gamin quality that was quite fetching. Where had she met her elderly husband? How had she ended up here, so far in the wilds of northern England? She must find this isolation trying after living in France, with the glittering social life available in Paris.

Eleanor put her curiosity aside. Now for the tricky part, she thought, trying not to dissolve into nervousness. In rushing to Lady Grabble's aid, she had forgotten her own qualms, but now they came slipping back to turn her stomach to jelly.

Fortunately, Lady Grabble was pouring out tea into thin china cups. "That will be all," she said to her housekeeper.

The woman looked mutinous for an instant, but she nodded and left the room, though when she pulled the door, it did not quite close behind her.

Lady Grabble's face, no longer flushed, showed annoyance for just a moment, then she smoothed her expression into polite calm. She handed a cup of tea to Eleanor, offered her a plate of raisin-dotted scones, then stood and, without comment, walked over to push the door completely shut.

Eleanor wished her hostess might have slammed the door in the housekeeper's ear; she had no doubt the servant was waiting outside to satisfy her curiosity about this unexpected visitor.

Lady Grabble took her seat and sipped her own tea, then looked up at Eleanor at last, her gaze candid. "Your visit is an unexpected honor, Lady Whitmund."

"Not at all," Eleanor muttered, bracing herself.

Her hostess continued, "My lady, I don't wish to appear rude, but have we met?"

"Not exactly," Eleanor answered, the words suddenly hard to find. "But we were both guests at the earl of Swindon's party in London."

Lady Grabble's already-pale cheeks turned suddenly ashen. "*Mon Dieu,* I—I—"

"You must have been witness to my brother-in-law Robert's very public arrest," Eleanor plowed on, not knowing how to back down now. "None of it is true; Lord Manning is innocent, you know. He was never a spy for the French; that is a spurious charge."

"No," the other woman agreed. "I am sure he is not a spy. I am *très* sorry for your brother-in-law. But why come to me? What do I have to do with this?"

"I have information that I must give him, a letter which will help prove his innocence. And I thought he might come here—he was seeking your location—"

"*Non, non!* But why?"

To Eleanor's shock, the other woman jumped to her feet,

twin spots of red the only color in her whitened cheeks. Her eyes were anguished.

"I cannot say anything to him—*c'est impossible!* You must not ask me."

Eleanor gazed at her in surprise. "I'm not demanding any—any public declaration. If Robert knew you before your marriage, I mean, if you and he were friends, he would never try to embarrass you, you know." Was this woman's husband so jealous that he would be angered just at the thought that she had once known a good-looking man, younger and of better estate than himself? Why was she so alarmed? Or had Robert courted her in earnest? Had they been lovers? Had he already forgotten Eleanor while he was in France, even before he was imprisoned? The thought sent a sharp pang through her. No, she would not believe it. Robert had loved her, had loved only her!

And yet—perhaps Eleanor had been totally wrong, perhaps this woman was not an ally. Perhaps Robert was not on his way here. She wished she had never come. Why had she thought she could pull off such a mad scheme? Katryn was the one who ran heedlessly into danger and possible scandal—not Eleanor. She should have stayed home and endured her loveless marriage. Perhaps Robert had indeed forgotten her, no longer in his heart of hearts clung to the love they'd once shared. Why had she been so sure—

The door opened again, and Eleanor jumped. She looked up to see the short, stout gentleman she remembered vaguely from the London ball. Sir Henry Grabble had graying hair and a rounded paunch, but his eyes were keen with intelligence. He crossed the room to stand beside his wife's chair.

"Going to introduce me, my dear?" he said, glancing at Eleanor's traveling costume. "I saw the carriage outside."

Eleanor tried not to look embarrassed. How had she thought she could barge into a stranger's house and expect to be welcomed, when concern for Robert's safety was the only thing they shared. Or she had thought they shared it. . . .

"This is Lady Whitmund," Minette said, her voice faint.

"Lady Grabble and I met in London," Eleanor added.

"How nice," Sir Henry said politely. "I didn't know you had any friends in London, my dear."

"We share the same dressmaker," Eleanor said quickly. "You know how women love to chat about fashion."

He raised his thick graying brows. "Indeed." His dark eyes took on a sardonic gleam. It wasn't necessary for him to point out that his wife could never have afforded the expensive modiste that Eleanor patronized regularly. Eleanor racked her brain to think of a more convincing connection between two women who lived in such different circles, but it was Minette who smoothed over the gaffe.

"No, I think we met first at the lace-maker's," his wife suggested. "At any rate, it had something to do with dress-making." She smiled; her agitation seemed to have subsided and her tone was more assured. "And I invited her to visit when she came to our county, *Henri*," the other woman added, to Eleanor's surprise.

Sir Henry nodded to Eleanor. "I see. Welcome, then, my lady. I hope you are enjoying your journey?" There was thinly veiled curiosity in his voice; this out-of-the-way estate was not on any direct route from London. And well-bred ladies did not travel alone.

"Yes, thank you," Eleanor answered. "I have relatives in the area."

"Really?" Sir Henry raised his brows. "Anyone I would know?"

He would know everyone in the county, Eleanor thought, in a panic. She cursed herself for such an obvious lie. She herself would never make a good spy, that was certain. She tried to think how to answer, but fortunately her host did not pursue the question.

Instead, Sir Henry looked back to his wife, who poured him a cup of steaming tea. As she handed it to him, their hands brushed for an instant, and Sir Henry smiled. Minette seemed to relax slightly.

The moment of glimpsed intimacy brought a lump to Eleanor's throat. She thought of her own fine London home, and the bed she had slept in alone since the night of the Swindons' ball. Sir Henry might be twice Minette's age and plain of face, but it was obvious he loved his wife.

Eleanor found her tea, at first sip quite palatable, suddenly bitter and hard to swallow.

They chatted of inconsequential topics and, to Eleanor's relief, Sir Henry asked no more questions. When they finished their tea, Minette showed her up to a guest room on the second floor; it was small compared to the rooms in Eleanor's own spacious house, but neatly done up.

"I hope this will be sufficient," her hostess said, her voice a bit anxious.

"It's very kind of you to offer me hospitality," Eleanor said sincerely. "I'm afraid I didn't think this journey through very well; I just wanted to help Robert, that was all."

Lady Grabble smiled somewhat ruefully. "Yes, I understand." She lowered her voice; they were for the moment alone. "*Eh bien,* Robert does have that effect on women, does he not?"

Eleanor blinked; was it true, then—had this woman and Robert been lovers? Perhaps her own expression was too revealing, because the Frenchwoman actually smiled for the first time, and her dark eyes twinkled for just a moment.

"Have no fear, Lady Whitmund," she said. "When I knew Robert in France, he could see no other woman, no matter how lovely; the vision he held in his mind's eye blocked all else. He had only one woman in his heart—and that woman was you."

Eleanor felt as if she had been given a precious gift;

Robert had indeed loved her; he had not betrayed the promise they had made to each other. How had she doubted him? Robert had been faithful, and a precious part of her past was still secure.

No, she was the one who had broken their troth, and it must haunt her the rest of her life. The old pain lanced through her, and she took a deep breath, then looked up to see the other woman watching her, her dark brows lifted.

Eleanor shook off the guilt that always dogged her and smiled at her hostess with real warmth. "Thank you," she almost whispered. "Thank you for that."

"I'm sorry that when he returned, you had already married," the Frenchwoman said. "*Quel dommage.*"

Eleanor flushed slightly, but the other shook her head. "No, I do not judge you, Lady Whitmund. One must be practical. *Moi,* I understand that, too well." For a moment, bitterness colored her tone, then she shook her head, as if pushing aside unpalatable memories. "I am only so fortunate that in my life, at last, I found love and security in the same man." Her dark eyes glittered with tears, which she blinked back; some instinct told Eleanor that they were tears of happiness, the mark of a storm-tossed refugee who had at last found her way home.

Everyone knew there had been much disorder in France over the last decades, with first the Revolution and its bloody reign of the guillotine, then Napoleon's also tumultuous rise to power. What danger and privation this woman had endured, Eleanor could not even guess. Impulsively, she put out her hand.

"Call me Eleanor, please," she said. "I hope we may be friends, in truth."

The Frenchwoman flushed a little with pleasure and pressed the offered hand. "*Merci,* you are *très* kind. And you must call me Minette."

"I should like that," Eleanor told her.

A clock chimed on the landing, and Minette's expression changed. "Ah, I must see about dinner; we keep early hours in the country," she said. "I'm afraid we sit down to dinner at five o'clock."

"Of course," Eleanor agreed without surprise; most of the gentry kept country hours when away from London.

"I will send you my little maid; she is not of the quality you will find in London, but she has a way with the hair," Minette said with perfect seriousness.

"Thank you," Eleanor told her. A manservant brought up her bags and told her that her carriage and team and servants had all been looked after, and when the girl came—fortunately of much less forbidding aspect than the old dragon of a housekeeper—Eleanor washed away some of the dust of the trip and changed her dress to a becoming but not ostentatious gown that was suitable for a quiet family dinner. She did not want to seem to put on airs, she thought; she was happy to have gained Minette's friendship, and hopefully her trust. So she wore only her pearl ear bobs and a simple necklace, and she kept her toilette simple.

When she left her room to go downstairs, Eleanor paused on the landing to look over the family portraits. Hearing footsteps behind her, Eleanor looked around, expecting Minette, but it was the housekeeper.

"Them's Sir Henry's grandfather and great-grandfather, my lady; the Grabble family is one of Yorkshire's oldest," the servant explained, her tone reverent. "Been landowners here for hundreds of years, they have."

Eleanor nodded; for once, the woman looked slightly less forbidding. Her loyalty to Sir Henry was impressive, if not her treatment of his wife.

"Have you been in service here a long time?" she asked politely.

"All my life, just about." The housekeeper lifted her chin. "I started as scullery maid, my lady, when I was twelve; I'm not too proud to admit it. But I advanced to become upstairs maid, and then parlor maid, and then housekeeper, and when Sir Henry was widowed, I took good care of him, I did. Till he went down to London two years ago and met this—this Frenchwoman and married her, just like that." Her tone expressed her amazement and disgust that her beloved employer would act so rashly.

Eleanor was not about to encourage this woman's obvious prejudice. "How wonderful that Sir Henry was able to find someone to comfort him after his loss. You must be very thankful for the new Lady Grabble."

She knew this was not true; it showed in every movement of the woman's angular body, but it was the sentiment that a loyal servant should express, and Eleanor didn't mind pointing out the fact. It was obvious that Minette had a hard time with her recalcitrant housekeeper.

The woman sniffed. "The Grabbles is a good *English* family," she said. "Always have been. And where this so-called lady came from—"

Eleanor frowned, allowing her voice to turn icy. "If you value Sir Henry, I'm sure you trust his judgment," she pointed out.

The housekeeper was not easily cowed. "Anyone can make a mistake, my lady, on short acquaintance. And he hardly knew this woman afore he married her. What kind of blood is she, to bring into such a family?"

Eleanor lifted her brows. "I'm sure Lady Grabble will only add to Sir Henry's well-respected family history."

"But how do we know that? What I say is, who knew her?" the servant repeated stubbornly.

"I did! Minette and I are old friends," Eleanor lied. She would have said anything to dispute this odious woman's disparaging words. "Her family is not wealthy, but they are eminently respectable."

The housekeeper's mouth pursed into a disapproving

frown, but she made a stiff curtsy. "If you say so, my lady," she said.

Still annoyed, Eleanor made her way past the servant and on down the staircase. She found her hostess in the parlor.

"I hope you are comfortable, my la—Eleanor," Minette said, her tone still a little formal. "My husband was called out to check on a tenant who fell from a haycock, *quel dommage,* but dinner will be served shortly. Perhaps you would like to take a turn in the garden while we wait?"

"I should love to, Minette," Eleanor agreed, her tone easy.

Minette smiled, a sweet, wistful expression that almost lifted the hint of old sadness lingering in the depths of her dark eyes. She led the way to the formal walled garden at the side of the old manor house and showed Eleanor rosebushes and flowering shrubs that made a pleasing picture.

"This is my planting." Minette leaned over to pluck a withered leaf. She broke off a just-opened blossom, luscious in its soft pink petals, and presented it to Eleanor. Minette's voice reflected obvious pride. "I have tried to revive the garden; Sir Henry's first wife was a renowned gardener, and it was neglected after her death; Sir Henry was too much reminded of his wife to wish to walk here. *Moi,* I have not her skill, but I have tried to tend the plants and preserve the harmony of the design."

"The garden looks wonderful," Eleanor assured her, holding the rose to her face so she could smell the sweet heavy scent. What a shame that Minette, who seemed to try so hard, should have to live her life in the shadow of the first Lady Grabble. "I'm sure Sir Henry appreciates your attention to the estate."

Minette smiled briefly, but her usual solemn expression returned almost at once. "This rose also has a lovely hue, *n'est-ce pas?*" she told Eleanor, moving to the next bush before a call from the garden gate interrupted her.

"Pardon, ma'am, but Cook says there's a problem with

the joint, and should she dress the chicken with parsley sauce or with that new French recipe that you gave her?" The little housemaid bobbed respectfully, but her tone was anxious.

"*Mon Dieu,* did I not tell her already which sauce to use?" Minette answered, her voice sharp.

"Yes, ma'am, you did, but Mrs. Hopple says it's too rich for Sir Henry's digestion, and—"

"*Mais non.*" Minette glanced at Eleanor and rolled her eyes in half-humorous dismay. "I fear there is another battle brewing in the kitchen; I must see to it, *moi.* If you could excuse me just for a moment, *s'il vous plaît?*"

"Of course," Eleanor agreed, feeling sympathy for Minette's continued battle with her housekeeper.

Shaking her head, Minette hurried back toward the house, the little housemaid almost running to keep up.

What a headache to have such acrimony in one's own household, Eleanor thought as she strolled back out of the walled garden and turned down the lawn toward the trees at the far end. Perhaps Sir Henry could not be persuaded to let go a servant of such long service, but really, this was not fair to his wife. Men never had any concept of how hard it was to run a household smoothly—

A movement in the trees made Eleanor pause, and she suddenly wondered if it was wise for her to have walked away from the house. But even though she was in the wilds of Yorkshire, there should be nothing here to annoy her. It was likely some farm laborer or tenant coming to ask Sir Henry for advice. Perhaps it was even Sir Henry himself, taking a shortcut back to the manor after seeing to his wounded farmer.

But no, this man was on foot as he came out of the concealing brush, and he was too tall, too well-built to be the elderly squire. In fact, the figure was strangely familiar—

Eleanor felt a burst of joy spring up inside her, rushing through her veins as swiftly as the best French champagne.

"Robert!" she cried. Dropping the rose that Minette had given her, she ran into his arms.

16

"Eleanor!" Robert exclaimed in shock. He had no time to do more than open his arms to catch her as she ran to him. She threw her arms around his neck, clutching him tightly, her face flushed with joy and relief.

It was—some part of his mind recognized as he stood stock-still, almost light-headed with astonishment—exactly the homecoming he had always pictured during those long dreary years in his French prison. Eleanor would look at him just so, and run into his arms and hold him tight. When he had laid his head against rough stone walls and narrowed his eyes to shut out the grim reality, he had dreamed of this, dreams so real that he could almost feel the warmth of her in his arms, and how her rose-scented perfume would tickle his nose, and how soft her hair would feel pressed against his cheek. Those fantasies had blocked the stench of the prison, the pain of his wounds, the constant aching loneliness.

And this time it was real, it was not a part of his desperate imagination, his endless daydreams. Eleanor was here, and she had run into his arms without hesitation. Her love for him lit up her blue eyes, eyes the color of a summer sky, and colored her whole sweet face. His heart leaped inside him as he saw it. He longed to lean forward and capture her soft lips. This was all he had ever wanted—

No.

It was not to be; it was impossible.

Eleanor was married to someone else, and so was he. Katryn—his wife, Katryn—was coming up behind him; she would witness this impulsive greeting. Robert tried to pull himself together. He had to put Eleanor away from him, but his body rebelled; it was a physical strain to ease her out of his arms.

He had to let go; he had to. He wasn't sure if he could, but he heard a footfall behind him, and knew that he must try.

Eleanor's expression faltered for a moment, as if she too were returning to reality, and it was she who stepped back. Robert still stood, as immobile as one of the statues dotting a formal garden.

"What are you doing here?" he asked, his voice shaking a little with suppressed emotion. He lowered his arms slowly; they felt so empty without Eleanor. She stood only a few inches away, but it felt like a league. He had told himself that he could forget her. How did one give up the dream of so many years?

"I came—I came because I have proof of your innocence," she told him.

Robert couldn't seem to take in the words; her voice was far away, but she was so close, so close, and yet forbidden. His long-held dream of happiness, snatched away once again. He tried to take a breath, tried to make his mind work. "Proof?"

"Oh, Robert, Cavendish showed it to me, and I stole it from his desk. It's in my reticule inside the house; you must come in and I will show it to you. Everything will be all right; your arrest—it was all a mistake."

"I see," Robert muttered, but his tone was blank. His life, his freedom—they mattered, he told himself—but he still felt too stunned to think. His freedom was restored, but what did it matter, if he was never to have Eleanor?

Behind him, Katryn felt her whole body shake. They had come out of the woods to see the low-built manor house ahead, and she had known that they had at last reached their goal; her heart had been beating fast with happy anticipation. This was where the answer lay, must, must lay, if Robert was to be absolved of the untrue accusation Cavendish had leveled against him.

And then to see Eleanor, to see her sister, who should have been in London, hundreds of miles away, pop up out of the garden and run into Robert's arms—Robert's willing arms—Katryn tried to push back her feelings of betrayal.

Had it all been for naught? Their mad flight across country, the risk to life and limb, even—she bit back a sob—even their night of glorious passion that had united them she had been so sure, like nothing before.

How fast Robert seemed to have forgotten. When Eleanor appeared, Katryn was again second-best, ignored, only a distant star faint on the horizon, eclipsed by Eleanor's radiant sunny beauty.

Katryn had never felt such crushing pain, such a mortal blow. Her chest seemed to have been cleaved in two; she even glanced down toward the travel-stained, grass-spotted bodice of her gown. The cloth was whole, without rent, yet she knew that her heart had been ripped apart. And by her own sister, her own husband. She took a deep breath, trying to control the tremors that still ran through her.

"Oh, Katryn," Eleanor said brightly, glancing her way but not meeting her eyes. "I have proof of Robert's innocence—isn't it wonderful?"

Katryn swallowed, trying to make her voice work. Katryn had risked her life and her reputation to stay with her husband, to help him in his darkest hour, and it was Eleanor who now offered him his salvation? Eleanor, who stood before them in her usual pristine beauty, who didn't have a hair out of place, nor a spot mussing her well-cut silk gown?

Katryn knew she was being small-minded and petty. Of course Robert's safety was the only thing that mattered. The fact that Eleanor had given it to him was beside the point. And Katryn, wrinkled and disheveled in her plain gray gown, her hair hanging almost into her face, dirty from days and nights on the road, first on foot and now riding an ill-groomed nag that left her smelling like a badly kept stable—oh, no, that wasn't important.

But she felt a strong urge to weep.

"Come inside," Eleanor said, reaching to take Robert's hand.

He gave it to her, of course, and Katryn bit her lip to hold back her instinctive protest.

"You must be starving," Eleanor babbled on. "How on earth did you manage to get here?"

Katryn could have answered that, told her of Robert's prison-tainted nightmares, of cold nights and frantic days and attacking felons, but she pressed her lips together.

Robert shook his head. "It's a long story," he said slowly. "Have you spoken to Minette? Is she really here; can she help me?"

"I don't know if—that is, don't worry; it's all going to be all right," Eleanor assured him. She led Robert toward the house, still clutching his hand.

Katryn followed a few feet behind them, stumbling a little despite the smooth turf. She felt all of twelve years old again, awkward and ill-made beside Eleanor's willowy beauty, and she hated her sister.

Eleanor, babbling something about her fears, her journey—*her* fears? *her* journey?—led them into the house through the side door and down the hall into the empty parlor. The room was small compared to those of Manning Hall, or even Eastborne, but pleasingly if not richly furnished. Old-fashioned wooden settees had been softened with the addition of embroidered cushions. A faded Persian rug covered the much-polished wood floor, and the stone hearth of the fireplace held a fire, comforting in its warmth.

Katryn realized she had been chilled for so many days that it had become almost normal. She stretched out her bare hands to the fire—she had left behind her gloves during the fight with the horse thieves—and felt her fingers tingle with the unaccustomed warmth.

The door to the hall opened again, and Katryn glanced around. A servant with a long face, her mouth twisted in disapproval, stared at them in surprise. The woman looked first to Katryn, staring at her dusty gown, then—perhaps dismissing her as Eleanor's maidservant—turned to focus her full wrath upon Robert, who stood a little apart from the two women.

"What are ye doing in the parlor, bothering your betters? Get round to the kitchen entrance, if you have any business here at all. If not, get yourself off—we'll have no beggars at this house. Go on, now, or I'll set the dogs on ye!"

"That will do," Eleanor interrupted before Robert could speak to defend himself. "This is another guest of Sir Henry and Lady Grabble. You may lay two more places at the table, and prepare a room for the added guests."

The housekeeper's nostrils flared. "I take my orders from Sir Henry," she snapped. "Not from you, my lady, fancy title or not."

"If this household is properly run, you'll take your orders from the mistress of the house," Katryn spoke before she thought. When the older woman jerked to confront her, Katryn met her gaze without backing away.

"And who gave you permission to speak, missy?"

"This is my wife, and she needs no one's permission to speak her mind," Robert put in, his tone calm but resolute. "Certainly not yours."

The comment warmed her, though it was a small balm to the enormous hurt that left Katryn still feeling hollow inside; she bit back her own response and waited to hear Robert continue.

But the housekeeper didn't hesitate to speak. "If the real Lady Grabble—*my* Lady Grabble—were alive, there'd be no such riff-raff littering her house in their dirty rags and shaggy beards. If you think someone dressed like yon is sitting down to the table with Sir Henry himself—"

Katryn flushed slightly, aware of the deficiencies of her own costume, and then glanced at Robert's rough-made garments, now ripped and soiled by their cross-country ordeal. She could hardly blame the woman for misjudging their station, but still, it was not her place to make such a decision; she should wait upon her mistress. Was Minette, the former courtesan, having a difficult time with her servant? Did this alarming woman suspect Minette's shameful past?

"How dare you?" Eleanor's usually mild voice was raised in unaccustomed anger. "This is Robert Manning, Viscount Holt, heir to the earl of Stonesbury! Just because a traveling accident has left him a little—a little disheveled, and has stripped him of his normal wardrobe, is no reason for you to be insulting, or to forget your place. Now go and summon your mistress and leave the decisions to her!"

The housekeeper sniffed and turned abruptly to stalk out of the room; heaven only knew what she would say to her mistress, or to Sir Henry himself.

Katryn had never heard Eleanor speak so, and she would have applauded her sister in any other circumstance. But now she noted Robert's admiring glance as he watched her sister, and she felt sick at heart. For an instant, her head spun. Despite her muddy skirts, she sank onto one of the oaken settees, her knees weak with despair.

Then a sudden thought sent her back to her feet as anger and apprehension gave her new strength. "Eleanor, would you hold your tongue!"

Her sister had been gazing at Robert, the love in her eyes

so palpable that Katryn might not even have been in the room. Now she looked at Katryn and frowned. "You don't think I should put down that awful woman and her snobbery?"

"I think you've just announced Robert's full name to the greater part of the North Riding!" Katryn pointed out, her tone as sharp as her sister's. "Do you want Cavendish to find him before we can establish his innocence? After all our efforts, you'll have him in the Tower yet if you're not more careful with your words."

Eleanor's fair skin flushed with emotion. "Don't be silly; weren't you listening? I told you, I have proof of Robert's innocence."

"You stole a letter from Cavendish?" Robert asked slowly. Was he still admiring her sister's soft blue eyes, her delicate complexion, her tall, slender frame? He had looked just so on the evenings he had sat with Eleanor in the drawing room at Eastborne, while Katryn watched from across the room, feeling that her heart would break. She felt even more miserable now, when she had had his love—or so she'd thought—for such a brief and wonderful night. And now his passion had waned; once again, his heart belonged to Eleanor.

Robert was speaking; Katryn tried to focus on his words and push down her own misery, hoping it did not show. Bad enough to be spurned; she had no wish to be pitied, too.

"Show me the letter, Eleanor," Robert said, his voice now urgent.

Eleanor opened the elegant reticule that she had left on the side table and took out a folded paper. Wordless, her eyes shining with anticipation, she held it out to Robert, who almost snatched it from her grip.

Katryn, her knees weak again, sank down onto one of the wooden chairs. The paper looked very fresh, she thought absently, to have come through the rigors of a military campaign. Was it true that this letter would save Robert? She prayed it was so, even if it would give him back to Eleanor. Even if she were left miserable and alone, she did not wish to see Robert dead.

Robert scanned the handwritten lines on both sides of the sheet, then went back and read the letter again more slowly. His expression was hard to read. But when he looked up, despite his struggle to compose himself, Katryn saw that despair had settled back into the lines around his mouth.

"Eleanor," he said slowly, "I know you took this in good faith. But the letter is a forgery."

"What?" Eleanor gasped and grabbed the edge of a tall settee to steady herself as if she might swoon. "Are you sure? How can you be certain, Robert? It must be genuine!"

He shook his head. "It is dated June 1814; Colonel Richmond was killed eight months before this letter was supposedly penned. In fact, I suspect that Cavendish wrote it himself. The handwriting is nothing like that seen in Richmond's other papers."

"Why would Cavendish do such a thing?" Eleanor demanded, her brows contracted over her blue eyes as she tried to work it out. "Why show me the letter and claim that it would prove your innocence?"

"Perhaps he wanted to find out if you knew where Robert was; did you tell him?" Katryn demanded.

"Of course not, I am not so foolish!" Stung, Eleanor glared at her younger sister.

"I should like to believe that," Katryn retorted. "But if you did not tell him, he has likely followed your path north. You have doubtless led Cavendish straight to Robert by your ill-planned flight. After all our dangers evaded, you will be the cause of his destruction!"

"My ill-planned flight! You were the one who insisted on going with him, despite any reason or logic." Eleanor's blue eyes flashed, and her soft voice rose.

"I was a help to him!" Katryn insisted.

"You must have slowed him down; just because he is too gentlemanly to tell you so—"

Gentlemanly? For a moment, Katryn had a mad desire to giggle; she thought of their bodies rolling and heaving in passion against a mossy, star-lit bank. Robert was not always such a gentleman as Eleanor seemed to think. Katryn raised her chin and met her sister's furious gaze.

"I am his wife," she said.

Eleanor gasped, one hand flying to her cheek as if she had been struck.

"I have the right to share good times and bad," Katryn continued doggedly.

Eleanor's face went as pale as it had been flushed, and she didn't answer. Suddenly all Katryn could hear in the small parlor was the crackling of the fire. Eleanor's eyes seemed blank, and she looked down from Katryn's steady gaze. Robert had turned his head away from them both; he stared at the fire as if all the secrets to the conundrum that bound the three of them together lay in its dancing scarlet depths.

They stood without moving, without speaking, as if they had been caught in some oil painting, motionless and mute. It could only have been a few moments, but it felt like an eternity. Katryn was caught up in her own private pain, and she could only guess what the other two suffered. Then the door opened, and the spell was broken. Katryn turned to see Minette in the doorway.

Eleanor, to Katryn's annoyance, took it upon herself to explain. "Minette, this is—"

"Robert!" Minette exclaimed, her voice husky with shock. "You are here, *non, non—c'est impossible!* I cannot do it."

They all gazed at her in astonishment, though Eleanor's expression might have been tinged with guilt, her sister thought absently.

"What?" Katryn put in, unable to be silent; she didn't totally understand, but she knew the answer might be vitally important to Robert's survival. "What can you not do?"

"Robert, you know—*n'est-ce pas?*" Minette's voice caught in a sob that she tried to contain. When she could speak again, she continued, "You know that I cannot—cannot tell—"

Robert nodded. "I understand your situation, Minette, and it pains me to have to ask. But you may be the only one who stands between me and the gallows."

Katryn shuddered, and Eleanor cried out in protest. But Minette, though tears glistened in her eyes, shook her head. "*Non,* I cannot," she repeated. "Besides, who would believe such a one as *moi?* They would laugh, the court, your judges, and it would all be for naught."

"No," Katryn argued. "You would be believed, they would have to—"

Minette seemed to brace herself, but her tone was resolute. "*Non,*" she repeated. "You must comprehend."

Robert hesitated, his expression twisted, as if not sure how to answer.

"I don't understand," Katryn cried, her voice shrill with fear and frustration. "It is not a small thing we are talking of—it is his life! Don't you know what you are doing? How can you say you will not help him?"

Minette lifted her chin, gazing at the three of them, all united against her. The Frenchwoman had backed against the closed door as if they might physically attack her. But her expression remained stubborn.

"*Non,* it is a small thing," she almost whispered. "I think you will have to see to understand. Come with me, quietly, if you please."

She opened the parlor door and went out into the hall. Not sure what their hostess could mean, Katryn hurried to follow. Eleanor came just behind her, and then Robert. All three of them followed the petite Frenchwoman along the hall, up the stairs to the next level, and then up another, narrower flight of stairs.

What on earth was she doing? Katryn wondered. Why would Minette take them up to the servants' quarters. But when Minette opened a door and led them into a small suite of rooms, Katryn understood, all at once, with blinding clarity.

Another fire crackled in a small fireplace; the walls were white and hung with delicate watercolors. A maidservant curtsied to her mistress, glancing at the visitors in obvious surprise.

"You may go," Minette told the servant, her tone abrupt.

The young girl looked surprised but did not try to protest; she picked up the mending she had been working on and left the room, pulling the door shut behind her.

Katryn barely noticed. She was staring at another piece of furniture that stood by the fire, close enough for warmth on a cold night, but not too close to the tin fire guard that protected against flying sparks. It was a cradle, and inside she glimpsed a tiny face pink with good health, blue eyes bright with anticipation.

The baby cooed in delight when it saw its mother's face bend over it. Minette reached down to pick up the child and held it close to her breast. Her expression softened into one of deep love as she kissed the baby on its forehead, smoothing the long lacy skirt of its dress.

"This is my daughter, Henrietta," Minette said, her voice gentle but her expression, as she glanced toward them, fierce with all the protective instincts of motherhood. "I would not—cannot—destroy her hopes for a future untainted by scandal. I want her to have everything that I did not—every chance for happiness."

"Why would helping Robert hurt your baby?" Eleanor demanded. "I don't see—"

"Hush, Eleanor," Katryn interrupted. "You don't know

the whole situation." Ignoring her sister's affronted gasp, Katryn dropped to her knees beside the cradle. "We would not ask if it were not so important," Katryn said to Minette, her tone low. She gazed at their hostess as if the two were alone in the room. "But you may be his only hope. And if his reputation is restored, he will inherit his father's title, you know. We would not forget what you had done. We could sponsor your daughter when she is of age, make sure she has the best possible chances for a good life, a good alliance."

Minette shook her head slowly, still holding the baby close to her. "*Non*. Who would wish to affiliate themselves with a girl whose family was tainted with such a scandal, whose mother—whose mother—"

"Minette, please," Katryn interrupted. "Your friends will understand—"

"My friends? You think so? And my husband?" Minette's expression twisted. She glanced at Robert, then as quickly away. "My husband does not know about—about all of my background, you see. I met him in London when a runaway carriage almost ran me down; he pulled me from its path, and he was so kind. I told him I had fled from France and its disorder. But if he knew—if he knew all, he would divorce me, and I would lose my husband, my home, and my child."

Katryn swallowed hard. It was true. A divorced woman had no rights to her children, no legal recourse. And if Minette had no family to go to—she would be homeless and penniless, reduced to the only trade she knew. Katryn remembered the lewd drunk who had tried to invade the bath during their brief sojourn at the London brothel and shuddered despite herself. Of course, she and Robert could shelter Minette, protect her, give her an allowance to live upon, but it wasn't enough. What reward could anyone possibly offer for testimony that would cause Minette to sacrifice her own child?

Her mouth dry, Katryn found no words ready, and it was Robert who answered.

"It's all right," Robert said quietly. "I do not wish to destroy your chances of happiness, nor ruin your marriage and see you lose your infant."

"Robert!" Eleanor protested. "It is your life."

"And it is Minette's life, and that of her child," he said. "I would not ask anyone to sacrifice so much for me."

He shut his eyes for a moment and saw his younger sisters' faces. They would face the scandal, the penury instead, he thought, his heart heavy. But when he opened his eyes again and saw the flush of gratitude on Minette's face, he knew he was doing the right thing. One family could not be ruined to save another.

Eleanor looked resentful; Katryn's expression was harder to read. She stood up, nodding slightly as if acknowledging her defeat, but her eyes were dark with sorrow.

"Thank you," Minette said, her voice very quiet. The baby whimpered a little; and Minette looked down and relaxed her too-tight hold. "I cannot give up my child. I thought you must understand when you knew."

"I don't understand at all," Eleanor snapped, her tone rebellious.

Katryn glanced at her sister, but this time she was silent, and no one answered.

Minette kissed the infant, then laid her carefully back into the cradle and called the nurse back to take charge of the nursery. Then she led them back to the second floor to another guest room, next to the one, Katryn found, that Eleanor had been assigned. Eleanor's expression was still sullen; she disappeared into her own room without any further comment.

"You would like to wash, *n'est-ce pas?*" Minette told them, as if determined to take refuge in the ordinary. Perhaps her nerves too had been strained to the breaking point by the stress of their confrontation. "Dinner will be ready soon, *j'assure,* and despite my housekeeper's arrogance, you will of course sit down with us. I'm afraid I have no clothes for you, Robert. My husband is—you are not at all the same size."

If their current circumstance had not been so desperate, Katryn would have laughed to think of Robert trying to wear garments donated by the short, portly Sir Henry. But laughter wouldn't come. She tried to steady herself; it would be good to wash her face and hands and try to pin up her hair, and then somehow, somehow, they had to think of a way, of another way, out of this quagmire.

She could not seem to realize that their last, best hope had failed them. Yet she admired Robert for his refusal to demand Minette's testimony—despite the fact that Katryn would suffer with him, face scandal and privation, and, most of all, feel the wrenching pain of losing Robert all over again. No, she couldn't think about that now; after a meal, after a few hours' sleep, something would come to her. Katryn would not, could not give up hope.

When they were alone in the bedchamber, she glanced at her husband. She wanted to go to him, throw her arms around him as Eleanor had done on the lawn, but something held her back. His face was grim, his eyes far away; he did not even seem to remember she was in the same room. Perhaps it was already too late for Robert and Katryn.

The maidservant brought up a pitcher of warm water and poured some of the liquid into the small china basin that sat on a table at the corner of the room. She set down the pitcher, curtsied and left the room.

Katryn cupped the clean water in her hands and splashed her face. She felt a wave of nausea but she pushed it back. Not now, she could not be missish now! She must clean up, and also try to do something to her hair. Robert might have precious little freedom left; she must try to look more presentable, not only because Eleanor was her usual elegant self, but so that Robert would have a better memory of his wife when he was once again hauled away to prison, perhaps even to the scaffold. No, no, she'd promised herself not to think of that now. Katryn dipped a cloth into the warm water, took the rose-scented soap, and concentrated grimly on her ablutions.

She paused when someone knocked at the door; Robert opened it. The little housemaid had returned. "I have a jacket and a shirt that you might wish to try, my lord. If you would step outside."

It took a moment for her words to register, then Robert nodded slowly. What did it matter what he wore? But he followed the servant out into the hallway and, to his surprise, he found Eleanor holding the garments.

Before he could remark, the maid disappeared down the hall. Eleanor motioned him toward her own room.

"Sir Henry wore these years ago, so they may fit your chest size, though I fear the sleeves will be too short. That's all she can do for you, however. Minette's husband has nothing that might fit your long legs, Robert, though I think I can mend some of the worst rents in those trousers. I have borrowed a needle and thread; come inside for a moment and let me see what I can do."

Her tone was matter-of-fact. After a moment's hesitation, Robert followed her into the next room. Eleanor shut the door behind them and laid the shirt on the bureau; she came closer and held up the jacket to measure it against the length of his arm.

"This should—should—" Her voice faltered as they stood so close together.

Robert's own resolve wavered, too. "Eleanor—"

She lowered the jacket and stared up at him, her blue eyes sparkling with unshed tears. "Robert, why can you not insist that this woman—that Minette must help you? I don't understand. Just because her background is not as exalted as her odious housekeeper would desire, that will not wreck her life."

Eleanor's voice was husky with emotion. Robert fought back the urge to comfort her. His desire to take her into his arms was so strong he had to tighten his hands into fists, trying to restrain himself.

"There is more to it than that," he tried to explain. Minette's secrets were not his to broadcast, and he fumbled with a logical explanation that would not give too much away. "But—but she does have reason to fear from public exposure, Eleanor. And if her husband chose to cast her off . . ."

"He would not do that; he loves her, I think," Eleanor said, her voice breaking a little. "She is lucky in that, no matter what else happens. Even stuck in this tiny estate in the north of England, and suffering from a termagant of a housekeeper, despite all of it, Minette is more fortunate than most of the women I know."

It was too close to a confession of her own situation, and Eleanor could not go on. A lump in her throat held back the words, and she found that her vision wavered as tears flooded her eyes. She tried to blink them back, but one slipped out, sliding down her cheek.

"Eleanor, don't—" Robert put out his hand to wipe away the tear, and then he was drawing her closer. He bent to kiss her lips.

Eleanor felt the pressure of his lips against hers, and her heart leapt with joy. In the garden, she had been the one who had run forward, her joyous surprise sending her into his arms. Robert had seemed too stunned to return her embrace.

This time, he pulled her into his arms with a strength that surprised her, and the kiss was all that she could wish for. Eleanor shut her eyes and surrendered to the moment; whatever came later, she would face. But right now she had

Robert, and she could lean into his arms and match his passion.

For a long and wonderful moment, everything was perfect; it was all that she had dreamed of during his long absence, before the terrible news of his death was delivered.

But then his kiss became more fervent, and Eleanor felt surprise mingle with her delight. This was not at all like the chivalrous, restrained kiss that she and Robert had shared when she had accepted his proposal of marriage. Robert had been a little diffident, but it hadn't mattered; she had been shy and thrilled by his least touch.

Of course, she and her husband had shared many conjugal encounters since their wedding night, but Edward was always gentle, and he knew just what she liked. The thought that he might have held himself back a little, for her sake, had never occurred to her before. But Robert—she had never expected such forceful, almost crude energy in his embrace.

She realized that he smelled of sweat and horseflesh and the dirt of the fields, like any farm laborer, and his cheek was covered with days-old growth of beard; the stubble scratched the tender skin of her face, and she winced a little and tried to draw back. But Robert was kissing her still, and he had pressed her against the inside of the door, holding her back against the hardwood as his tongue slipped inside her opened lips, his passion clearly growing.

He ran his hand lightly over her breast, cupping it within his palm, and his body was hard against her own. How could he act so, when they were not even in bed, were still fully clothed?

Alarmed and confused, Eleanor tried to push him away. This was not the careful, controlled suitor she remembered from her girlhood. This was nothing like her wistful daydreams, not what she had wanted. . . .

It took Robert several moments to realize that Eleanor

was no longer responding to his embrace. She stood inside his arms and her body had stiffened, but not with passion; he released her slowly, not sure what was wrong. This was a kiss he had dreamed of for years. But Eleanor gazed up at him now with a strange expression.

And he realized that something had been missing even before Eleanor drew back. He had been seeking in her, without quite realizing it, the same heartfelt, untrammeled passion that Katryn had revealed to him; he had expected Eleanor to meet his body's need and answer it with appetites of her own. Instead, she had pulled back, and she gazed at him now with doubt clouding her blue eyes.

"Robert," she whispered, then she hesitated and bit her lip. "You—you are so changed."

He glanced down at the homespun garments he wore, tried to see himself through her eyes, dirty and unshaven and disreputable, perhaps even somewhat dangerous. Changed? If he hadn't felt a swift moment of sadness, he might have laughed. Years of warfare, years in prison, now his life and his family's future at stake in a desperate search for the truth—of course he had changed. It would take time for Eleanor to know him again, but—

Eleanor stepped back. "I think you had better go before anyone comes," she said softly, not meeting his eye.

It was a dismissal, and he retreated a little farther. "You're right; I don't wish to cause you—or Katryn—embarrassment," he told her, feeling a sudden wave of guilt. He should not have yielded to temptation in such a way; it was very wrong. But he gazed at her, trying to remember this moment, and unrequited longing made his voice husky. "Whitmund is a lucky man."

Eleanor's mouth twisted, and he could not read her expression. Perhaps he had made her feel guilty, too; it had not been his intent.

"Eleanor—"

She interrupted, reaching for the shirt and cravat and holding up the evening jacket that only moments ago had been crushed between them. She handed the garments to Robert. "Here, take these and try them for size. And here is a cravat, too, though sadly old-fashioned. I do hope they fit. You make a strange sight, indeed, just at the moment. I will see to your trousers another time. Katryn never did have much of a hand for needlework."

Her tone was wry, but she managed to smile at him. Robert took the clothing she held out and followed her as she reached for the brass door handle.

When she swung the door open, her eyes widened, and just behind her, Robert stiffened in shock.

The hallway was no longer empty. Katryn stood in front of the bedroom door, staring at them both in disbelief.

17

Katryn looked from one to the other, her expression blank with shock. Robert felt a wave of guilt; he hadn't meant to hurt her. He thought for an instant that she might turn and flee. He should have known better.

"How dare you!" Katryn demanded, folding her arms and facing them both squarely, her green eyes hard with anger.

"It's not what it seems," Robert tried to interrupt. "I only—"

"W-we were only—the jacket—I wanted to see if it fit," Eleanor put in at the same moment, stuttering a little in her haste to get the words out.

"Oh, I know what fit you are interested in," Katryn snapped, glaring at her sister.

"Don't speak like a fishwife!" Eleanor fired back. "Remember your station, please! You might show a little breeding."

"And this is how you show yours?"

In one corner of his mind, Robert couldn't help feeling a quiver of laughter. If this were not so serious—if he had not behaved very badly indeed—he would smile for real.

Eleanor's blue eyes were narrowed, their expression almost as severe as Katryn's. "I was only helping with his clothes. I borrowed a needle and thread from the maid; you know you have no hand at stitchery."

"I can sew quite as well as you," Katryn retorted. "And I can take care of my own husband, thank you very much!"

"If I hadn't thought that he needed assistance, I should never have offered—"

"Don't patronize me!" Katryn interrupted. "Just because you are older—"

"Just because you never listen to your elders—"

Robert thought of the goose fight he had once witnessed as a child, the two fowls with their wings raised, beaks extended, feathers flying, hissing in truly ferocious display as they stabbed and feinted. It had taken a large pail of cold water to break it up, he remembered. He wasn't sure there was enough water in the manor to accomplish the same thing, now.

He was wrong. The young maidservant approached from the end of the hall carrying a pitcher of hot water, and Eleanor suddenly remembered her dignity.

"I will not exchange words with you in front of the staff," she said, lowering her voice abruptly. "When you can discuss this in a mature manner—"

Katryn seemed ready to battle on. "If I ever get so 'mature' that I stand by and watch my own sister and my husband carry on behind my back—"

Now the servant was eyeing them with obvious curiosity. Eleanor, her lips pressed into a thin line, turned on her heel and slammed the door on them both. Katryn frowned.

Would she listen to his apology? "Katryn—"

Now it was Katryn's turn to wheel and march back into the next room, slamming the door soundly as he tried to follow. He knocked on the door gently, then tried the handle.

It was locked.

"Katryn, please let me in." He spoke quietly into the time-worn oaken grain of the door, feeling both ridiculous and chagrined. "I am sorry, truly, but it was not what you think. Eleanor was only helping me with a jacket."

The excuse sounded foolish to his own ears; he couldn't imagine what Katryn was thinking. No, he *could* imagine, and none of it was good.

He tapped very lightly, but there was still no response. Robert sighed. This day only seemed to get worse and worse. In a moment, he heard the maid return along the corridor and he turned his head.

The servant's dark eyes gleamed with curiosity. Likely this out-of-the-way manor hadn't had so much to speculate about since Minette herself had come back with Sir Henry from London, the new and unexpected bride.

"Would ye be needing anything else, sir?" the maid asked, her tone polite but her expression too eager.

Robert tried to pull his thoughts together. "Actually, I would very much like the use of a razor," he told her, rubbing his whiskery chin. "My kit, not to say my manservant, is not with me at present, but if your master would be so kind—"

The maid wrinkled her forehead. "Sir Henry ain't back as yet, sir, but I 'spect I could let you use his second-best razor."

"That would be fine," Robert agreed gravely. A rough beard was much easier to deal with than an angry woman, anyhow. Or worse, two angry women.

"I'll just fetch it for you," she said.

Robert followed her down the hall instead of lingering foolishly outside his own door. At the end of the corridor, however, he waited while the servant went into her master's room to retrieve the blade. He had no wish to enter any more strange bedrooms this day; he'd gotten himself into trouble enough already. When the maid brought the straight razor, he took it carefully and walked back to his assigned room.

This time when he tried the doorknob, it turned easily.

Heartened by this evidence of his wife's relenting—if she would just listen to him, he would most humbly beg her pardon—Robert hurried inside. But his mood darkened again as he saw that the room was empty.

His first impulse was to rush after her; Katryn had perhaps gone down to the drawing room to wait for dinner to be announced. But what if she hadn't? He would look a total fool wandering around the house half-dressed. Taking a deep breath, he shook his head. No. No wild-goose chases—better to give her time for her anger to abate, then maybe she would listen to his apology. He had been wrong to go into Eleanor's bedroom, knowing his own weakness, knowing that a mistaken interpretation of his actions could wound his wife. After Katryn had done so much for him, it was ill-met of him to repay her in such a fashion.

He poured fresh water, now a little tepid, into the flowered china bowl and set about removing several days' growth of brown beard.

Jerod Cavendish stood inside the tiny, out-of-the-way shop that displayed the traditional three gilt balls over its entrance. The small man with the olive skin who watched him seemed already to sense his desperation. He held Jerod's watch in his palm, touching the gold face with an experienced fingertip.

"As I said, sir, two guineas is the best I can do. It's not in the best of shape, and—"

"It's worth five times that or more!" Jerod exploded, striving to hold back his anger. "If I were in London in reach of my usual man—"

He paused, realizing he had said too much; despite his silence, the man's expression seemed to mask hidden laughter. Did the little weasel realize that Jerod had often had to resort to moneylenders, that he lived his life on the edge of financial ruin?

Frustration rose inside his throat like bile, bitter and foul-tasting. If only Whitmund had not thrown him out of the carriage—the arrogant fool would pay for that, one day. To have come so far, to be so close, so close—and still unable to complete his masterful plan. And now to have this little rat of a man stand between Jerod and its successful fruition—the rage he felt turned his vision crimson and would no longer be contained.

Something in his expression must have alerted the other man, because he dropped the watch hastily upon the polished table that stood between them.

Jerod reached to grab the little man's throat, but found his own hand caught in an unexpectedly strong grip.

"I wouldn't, if I were you, sir," the other man said, his tone hard. "If my proposition doesn't please you, you can go elsewhere."

"There is no one else willing to lend money in this accursed rathole," Jerod snapped. "As you well know. I inquired before I came here."

The man nodded gravely. "Indeed."

"It's not enough," Jerod repeated, his voice hoarse with the unfairness of it all. "I need a horse—I must get there before Manning—before he escapes me. I must!"

The man's bland, self-satisfied expression didn't change. "I regret that two guineas is the best I can do, sir."

Jerod had a dagger in his boot; if he could reach it before the man gave the alarm—he must have a fortune tucked away in a strongbox somewhere in his shop. But then a flicker of movement at the side of his vision made Jerod pause. A stout woman in a plain brown dress had come into the shop.

"Yes, Mistress Lindley, I'll be with you in just a moment," the moneylender called out.

Jerod threw one quick glance at her fat, foolish face. Just

the sort of woman to erupt into hysterical screams and bring the whole village down upon him.

Cursing, he picked up his watch and strode out of the shop, ignoring the affronted expression on the woman's face, and let the door bang shut behind him.

He would not be bested—he would not! There had to be another way.

Downstairs, Katryn found herself alone in the parlor when she opened the door. She walked across to stand before the fire, which needed tending. The blaze was low, and the temperature in the room had cooled, much like her own heart. Her anger at Eleanor had faded into a chill despair.

It was obvious now that Robert would never love her, and she had a decision to make. He didn't even come after her to argue his innocence; he had protested little. Not that it mattered; she knew Robert and Eleanor's history and how long their attachment had endured. She had been a fool to think that she could ever wean him away from his first love. A fool, a fool, she thought bitterly. A fool to think she could settle for being second-best, that she could be happy with only scraps of his affection. Where had her mind been, or her pride? She would end up spending her days much like Minette, scorned by her housekeeper as a poor imitation of the real thing. Only in Katryn's case, it would be much worse—it would be her husband, not her servant, who could not accept her.

Despite the heaviness inside her, Katryn could not help looking up when the door opened again, but it was only Minette, followed by her husband, Sir Henry. Katryn curtsied to the stout older man as Minette made the introductions, hoping he didn't stare at her drab outfit. She had done what she could to repair her appearance, but the gown was still plain and obviously travel-stained, ill-suited for sitting down to dinner.

"Lady Manning's husband will be down shortly," Minette added.

Katryn couldn't imagine how Minette had explained their presence, but Sir Henry's greeting was polite enough, if short and to the point.

"Happy to make your acquaintance, my lady. I understand you're in something of a bind."

Katryn opened her mouth to reply, then wasn't sure what to say. Minette broke in, her eyes bright.

"The accident to your carriage—it was so distressing, *n'est-ce pas?*"

"Yes, indeed," Katryn agreed cautiously. "Very upsetting."

Sir Henry gave a snort of laughter. "Upsetting—yes, to be sure."

She smiled, too, though she hadn't meant to jest.

"So fortunate you knew where to find your sister, Lady Whitmund," Minette went on. "So you can all journey on together in her carriage until your own is repaired." The unspoken desire to see them journey on as soon as possible was strongly hinted at; it hung in the air like smoke from the fire, Katryn thought. Yet who could blame Minette for wanting this whole explosive set of visitors out of the way before their shaky deception crashed into rubble, brought down by its own mendacious weight?

Eleanor came into the room as Minette was speaking. She glanced at her sister, her expression cool, then turned to speak politely to their hostess.

Robert entered last. "I'm sorry to be so long, Lady Grabble, Sir Henry," he said. "You must forgive my somewhat unconventional appearance."

"Of course." Minette introduced him to her husband, and the two men eyed each other warily.

"Evening, my lord," the older man said. "Had a little problem with your wardrobe, eh?"

"Yes," Robert agreed, and wisely refused to elaborate. Instead, he looked quickly at his wife, but in that strangely assorted company, there was little he could say to Katryn, or she to him.

Katryn did not try to hold his gaze. It was just as well, perhaps, that they could not speak privately, as she suddenly knew what she must say, and she had no idea how she could tell him. The resolution was barely formed, but she knew that it was the right choice.

Minette directed them all into dinner, and Robert, as the only male guest, took her into the dining room on his arm. They made a strange pair; he wore his borrowed, out-of-date evening coat and shirt and cravat with the same rough trousers he had arrived in. Minette, petite and almost child-like at his side, was dressed in tasteful if not quite up-to-the-minute style in lavender silk.

With unexpected gallantry, Sir Henry offered an arm to each remaining lady; they walked in together, Eleanor on one side and Katryn on the other. But Sir Henry spoke little to either of them and seemed instead to watch Robert talking in low tones with Minette. Katryn did not speak to Eleanor; it would have been too awkward to converse over Sir Henry's balding pate, and what could she have said in front of the whole ill-assorted group?

The much-delayed dinner had not improved by the waiting; the roast was overdone, and the sauce lumpy. Katryn thought briefly of the cook fighting with the housekeeper and Minette trying to keep them all in line—it was a wonder anything edible ever came out of that kitchen.

Never in her life had Katryn endured such a strange and difficult meal. So many people at the table knew so many differing fabrications of the truth that it was hard to remember what could be safely discussed. They were wont to fall into long, awkward silences, while they plowed their way through the dishes offered to them by the maidservant.

Eleanor tried to talk of gardening, but even that unexceptional topic had its thorns. "That large rosebush you showed me has such a delightful hue," she told their hostess. "I'm sure your special touch has aided its growth."

"*Mais non,* that one was planted by the first Lady Grabble," Minette explained, her tone diffident. "She was a wonderful gardener, is that not so, *Henri?*"

Her husband looked up from his plate for a moment. "Ah, yes, just so." Then he went back to his roast, as if impatient with trivial conversation.

Despite all the uncertainties, Robert ate the plain fare with obvious appetite; they were both still famished from their long and difficult trek. Katryn knew that she should eat, too; her stomach was empty, but it also quivered with all the emotion she strove to contain, and that made it hard for her to swallow. She chewed slowly, trying not to think of the past or the future, or even Minette's urgent need of a decent cook.

"Yorkshire is a lovely county." Eleanor still labored to continue a normal dinnertime conversation. "I'm sure you must enjoy its many unspoiled natural vistas, especially after the busy London streets."

Minette flushed, and Robert dropped his fork with a clatter. Katryn bit back an exclamation and glanced at Sir Henry. His gaze remained doggedly fixed on his plate.

This time, the silence seemed to crackle with unspoken tension. Eleanor, not understanding why her innocuous comment could cause strain, looked from Minette to Robert, her expression puzzled.

"Um, yes, Yorkshire is much more pleasant than London," Katryn put in, trying to ease the moment. "Rural scenes are always a delight after the crowded streets"—her voice wavered, and she forced herself to continue—"after the busy congestion of a city. I'm sure you're both very lucky to live in such an area of rural serenity."

"Um . . ." Sir Henry chewed hard and swallowed. "No doubt. Don't you and your husband have a country estate, Lady Manning?"

"Well, yes," Katryn agreed. "Of course." Any person of rank would have; the question was almost rhetorical. "As does my sister," she added with bright archness.

"Tell us about your estate, Lady Whitmund," Minette said, picking up the conversational gambit. "I'm sure it is *très belle*."

Eleanor stared hard at the silver candlestick in front of her plate, as if trying to pull her thoughts together.

"Um, Whitmund Hall is not huge, but it has been in my husband's family for two hundred years."

If the housekeeper were within earshot, she would tell them that Sir Henry's family line was older, Katryn thought. She glanced at Robert, wishing she could share the joke with him, then, her heart sinking, remembered. No, that time was past.

"The park is very pleasing, and the garden makes a good vista, too, though I'm sure your roses are more handsome," Eleanor told Minette, her lips curving sweetly. "The new bushes you have added complement the original design of the garden so nicely."

Minette smiled, looking gratified. "You are too kind. I must show you a new cutting after dinner."

Eleanor was always charming, Katryn thought, quelling the desire to toss a chunk of potato at her sister. Everyone liked Eleanor. Everyone loved Eleanor. Most especially, Katryn's husband.

Fine, then, she and Robert could be happy, together. Katryn had had enough. She no longer worried how she would tell him; she could barely keep the words inside her lips.

Minette and Eleanor continued to chatter about gardening until even Eleanor ran out of polite chitchat, and silence once more fell heavily over the table. Head down, Sir Henry attended to his dinner, seeming to feel no obligation to entertain these unexpected, poorly explained visitors. Katryn was afraid to open her mouth, afraid of what rash accusations might pour out, and Robert was quiet, too. If Katryn had not had much more on her mind than a ruined dinner party, she would have felt sorry for Minette.

Thankfully, they had reached the last course and Katryn could foresee this awful dinner ending soon, when the housekeeper herself suddenly appeared in the doorway.

"You have *another* visitor, Sir Henry," she announced, looking grimly pleased.

Katryn felt fear flash through her. Cavendish! Had Cavendish found them? She looked across at Robert, who had gone still, with the fork halfway to his mouth. He looked frozen; slowly, he lowered the food back to his plate and seemed to brace himself.

Eleanor's eyes were big, and even Minette had gone pale. Only Sir Henry looked as unmoved as ever, though his eyes were alert. "Show 'em in, then," he told the housekeeper.

In her best this-is-more-like-company-should-be voice, the woman announced, "Lord Whitmund."

Then Whitmund stood in the doorway, his many-caped coat splashed with mud, his hair wind-tossed, his square face weary, and his expression grim.

Katryn saw Robert relax just slightly, and she drew a deep breath, hoping her heartbeat was not as loud as it seemed in her own ears. Not Cavendish, not yet.

Eleanor jerked, and the wineglass she had been about to sip from slipped out of her hands and fell, splashing the last drops of red wine across the white linen cloth. "Edward! What are you doing here?"

He ignored her question, glancing instead toward the head of the table.

"Your servant, sir," he said to Sir Henry. "Pardon me for barging into your home without invitation."

Sir Henry shrugged. "Seems to be our week for company," he pointed out, his tone wry. "My wife will have another setting put out for you."

Minette, who had watched the wine spill anxiously, was already signaling to the maidservant, whose eyes were almost as big as Eleanor's. More fodder for the servants to gossip about belowstairs.

Whitmund shook his head. "Thank you, but I am not hungry. Eleanor, I would speak to you privately. If you would excuse us, Sir Henry, Lady Grabble? Family matters."

Sir Henry nodded. "Thought it might be," he said, and reached for another sip of his wine.

Minette stared at this new arrival and muttered something beneath her breath; she looked worried.

Eleanor had flushed, but her expression was again composed as if she realized that she was the focus of everyone's attention. Still, when she rose from the table and walked toward the door, she wavered a little as if her legs were unsteady. Whitmund followed her out of the dining room.

Outside, Mrs. Hopple stood a few feet from the door. Odious woman! Eleanor threw her one icy look and then ignored her.

She and her husband walked in silence to the parlor—Eleanor was not sure where else to take him, and hopefully the rest of the party would stay at table for a while longer. They went inside and Eleanor, remembering the nosy housekeeper, shut the door firmly behind them.

When Whitmund motioned for her to sit, her mind—which had seemed to go blank at the first sight of her husband's unexpected arrival—began slowly to function again. Her first thought was so alarming that she put one hand to her mouth.

"The baby—he is not ill? Whitmund, tell me little Fitz is all right!"

Whitmund seemed to relax just for an instant; he shook his head. "The child is well."

Eleanor felt dizzy from relief; she almost fell into one of the settees. If her son had fallen sick while she was hundreds of miles away, she could never have forgiven herself. Then why was Edward looking so grim? He must be truly angry at her—so angry he would never forgive her. Perhaps, perhaps he would divorce her over this. She tried to prepare herself for the worst.

"Why have you come?" she whispered.

He took a step closer to where she sat on the wooden settee, and she shrank back instinctively, his expression was so agitated.

"Why have I come? My wife leaves home with the slightest of explanations and journeys hundreds of miles to join a man who—who has been publicly accused of treason, and you ask me why I have come? Have you been traveling with him, Eleanor? Did Katryn agree to such an arrangement?"

"Of course not, it's not like—like you mean, at all." Eleanor bit her lip to hold back the tears. She had never dealt well with other people's wrath. Edward had never before shouted at her; he seldom became agitated, and he had never acted this way in her presence. But she must endure this the best she could; he did have cause for his anger.

"Robert is not guilty—" She tried to speak, but her husband interrupted.

"That is for a court to decide; I will not have you drawn into the scandal or, God forbid, accused of complicity yourself. I must protect you from your kind heart, Eleanor. We will turn Robert over to the authorities."

She felt hysterical laughter in the back of her throat and controlled it only with the greatest effort. To the local magistrate, their host, in fact, who sat a few rooms away sedately eating his stewed prunes. But he would be dangerous enough to Robert, despite his mild appearance, capable of sending him back to London in chains.

"No!" she said. "You must not; he is not guilty, I know he could not be a traitor. That was why I came in the first place, Edward. Cavendish lured me to his rooms with the promise of important information. I took a letter from his desk that I thought would clear Robert, but now Robert says it is a forgery, and Katryn fears I have led Cavendish to Robert."

Whitmund frowned. "You have," he said gruffly. "I journeyed most of the way with that wretched man. But it is not our concern, Eleanor. We must leave this to the law to sort out."

"How can it not be our concern!" Eleanor forgot her own fears to defend Robert. "He is innocent. If Cavendish could lie about the letter I saw, how can we trust his accusations, his sources? You know he has so much to gain from Robert's death!"

Edward grimaced. "I understand, but it is you I am most concerned about. My family honor is involved here, too, you know, and our son's well-being. It is not just his health we must guard. You must think what you are doing. Do you wish to see me in gaol for abetting a criminal?"

She flushed again. "Of course not! But we cannot be the cause of his capture; he must have the chance, the time he needs to clear his name."

"Even if our family suffers for it?" Edward's voice rose again, and his tone was bitter. "But why do I bother to ask; you made your preferences clear when you left home to follow him, Eleanor."

She had to force herself to answer calmly. "I know that it looks bad, Edward," she said, her voice barely above a whisper. "But I did have good reason for coming here."

"Oh, I know the reason!" he snapped, his tone so savage that she shrank back even farther, bumping into the hard wooden back of the settee. Her heart pounded, and it was difficult to breathe. She had never, ever seen her husband in such a state.

"I know how you feel about Manning," he went on, pounding one fist into his palm. It made Eleanor wince; would he strike her? Edward had never done such a thing, though some husbands did. She had never been afraid of him before, but then, she had never before seen him like this.

Eleanor tried to interrupt, tried to say something that would calm him. "No, no, really, I have done nothing to disgrace you, I promise. Don't be angry, please, don't."

He hardly seemed to notice. "I know that he has your heart, has always had your heart. I know that you married me mainly because your parents urged it, Eleanor."

He had never spoken about this; Eleanor felt faint with shock. "You did—I mean—you do?"

"I knew at the time that I was taking a grave risk—that you might never recover from the loss of your first and greatest love. But gaining you, having you as my wife, seemed worth the gamble. I thought—I hoped that I could win your heart after enough time had passed. I never expected that Manning would return from the grave. No sane man would have."

She tried to understand his meaning, but her mind still seemed to move so slowly, like an injured rabbit caught in a snare. Speechless, she stared up at him.

"Eleanor, I will not stand idly by and watch you throw yourself after the man you were once promised to marry." He had stopped making such alarming blows into his palm, but now he resumed his pacing up and down the room. "I cannot do it."

It was the worst, then—he was going to demand a divorce. Eleanor felt cold all the way through; she thought of her small son, how he would grow up without her, and she wanted to weep.

"I—I am sorry to have distressed you," she managed to say, then the tears she had so far kept back closed her throat. In a moment, she would dissolve into a heap, and she hoped he would throw his ultimatum at her and then leave, so she could fall apart in some semblance of privacy. Obviously, he had not come to listen to her apologies. What had she been thinking when she'd left London on such a whim—it had been foolish past measure. Now she would pay the price.

"I won't let you go, Eleanor!"

It was not at all what she had expected, and Eleanor jumped, wondering if she had heard him correctly. "What?"

Edward took a long step and came back to face her. She gazed up at him, her eyes still swimming with unshed tears, and blinked to try to see his face more clearly. She found that he stared at her earnestly, and some of his earlier agitation had faded into what seemed to be grim resolve.

"I know you love Robert, and I cannot in good conscience blame you. He was your first love, he is better favored than I, more charming with the ladies, and he carries the glory of his soldiering."

Eleanor couldn't believe what she was hearing. "Edward—"

He interrupted. "No, just listen. I know you feel you will love him forever, but I must have more time to change your mind. Eleanor, I love you with all my heart. I am a blunt-spoken man, and I have no gift for flattery or enticement. But I will love you always, honor and respect you. And I will not stop, I will never stop, until your heart is mine. You must give me that chance."

He loved her? He hadn't just married her for her position, her dowry, her respectable name? Their courtship had been so subdued—mostly her own fault, Eleanor realized, looking back for an instant; she had been weary with grief, her heart out of reach—their marriage so sedate and polite, she had not really thought—

"You love me?" she said it aloud, her voice barely audible to her own ears.

"You are my wife, and I love you," Edward repeated. "Will you give me the opportunity to woo you, this time for good?"

"Oh, Edward." She put her hands to her face for an instant; the tears came despite her best efforts, but they were no longer tears of despair. "Oh, Edward."

She blinked and saw that he watched her anxiously. She dropped her hands and held out her arms, and, to her infinite relief, he reached for her and pulled her into a warm embrace.

Eleanor laid her head upon her husband's chest, feeling that after a long and difficult journey, she had come home at last. And somewhere on the edge of her thoughts, she felt a passing moment of pity for her sister.

18

After Eleanor and Whitmund had left the dining room, any further attempts at conversation seemed impossible. There was too much tension in the room to make bland comments about the weather or polite lies about the truly awful food. Katryn had pushed the roast around on her plate and ignored the stewed peaches and prunes; her stomach felt uneasy. The last course was one of cheese and fruit, and despite her inner agitation Katryn accepted a small red apple and cut it neatly into quarters, relieved by its tart, unspoiled flavor. Even the cook had not managed to ruin this course.

She glanced across the table; Robert stared into his glass of red wine as if his thoughts were far away. Did he wonder, as she did, where Cavendish could be? If Whitmund had arrived here, how far behind was Robert's dangerous cousin?

As her worry increased, the morsels of apple seemed to catch in her throat; Katryn coughed and had to take a sip of her wine. She wondered if they would sit here all night, caught in some terrible spell, doomed to inedible food and mute dinner partners. She felt the strange dizziness again, and had to catch hold of the edge of the table. This was no time for nerves, she must be calm! When she looked up, she saw that Minette was trying to catch her eye. At last! Katryn pushed her chair back when Minette did the same.

"If you will excuse us, my dear," Minette said to her husband.

He nodded, and the ladies stood, to withdraw to the drawing room. Katryn wondered what Eleanor and Whitmund were doing right now. Could Whitmund be as furious as he had seemed? Katryn felt a moment of sympathy for her sister; it was brief. Surely Whitmund could not be angry at his wife for very long. Eleanor would bring him around, she always did, Katryn thought with a strange sense of fatigue. She was tired, so tired of seeing her sister always get what she wanted. All their lives, Katryn had witnessed Eleanor's charm and beauty win men over, soften their anger, beguile their attention. Why should it be any different this time?

She had somehow expected that Eleanor and her husband would have withdrawn to their bedroom, so she was startled when Minette opened the door to the small parlor and they found Eleanor and Edward standing very close together in front of the fire. They had obviously been embracing, and Katryn felt both relief for Eleanor's sake and a sad twinge of envy. Of course Whitmund loved her sister; how could he not?

Eleanor was blushing. She nodded to their hostess. "As— I—we—that is—"

"Ah, *très bon*," Minette said, her tone gravely pleased. "You have repaired the misunderstanding, *n'est-ce pas?*"

"Yes," Whitmund agreed, smiling just a little. "I must thank you for your hospitality and your assistance to my wife, Lady Grabble."

"It is a pleasure," Minette assured him. They all sat, Whitmund staying unfashionably close to his wife, holding her hand in his large, capable grip. Eleanor was still pale, but happiness shone from her blue eyes like a candle lighting the dark.

Katryn felt another pang. Where was Robert? She had to tell him her decision before she lost her nerve. She hoped he and Sir Henry would not sit long over their port.

Fortunately, the two men rejoined the others very shortly. Robert glanced quickly at Eleanor, at Whitmund, and then at Katryn, who did not meet his eyes, then he walked over to stand in front of the fire. Sir Henry did not sit, either, but went quickly to his wife.

"Sorry, m'dear," he told her. "One of the farmers at the edge of the county's at the back door—horse seems to be missing. Bad business."

"But, *Henri,* you are going out again? What can you do? Let them search the fields. The beast has no doubt broken through a gap in the hedge or jumped a fence, yes?"

"No doubt, but the man's asking for help, and I must see to it." Sir Henry patted his wife's hand. "Be back soon, I hope, but don't wait up."

He strode off down the hall, leaving Minette looking distressed, as well she might, Katryn thought, with such a strange assortment of guests to entertain alone.

Conversation was almost as difficult as it had been at dinner; Eleanor and Whitmund were only interested in each other; Robert stared into the fire; and Minette, as if despairing of any kind of social pretense, took up her embroidery and applied herself to her stitches.

Katryn could not sit still any longer. She needed to be alone with her husband. She could ask Robert to join her in their room, but she felt her cheeks heat at the interpretation the others would put upon that. And in fact, she didn't think she could tell him her decision with the bed looming so close behind them—as if in mute testimony of the joys they had shared, despite all the obstacles between them.

"Robert," she said suddenly into the silence. The fire popped, and Robert turned toward her, his brows knit. "I should like to show you the garden; Lady Grabble has done a lovely job of it, as Eleanor told you at dinner."

"In the dark?" Minette said, looking up in surprise.

"The moon is likely out by now, and we can take a candle," Katryn continued, her tone stubborn. "I—I should like for you to see it." She met her husband's inquiring glance, and he nodded.

"Of course, if you wish it." His tone had the old polite but noncommittal tone, evidence of the renewed presence of that invisible wall between them that she had hated for so long. At least she would no longer have to endure his careful courtesy, almost worse than outright rejection. Katryn felt both a terrible sadness and a strange relief; she looked away before her feelings might show in her face. She stood, and Robert came to her side.

"If you would excuse us," he said to their hostess.

Minette looked at them, her expression perplexed. "*Mais oui,* of course," she said. "Never has my garden had so much attention paid to it, *c'est fantastique, non?*"

Katryn bit her lip, but she took a candle from a side table without asking and almost ran to the door; she knew, even without looking, that Robert followed. He had never entered a room without her knowing it, without her feeling his nearness, never in all her life. When he walked into a room, the light seemed brighter, the air sweeter. How would she live without any hope of having him walk unexpectedly into her presence—no, she must not think of that, not now.

She hurried her steps, making the candle flame flicker. Katryn ignored the housekeeper's curious stare when they passed her in the hallway as they went toward the side door. Was the woman listening at keyholes again? Robert walked beside her, and though she felt his gaze on her face, he said nothing.

Only when they walked out into the night air, the moon

half-hidden behind dark clouds as she led the way to the walled garden, did he speak.

"What did you wish to say to me, Katryn? I know we are not here to look at the roses."

She took a deep breath, trying to hold on to her hard-won resolution.

"If you are still angry at me, I can only beg your pardon," he went on. "It was very wrong of me to go into Eleanor's bedchamber. I behaved badly; it will not happen again. I did not mean to embarrass you—"

She broke into his too-formal apology. "It's not that. It's—it's everything, I'm afraid. This was a mistake, Robert. The marriage, all of it. I'm going to leave you."

His mouth dropped open, and he stared at her, an expression in his eyes that Katryn found hard to meet. She stared down at the flickering flame of the candle; it seemed to tremble in her hand.

"I thought it would be enough, being your wife, bearing your name, knowing that you would always"—her voice wavered just a little—"offer me courtesy and respect, even if you could not love me, even if Eleanor would always be your first choice, the object of your truest passion—"

"If this is because of the—the incident with Eleanor—" he tried to interrupt, but she waved his comment aside.

"No, it's more," she repeated. "I thought I could be your wife without having your heart, but it won't work. I'm beginning to feel that we are living a terrible lie, and it hurts too much. I thought I could not live without you, Robert, but I think—I think perhaps my feelings have changed. I won't stop trying to prove your innocence, but I believe it would be better if we part."

He gazed at her; his expression was stark in the moonlight, his face heavily shadowed, but she thought he looked numb with shock. He whispered something—she thought it was her name, but she couldn't quite make it out.

"I know that you must have a son because of the entailed estate and I—I don't mean to ruin you; we—we will discuss that later, but just now, I need some time. I just—I just can't do this any longer, Robert. I'm sorry."

"Katryn—" She heard a strange timbre in his voice; he sounded almost ill, but she had already turned away and she didn't dare look back.

She knew this must be a blow to him, to his plan for saving his family, saving his estate. But he had not thought of her when he made the plan, had not considered her feelings, her response. So be it; his grand scheme would have to be put aside for a time. She would see him safely to some place of seclusion, and then she would leave with Eleanor and Whitmund.

No, perhaps not. She wasn't sure she could bear riding all the way back to London with two reunited lovebirds holding hands, speaking softly in such obvious harmony and affection. Every tender glance would score her like a hot poker, remind her too vividly of what she herself could not have. It appeared that Eleanor was managing to forget her first love, but Robert had not.

Perhaps Katryn would borrow the fare from Eleanor and take a public coach; it was not respectable for her to travel alone, but after their wild flight north, no breach of propriety would shock her now.

Shivering, Katryn felt suddenly cold; she clutched the candlestick more tightly and quickened her steps toward the house. She had expected some relief when she told Robert her decision, but she felt only empty and very, very sad.

Behind her, Robert felt as if he had been blindsided, struck a massive blow by a heavy weapon. He had been shot, once, during the war, and the shock had been much the same. One moment he had been astride his horse, the next he was flying off the horse's back, landing with a jolt on the hard earth of the battlefield, his arm bleeding from the portion of shell that had embedded itself in the tender flesh.

He felt just as violated now, just as stunned. His knees trembled and his legs couldn't seem to hold his weight; he found that he had sunk to his knees on the firm soil of the garden path. It was an attitude of penitence, but Katryn didn't see him. She still walked away from him, strode steadily toward the gate, and the silvery flickering of her candle wavered as she turned out of his sight. With the candle, she took the light from his life—the light that emanated from her loving heart, the warm glow that chased away his demons. He was losing her. . . .

Without even the shimmer of the candle to lighten the blackness, with the moon now hidden by clouds scuttling across the night sky, Robert knelt in deepest shadow. He could smell the scent of the flowers around him, hear the rustle of shrubbery in the breeze, but he could see nothing. He might have fallen into a dark well—and he felt just as lost, just as isolated.

Oh, Katryn, he thought, with a wave of emotion that he could not even identify. *I did you such wrong, to ask you to submit to such a mockery of a marriage. And then to drag you from your home, to take you into danger and privation, living like gypsies and beggars in the moors and byways . . .*

But instead of the hardships, he thought of their glorious passion, remembered lying in green grass with swaying tree limbs high above them, the smell of growing things and the rustle of birds taking wing, their sylvan refuge interrupted by the tumult of human lovemaking—most of all, he remembered Katryn in his arms, her skin soft, her voice husky as she responded to his ardor with an honest passion of her own. He had to swallow hard.

No, even without her words, he knew the truth. It had not been the difficulty, the danger that had driven Katryn away. He had lost his wife—*his wife*—because of his blind-hearted refusal to give up his first attachment, his youthful adoration of the glorious Eleanor. Suddenly that seemed such a long time ago; he had been a different person then, and so had Eleanor. Why had it taken him so long to see it?

He had dwelled so long on the fantasy during his interminable days in prison that he had lost sight of the reality, the real person that Eleanor now was. When they had shared the one stolen, guilty kiss, she had said that he had changed, and it was true.

And Eleanor had not. Oh, she had married, had borne a child, so she was not exactly the same pleasing, biddable girl he had proposed to, but in essence her soul was little altered. She was still beautiful and sweet and gentle, just the kind of angelic vision a young man could aspire to.

But Robert was not the same, altered by the harshness he had faced, the obstacles he had surmounted. He had gone into battle, been thrown into prison, fought for his life a hundred times, while Eleanor was safe at home in the bosom of her loving family.

It was no wonder Eleanor didn't understand him, no longer knew who he was. For a moment he tried to picture Eleanor on the run with him, Eleanor fighting horse thieves and murderers in a lonely wood, and his mind refused to frame such a scene. Eleanor would never have dreamed of doing what Katryn had done.

It was Katryn who had had the courage, the determination, the whole heart, which had never failed him; probably, she had always had that kind of spirit. He had just failed to see it, dazzled as he was by Eleanor's golden beauty. Eleanor would have been—surely was—a sweet, gentle, loving wife, but compared to her sister, life with Eleanor would have been—well, somewhat tame.

He felt a flicker of disloyalty in thinking it, but he knew it was true. The love they had once had for each other had been part of youth and inexperience and the innocent naïveté of two young people first dabbling in love. And its time had passed.

His love for Eleanor was only a gentle memory, ready to be put into the deepest recesses of his mind. He would always be fond of her, always value her. But he loved Katryn.

He loved Katryn. How could he have been such a fool!

Katryn had done so much, had given to him so freely, had charged into danger by his side, never thinking of herself. And he had lost her now, lost the possibility of a rich, deep, many-layered love of a kind that two adults could offer to each other, perhaps the most precious commitment that he would ever have the chance to make.

He had been such a terrible fool. Katryn would probably never forgive him the slights, the inadequacies that he had served her—he had given her brass coin, dross, when she deserved only the purest gold.

Oh, Katryn, he thought, sick at heart. *How can I win you back?*

Not by cowering in a garden like some craven half-man, that was certain. He staggered to his feet and headed for the gate; he would not give up without a fight. They had come too far together for their marriage to end like this. Perhaps it had begun in a fog of self-deception—perhaps he had not recognized her spirit, her beauty, her incredible heart when he should have. But there must be some way that he could make up for his horrible mistake.

He must have her, no matter what it took!

Katryn strode blindly toward the house. The sky had darkened as clouds momentarily blocked the moon, and the candle was her only aid, its pale light flickering across the lawn. But she could make out very little; tears fell silently and steadily down her face, and she had to blink hard to clear her vision.

It was right what she had done, it had to be right. But she

felt so weary, so empty that she longed for a quiet place and a long, long sleep. Perhaps she would wake better able to face the world, to face a life without Robert.

She blinked again, trying to make out the path, and trod too hard on a pebble. It slipped beneath her, and her ankle twisted. As she jerked, the candle flame dipped, almost going out. She tried to steady it, tried to steady herself, but she thought that despite her efforts, she was going to fall. She lurched—

And a man's hand grabbed her arm, pulling her up, holding her erect.

Robert! Katryn's heart leapt despite all her resolution. He had followed her, he had—he had—

Then someone spoke, and it was a man's voice, but not Robert's. The voice was harsh, the tone mocking, and as she recognized the speaker, she jerked again from shock; as fear rushed through her veins like a cold river.

"Easy, Lady Manning, I would not have you unconscious at my feet—at least, not just yet. You still have a role to play in our little comedy of errors."

Cavendish!

19

How had he found them? It was a useless question; if Whitmund had found it possible to track Eleanor, so could Cavendish. Katryn tried to twist away from his hand, but his grip was too strong.

"Let go of me!" she demanded, fear sending shivers up her back. "You have no right to put your hands on me."

"I act only as would any loyal subject of the Crown," Cavendish told her, his tone too smooth. She could hear the gloating in his voice; he thought that he had won, that he stood on the threshold of victory. She bit back a sob.

"I need only announce your husband's duplicity to the local magistrate—whose estate this is, if the hag I questioned at the last farmhouse spoke correctly—and then your precious spouse will be dragged away to London, to the ignominious fate a traitor deserves."

"On your word? You think that Sir Henry will trust a lying, scheming rascal such as you?" She almost spit the words into his face.

"Have a care, Lady Manning." His grip tightened painfully, and Katryn hoped that he could not detect how she winced. She did not want to show him how frightened she was.

"Of course I have papers with me which will substantiate

the charge; I'm sure this Sir Henry is a reasonable man, and he will take the proper actions."

"Papers as false as the letter you allowed Eleanor to take away? We know that it is a forgery; I would bet that these are, too."

"Oh, no, dear lady." He was relishing the moment, even as he pulled her toward the manor house. He seemed to delight in his anticipation of his final triumph; she could hear it in every word he spoke. "The letter from Colonel Richmond that I held up at the ball is quite genuine."

"And how would you of all people have come across it?" She tried to drag her feet on the grass without being too obvious, pulling against his strong grasp, trying to stall for time. Where was Robert—still mulling over her declaration? Perhaps he was too angry or too embarrassed to return to the house right away. Oh, why hadn't she waited! She was always too impulsive; Eleanor had told her that often enough.

Cavendish must not reach the house. He didn't know that Sir Henry was away from his home, but the magistrate would surely return soon, and then—Robert would be lost. How could she warn Robert? He must flee—

"I have my sources; if you pay enough, there's always someone who will dig deeper, even in the War Office—did you think I'd have destituted myself for no reason?"

"No one will trust your sources," she snapped, trying again to pull away from his grasp.

"Careful, Lady Manning." Cavendish's tone lost some of its smoothness. "Do not press me too far; I warn you. I suspect you are only a pitiful dupe of your too-handsome husband, but nonetheless, I can be harsh if I need be."

Pitiful? Dupe? She swung the candle at him, but the wax taper snapped easily as he pushed it aside, and the small flicker of flame died, making the darkness around them even denser.

Katryn refused to give in. Anger made her stronger; she

dug in her heels, still trying to pull away, or at least slow their inexorable approach to the house. "Unhand me! This is not the behavior of a gentleman."

This time he jerked her so hard that she lost her footing completely. She was falling, falling—the ground rushed to meet her, and for a moment she was too winded by the impact to fight back.

"Don't dare call me less than a gentleman!" Cavendish snapped, all his urbanity vanished. "I am as good as any gentleman born, and if Fate had been more fair, I would be standing in Manning's place right now! Don't you dare insult me!"

He leaned over, holding her down against the smooth turf of the lawn. Katryn tried to get her breath. Before she could manage any resistance, he had bent his knee against her thighs; the pressure was painful.

"Do you wish to hold on to your title, your position?" he half-whispered. "Perhaps I will offer you the chance—perhaps I shall taste the pleasures that Manning has sampled before me; perhaps it is not only his house, his estate, his fortune that I shall inherit."

Furious with fear and rage, Katryn struck at him, but he grabbed her hands and held them down, leaning heavily over her to kiss her. His breath was hot and smelled stale and fishy, his lips felt too damp; she felt her stomach roil. She couldn't breathe; he was lying across her chest, one of his hands now tugging at the neck of her gown.

She heaved beneath him, trying to push him away, but he was too heavy, and his free hand now encircled her throat, the pressure intense. She trembled from the pain, felt a darkness threaten her deeper than the moonlit night around them, saw stars shooting as her consciousness ebbed.

Then his hand dropped away, and she felt him pulled bodily off her.

"You'll die for this, Cavendish!"

Robert. Thank God in heaven, it was Robert!

She heard the sound of a blow, but for a moment Katryn could only concentrate on breathing, on drawing in precious air, on the soreness of her throat as she gasped for breath. Then when her vision cleared, she saw the two men grappling, and fear itself almost choked her all over again.

"Robert!" She pushed herself to a sitting position and tried to see them better just as a cloud slipped over the moon. The darkness deepened as the two figures struggled—she could not make out the faces. Then the cloud slid away, and the moon's pale light again lit up the tableau.

They were locked in a ferocious struggle, both men too intent, too focused to waste any breath on insults. As she watched, Robert pulled one arm free and punched his cousin's face—the face whose features were so like his own. Katryn heard the hollow thud as the blow fell, and Cavendish's muffled grunt of pain.

But Cavendish refused to give up. He swung back, and Robert ducked, then sent a blow into his opponent's stomach.

Cavendish groaned, but when Robert punched again, Cavendish grabbed his hand and twisted his whole arm. This time it was Robert who made a queer sound in his throat.

Had Cavendish broken his arm? Katryn clenched her fists in useless fear. But there was no snap of bone, and now, through some movement that she could not make out clearly, Robert had shaken himself free. The two men circled on the lawn, watching each other grimly. They were of much the same weight, but Cavendish was better rested, better fed than Robert after their long, difficult journey. And although Robert was well schooled in hand-to-hand fighting, Cavendish seemed to know enough dirty tricks of his own to make the outcome uncertain.

Should she call out for help? But then Cavendish would air his accusations, and Sir Henry might take his side, sending Robert back to a London gaol. What on earth could she do?

Then Katryn realized that she knew Cavendish's weakness; he had revealed it during the earlier attack on Katryn herself. Cavendish's Achilles' heel—

"This is no way for gentlemen to behave!" she shouted at them. "Cavendish, you are acting like a street thug. You should be ashamed!"

For a long moment, she thought they were too intent on each other to hear her, but then both men glanced her way. Robert looked only surprised, but Cavendish snarled, his lips drawn back into a grimace that twisted his whole face.

"I am a gentleman, damn you!"

"Then act like one," Katryn threw him the challenge, not sure if it would work. To her horror, her gambit worked—too well.

"So I will," Cavendish snapped, still breathing hard. He drew himself up and glared at his opponent; it must gall him that Robert was at least an inch taller. "I will issue a challenge, Cousin, a most *gentlemanly* challenge."

Robert snorted in obvious disbelief. "Is this a jest? I'm in no mood for sport, Cousin."

"Would I mock myself?" Cavendish's eyes were eerily pale in the moonlight.

"And are you sending your second to call upon me? Is he hiding in your back pocket?"

"No," the other man retorted. "We'll settle this here and now. I'm sure Sir Henry has suitable weapons, and the light will be better inside. Let us retire to the house. Unless you refuse to fight me?"

"Nothing would give me greater pleasure," Robert answered, his tone equally grim. "In fact, I believe we had an appointment, made days ago in London. Now is as good a time as any to see the matter to its end."

"No!" Katryn cried out, but neither man seemed to listen.

They turned toward the house, and she followed, almost running to keep up with their quick stride.

Robert slowed a little to reach for her hand. "Are you all right, Katryn?" he asked quietly. "He didn't injure you?"

"No, but—but you must not do this," she whispered. "Cavendish has often boasted of his ability with the sword—he sees it as such a gentlemanly skill. And you are still exhausted from days of walking—"

"I must." He pressed her hand. "I cannot turn my back on a serpent, dearest. The danger must be addressed, here and now."

She was so distressed by his answer that the endearment did not register, not until they all three had entered the house and met the housekeeper in the hallway; Mrs. Hopple stared at Cavendish in surprise.

"Ye have brought in more unmannerly friends! Do ye think my master's house is a common hostel?" she demanded.

Cavendish touched his cravat, which had lost its elaborate arrangement, and tried to pull his jacket back into place. "Mind your place, woman," he snapped. "I am told your master is of a long lineage—"

"One of the oldest families in Yorkshire," Mrs. Hopple responded, drawing herself up.

"Then he must own a pair of dueling swords."

"Aye, his grandfather's, but—"

"Then bring them, at once, and some wine, and show us to the largest room in the house," Cavendish went on, his tone still heavy with what he must believe was aristocratic arrogance. "And we need candles for light, lots of candles. This is an affair between gentlemen!"

Mrs. Hopple looked in amazement from Cavendish to Robert, then back to Cavendish, and bobbed a curtsy. She *would* respond to his cavalier-style insolence, Katryn thought; it was just like the woman.

"Ye'd best come up to the attic, then, m'lord." The house-keeper unconsciously gave Cavendish the title he so longed for. "I will bring the swords and candles."

"And wine," he reminded her, lifting his chin as if the homage was only his just due.

"Yes, m'lord," she agreed. Taking a candle from a side table, she led them all toward the stairs.

Robert pressed Katryn's hand, as if he knew that she had been about to object again. She pressed her lips together, trying to think. This duel was insane. Yet—yet would Robert have a greater chance to win his freedom in this illegal but private fight than he would at the hands of the law?

She wasn't sure. But Robert wished it, had demanded the right, and she hesitated to call for outside assistance that might too easily turn against him.

They climbed several flights of stairs, the last narrow and ill-lit, then found themselves at the top of the house, in an open room only slightly cluttered with boxes.

Robert began to push several old chests out of the way, and eyed the dusty wood floor as if mindful of the footing that would be so crucial once the fight began. Across the room, Cavendish pulled off his disordered cravat and his coat and rolled up his sleeves.

Robert was doing the same with his borrowed dinner jacket. He also pulled off the heavy, ill-cut workman's boots he had been wearing for days; they would slow him down too much, Katryn realized, when speed and nimbleness could make the difference between avoiding and receiving a fatal thrust of the blade.

The housekeeper had left the candle and disappeared; would she tell her mistress what strange events were transpiring in the attic? Any good servant would, but with the relationship that existed between Minette and her grudging housekeeper, Katryn suspected that this time, the secret might be kept.

If anything, Mrs. Hopple seemed to be taking a macabre delight in the proposed duel, Katryn thought, her spirits sinking even lower. And after all, she could always inform on them when the contest was over. But which man would survive? Katryn had no doubts that Cavendish meant to fight to the death. She swallowed hard, feeling the soreness in her abused throat.

Very shortly, the housekeeper returned bearing a long case; she set it carefully upon a dusty three-legged table, and then turned back to descend the stairs.

Cavendish strode across to open the leather case. Inside, two dueling épées rested, their blades shining in lethal splendor. Katryn shuddered when she saw them. Cavendish gave a wolfish grin and lifted one, then swung it lightly through the air, testing its weight and balance.

"It will do," he said. "Manning?"

Robert approached warily and accepted the other sword, then whipped it through the air, gauging it in his turn. The two men focused on their weapons.

Katryn wrung her hands—could Robert defeat his cousin? How had their long struggle come to a climax in this dusty, shadowed room?

The housekeeper returned too soon bearing two large candelabras, which she placed at opposite sides of the room, to even the light as much as possible. She had not yet brought the wine he'd asked for, but Cavendish, flexing the sword lightly, did not seem disposed to wait any longer. Perhaps he meant to save the drink for a victory toast, Katryn thought, her stomach clenching with fear.

"Cousin?" Cavendish said, his tone formal, but his enmity still apparent.

"I am ready."

"Then *en garde*." Cavendish sprang into attack so quickly that Katryn gasped, then bit her lip to keep any more sound from escaping; she must not distract Robert.

Her husband brought up his sword smartly, blocking the other blade just in time; it slid aside before it could reach his heart, but though the strike had been blunted, it did not fail totally. The blade caught Robert's arm and, to her horror, Katryn saw a spot of red stain Robert's borrowed shirt. He was hurt!

Robert didn't seem to notice. He met Cavendish's frenzied attack again and again, beating back his cousin's feverish blows. The two blades flashed through the air, almost hypnotic in their fierce grace, glinting in the candlelight, moving too quickly for Katryn's eyes to focus clearly upon them. The swords sang as they met and disengaged, then met again, and the sounds of metal striking metal seemed very loud in the almost-empty room.

How could Minette and Eleanor and her husband be sitting so calmly somewhere below, unaware of the life-and-death struggle taking place here? Katryn pushed the thought aside; she had no time to think of anything but the fast-moving fight before her.

Cavendish took two long strides forward, his épée moving so quickly that it seemed to flicker before her eyes. His skill with the sword had not been exaggerated, Katryn saw, her fear growing. He slashed at Robert's neck, but again, just in time, Robert met the attack and pushed back the slender blade.

Then Robert feinted, and before Cavendish, almost overbalanced in his eager rush across the room, could regain his equilibrium, Robert's blade slid through his guard and slit the side of his cousin's jacket.

Cavendish winced, but he recovered in time to push away the blade before it sank too deep. But now he too was wounded; drops of blood fell onto the floor, where their footprints had already scattered the light layer of dust, crimson splattering the dark grain of the wood.

Katryn bit her lips, almost afraid to breathe. Now Robert

was on the attack, pushing Cavendish back, back, Robert's
blows falling furiously, his sword moving with deadly pre-
cision. Cavendish was breathing faster, trying to meet each
careful thrust, each shimmering lunge of the weapon. Robert
struck again, and Cavendish parried in time, but his riposte
was barely adequate. The blades rang loudly beneath the
slanted roof, then Robert pulled back his sword and before
Cavendish could lift his own weapon, Robert jabbed, his
aim straight and true.

The sword caught Cavendish just above the heart, im-
paled him like a fowl on a cooking spit. Cavendish staggered a little from the impact and dropped his weapon. It fell
to the floor, clattering, and no one moved, no one spoke.

Katryn held her breath. Would Robert kill his cousin here
and now? She watched her husband's grim expression, the
hardness of his gaze. She wasn't sure she had ever seen him
like this. If this was what the soldier, the prisoner of war had
become—he had changed even more than she had suspected. Had he grown too violent, too savage to live the life
he was trying to reclaim? He might be lost to them all,
whether or not he could ever disprove the false charges of
treason.

The tableau lasted a heartbeat, a lifetime. Then instead of
going for the kill, Robert pulled his sword back. Cavendish
slumped, falling in a loose heap to the floor. Blood soaked
his shirt, but it did not look to be a life-threatening wound.

Robert blinked, staring down at the man who had cost
him so much. Cavendish's face was white, his brows lifted
a little as if in surprise that he should be the one lying
wounded. Not what he had planned, Robert knew. Plans had
a habit of changing.

Robert himself was still gripping his sword very tightly;
he tried to take a deep breath. He had wanted to kill this
man, this lying, scheming weasel who had dared to attack

Robert's wife, who had tried to ruin his family. He had wanted to—but he had not.

"A good choice," someone said quietly from the stairwell.

Robert jerked in surprise. It was Whitmund who stood there, gazing at the whole scene with grim appreciation.

"Dueling is illegal, after all, and a death on your hands would not exactly help your case," his brother-in-law pointed out dryly. "When it comes before the law, as it must."

He climbed the last steps up into the attic—how long had he been watching? Behind him, Eleanor followed, her face pale with alarm, and then Minette.

But Robert had eyes for only one lady, his lady. He turned to find Katryn.

He heard her cry out, then to his surprise saw her run forward, but not into his arms. Too late, from the corner of his eye he detected the glint of another, smaller weapon in Cavendish's hand. Too weak to stand, his enemy struck from below, like a serpent, a lethal slashing blow toward Robert's abdomen.

Whitmund shouted, but he was too far away to act. Eleanor screamed.

Robert had relaxed too soon. Barely in time, he lowered his own blade to block the knife before Cavendish could gut him like a hog hung for slaughter. But though his sword caught the dagger's edge and held it back for an instant, his stocking feet, wet from the blood that had dripped to the floor, slipped. He could not regain his footing—he fell forward, his sword flailing uselessly. Cavendish pulled back his weapon and struck again.

It was Katryn, snatching up a brass candlestick, who deflected the dagger, Katryn who pushed the blade aside, but not without cost to herself. The sharp edge rang against the brass, then slid across it to slice her arm.

She exclaimed in shock, even as Robert, now on his

knees, lunged to grab Cavendish's neck, squeezing until the other man gasped and dropped his last, hidden weapon.

"You miserable coward," Robert snapped. Then he released Cavendish's limp body, not caring how hard the man hit the floor, and he grabbed his wife.

For once in her life, Katryn looked truly ready to swoon. Her arm was bleeding; Robert reached for something to stop the blood, and Minette, practical as always, was there to offer the borrowed cravat he had earlier discarded. Robert dabbed at the blood, his whole body cold. That Katryn could come to harm—suddenly nothing else mattered, nothing at all.

He blotted more of the blood and found, to his immense relief, that the cut was wide but shallow. He glanced at Minette. "If you would bring warm water and clean cloths, I will bind it."

Minette nodded and hurried to the stairwell. Mrs. Hopple stood on the steps, for once looking nonplussed.

Katryn's head was spinning, but she heard Minette say quietly to the woman, "This may be too much even for my husband! I would suggest that you should begin your packing."

The housekeeper gasped.

Katryn had a wild desire to giggle. Minette would get rid of her awful housekeeper, Robert was not dead, Cavendish was foiled. Then the laughter died within her. The original accusation remained—the charge of treason that could still destroy him.

"Katryn, lie still," Robert murmured. "I must tend to your wound. Does it hurt much?"

It stung abominably, but she didn't care. Robert's arm cradled her, and she had his total attention. His brown eyes were dark with emotion; he seemed to have forgotten everyone else.

"Katryn," he said very quietly, his voice intense with feeling, "you must never, ever do such a thing again. You could have been killed."

"I'm sorry to distress you," she murmured, meaning not a word of it. It had been worth the small hurt to see Robert so upset, all for her.

"If I had lost you, nothing else would have mattered," he told her. "I know you don't believe me now, but you must give me another chance, I beg of you."

Katryn blinked at him; the sincerity in his voice was unmistakable—and yet, could she take the gamble? Dared she risk her heart one more time?

Minette interrupted, returning with water and clean rags, the little maid behind her with more bandages. "Here, she must not bleed, not in her condition, *mais non.*"

She knelt and held the basin so that Robert could rinse the blood from Katryn's wound. Katryn braced herself against the sting, then her eyes widened. Her condition? She thought of her spells of faintness, her nausea. Could it be? Then another voice boomed from the stairwell, and her moment of happiness faded beneath renewed alarm.

"The nerve of the rascal! A stolen horse in my own stable, brazen as you please. Where is the villain?"

Katryn froze; she tried to grab Robert's hand. "It's our mount—the one we took from the robbers. I knew it had to be stolen," she whispered. "You must go; leave me!"

"Never," he told her, seeming maddingly oblivious to his danger. "Never again."

She was caught between joy at his words and fear for his safety. "But, Robert—"

"I have the description of the thief"—Sir Henry puffed a little as he climbed the last of the stairs—"and he will rue the day he stole a horse in my county!" Their host glanced around the room, his gaze pausing when he saw Robert kneeling over his wife.

But to Katryn's surprise, the older man turned away, scanning the attic till he saw Cavendish, his fine linen shirt sodden with blood, lying on the bare floor. "You! You're the one."

Cavendish had recovered enough to lift his lips in a ghastly caricature of a smile. "How can you be sure, you old fool? That man looks so much like me."

Katryn drew a deep breath. It was true; Robert and his cousin shared much the same countenance. To a stranger . . .

Sir Henry shook his head. "A well-dressed gentleman, slim and dark-haired, the farmer said he saw taking his best mare out of the field. Yon lord's not what I would call well dressed; decked out like a scarecrow he is, no matter how many titles he possesses. You're the one who will go to gaol, fine sir!"

Cavendish's face twisted. "I think not, not when you see what I have to show you. . . ."

It was here, then, the moment they had dreaded for so long. Katryn winced, and Robert took her hand. "Be brave," he whispered.

Cavendish tried to reach inside his jacket, but his arm seemed limp. Whitmund came closer. "What secret are you keeping now, Cavendish?" To the women, he added, "I'm afraid we must stop his bleeding, you know. He does have a more serious wound than Katryn."

"No, no." Cavendish tried to push Whitmund away, but the bigger man would have none of it. Cavendish struggled against his hands, but Whitmund soon prevailed. Robert's cousin was too weak from loss of blood to prevent this forceful disrobing as Whitmund stripped off his jacket.

First, Whitmund pressed a pad of cloth to the deepest wound to slow the bleeding, then he turned aside to pat the bloodstained coat. There was something in an inner pocket. In a sudden intense silence, as everyone in the attic room watched, he pulled out a wad of papers.

"No!" From the floor, Cavendish reached for the packet, but Whitmund easily pushed him back.

"And what do we have here?" Whitmund removed the outer wrapping, now heavily stained with blood.

Robert pressed Katryn's hand once more, then moved closer so that he could see what Whitmund held. He knew what his brother-in-law would find, but he was surprised that his cousin had carried the irreplaceable letter on his person. Had Cavendish been afraid to allow the precious letter out of his sight, or did he feel he needed it to support his charges? It was Colonel Richmond's letter, accusing Robert as a French agent, the same one Cavendish had brandished at the London ball. Robert looked again at the faded ink, the familiar handwriting, his heart heavy. Here, still, was the charge that could yet destroy all his hopes.

But then Whitmund detached the folded paper and they all saw something else—beneath the first letter was another. Robert felt light-headed for an instant. It could not be . . . he could not have . . . at last—such incredible good fortune.

But when Whitmund unfolded the creased sheet carefully and began to read aloud, he knew.

"This is written by my hand, to affirm that I have ordered Robert Manning to go behind French lines and to play a role as informer to Napoleon's forces . . ."

It was true—this was the second letter, the document he had never dared hope to find, his commander's avowal of Robert's true mission. This piece of paper would affirm his innocence.

Whitmund's voice faded, but he held the fragile piece of paper as if it were a precious gem. Robert took a long breath, barely able to believe the document still existed, that this was not just another dream.

No one else spoke until Katryn exclaimed, "That—that means you are innocent, doesn't it, Robert?"

"Oh, yes," he said slowly. "It does. It is good news indeed."

Looking across at Cavendish, whose features were twisted again with futile, unending hatred, Robert asked the man, "Why? Why did you not destroy it? You could have so easily tossed it into the fire, and then I would never have been able to prove that I was not a traitor, that the first letter was written only to set up my double identity."

Cavendish swallowed hard, and his voice was brittle with frustration. "I wanted to 'find' it after you were safely dead, and the title mine. Of course I didn't want such a scandal to taint our family name forever, to stain our honor past reclaiming."

The man seemed quite unconscious of the irony of his reasoning. "Of course not," Robert agreed. "Whitmund, perhaps you will take charge of the documents, and guard them most zealously?"

"With pleasure," the other man agreed, his eyes glinting.

Minette sighed. "Someone must still bind this villain's wound," she reminded them tartly. "I will not have him dying in my house; bad enough that our housekeeper has allowed this most illegal duel to take place—"

"What?" Sir Henry exclaimed. "A duel? In my house? And Mrs. Hopple knew about this?"

"Indeed, my dear," Minette assured him. "Who do you think gave them the use of your grandfather's swords?"

Sir Henry's round face turned slowly a deep crimson. "In my own house—the magistrate's house!—would she make me the laughingstock of the county?" He turned and stamped back down the steps.

Minette's lips curved, just a little. Then she stood, picking up the rest of the bandages. "My lady, if you will attend to your sister?"

Eleanor came forward cautiously, as if not sure that Katryn would allow it. "If you don't mind," she murmured to

Katryn, kneeling beside her sister and offering her arm for support.

Katryn smiled ruefully. "Of course not," she said. "I do still feel very weak." Later, she thought, later she would tell Robert—tell everyone—her happy secret. A baby with Robert's dark eyes, perhaps a son in his own image . . .

Eleanor shook her head. "I can't imagine why," she said, giving her sister a quick hug. "Oh, Katryn, always so impulsive—but this time, with excellent results! You did make my heart almost stop."

Robert left Cavendish to Minette's deft hands and Whitmund's watchful eye and came closer to observe the two sisters. One tall, one of medium height; one fair, one dark; one willowy, one more generously curved. They would both forever mark milestones in his life. But he loved only one, and he must make his feelings clear.

He dropped to one knee on the dusty floor in front of them. "Eleanor, we were once sworn to each other," he said and saw Katryn wince. Eleanor met his gaze, her own expression grave.

"But we have changed," Robert went on gently. "We were truly in love then, though we were both very young, and we will always have that memory. But now—"

Eleanor smiled and glanced for a moment at her husband. Whitmund had gone very still. "Now, you are not the man I knew," she agreed. "And perhaps, I am not the woman you desire."

Robert relaxed just a little at her understanding, but the biggest challenge still lay ahead.

"I'm glad we had the time we did," Eleanor continued, her voice soft. "But now I—I love my husband, and he loves me." She gazed proudly at Whitmund, and the big man exhaled gustily as if he had been holding his breath for some moments.

"And I love my wife," Robert continued, looking now at

Katryn, whose green eyes glistened with a suspicious moisture. "I love her more than I have ever loved anyone or anything, more than my life, more than my family. And though I have treated her badly, though I was blind to too much for too long, I must beg her forgiveness. I must ask her—I must ask you, Katryn, to give me another chance."

Katryn stared up at him, and for a long, long moment, she didn't answer.

This was the proposal she should have had in the beginning, she thought in some corner of her mind. Was it too late? Did she still love him? Had her childish adoration grown into the kind of love a woman should give a man? The silence grew, and no one moved.

"Will you be my lady, my wife, dearest always to my heart?" Robert asked, his voice very quiet, as if no one else were in the room, or, at least, as if none else mattered.

Slowly, slowly, Katryn smiled. "I will."

Epilogue

When the midwife finally allowed Robert back into the bedchamber, Katryn had been washed and dressed in a fresh cambric gown. Eleanor had threaded a scarlet ribbon through her brown hair to pull it back from her face; Katryn had no patience just now for more elaborate dressing—she had more important matters on her mind.

She was weary after her labor, but the pain was already fading into a distant memory. She gazed down at the sweet face of the baby lying in her arms, staring at the blue eyes and tiny lips, feeling such love that it surprised her once again.

"Katryn?" Robert came into the room cautiously, his voice pitched low. "You are not asleep?"

"Of course not," she said. "I was waiting for you. Is the babe not beautiful?"

"Perfect," he agreed, but she saw that he was gazing at her. "I was worried about you, dear heart. If I should ever lose you—"

"Nonsense." Katryn smiled up at him. "Look at the babe, dearest. Did you ever see such a sight?"

"I think she will look like her mother," Robert said, putting out one finger to cautiously touch the little hand that had escaped the swaddling. The baby had already suckled;

she blinked at her father for a moment, then closed her eyes in glorious indifference to his presence.

"You don't mind that it's—she's a girl?" Katryn asked, her tone just a little anxious.

"Of course not. Another small Katryn? How could I be unhappy with such a blessing? Mind you, if she has your determination, we shall have a challenge before us." He laughed gently at her indignant frown.

"How could you say so!"

Then a soft knock interrupted, and they both glanced toward the door. "Yes?" Robert called.

Eleanor pushed open the door and looked inside. "May the boys come in for a moment?"

"Of course," Katryn agreed.

Eleanor's son Fitz led the group; he was the oldest and took his position quite seriously. He had inherited not only his father's brawny frame and big ears, but also his sense of responsibility. Behind him came his younger brother, James, and two more little boys.

The youngest of them all, William, hurried forward and in his haste almost fell over the rug beside the bed. Young Rob grabbed his arm and jerked the toddler back to his feet. "Mind your step," the taller boy said. "You mustn't upset Mama."

Katryn looked at her sons and smiled, feeling as if she might dissolve from the warmth of the love she felt for all her family. "Of course he won't upset me, will you, William love?"

"No." Will reached up to touch his mother's hand. Then he stretched, standing on tiptoe to better view the bundle in her arms. "Is it finished, the baby?" Will asked his father.

Robert took a boy in each arm and lifted them to see their new sister. "Quite finished."

"Then why is she so red and wrinkled?" Will asked.

"Ha, you were just the same," Rob answered for his father. "Nurse told me. And you smelled, too."

"Did not!" Will struggled in his papa's grip, eager to defend his honor, till Robert gently shook them both.

"Mind your manners, young sirs, or I will upset the both of you."

They subsided, and in a moment Robert kissed each boy on the top of his head, then bade them give way to their cousins, Fitz and James. When all the boys had had a glimpse of the infant, Eleanor came and shooed them out.

"Shall I put her into the cradle?" Eleanor asked her sister. "We mustn't overtire you. Mrs. Mingle will be back in very soon; she's having a cup of tea with the two grammas, comparing recipes for healing broths. She may be the best midwife in three counties, but you know what a tartar she is; she'll banish us all from the room so that you can sleep."

"Yes, please. I am a little fatigued." Katryn surrendered the baby, whose eyes were shut, and the two sisters exchanged a look of perfect harmony before Eleanor placed the baby into the white cradle

"I should go," Robert said, "and let you rest."

"Not just yet," Katryn whispered. "I want a moment, just the two of us."

So as Eleanor quietly left the room, Robert bent closer and slipped his arm around Katryn, cradling her much as she had held the infant a minute before. He thought how dear she was, how incredibly precious. He loved the children, every one, but not even they could move him like his lady wife, who every day continued to surprise and delight him. He tried to tell her so, but she only laughed beneath her breath.

"Hush," Katryn told him. She could hear the determined tread of Mrs. Mingle coming ever closer down the hall. "And kiss me quick."